Willow Hall Romance

Willow Hall Romance

Romance

A Pride and Prejudice Variation Series

LEENIE BROWN

LEENIE B BOOKS
HALIFAX

Contents

So Very Unexpected

At All Costs

Dear Reader,

It all started with a picture of a sunset and a writing exercise on my blog (leeniebrown.com). However, what was supposed to be a few minutes of practice, grew and stretched and became something much larger.

Those writing exercises have now produced several published works, including the collection you hold in your hands.

While some things about how I create these stories have evolved since that first writing exercise, the tradition of posting a portion of a work in progress continues each Thursday. In fact, there is a new story posting there now.

Happy Reading!

Leenie B.

"I had anticipated calling on your brothers at least once before returning to my party in London. They will be travelling with me to Pemberley when –" He stopped speaking as Elizabeth approached. "Miss Elizabeth," he said in surprise.

Philip, who had also approached at just that moment, noted the slight stiffening of his friend's posture and the way he fidgeted with his hat as he greeted the Abbots' guest. Shifting his eyes to Elizabeth, he smiled. So that is how it was, was it? Her cheeks were quite rosy, and her eyes were demurely lowered as if afraid to look at the man in front of her.

"Mr. Darcy," she said with as much of a curtsey as one could make when her hand was being held by a gentleman. Her eyes grew wide at the thought, and she tugged her hand away from Marcus as gently as she could. "Thank you, sir," she said softly. "I believe I have recovered."

"You are unwell?" Darcy, without thinking, took a step toward her.

"I merely stumbled, Mr. Darcy." She once again attempted to smile reassuringly.

"You did not injure yourself?" Darcy barely held his place. His every instinct wished to see to her safety, but, he reminded himself, he had not been granted that privilege.

It was as she had feared. The meeting was uncomfortable and with an audience, which made it even more strained. "I am well. It was just a momentary lapse in grace. Fortunately, Mr. Dobney was there to prevent any injury."

Darcy suddenly became aware of the man standing next to Elizabeth. "Marcus," he acknowledged with a nod. The same feelings he had endured when Elizabeth had laughed and talked with his cousin at Rosings, rose within him. Darcy attempted to remind himself that she had refused him, that he had removed her from his heart, but his heart was not listening. Instead, it was demanding that he remove Marcus Dobney from his place at Elizabeth's side. Of course, he would not do such a thing; he had no right or reason for such an action. Again he attempted to remind his heart that it had been rejected.

Philip bit his lip to keep from chuckling and pulled his wife a bit closer to his side as he watched Darcy fight to control himself. "Mary Ellen must cease all attempts to match Marcus with Miss Bennet, or I fear," he whispered, "he and Darcy will be coming to blows."

Lucy, who had also been watching the meeting, looked at her husband, a slight smile tipped the corners of her mouth up showing her delight. "I believe you are right," she whispered in agreement. Then she tipped her head toward Darcy. "You might wish to greet him. It may be the distraction he needs."

Philip winked at her and followed her suggestion. "Darcy, it is a delight to see you." He waited patiently for the gentleman to acknowledge him.

Slowly, Darcy turned toward him, a smile spreading across his face. "Ah, Philip, Mrs. Dobney."

"Lucy," Lucy corrected, "we are among friends. Will you be with us long?"

A short conversation about Georgiana and some estate matters followed this, and Elizabeth was glad for the moment to compose herself. He had greeted her so kindly. Perhaps, she had not completely lost his good opinion. The thought both caused her heart to hurt and flutter in the same rapid beat.

"I take it you have met the Abbots' guest before today." Philip felt Lucy nudge him in the side, but it was too late, the words had already been spoken.

"Yes, I have." Darcy's answer was short, which to anyone who knew the man as Philip and Lucy did was a sign that there was information he did not wish to impart at this time — perhaps later in a more private location, but not as they were in a group.

"My father's estate borders Netherfield," Elizabeth explained, feeling the need to fill the moment's silence that followed Darcy's answer. "It is not more than a three-mile walk."

Her heart was still racing, but her mind had begun to function more normally. They could meet as friends; surely he would be willing to do so. She cast a questioning look towards him, and thankfully, her mind fell upon a topic which might put everyone at ease. "Mr. Dobney,

Mary Ellen," she said turning toward them, "Mr. Darcy could tell you about Jane. I believe he knows her to some extent, and his opinions may be less partial than mine, for I do tend to see only the best in her."

Darcy looked startled for a moment. "I know very little of her. I fear I might do her a disservice."

"Not purposefully, I am sure," Elizabeth said softly. "You seem the sort of man who would never injure another without cause. I am not wrong, am I?"

Darcy searched her eyes. Did she mean what he thought? Had his letter served its purpose in correcting her misconceptions? Might she welcome his presence? "You are not wrong."

She smiled and her stomach flipped as he smiled in return and the wall that seemed to part them crumbled at her feet.

"Miss Bennet, Jane," he clarified, "is," he paused, "an angel. She is both beautiful and kind. She seemingly keeps her emotions under good regulation. She did not complain once while she convalesced at Netherfield — and she was quite ill." He tilted his head and looked at Elizabeth. "As far as I could tell, she has but two faults. She is altogether too pleasant, and she smiles too much." He could not help the delight he felt as he saw Elizabeth's brows raise and her eyes sparkle.

"And it is a good thing she does," Elizabeth replied, "or

I would not have seen a smile the entire time I was at Netherfield."

Darcy chuckled. "Bingley smiles."

"Very true. I have been corrected once again." She turned to Mary Ellen. "If it had not been for Mr. Bingley, my stay would have been very," she tapped her lip as she considered her choice of description, "dreary."

"Dreary?" Darcy said in surprise.

"Yes, Mr. Darcy, dreary." Elizabeth tilted her head. "Or do you prefer dull, mundane or prosaic?"

"Surely, it was not so bad as that," interrupted Mary Ellen. "I cannot imagine Mr. Bingley allowing it to be so."

Elizabeth laughed. "Indeed. Mr. Bingley is as lively as he is pleasant."

Darcy agreed with the statement but refused to allow that he, himself, had been dreary. "I was not silent, and I did not stay in my rooms. I think I did an admirable job of being pleasant considering the circumstances." He smiled at Mary Ellen who was looking rather confused. "Bingley's sisters."

Elizabeth heard Marcus groan softly. Apparently, Hertfordshire was not the only place where Caroline and Louisa were not admired.

"Ah, Mr. Darcy," Mr. Abbot exerted himself into the conversation. "It is a pleasure to see you, sir. All is well, if that was the purpose of your call. The fence has been fixed and the sheep are happy for it."

"You must come in and have some refreshment, Mr. Darcy," added Mrs. Abbot. "Travelling even a short distance on such a dry day can make one thirsty."

Darcy bowed and accepted her offer. He would call every day to check on Willow Hall and its tenants if it meant he could spend time with Elizabeth. He fell into step with her as they entered the house. "Why am I telling my friends of your sister?"

"I have just had the most delightful letter informing me of her arrival in a week's time."

"She is coming to Willow Hall?"

Elizabeth nodded. "She is travelling with my aunt and uncle Gardiner. Aunt Gardiner and Mrs. Abbot are sisters, you see. Uncle had planned to take me with them on a trip around the lake district, but his plans had to be altered. So, I was sent on ahead, and now Jane shall be able to accompany them."

"Will you be staying long at Willow Hall?" he asked hopefully. If she were staying, he might have a chance to convince her of his worth.

"Two months complete."

Darcy looked about the room. The others had taken seats and were in discussion with each other, but he still spoke quietly even though they were a few paces away from the others, standing just inside the door to the room. "Might I call on you and introduce you to my sister?"

A small amount of peace washed over her. He was not

averse to remaining acquaintances. "It would be an hon-our, sir."

"I must return to London next week, but at the end of the month, I shall return. Georgiana will stay behind at Pemberley. Lucy will see that she is well, and if you will visit, I shall not worry about her being bored or lonely while I am gone."

Elizabeth could hear the care and worry in his voice for his sister.

"You should know," he continued after a short pause, "Bingley and his sisters will be with me when I return."

"Mr. Bingley?" Elizabeth's eyes grew wide, and her hand flew to her heart. "But, Jane...oh." She had hoped that a tour of the country and a stay at Willow Hall might be beneficial to Jane's state of mind, but if Mr. Bingley were to be here...

"That is why I am telling you," Darcy said softly. "Shall we join the others?" He asked motioning toward where a lively story was being shared by Mary Ellen.

Lucy rested her chin on her shoulder and watched Darcy and Elizabeth conversing. It was obvious to her that they were good friends, if not more. She had never seen Darcy stand so close to a lady or speak at such length. Elizabeth must be the lady about whom he had written to Philip. Her brows furrowed. Those letters had not spoken of a happy man. Philip had been quite uneasy about sharing parts of them with her, but he was equally as uneasy about what he feared was his friend's state of mind.

However, there was no sign of that desperate man here. Elizabeth was lovely. It was not hard for her to imagine Darcy losing his heart to such a lady. They would make a good pair. Mary Ellen's laugh brought her back to the conversation. She sighed. Hopefully, Mary Ellen would be content to have Elizabeth for a neighbour instead of a sister, for after the help Darcy had given her in ridding her of her uncle and achieving her current happiness, she would do her best to see the favour returned.

Chapter 3

Darcy paced beneath a large oak tree, stopping now and again to cast a glance down the path toward Willow Hall. Elizabeth had mentioned taking a walk each morning on this path. Being unfamiliar with the area, she dared not venture too far from the house, so Mr. Abbot had shown her this pleasant path that would take her to the lower field where the remains of a wall stood. It was, she said, much better than repeating the same small circuit in the garden. She had laughed at the idea of growing dizzy with all the turning.

Darcy chuckled at the thought as he made a circuit of the tree and then continued pacing. Perhaps he should have told her that he planned to meet her, but the idea had not come to him until last night when he was sitting in his library wishing she was there.

He removed his hat and ran his hand through his hair. He knew it was dangerous to be allowing himself to hope as he was, but she had seemed welcoming yesterday. She had even agreed to meet his sister. Surely, if she were set against him, she would have refused, or so he thought.

Again, he took a circuit of the great old tree, and this time, as he rounded it and faced Willow Hall, he saw her. He immediately put his hat on and then took it off. He ran his hand through his hair once again and replaced the hat, only to remove it a few seconds later as he waited for her to come close enough to greet.

"Mr. Darcy," Elizabeth called, a smile lighting her face as she approached. "I see you still practice the exercise of walking each morning, although, it would seem you have wandered very far from your home."

He chuckled at the teasing tone of her voice. "I was actually riding," he said as she joined him.

She peeked around him. "Is your horse behind the tree then?"

He shook his head and offered her his arm. "No, I left him at the wall and walked up here in hopes of seeing you." He placed his hat back on his head. "I hope I was not being too forward in doing so. I do not want to intrude on your solitude."

"Your presence is not an intrusion, sir." Elizabeth watched the path before her. If she was to be honest, she had hoped to meet him on her walk, for there were things which she needed to say to him, things that could not be discussed in company, things she had wished to say for months now. "I must apologize," she began.

"No," he interrupted. "You said nothing that I did not deserve to hear."

"That does not make it right," she argued.

"Neither one of us was without fault on that occasion," he conceded. "I had hoped we might move forward as..." He stopped walking and looked at her, the corner of his bottom lip pulled between his teeth in uncertainty. "I had hoped," he began again, "that we might move forward as friends." He noted how the light in her eyes faded and her lips no longer smiled as widely. "I was certain when I left Rosings that I would never see you again, and then yesterday, when you were here, and you welcomed me, I began to hope..." His voice trailed off, but his eyes held fast to hers.

"As friends?" The word dug at her heart.

"It is not what I would truly wish," he said softly, "but, I am determined to be happy with mere friendship if you would allow it."

She tipped her head to the right, and her eyebrows drew together just slightly as she looked at him. "What do you wish?" Her heart drummed fast and heavy in her chest as she voiced the question.

He smiled sadly. "My wishes and desires remain as they were."

Her cheeks reddened, and she had to look away as she asked, "And what if my wishes have changed?" She looked back at him briefly before looking away once again. "Is there any hope that we might ever be more?" She shook her head. "I know I do not deserve it, but might I have a second chance?" Nearly before she had finished speaking the words, she found herself wrapped in his embrace, and then just as quickly, she was standing on the path looking at his back.

"Forgive me. I should not have — "

"I am uninjured, sir," she interrupted.

"But I had no right — " Her smile as he turned toward her snatched all thought from his head.

"I am uninjured, sir," she repeated. "In fact, I find I am quite well — more well than I have been in months." She began walking for fear that if she stood still he might embrace her once again, which was an action she would happily allow and even return.

Elizabeth heard Darcy's hurried steps as he came to walk beside her. Joining her, they continued down the path for some minutes in perceived silence, but although there was no word of conversation spoken, their closeness and the comfort of such nearness spoke where words could not as each considered the other with varying degrees of delight. Hope filled each heart.

As they approached the wall which stood in the field just beyond where the trees ended, Darcy finally spoke. "You would welcome my addresses?"

She nodded and peeked at him, thankful for the brim of her bonnet that kept him from looking at her directly. It was not that she was necessarily shy, but speaking of one's heart to the object of that heart's desire was naturally uncomfortable when one had never done such a thing before. In fact, this was the first time that Elizabeth's heart had ever desired any person and his good opinion as it desired Darcy and his opinion. "I would. Very much."

Her hands twisted together slightly and her heart kept its loud and rapid beat in her chest as she continued, for though the topic was a new one, she would not retreat from it, no matter how much her mind begged her to do just that. "I have long regretted my words and my refusal. No, do not acquit me of my words or behaviour. I must speak what I have been contemplating." She looked at him, and he nodded. "My discernment of your character was so faulty that I am truly ashamed of what I said."

He held his arm out to her as they exited the trees. "Please?" he pleaded as she looked at his arm with indecision. "I shall control myself," he murmured.

A small giggle escaped her, and she placed her hand on his arm. The contact of her gloved hand on his jacketed arm and the small act of drawing closer to him did nothing to calm the beat of her heart, but it did bring a peace and reassurance to her mind. "Your words were not untrue. My family has its faults, and my standing is not so great as yours. My relatives do not hold titles or large amounts of land. My father, while I love him dearly, is not so attentive to his duties as he should be. He finds too much enjoyment in the follies of not just others but also his family. Though

I have tried, I cannot absolve him of his guilt in the behaviour of my mother and youngest sisters. I have attempted since that day when we last spoke in Kent to sway his opinions and provoke him to action, but I have not succeeded."

Darcy did not miss the pain in her voice and, in response, covered her hand with his free one, squeezing lightly in an attempt to comfort her. His comments about her beloved father were the ones which had caused him the deepest amount of regret. Had someone said such things, whether true or not, about either of his parents, he would have been, at least, as angry as she had been.

"The one thing which I still struggle with to some degree is your interference with my sister." She felt his arm tense beneath hers. "I cannot fault you for seeing to the care of a friend, but I cannot forget the despondence of Jane. On this matter, I still find my mind divided." She paused. "As for the last matter," she looked away and shook her head, "my self-reproach is most severe. I know better than to listen to tales and take them as fact without allowing for a careful examination of both sides. How you could ever forgive me for such behaviour only accentuates my deficiency in considering your character wanting."

They had reached the wall by this time and stood there with her hand still clinging to his arm, and his hand holding it there firmly. Neither wished to part from the other even for a moment.

"You need not explain your actions to me," Elizabeth

continued. "Your letter has done so each day." She pulled the well-worn paper from her pocket. "It has been both my reproach and my comfort for these many months, for it is both a reminder of my foolishness and a soothing substitute for your presence because it is your voice I hear as I read it." She put the letter back in her pocket. "I have, since the third or fourth reading of your letter, longed to be able to withdraw my refusal, to turn it on its head and happily accept, but I dared not hope for such good fortune until now."

She drew a deep breath and released it, then turning to face him and taking both his hands in hers, she said, "I have been as foolish as any member of my family. I cannot promote myself to you as worthy of your status or your name, and my portion is not great. However, if you will have me, I can promise to always strive to bring you the honour you deserve and to continue to love you as I do now, most ardently."

"I fear I have lied," he said with a smile.

Her brows drew together as she searched his face. Confusion created by the gravity of his words and the joy of his smile was clearly written on her face. He freed one hand from her hold and placed it softly on her cheek. "I have lied," he continued, "for I am uncertain that I can keep myself under regulation when such loveliness stands before me offering herself to me. I can think of nothing in this world that would keep me from accepting you." He brushed his thumb across her cheek. "I would marry you this day, if I were able." His thumb brushed her cheek once more. "But," he continued, "first, I must speak to your father." His eyes grew worried. "Will he allow it?"

A smile lit her face. "If he does not, mention it to my mother, and he shall soon change his mind." She laughed with him at the thought, but then sobering, she added, "I shall write to him, so that he might be assured that this is my wish."

"You truly wish this? You would have me, arrogant man that I am?"

"I would."

He tossed his hat on the ground and taking her face in his hands, bent to kiss her.

The sensation of his lips pressed against hers took Elizabeth by surprise, and without her willing it to do so, her body leaned into him and her arms wound around his waist as if they knew exactly what to do.

It was no wonder some ladies found themselves in compromising positions when their senses were so attacked as to be wholly outside their own power Elizabeth thought, as she stood some moments later, wrapped in Darcy's arms, her head on his chest. Her mind even now knew that standing here, embracing and being embraced, was not proper, but her body was not willing to listen to anything but the beating of his heart, which matched her own rapid pulse. It was with regret that she followed his lead and slowly stepped away from the embrace when finally both hearts had returned to a more normal rhythm.

"I must go on," said Darcy, "and you must return to Willow Hall." His hand caressed her cheek, and his smile looked almost sad. "I will call later at a proper time, if you are agreeable."

She nodded. "I would be happy to receive your call, Mr. Darcy."

"Fitzwilliam." His voice was soft. "You must call me Fitzwilliam for I intend to call you Elizabeth." There was a stubbornness to the set of his mouth and eyes as if he were prepared to defend his decision.

She raised an impertinent brow and attempted to keep from smiling but could not. "Will it not seem strange to the Abbots if we address each other so informally?"

He chuckled. "Indeed it would, but I do not intend to call you Elizabeth save when we are alone as we are now. I have referred to you as such in my thoughts for some months now." He shook his head. "Nay, nearly a year."

"A year?" She looked at him in question, not only because of the length of time that he had considered her, but because in contradiction to his words of needing to leave, he had tucked her hand into the crook of his arm and was walking with her back toward Willow Hall.

"I do not know exactly when I began to think of you in such familiar terms, but I am fairly certain that it was after your stay at Netherfield." He smiled sheepishly at her. "You were charming."

"I was not," she disagreed. "I was disagreeable."

He shrugged. "It was most charming."

She laughed and held his arm more tightly as she stepped towards him as if there was something about his person that drew her to him. "So I have not only promised myself to an arrogant man, but one who finds argument and debate to be charming?"

He nodded. "So it would seem."

She heard him sigh.

"Do you regret your answer?" he asked.

Elizabeth shook her head and then lay it against his shoulder. "Not this time."

The letter in her pocket reminded her of just how fortunate she was to have been given this opportunity to correct her mistake. "I shall never regret it," she added softly.

She smiled as she heard him sigh once again, only this time instead of holding concern, it was an exhalation of peace. So they walked, slowly, toward the tree where he had met her that morning, where he gave her a second kiss, and where he stood watching her until she reached a turn in the path.

As Darcy stood looking at the path where Elizabeth had been, he considered his good fortune in not only having found her again but in being accepted. He wanted to whoop and toss his hat in the air, but that particular article of clothing was still on the ground next to where he had kissed her the first time.

A smile spread across his face. She was his, or nearly so. He would leave early for town so that he would have time to speak with her father, and then, he would plead a need to see his sister to Bingley, so that he might return to Derbyshire sooner than originally planned. And once returned, he would make known to one and all that she was his.

Plans in place, he drew in a deep breath, released it quickly, and headed back to the wall to find his hat and his horse.

Chapter 4

Days passed. Calls were made and received. Friendships were begun and strengthened. Life and love, like the fields where the labourers toiled, blossomed and flourished. All seemed idyllic, but on such serene and happy times, there must of necessity encroach some form of displeasure or discontent. For Darcy and Elizabeth, this came in the form of a necessary separation of a fortnight, which is not so very long — unless one is in love. And Darcy and Elizabeth were in love. Though they had not spoken of such things, even in private, to any of the friends who surrounded them, there was little doubt in anyone's mind that the two were more than mere friends as they claimed.

Darcy's agitation as he prepared to leave nearly a week after his arrival was quite obvious to Philip, who had, at his friend's request, called at Pemberley. He sat silently waiting in Darcy's study as Darcy shuffled papers and muttered under his breath about business that should have been sorted out but was not.

Finally, his desk cleared of all pressing matters, Darcy

leaned back in his chair and began the necessary conversation. "I am reluctant to leave."

Philip nodded. "That is obvious."

Darcy raised a brow.

"You become testy when faced with a duty you do not wish to do but feel must be done," Philip explained.

Darcy sighed. "I apologize. I am reluctant to leave Georgiana." It was partially true. "And because of my reluctance, I wish to ask a favour of you." He ran a finger along the edge of a pile of papers on his desk and allowed his eyes to follow it. He could still not speak of his failure in regard to his sister without some degree of shame. "You and Lucy know of the damage done to her last year."

"She seems recovered," said Philip.

"Yes, and I thank you and Lucy for that. Had you not been willing to take her in for those few weeks while a new companion was obtained, I am certain her recovery would not have been so quick."

"I cannot take credit for that, my friend. It was Lucy." He smiled. "Who would have thought that having nearly had her reputation ruined by her uncle would have been a blessing?" And in truth, it was the commonality of having lost parents and been preyed upon by men who should have been trustworthy which had bonded the two ladies together during that time.

Darcy reluctantly nodded his agreement.

"Lucy's father could not prevent her uncle from acting

as he did, any more than you could have prevented Wickham's actions. You may be master of a large estate, but you are not God. Therefore, you cannot discern the intentions of any man save yourself." Philip tried to keep his voice from sounding too much like he was delivering a message from the pulpit rather than sitting in the home of a friend, offering encouragement.

"I have tried to believe that," said Darcy, "but the fact remains —"

"The fact remains," interrupted Philip, "that what has happened in the past cannot be undone. Your sister will be well. Lucy and I will see to it." He leaned forward in his chair, a small smile on his face. "And I do not believe for one moment that it is leaving your sister that has you in such a state. There have been several occasions over the past year when you have left her to deal with business. I do believe, however, that her experience of being taken in during your absence has you worried that the same may happen to Miss Bennet."

The speed with which Darcy rose from his chair and crossed to the window was all the confirmation that Philip needed. He waited patiently for his friend to speak.

"I lost her once." Darcy's shoulders drooped and his voice was soft. "I narrowly survived the experience. I am not sure I would survive a second time."

Philip tipped his head to the side and studied his friend's back. "So she is the lady of whom you wrote?"

Darcy nodded.

"I suspected as much." Philip rose to join his friend at the window. "Do you fear she is inconstant in her affection? Or does she still withhold her heart from you?"

"No," said Darcy, "she has given me no reason to doubt her, and yet, I do." He expelled a loud breath as he tried to relieve the feeling of guilt such thoughts brought to him. "And I should not."

Philip clapped him on the shoulder. "Do you see the beauty of the garden?"

Darcy gave him a puzzled look.

"An illustration, my friend," Philip answered with a smile before turning his gaze back to the paths lined with blooms and greenery. "The caretaker no longer worries about the growth of the shrubberies or the trees or the flowers, but when they were newly planted, he did. Presently, he tends and nurtures their growth, but he no longer fears they will not bloom. The same is true of love. Although I still nurture the love that I share with Lucy, I no longer fear it will not bloom. However, you are in the first throes of love, so naturally fears will follow." Philip leaned against the window frame. "A little faith is what is needed. Tell me," he continued, "what is the worst that could happen during your absence?"

"Fire, accident, disease — "

Philip held up a hand to stop the flow of disastrous events. "I really should know better than to ask such a question of you." He chuckled. "Allow me to rephrase my question. Who, in our acquaintance, would attempt to steal her away from you?" He held up his hand again to forestall Darcy's answer. "Wickham is not here, and the only unattached gentleman Miss Bennet knows well is my brother." He lowered his hand.

"There are others in your parish," Darcy protested rather weakly.

Philip shook his head. "Miss Bennet met many of them before you arrived and even with my sister trying to arrange a match between Miss Bennet and Marcus, she has shown no interest in any. In fact, she was quite uncomfortable with all of Mary Ellen's attempts. You have nothing to fear."

Darcy's brows furrowed, and his mouth turned down in a small frown as he thought.

"Lucy and I will do all in our power to see that Miss Bennet is just as attached to you when you return as she is now." Seeing his friend's features did not relax, he added, "I shall write to you straightaway if any new gentlemen enter our neighbourhood. I shall even offer my sister as tribute in Miss Bennet's stead." He lay his hand on his heart and affected a somber expression as he said the last.

Darcy relaxed and shook his head. "You are a good friend." He chuckled. "So good a friend that I will not mention your offer to Mary Ellen."

Philip laughed. "I thank you for that."

~*~*~

Elizabeth folded the letter and dried her eyes. She leaned her head against the tree and looked up into its canopy. She was uncertain how long she had sat there trying to compose herself. Her emotions had been anything but complacent since yesterday. She shoved her handkerchief into her pocket and drew first one deep breath and then another. It would not do to return to the house looking as she imagined she did now. She closed her eyes. She had thought her tears had been expended before sleep last night. She chuckled lightly at herself. Who in her family would believe that the man she had so vehemently opposed in all things had now become the source of both her delight and sorrow?

It had been a delight to see him waiting for her under this very tree this morning. She had thought yesterday was the last she would see him until the month's end, but he refused to leave until he had seen her once more. So, while his coach and four sat on the side of the nearby road, he had come to stand under this tree until he had been able to give her the letter she now held. For a man of few words, his ability to write a letter and express his soul in those words was truly amazing. She lifted the paper that held his professions of love and longing to her lips and gave it a kiss. "And I love you, Fitzwilliam," she whispered before tucking the new letter into her pocket next to the old one.

With one more deep sigh, she felt ready to continue her walk and face the day.

Jane and the Gardiners would be arriving the day after tomorrow. She must think on that. She rose, shook any bits of dirt or leaves from her skirts, squared her shoulders, and, affixing a smile to her lips, began walking in the direction of Willow Hall. Several times while she walked she had to remind herself to smile, to hide the pain that was in her heart, and every time she did, she wondered anew at how Jane was able to smile so very much.

"Ah, there you are," called Mrs. Abbot when Elizabeth neared the house. "I was afraid you might have gotten lost on your rambling." She tilted her head to the side and gave Elizabeth a searching look. "You look a bit worse for the wear this morning. Are you well?"

Elizabeth nodded. "I am well, although I must admit to not having slept soundly last night."

"Then you must take a rest after you have had your breakfast." She took Elizabeth by the arm and walked toward the house with her. "I dare say, with Mr. Darcy being gone, we will have fewer visitors today."

"I believe you are correct," said Elizabeth, the thought doing nothing to aid her in her attempts to smile and be pleasant. "However, the house will be full soon."

Mrs. Abbot squeezed Elizabeth's arm. "I am quite excited," she admitted. "I have not seen Marjorie in nearly a year. She was with me for Aiden's birth, you know."

Elizabeth nodded and allowed Cecily to prattle on about how delightful her younger son was and how he had nearly taken a step yesterday, which was at least a full month ahead of when his brother, Lucas, had attempted such a feat. The Abbot brothers were delightful. Elizabeth had spent many hours of her stay with them, reading books and building blocks, just as she had done with Aunt Gardiner's children when they were young.

"One day," Cecily was saying, "you will have your own children to crow about." She sat a cup of tea before Elizabeth. "Will it be soon?" she asked with a sly smile.

"I do not see how it can be," said Elizabeth with surprise. "It is still the practice to marry before having children, and I am not married."

Cecily laughed heartily at the comment. Gathering herself, she clarified, "I apologize for being unclear. I had meant will you be marrying soon, so that our little ones might grow up together?"

Elizabeth took a sip of her tea and slowly lowered the cup back to the table as she sought for a way to answer such a question without saying too much. She and Mr. Darcy had agreed that their understanding was to be of a secretive nature until he had been able to secure her father's approval. "I cannot say." Her cheeks glowed rosy. It was not a lie. She could not say without breaking her promise to Mr. Darcy, and yet, her heart felt it a half-truth.

A smile spread across Cecily's face. "Then, I shall not

press you on the matter until Mr. Darcy returns." The words were spoken in a loud whisper.

"Thank you," said Elizabeth. "I simply cannot say," she repeated.

Cecily patted her hand. "But it is not that you do not know."

Elizabeth's cheeks felt as if they were on fire now.

"I will say no more." Cecily pretended to lock her lips and place a key into her pocket.

Elizabeth rolled her eyes and shook her head.

"A fortnight is not so very long," Cecily commented as she lifted her own cup of tea and gave Elizabeth a wink. "He will be returned before you know it. I remember when my Harry would be gone for some reason or another — all related to business, of course."

Again, Elizabeth smiled and nodded and continued on with her breakfast while her friend told her story after story of the year before she and her husband were married and a bit about the year following.

"He was such a diligent worker. I am sure there is not another like him in all of Derbyshire." She paused to sip her tea. "And the Lord has rewarded us for it. Willow Hall is beautiful. My children are strong and healthy, and my Harry is no longer called away as he once was." She took another sip of tea. "He is still a hard worker. The best of men is what he is." She finished her tea. "Now look at me, talking and talking about my blessings and not allowing you a word."

"I enjoy hearing of your blessings, Cecily," assured Elizabeth. Indeed, it was what she had needed to take her mind off the events of the morning.

"Well, now," said Cecily after scrutinizing Elizabeth's face. "I must say you look better for having eaten." She stood. "Time for a rest."

Elizabeth sighed.

"No, I will not stand for you wearing yourself out and becoming ill." Cecily's hands were placed firmly on her hips, and although she was not more than six years Elizabeth's senior, she looked for all the world like a well-practiced matron. "One hour," she said definitively. "We shall not have visitors for at least one hour, so you are to lie on your bed until that time has passed."

Elizabeth rose to do as instructed but instead of allowing Elizabeth to pass, Cecily stepped in front of her and drew her into a firm embrace. "He will return like the wind. It was in his eyes," she whispered. Then, she gave Elizabeth a kiss on the cheek and allowed her to continue on her way.

Chapter 5

An hour is an incredibly small amount of time to lie on one's bed if weary, but when one's mind is filled with thoughts such as Elizabeth's was, it can be a very long time indeed. Feeling no more rested now than when she had first lain down, Elizabeth rose and readied herself for the possibility of callers.

"Oh, my, this is excellent news!" Cecily's voice carried from the sitting room and climbed the stairs to where Elizabeth was descending.

"Elizabeth! Elizabeth!" she called as she hurried into the hall. "Oh, Elizabeth, you will never guess, but it is the most excellent news." Cecily waved the letter she held. "Our sisters will be here tomorrow."

"Tomorrow?" Elizabeth said in surprise.

Cecily's head bobbed up and down, her smile seeming to grow with each bob. "My brother Edward concluded his business early, and so they will arrive early." She clasped the letter to her chest. "Oh, I must alert Mrs. Smith. There is so much to be done."

"I dare say there is little to be done," said Harold Abbot as he watched his wife hurrying down the hall in search of the housekeeper.

Elizabeth laughed. "Very little needs doing. The beds have been made for three days now, and the rooms have been aired. I suppose it is just a matter of informing the cook of a larger number of guests for meals."

"And cutting fresh flowers," said Mr. Abbot.

Elizabeth sank into a chair in the sitting room and placed her workbasket on the floor next to her chair. She pulled out a piece that she had begun last week and prepared to work on it. "I suppose the flowers will be best gathered in the morning," she said.

Mr. Abbot agreed but worried slightly that his excited wife would not be able to wait so long to prepare. "I say, you do not seem so excited to see Jane as Cecily is to see Marjorie," he commented with a laugh.

"It has not been a year since I last saw Jane," explained Elizabeth.

Mr. Abbot smiled at her as he opened his book. "I dare say you would not be so exuberant as Cecily even if it had been a year. We each express our delight in different ways. Cecily happens to be more demonstrative than most, although not improperly so. Had we had company — beyond family — when the letter arrived, I know her excitement would have been better contained. However, I cannot fault her for her exuberance. It is a wonderful thing to have people you love visit after a long absence."

"Indeed," said Elizabeth. "I cannot imagine having so long a time away from Jane."

Mr. Abbot peeked up from his book and winked at her. "A hazard of marrying someone who is not local. But Edward is a good man and has done well for himself. It was a good match." He chuckled. "Not that I was even courting Cecily when Edward stole Marjorie away from Lambton." He lifted his book to read once again. "It would be nice to have more family settle in the area," he muttered.

He had not lifted the book quite high enough to hide the knowing smile that accompanied the statement, and Elizabeth was positive that it was done purposefully. The Abbots were so happy in their marriage that any news that hinted at another possible happy match always brought out their teasing natures.

Elizabeth shook her head and applied herself to her work, allowing the comment to go unanswered. She knew that neither Cecily or Harold would be indiscreet or excessive in their comments. She would merely have to endure a few remarks made in private and intended to let her know of their understanding and support.

It was a far cry better than what she would experience at home once her betrothal was made known. Her mother was not discreet, nor did she know how best to express her delight.

Elizabeth closed her eyes for a moment and sent a silent prayer toward heaven that her father would not tell her mother of the betrothal until after Mr. Darcy left. She knew Mr. Darcy was willing to accept her despite her mother, but there really was no need to make the acceptance more difficult than it needed to be.

As she stitched, her thoughts wandered from her mother, who was certain to be excessively excited, to her younger sisters, who were equally as likely to cause embarrassment. She sighed. At least Lydia was not at home. There might be some hope of Mary and Kitty behaving appropriately. So her thoughts continued for some time, and she was just beginning to think they would have a very quiet afternoon when the crunch of carriage wheels on the gravel of the drive wafted through the open window.

"At last," said Mr. Abbot, snapping his book closed. "I was afraid I was going to have to read for an entire afternoon." He winked again at Elizabeth, who smiled in return. Mr. Abbot was almost as fond of reading as her father or Uncle Gardiner. To have to pass an afternoon or evening with only a book as company would have been a very small hardship.

"It looks like Mr. Dobney," he said as he peered through the window. "He appears to have his sister and some other gentleman with him." He cocked his head to the side. "I do not think I have met him."

Elizabeth joined Mr. Abbot at the window to catch a glimpse of the stranger.

"Not a bad looking fellow," muttered Mr. Abbot.

Elizabeth had to agree. The gentleman seated next to Mr. Dobney was handsome. "But looks do not signify character," she added to her agreement.

"Quite so," Mr. Abbot agreed as they moved away from the window and took their seats once again until the party was announced and they rose in greeting.

"May I present my cousin, Captain Harris," said Marcus. "He arrived quite unexpectedly last evening."

Elizabeth noted the pointed look that Marcus gave to the man beside him.

"I promise I had written of my intent to call on my cousins," Captain Harris defended himself. "In fact, the letter arrived this morning."

"His directions were so poorly written," said Mary Ellen, "that it is a wonder we received it at all." She smiled at her cousin and spoke with a teasing tone. "But we did." She took a seat on the couch near Elizabeth and Captain Harris joined her once all the proper introductions had been made.

"You are in the militia?" Elizabeth queried.

Captain Harris gave a sharp nod of his head. "I am, but I have been given some time to visit family. However, it will not be so long as it could be since the distance between Brighton and Derbyshire is not small."

"You are in Brighton?" Elizabeth asked with surprise. "You are not part of Colonel Forester's unit, are you?"

"No." Captain Harris shook his head firmly. "Colonel Fitzwilliam's." He tapped Mary Ellen's knee lightly with his own, causing her cheeks to flush.

"Mr. Darcy's cousin?"

"You know him?" asked Captain Harris.

Elizabeth nodded. "I met him in Kent at Easter. He is very pleasant, but I did not see him as a colonel, only as a guest of his aunt, so your opinion of him might be very different from mine, Captain Harris."

Captain Harris smiled. "I hold my colonel in highest regard, Miss Bennet. He is among the best."

"It is good to hear my judgement of him was not mistaken." Elizabeth was sure it sounded like the correct thing to say, but to her, whose judgement had been so very flawed regarding so many people, it was much more than a comment to be thrown away. It was an acknowledgement that she was not totally without sense in judging character.

"Now, Colonel Forester has the marking of one day being a fine colonel, but..." He shook his head and clucked his tongue softly, "he has been given quite the challenging band of recruits. A rather ragtag and bobtail lot they are."

Elizabeth's brows rose in surprise. She had not thought the regiment from Meryton was so very bad.

"Oh, not the whole lot, that is very unfair of me to

say." Seeing her expression, he adjusted his estimation. "It seems it is always just a few who make the reputation of the whole."

She could not disagree with that, although she felt as if she should, for his judgement seemed presumptuous. Colonel Forester had been a very agreeable man, and she knew that he did not use discipline sparingly. "Do Colonel Forester and his wife get on well?"

The question was asked but remained unanswered for some minutes as Cecily finally returned to the room just before the tea tray, requiring that introductions be made. Finally, when tea had been served, Captain Harris returned to their discussion.

"I do not wish to offend," he said softly, "but Mrs. Forester is a bit silly, although I am certain that much of that has to do with her age. She is not very old." He took a sip of his tea. "She has a friend staying with her. A bit of a flirt." He took another sip of his tea. "Oh, what is her name? I should know it. I am sure I have heard it in a half dozen or so conversations."

Elizabeth sighed. "Miss Bennet."

Captain Harris grimaced. "A relation?" he asked.

"My sister."

"Well, I have put my foot in it now, haven't I?" He shook his head and smiled sheepishly.

Although Elizabeth was indeed mortified to hear a complete stranger refer to her sister as a flirt, she was glad to hear something of how Lydia fared. Jane had shared some of what Lydia had written to Kitty, but it was all uniforms, handsome men, and soirees with a bit about the sites and sea at Brighton.

"I would rather the truth than a pleasing lie," said Elizabeth with a smile. "I am sorry to say that my youngest sister is an incurable flirt. Please tell me that she has not done anything to bring utter shame to her family." She held up a finger. "But only if it is the truth. I shall prepare myself for the worst, of course."

"She is a trial to you?" asked Mary Ellen.

"She acts without thought," Elizabeth said quietly. "She has a lively spirit, but it has been left unchecked." Her cheeks burned with the admission that her father had not done his duty by his family through allowing Lydia to continue as she always had.

"That is unfortunate." Mary Ellen placed a hand on Elizabeth's.

Elizabeth nodded her agreement.

"I assure you," said Captain Harris, "that beyond flirting, I have not heard of anything improper." He grimaced once again. "However, the objects of her flirtation leave something to be desired."

Elizabeth shook her head and closed her eyes. She knew of whom he spoke. "Mr. Wickham is still among that number?" To her surprise, she felt Mary Ellen's hand tighten on hers. The action made the small nervous fluttering sensation in her stomach, which she felt each time she thought of Lydia in Brighton, grow to a churning. The look of concern in Mary Ellen's eyes when Elizabeth looked at her did nothing to quell the nerves.

"He is." Captain Harris' voice was grave. "He is not a proper companion for any young lady."

Elizabeth sighed. She knew this to be true now. How she longed to go back to last fall and reform her impressions of him then. Perhaps, if she had taken a more careful look at what Mr. Wickham said and how he presented himself, she might have saved her family and Lydia the association. But, she had not, and now she must bear the weight of that error. "I know," she replied softly.

Captain Harris's smile was sympathetic. "I fear he missed his calling by joining the militia. He is far better suited to the stage, for he certainly knows how to play a part."

Elizabeth nodded. "That I also know."

"As do many," said Mary Ellen. "He is quite convincing." She turned to her cousin. "Perhaps it should be suggested to him. I am certain the fame and fawning which would accompany such a profession would be very appealing to him. A letter to Colonel Fitzwilliam, perhaps?" She spoke lightly as if teasing, but her eyes were serious.

Captain Harris' brows furrowed for a moment before he chuckled. "I shall make mention of it to him; however, I shall have to do so soon, as he is set to depart Brighton for town and then Derbyshire in a week's time. I am not sure a post would reach him in time."

"Oh," said Mary Ellen with a wave of her hand, "we shall send it express, and I shall write the directions so that it will not get lost." She giggled softly as if it were a great joke, but Elizabeth noted how Mary Ellen's grasp on her hand had not yet loosened. It was obvious that the young woman was more fearful than she allowed in her comments. Perhaps she knew of Georgiana's ordeal. She was friends with both Mr. Darcy and his sister.

"Colonel Fitzwilliam is to come to Derbyshire?" Elizabeth asked.

"Aye, he is planning to visit his cousins and his parents, of course. Lord and Lady Matlock have retired to their estate for the summer. I am to remain here until he is to return. Then I am to accompany him, as his current escorts will be given a few weeks to visit their families. Our unit, you see, originates from the towns around here." He tipped his head and peered at Elizabeth, whose brows were furrowed quite deeply as she thought. "Is there something troubling you, Miss Bennet?"

"I was merely wondering why, if Mr. Wickham is from Derbyshire, he is in Colonel Forester's unit and not yours."

"His home is now in London." Mary Ellen's comment was quick.

"Oh," said Elizabeth softly. From the sharpness of her

companion's reply, she was fearful that she had offended but did not know how or why.

Mary Ellen, finally, released Elizabeth's hand and gave it a reassuring pat. "He is no longer welcome here," she said softly. "I dare not say more, for it is not my tale to tell." She bit her lip and studied Elizabeth's face.

"Very well," she said after a moment, "I should not say, but since your sister is well within his sphere of influence, you may wish to speak to Lucy regarding Mr. Wickham, but, please, when you do, be gentle. It is not a pleasant tale."

Elizabeth's heart sank. Lucy, too? How many people had this man injured? Her spirit was troubled for the remainder of the visit and well into the evening. No matter how many times Cecily managed to speak of the arrival of Mrs. Gardiner and Jane, Elizabeth's spirit would not be lifted for more than a few moments.

Finally, as she prepared for bed, she determined that tomorrow, before Jane arrived, she would call on Mrs. Dobney. It was better, she supposed, to hear the sordid tale than to imagine what it might be. Then, she would also be better able to decide if she should write to her father. Perhaps if he knew details of the character of some of the men at Brighton, he would see reason and have Lydia returned home before anything irreversible could happen. Plan in place, she blew out her candle and snuggled under the covers.

Chapter 6

Elizabeth stood just beyond a low border, watching Cecily play with her children in the garden. The ball rolled toward the large tree that shadowed the far corner, and Lucas Abbot, the elder brother at nearly four years of age, ran after it while Aiden Abbott, the younger brother and just three months past his first birthday, swayed slightly and then took one wobbly step followed by another equally unstable step before falling with a plop to the ground. The action of dropping so ungracefully to the ground did not please the young child. His scowl before he took to crawling after his brother made Elizabeth smile. He was a determined young man. A little fall was not going to stop him from pursuing his goal, which at this moment was the ball with which his brother was taunting him.

Cecily waved to Elizabeth. "Come, join us."

Elizabeth, having just returned from what had proven to be a rather disturbing call at the parsonage and wishing for some time to think about all Lucy had shared with her, would have made her excuses and gone into the house.

However, the motion of his mother had turned Aiden toward Elizabeth, and the ball was seemingly forgotten in favour of the new arrival.

"Izabef!" Lucas, ball in hand, reached her before his brother could. "Will you play ball with me, Izabef?"

Elizabeth tousled the boy's hair. "Of course. Do you wish to run before I throw it?"

The young man's head shook furiously from side to side. "I want to race it."

"Very well." Elizabeth took the ball from his hands and squatted down. "Ready," she warned. "Go."

The ball rolled along the grass, passing just beside Aiden, who stopped and sat, looking first at Elizabeth and then the ball — clearly unsure which should get his attention.

"Aiden," Elizabeth called. "Come." She bent down and held out her hands toward him. The smile he turned on her would have been enough of a reward in itself, but the feeling of chubby little arms encircling her neck and a head nuzzling into her shoulder was even better.

"You are a natural," said Cecily as she took Elizabeth's arm and led her to a bench not far from the tree at the end of the garden.

Shadows of shade danced across the bench as the breeze rustled the leaves of the less mature tree beside it. Lucas had returned with his ball, wishing for it to be tossed once again. Cecily obliged him.

"It is his favourite game. He can roll it himself, of course, but he prefers running after it when someone else has rolled it. See how he tries to reach the tree before the ball?"

"I do. He is very quick."

Elizabeth sat Aiden on her lap and squeezed him tightly. He snuggled into her arms and stayed there peacefully for a moment until Lucas once again returned. Then, with a babble that sounded like ball, he began twisting and turning to free himself.

"Very well, young man." Elizabeth stood him on his feet. He teetered a bit, but this time he managed three steps before landing on the ground. "He will be chasing after Lucas before long."

"That he will," said Cecily proudly. "They do keep their nurse busy. When I looked in on them this afternoon, she looked as if she could use a few quiet moments, and I could not resist the beautiful weather. So, here we are. My duties are complete for the moment, and I am free to enjoy the garden with my dear boys. It is one of the great pleasures of motherhood."

Elizabeth closed her eyes and drew a deep breath. "It is a lovely day," she agreed. "I would also choose to sit in the garden on a day like today if I could not take a walk."

"Your walk was pleasant?" It was more than a pleasantry. Elizabeth could hear the curiosity that lay behind the nonchalance of the comment.

"It was." Elizabeth's smile was teasing. She knew what

information Cecily sought. "Not a cloud in the sky. A soft breeze to cool me, and a few birds to add their choruses to my reverie."

"And Mrs. Dobney is well?"

Elizabeth nodded. "Quite well, as is Mr. Dobney."

Cecily sighed. "Are you going to make me ask?"

Elizabeth giggled at the exasperated look on Cecily's face.

"Very well," said Cecily, "was your talk enlightening?"

"Very." Elizabeth assisted the child who was tugging at her skirt to stand. "I must write to my father. Mr. Wickham's character is..." She searched for the best word to describe him. "Reprehensible, completely, utterly reprehensible."

"I have heard enough to agree." Cecily rolled Lucas' ball and, as he scampered after it, turned toward Elizabeth. "I shall not ask you the details, though you know the suffering I must endure not to do so." She laughed as she pulled herself straight and primly folded her hands in her lap. "I will not be like my mother. I absolutely refuse to be a tattler like she. It is not right, no matter how tantalizing and delicious the topic." She sighed, her spine curving as if under a great weight. "Doing right is often very hard."

Elizabeth wrapped an arm around Cecily's shoulders. "It is." She squeezed her friend closely. "I only wish I had done what was right and not listened to Mr. Wickham's tales."

Cecily snaked an arm around Elizabeth's waist and returned the squeeze. "Regret touches us all at one time or another. The trick is to seek forgiveness and proceed with greater wisdom."

She released Elizabeth from her embrace so that she could roll the ball one more time for Lucas. Then, she looked at Elizabeth. It was not a casual or playful glance. No, this was a look that spoke of the seriousness of the words to be spoken and of the love that the speaker had for the hearer.

"A mistake must be forgiven not only by the person wronged but also by the one who committed the error. I believe you have the forgiveness of the person injured." She smiled as Elizabeth nodded. "But do you have your own forgiveness?" She patted Elizabeth's knee.

"Come. We must return these young gentlemen to their nurse so that we might have a few moments of rest before our sisters arrive." She stood and looked over her shoulder at Elizabeth. "I shall catch Lucas if you will take Aiden." She waited for no reply but called to her eldest and dashed toward the tree.

Lucas squealed and darted behind the tree where he stood peeking around it looking for his mother. Elizabeth laughed at the increased squealing and giggling that came from the child as his mother grabbed him and swung him about in a circle before instructing him to get his ball and follow her.

"You heard your mama," Elizabeth said to Aiden. "It is time to return to the nursery." She took hold of each of his pudgy little hands and hoisted him to his feet, allowing him to walk a short distance before snatching him up and carrying him the rest of the way.

~*~*~

Lucy pushed the door to Philip's study open slowly, peeking around it to see if she would be disturbing him. He glanced up from the book he was reading and smiled. Taking that as his welcome, she slipped into the room.

"You had a visitor this morning?" Philip placed the book to the side and leaned forward, resting his elbows on the desk as he crossed his arms.

"I did." Lucy arranged her skirts around her legs. She and Elizabeth had spoken in confidence, but after a time of consideration, she had decided that it was better to share what had been said with her husband than to keep it to herself. Philip was not one to tell tales, and he was a good friend of Darcy's.

"We spoke of Wickham." She knew it was not exactly the softest way to begin this conversation, but then, why try to speak softly of a man such as Wickham? Philip knew as well as she did the sort of man Wickham was. "And my uncle," she added.

Philip's eyes grew wide.

"Your cousin has arrived, and he and Mary Ellen called on the Abbots."

Philip's brows furrowed as he attempted to piece together the puzzle of information his wife was presenting.

"It seems Wickham is in the militia."

Philip nodded slowly. Now it was beginning to make a modicum of sense.

"His unit was stationed for the fall and winter in Hertfordshire."

Philip nodded again. "I believe one of Darcy's letters mentioned having seen the man."

"He befriended Miss Elizabeth."

Philip expelled a slow breath. Not only was the reason for Miss Elizabeth's visit becoming understandable, but several comments from Darcy's letters were also gaining clarity. "He told her lies about Darcy."

Lucy nodded. "And she believed him. She feels dreadful about having done so." She peeked up at her husband. "Darcy has forgiven her, of course." She considered telling him about Elizabeth's tale of Darcy's failed proposal and the letter he had written her but decided it was not necessary as Philip quite likely already knew of those details. And from the look of understanding on his face, she guessed that her theory was correct.

"That is not the reason she wished to speak of Wickham, however. As you know, Miss Elizabeth has several sisters."

Her husband nodded his agreement.

"The youngest, Miss Lydia, is sixteen and quite taken

with Wickham." When she had heard it from Elizabeth, Lucy had felt as if someone has tried to steal her breath, and she saw that same look on her husband's face. "Miss Lydia has gone to Brighton with her particular friend, who happens to be the wife of the colonel in charge of Wickham."

Philip sank back into his chair and shook his head. "Who would send one so young to such a place as Brighton?"

"Miss Elizabeth said she tried to convince her father that it was not a good idea, but she could not give him her full reasoning as she did not wish to betray a confidence."

"She knows of Georgiana?"

Lucy nodded. "She does, and your cousin has made her aware of a continued flirtation between Miss Lydia and Wickham." She drew a deep breath and expelled it. "I have given her permission to mention some of what happened to me to her father. She will not name me but will provide general details of what she has heard of Wickham. She is hopeful that in so doing, her father might find it necessary to have Miss Lydia returned to Hertfordshire."

They sat quietly for a while — Philip drumming his fingers on the desk as he thought and Lucy watching him. Finally, Philip rose from his chair. "I believe we must visit my cousin, my dear. I am surprised he has not come to call already."

He came around to the front of the desk and extended

his arm to Lucy. "And then, I must write Darcy a letter informing him of Captain Harris' arrival."

"You must?" Lucy asked in surprise.

Philip chuckled. "I promised I would write if any new gentlemen arrived in the area — not that I fear my cousin will persuade Miss Elizabeth away from Darcy. However, I should not like to be on the receiving end of Darcy's displeasure should he hear that Harris is here, and I did not inform him."

Lucy laughed. "I doubt there is anyone who could steal Miss Elizabeth away from Darcy."

"Yes," agreed Philip, "but having almost lost her once, he is unwilling to take the risk once again."

Lucy collected her bonnet from the table in the entry as Philip requested his curricle made ready. "So, it is as I expected?"

He opened the door and allowed her to exit before him. "Indeed, if all goes well in Hertfordshire, we shall soon be adding Miss Elizabeth to our numbers here in Derbyshire." He looked down at his wife's beaming smile. "But," he cautioned as they stood waiting for the curricle to be brought around, "we are not to know."

Chapter 7

Hertfordshire

Mr. Bennet gave the gentleman who entered his study an inquisitive look. "It is a surprise to see you, Mr. Darcy." He motioned for him to take a seat. "Is this a social call?"

Darcy did not miss the skeptical tone of Mr. Bennet's question.

"I am not fond of social calls," Darcy admitted knowing that such a comment was bound to earn him a chuckle at his own expense — which it did.

"I find them tedious myself," Mr. Bennet replied. "So if it is not social, I must assume we have some business to discuss, although I cannot say I have any inkling as to what business we might have."

"I have been in Derbyshire," Darcy began.

"You have seen my Lizzy? Does she send news?"

"I have, and she does." He took the letter Elizabeth had written to her father out of his pocket and handed it to Mr. Bennet.

"You could have left it with Hill." Mr. Bennet took the letter. "Were you instructed to await a reply?"

"I was not instructed," said Darcy, "but I will need a reply."

A look of skepticism mixed with intrigue crept across Mr. Bennet's face. "Elizabeth has been in Derbyshire for some weeks now. Have you been there with her that whole time?"

Darcy wished the man would just open the letter instead of plying him with questions. "No, just the past week and not even all of that. I was in town but travelled home to accompany my sister on her return there and to check on my tenants at Willow Hall."

"Willow Hall is yours?"

"I purchased it last year before I travelled to Netherfield with Bingley."

Mr. Bennet nodded and looked thoughtful. "So Sir William was not exaggerating when he said you owned half of Derbyshire?"

"I would not say half, but I do own a significant portion," Darcy admitted.

"Sir William can get carried away," explained Mr. Bennet. "The sky is always sunnier than it truly is, so to speak. He is a very pleasant sort of fellow and a true friend with a kind heart, but his version of reality is always slightly better than it is, or so I find." He turned the letter over in his hand. "I assume you wish me to read this before you divulge your reason for being here."

"I thought it best to let your daughter have her say first."

Mr. Bennet's lips twitched. "A wise man," he said as he broke the seal.

Darcy chewed the inside of his cheek while Mr. Bennet opened the letter that Elizabeth had sent. Breathing had never felt like such a task before this moment. Darcy's fingers itched to loosen his cravat, but, with no small amount of effort, he held them still in his lap except for one thumb that tapped against the inside of his knee.

Mr. Bennet pushed his round spectacles up the bridge of his nose slightly before turning his attention to what his daughter had written.

Darcy knew what it said, for Elizabeth had shown it to him — not that he had asked to see it. No, he would have delivered it without knowing an ounce of its contents, but Elizabeth was determined that there be no secrets between them. He shifted slightly in his chair as Mr. Bennet made a slightly startled, chuckling sound. Finally, the gentleman placed the letter on his desk, removed his spectacles, and leaning back in his chair, studied Darcy.

If having to wait for the man to read the contents of the letter was uncomfortable, being the object of that man's scrutiny for a period of several minutes was nigh unto torture. Darcy wished to have the ordeal over, but he would not speak first.

At length, Mr. Bennet leaned forward once again, replaced his spectacles, and picked up the letter for a second perusal. "It seems, Mr. Darcy, that my daughter has taken a liking to you after all."

"She has, sir."

"She is not one to change her opinion of a person once it has been firmly made," he peeked up at Darcy, "unless she has been proven wrong, and the evidence would have to be nearly irrefutable. She is nearly as stubborn as her mother."

He chuckled. "Do not worry, Mr. Darcy, she has far more sense than her mother. Your life should be decorated with fewer flutters of nerves than mine ever has been." He placed the letter on the desk. "I suppose we should consider the particulars of the arrangement, but I will not deny my daughter her wish so long as the details are agreeable. So," he waggled his eyebrows as he placed his spectacles on the desk next to the letter, "you may breathe now. I really am not so formidable."

He sighed as a raised voice and a slamming door were heard above them. "If I were, I am sure my house would be more serene." He settled back in his chair, propped his elbows on the arms of the chair, and tucked his fingers into the small pockets on his waistcoat. "I do suppose I should do the proper thing and hear your reasons for wishing to marry my daughter and into this family." His eyes narrowed slightly and his tone was serious as he said the last few words.

"There is only one reason, sir. I love your daughter and always shall." He felt the flush that such admissions might necessarily bring creep up his neck and warm his ears. "I know that my behaviour when I was last in Hertfordshire was not what it should have been. I was dour and disagreeable. I said things that were both unpleasant and untrue. Neither my words nor my actions were gentlemanly, and I must apologize." He held Mr. Bennet's gaze. "They cost me dearly." He swallowed and drew a breath before continuing. "Your daughter refused my first proposal of marriage."

"First?" Shock suffused Mr. Bennet's face.

"Yes, sir. I offered her my heart and my hand when she was visiting her cousin in Kent." He smiled wryly and shook his head. "I assure you I was most handily and heartily chastised for my prior behaviour."

Mr. Bennet chuckled at the admission. "She has a sharp tongue and a temper, that, although it is not quick, it is fearsome."

"That she does," Darcy admitted. How her words had cut him and flared his own indignation! "Her anger was not unjust."

"It will be part of what she brings to your marriage," Mr. Bennet cautioned.

Darcy nodded. "Of that I am aware, but I believe we have come to understand each other better since that day, and such knowledge might save me from earning her displeasure too often."

Again, Mr. Bennet chuckled. "So you are wise enough to know that yours will not be a marriage without argument?"

"I hope I am."

"Very good." He cocked his head to the side and studied Darcy once again. "Perhaps I should hear the facts that swayed my daughter to alter her opinion of you."

"You will not withdraw your consent?"

"My Lizzy is no fool, Mr. Darcy. If she finds good in you despite whatever it is that you are reluctant to share, then there is good in you. My consent shall stand." His eyes twinkled. "However, if it is of a very distressful nature, I may require you to stay for dinner with my wife and daughters."

Darcy grimaced as he knew that what he had to say was not flattering. "You might wish to inform your cook there will be an extra plate at dinner."

Mr. Bennet's brows rose.

"I was not lying when I said I behaved poorly," explained Darcy. "There were several charges laid at my feet by your daughter. One of those charges has to do with my friend."

"Ah, so you did separate them." Mr. Bennet's lips were set in a firm line, and his eyes lacked any merriment.

At such a response that confirmed what Elizabeth had

said of Jane's despondence, Darcy felt the guilt he had carried over such actions grow. He would not be pleased with anyone that caused such heartache for his sister. Nor, if he had several sisters or daughters to see well-situated, would he willingly forgive that person for possibly dashing the possibility of a good match. He hoped that Mr. Bennet would be less reticent.

"I did. I had not observed a strong attachment on Miss Bennet's part, but I had seen enough to know that my friend's heart was in grave danger of being seriously injured if she did not return his admiration."

Mr. Bennet sat quietly for a moment before saying, "Yes, yes, Jane is far too calm for her own good. I wish she had just an ounce more of Lizzy's pluck." He shook his head. "It is not a flattering admission, but not being of the female gender, I find I can understand the decision better than my Lizzy would. She and Jane are quite attached, as I am sure you are aware."

"I am," Darcy admitted. He drew another deep breath. Confessing to one's follies was not easily done. "At Easter, when I proposed to Miss Elizabeth in Kent, I explained my feelings to her by telling her about the many obstacles I had to overcome before I could follow where my heart led."

Amusement played at Mr. Bennet's mouth. "She does not have the connections a family such as yours would welcome."

"Indeed."

"That was badly done," muttered Mr. Bennet.

"Indeed," repeated Darcy. "I am ashamed to say that I spoke ill of your family." Again, as a shadow of sadness passed over Mr. Bennet's face, Darcy felt the shame of his words deepen in his chest. "It was wrong. My family is not without fault and to hold others to a standard that my family does not even meet was pure arrogance."

"Is that all?" Mr. Bennet asked.

Darcy shook his head. "I wish it were, but it is not. However, before I relate the rest, I must have your assurance of secrecy as part of the tale involves both a friend and my sister. I have told Miss Elizabeth the portion of the tale as it relates to my sister, but not the part about Miss Tolson. I had not thought to tell her about that, but I understand your youngest daughter has gone to Brighton."

Mr. Bennet's brows furrowed. "Of course, I will say nothing." He stood and crossed behind his desk to the side of the room away from the windows. He lifted a decanter of port and with his eyes and a tip of his head inquired if Darcy would like a bit.

"Please," Darcy accepted. He always found it easier to speak of Wickham when there was something to warm his throat and push down the bile that arose. How close he had come to losing his sister! No matter what counsel he gave himself or received from a friend, he could not discuss the story without feeling his failure — even now, a year after the incident.

Mr. Bennet refilled his glass twice over and Darcy's once during the recital of events leading to Darcy's purchase of Willow Hall to protect Lucy from her uncle and Wickham's scheming. Then, as both men cradled empty glasses in their hands, Darcy shared about Georgiana's near elopement.

Mr. Bennet tipped his glass this way and that, catching a bit of afternoon sunlight with one of the cut-out designs and separating the light into a rainbow of colours. "You have given me much about which to think." He placed his glass on the desk. "However, that will have to wait. I believe, we have a marriage agreement to discuss." He pulled out paper and pen for making notes. "You will, of course, be required to stand by my side when I tell my wife. That should bring us to even. You have spoken ill of my Lizzy and my family — not all unjustly, I am certain — but there must be some recompense." He chuckled. "It will be like nothing you have ever witnessed before, I can assure you of that."

Darcy did not quite catch the grimace that accompanied such news. This made Mr. Bennet chortle even more as he dipped his pen in the ink. "Shall we start with what Elizabeth will bring to the marriage — other than her mother."

~*~*~

Darcy was, of course, also subjected to supper with Mrs.

Bennet and her daughters as he had suspected he would be. Whether it was as additional penance for his previously poor behaviour or as a means to gain Mr. Bennet a conversation partner, he was not certain.

After their meal, he made his excuses and attempted to leave, but Mrs. Bennet was not to be moved from the fact that travel at such an hour was entirely unwise. And so, after a time of entertainment and chatter, much of which he only marginally enjoyed, Darcy found himself tucked into the guest room at Longbourn. It was small but tidy and welcoming.

A footman was dispatched to attend him, and then, with a borrowed book, he was left to himself. Propping a pillow behind his back and tucking the blankets about his legs, he made ready to read a few lines of poetry before attempting sleep. Down the hall, which was not so very long, he could hear the shuffling of furniture and closing of doors as the others prepared for sleep as well. A humming came from the same direction, grew louder as it passed, and faded as it disappeared, he supposed, behind the door that led to the servants' stairs.

He shook his head. How different this was from what he had become accustomed to! This was the noise which, to Elizabeth, was familiar. He considered his evening. Yes, it had been uncomfortable, but it was not due to the Bennets. No, it was due to his own inclinations for solitude. With a smile, he opened the book of poetry. He was certain he could get used to a bit of the noise associated with a family such as this.

A door opened down the hall, and there was the scurrying of feet and a good night was called from one sister to another. He grimaced slightly at the force with which the next door had been closed. Yes, he could get used to such noises, but it would take time, and he might need to take them in small doses, at first.

The book had fallen open to where it had been marked with a paper. Unfolding the paper, Darcy found a drawing entitled *What Walks We Take, What Books We Choose*. There was a rough form of a girl and her father walking along a path toward a rise in the distance. He held the picture closer to the candle and examined it carefully. The figures seemed to be carrying something, which he assumed from their square shape and the title, were books. He chuckled. It was obviously the work of a young hand. He continued to look at the picture for a moment. Finally, his eyes came to rest on the artist's signature.

To my Papa,
With all my love,
your Lizzy

With a smile, he folded the paper once again and tucked it back into the book and began to read. For a few moments he disciplined his mind to pay attention to the words that Mr. Cowper had penned, but eventually, his mind refused to cooperate, and taking one last look at a young Elizabeth's gift to her father, he set the book aside, blew out his candle and prepared to sleep.

Chapter 8

The next morning, Darcy was again assisted by the same footman who had helped him the night before.

"The master has requested you attend him in his study," the footman said as he helped Darcy into his boots and jacket. "He has had some tea and muffins made ready there."

Darcy thanked the man for the message and made his way to Mr. Bennet's study.

"Ah, there you are. I figured you for an early riser." He put down his pen and motioned to the tea on the corner of his desk. "I prefer a quiet cup in here before facing the rest of the house."

He took his cup and settled back in his chair. "On occasion, I am joined by Jane and Lizzy. Mary rises just as early, but she prefers to find a corner near the window in the drawing room, so that she can read before her mother finds her and sets her about her tasks for the day. I imagine, from the soft footsteps I heard just a few minutes before you arrived, that she is there now."

One eyebrow cocked as a smile played at his lips. "My wife and two youngest are not late risers by any means, but they are not early either."

He placed his cup on the desk. "You slept well?"

"I did, thank you."

"Very good. I did not." He sighed. "Lizzy warned me of the danger that sending Lydia away might pose, but I did not think it so bad a thing. Colonel Forester seemed a respectable sort of fellow, and he assured me he would hold her to the rules of propriety," he sighed again, "at least as far as a high-spirited young lady like Lydia can be held to them."

He picked up the paper that lay on the desk in front of him. "I am sending an express to Colonel Forester this morning and will depart today for Brighton to retrieve Lydia." He sighed for a third time. "It will not be a pleasant task, I assure you. Between the wailing that will occur before I have left my door to the wailing that will accompany me from the shore until I return –" He shook his head. "It is no more than I deserve. I should have listened to reason, but I did not." He folded and sealed his letter.

"It seems a reasonable plan." Darcy was relieved that Mr. Bennet had come to the conclusion that action needed to be taken immediately. Even so, he still felt a small measure of trepidation that even with such swift action, it might be too late. But he knew also that other than riding through the night, the trip could not have happened any sooner. "Will you allow me to return your hospitality by spending the night at Darcy House?"

Mr.Bennet smiled sheepishly. "Gardiner has already departed for Derbyshire, so I had hoped you would offer," he admitted.

Darcy smiled at the admission and made one of his own. "My motives are not so pure as you might assume."

Mr. Bennet raised a questioning brow.

"I expect to see Bingley this evening."

Mr. Bennet laughed. "I shall stand by your side, but I'll not be your second."

Darcy laughed with him. He hoped that having Mr. Bennet there might soften the response he knew he faced — and rightly so — from his friend. Bingley was amiable to a fault, but he was not without a temper. More than one chap at school had had an eye blackened or a lip split by Bingley, usually over some comment concerning his connections to trade and, often, followed by the comment,

"Ah, tradesmen, ruffians, the whole lot, is that not right?"

The injured would assuredly agree, which was as Bingley planned, so that he might then add,

"I should hate to have anyone think you a liar, so you may thank me for keeping your point valid."

All this Darcy shared with Mr. Bennet.

When Mr. Bennet had finally stopped chuckling over the information and had repeated *"thank me for keeping your point valid"* for the fourth time. He took a sip of tea and commented, "I hadn't thought him to be so quick with a quip."

"He is not, but occasionally, he will surprise you," said Darcy. "He is, however, quick with his hands, so if you would stand in front of me, I should feel much safer than if you stand beside me." Darcy smirked as Mr. Bennet raised his brows in surprise. "No need to fear, sir. Although I have become well-versed in the art of teasing through my cousin, Colonel Fitzwilliam, I do not engage in the activity very often. Often, the moment has passed before I have thought of a reply." He lifted a shoulder in a half-shrug. "My nature is more serious, I suppose."

Mr. Bennet chuckled again. "I doubt you will remain so serious for long."

Darcy returned Mr. Bennet's grin. "I am not opposed to change — at least not completely."

"Just not quick to make it?" Mr. Bennet raised a brow, peering over his cup, as he finished his tea.

"Guilty as charged," said Darcy with a small bow of his head. "However, when a change is for the better and a reasonable explanation has been given, the alteration is made posthaste."

"Nothing by halves, is it?"

"Very little."

"You and my daughter are very similar in that way." He stood, his sealed express in his hand. "I shall send this off and then inform my wife of my plans. You are welcome to take refuge in here for as long as you wish. Breakfast will be spread out in about a half hour's time, and we can leave quite soon after."

Darcy thanked him and poured a second cup of tea. Then, selecting a book from one of the shelves, sat down to enjoy it and his beverage in relative peace as voices were heard above stairs and a servant or two scurried to answer.

~*~*~

Finally, when all the details necessary before a trip had been seen to, Darcy allowed Mr. Bennet to climb into the carriage and arrange himself comfortably before entering the coach and taking the seat opposite of the gentleman. They were just moving away from the front of Longbourn, and Mr. Bennet was complimenting Darcy on the fineness of the carriage when a rider entered the drive.

"What can that be?" asked Mr. Bennet as Darcy tapped on the roof to get the carriage to stop.

"Ho, there!" Darcy heard his coachman call to the rider. "The master be inside the carriage if ye be looking for him."

"Indeed, I am," returned the rider as he slowed his horse and swung off in a fluid motion, landing next to his mount as it stopped. "I've a message for 'im." The rider pulled a letter from his bag and approached the carriage as a footman opened the door. "Mr. Thomas Bennet?" The rider looked between the two gentlemen in the carriage.

"That would be me," said Mr. Bennet, accepting the letter and thanking the rider, who was gone nearly as quickly as he had appeared.

Darcy watched Mr. Bennet's eyes grow wide and his skin pale as he read the message. "Is something amiss?" he asked quietly.

Mr. Bennet replied by passing him the letter.

Sir,

I must inform you of some unfortunate news and my failure. Miss Lydia went out to the shops this morning with her maid, and neither has returned as of the time of my writing this letter. (It is now six o'clock.)

We have searched the area, to no avail. However, I have heard that she was seen boarding a mail coach bound for London. I wish this was the extent of my news, but I must inform you that the mail coach also carried three of my men, who are enjoying a period of time away from their duties. One of these men, Lieutenant Wickham, has paid particular attention to your daughter and she to him. It is rumoured that they do not intend to stop in London but continue on to Gretna Green. I have no evidence to support this claim save the departure of both, but I could not in good conscience omit that information whether substantiated or not. There are men already on their way to London to try to apprehend Miss Lydia before it is too late to do so.

I must humbly beg your forgiveness in this matter...

Darcy scanned the remaining few words of apology before handing the letter back to Mr. Bennet.

Mr. Bennet shook his head. "Had I listened to Lizzy," he muttered.

"Had I told you of Wickham earlier," said Darcy.

"Ah, we are a sorry pair, are we not? Sitting here regretting what cannot be undone." Mr. Bennet tucked the letter in his pocket. "I'll not make mention of this to my wife just yet. It would be best to see if we can find out anything once we get to town. However, if we might take a few moments for me to write a reply to Forrester and then have it posted at the first stop along the road?"

"Of course," said Darcy. "Time is of the essence."

"Indeed," agreed Mr. Bennet. "I shall be mere moments." He climbed down from the carriage as quickly as he could.

Darcy climbed out and stood next to his carriage, watching as Mr. Bennet met his wife, who was fluttering on about what the rider could have wanted. "Just some business that needs attention. Nothing to worry about at present, my dear," he said as he took her arm and wound it around his.

Darcy was glad when just a few moments had passed and Mr. Bennet once again appeared.

"All is well within," Mr. Bennet assured him. "None the wiser." He settled into his seat. "I do not like the idea of being away while she is in a state." He peered out the window toward the house. "But I spoke to Mary, and she will care for her."

The tone of the comment took Darcy by surprise. He had expected a less worried tone or perhaps a funny quip about nerves and females. But from the way the man looked back several more times, Darcy got the feeling that though the man across from him may not act the part of a smitten husband or a doting papa, he was far from the unconcerned husband he portrayed.

Once Longbourn was well behind them, they traded a few pleasantries and then each indulged himself in a book. It was a quiet trip, but not uncomfortably so. It seems that each man respected the need of the other for solitude. There were a few moments of friendly discussion at each stop and occasionally as something came to the mind of Mr. Bennet that he felt needed to be pondered, but aside from those few and well-dispersed interactions, the remainder of the trip was silent within the carriage, save for the shifting for comfort in seats and the turning of pages.

Mr. Bennet closed his book and placed it on the seat next to him. "I do not know where to begin," he said looking out the window toward the city that was before them.

Darcy also closed his book. He could well imagine the concern that ran through Mr. Bennet's mind. "I may know of a few places to check if Wickham still associates with the men he once did." He smiled ruefully. "They are not pleasant places, so I will send someone to inquire before venturing out myself. That should also make the search swifter."

Mr. Bennet nodded thoughtfully. "I admit I know little of London besides Cheapside and Gracechurch Street. I leave the exploration of shops to the ladies." He chuckled lightly. "Aside from the occasional foray into a bookshop."

"You shall have to allow me to show you the sites on some visit." The carriage was winding its way through the streets. "I imagine the museum would be of interest to you?" He nearly laughed as the gentleman's eyes could not hide his delight at such a thought. "But for tonight you may have to content yourself with my library."

This, of course, prompted one of the longest discussions of their journey as Mr. Bennet inquired about particular authors and books, and Darcy delighted in telling him of all he asked plus a few of his prize acquisitions.

"I believe you shall be my favourite son," declared Mr. Bennet. "And to think I thought it might be Mr. Bingley since he is so amiable." His lips curled into a small teasing smile and his eyes twinkled. "I mean him no ill, but he is not the most studious of men." The smile grew. "And I may not even gain him as a son unless he, or one of his friends, can convince Jane he is not fickle."

Darcy shook his head, a small smile curling his lips. "Indeed, I hope that if your daughter's happiness depends upon it, it can be accomplished. However, it must be noted that this particular friend, though he may do all he can to convince Miss Bennet of Mr. Bingley's worth and inno-cence, is not known for his eloquence with the Bennet ladies."

Mr. Bennet reached across the carriage as it drew to a stop and patted Darcy's knee much like a solicitous father might. "Ah," he said with a wink, "but you are learning."

Chapter 9

London

Lydia folded her arms and stood in front of Wickham, blocking his path to the establishment behind her. People bustled in and out of the inn. One young gentleman paused for a moment, looking curiously at the pair before moving on. A maid slowed her steps as she passed them, and Wickham's lips curled into a smile as he winked at the young girl. Lydia rolled her eyes and shook her head. Staying here as Wickham had suggested would not do.

"You will take me and my maid," Lydia waved a hand at the poor frightened servant, who stood fidgeting behind her mistress, "to Derbyshire. My sisters are there, and I wish to join their fun."

"I will do no such thing," he said, taking a step to the side.

She placed herself between him and the inn once again. "I cannot stay here."

He shrugged. "Where you stay or where you go is none of my concern." There was no way he would willingly go to Derbyshire. Mr. Williams had told him that to show his face again in the area would likely lead to unpleasantness, and old Williams was just the man to ensure it happened. He might be the constable, but, rumor had it, he was not above seeing justice fulfilled outside of due process. His men had appeared rather suddenly after Tolson's accident last spring. He shook himself. No, Williams was not a man with whom he wished to trifle. Wickham appreciated life and wished to keep his.

And then there were Darcy and his cousin, Fitzwilliam. After last summer's botched play for Miss Darcy's inheritance — well, it was best if he stayed clear of those gentlemen. Darcy would likely not kill him, but he could not guarantee the good colonel would not find a way to follow through on the threats he had snarled at Ramsgate. Wickham had been enduring the constant glares and sudden appearances of that man at Brighton. More than one amorous rendezvous had been scuttled due to him. Wickham was looking forward to a few days without supervision.

Lydia matched Wickham's step to the side again. He could not leave her here on the streets of London when she needed to find her way to Derbyshire! He simply could not. She had expected a bit more cooperation from him than a flat refusal. He had always willingly done what she asked before. It was not an eventuality for which she had not prepared, but it was not exactly what she had expected.

"I cannot go to Derbyshire," said Wickham. "Town is my destination, and I'll go no farther."

Lydia fluttered her eyelashes and smiled. It was a technique that had worked before. Perhaps it might be more effective now than just demanding. "Oh, but you must."

He shook his head. He was not going one mile closer to Derbyshire unless forced, and he doubted very much that the feather-brained chit before him would be able to force him to do anything. He smiled as her smile turned to a frown before becoming something of an indifferent pout.

Well, if it must come to that, it must be done. Lydia flicked a piece of lint from her sleeve. "I am afraid you are wrong, and you must see me to Derbyshire."

"I do not see why I must," he replied, trying once again to slip around her and being thwarted by her matching his move. Agitation showed plainly on his face.

"Well, you see," Lydia began, smiling lightly while watching Wickham's face carefully. That look of displeasure was certain to deepen in a moment, and she must watch for signs of anything more than words being hurled at her. "I know that you cheated Saunders out of money last week." Her smile widened. "I have it in writing. Not your own, mind you, but a very close representation. The signature, however, is yours."

Wickham's brows drew together, and his mouth dropped open slightly. "You forged a note?"

She shrugged and fluttered her lashes again, feigning as innocent a look as she could. If her expression were to be honest, it would have been one of delight at having surprised someone who thought himself so clever. "Forged is such an ugly word. I prefer created. It really is not hard to do, you know. I can copy all my sisters' writing."

Wickham answered her charming smile with one of his own as he glanced around their surroundings. "I could just take it from you," he said quietly while eyeing her reticule.

She held her bag out towards him. It was an action that once again startled him according to his expression. Although she had not expected to have to use her full plan, she was finding it quite delightful to do so. There was something exhilarating about matching wits with another. Perhaps this was why Elizabeth was always debating?

Lydia wished to spend a moment contemplating that startling idea, but there was not time. She needed to convince Wickham to take her to Derbyshire and the sooner the better. Since he had not taken her reticule, she pulled it back, opened it, and looked inside.

"Oh, I do not have it with me." She closed her bag. "But then having it with me would be foolish, would it not? It could get lost or stolen." She giggled. "Kitty has it."

Her smile faded as his scowl darkened. It was time to tell him the whole of just how much he should wish to assist her. "Along with the note about your cheating, she also has two letters of distress from me accusing you of threatening to harm me that she is to give to my father and Mr. Darcy."

"Darcy?" Wickham's brows rose in surprise.

"He did not seem to like you." She had not seen anyone look at another with such hatred as Mr. Darcy had looked at Wickham when they met him on the road from Meryton. And, knowing Mr. Darcy was a wealthy man and more than a little enamoured with Elizabeth, she doubted he would spare any expense in seeing to her rescue. She might not enjoy the man's grave countenance, but he was a true gentleman, no matter what Elizabeth might say to the contrary.

Wickham snorted. No, Darcy did not like him. He rather knew that the man hated him. "It does not take a great deal of observation to know that."

His reticence to fall into line with her wishes was beginning to annoy her, but she would not allow him to know, of course. So, she shrugged one shoulder with as much nonchalance as she could muster. "It does not matter if it took an extraordinary amount of deduction or just a trifle. I am certain he will act accordingly if he hears you have endangered me." She fluttered her eyelashes again.

Darcy's parting words when he left Ramsgate played in Wickham's mind. "I will save you this once, but should I hear of a word of this being spoken to anyone or if you should attempt to prey on another lady of my acquaintance, I will allow Fitzwilliam to do as he wishes." A letter suggesting any sort of injury to Lydia reaching Darcy would not be in Wickham's best interest.

"You do not have the directions to send such a letter, and he shall not be returning to Hertfordshire, I should say. He liked very few in the area, and there is nothing to draw him back since his friend seems unlikely to return."

He really did not think anyone could best him, did he? Lydia sighed. "Do not take me for a simpleton, Mr. Wickham. I am the youngest of five sisters, and I know how to get what I want. I assure you I have addressed the missive appropriately. Kitty will send it in five days' time if she has not heard from me, and I will not write to her until you and I have reached Derbyshire."

Wickham stared down at the silly chit with disgust. She had given no indication that such a devious plan, or any plan for that matter, could be formulated in her pretty little head. "Very well," he muttered through clenched teeth. "We will leave in the morning."

She shook her head. "No, we will leave now."

"We cannot go until there is a coach on which we can buy passage. I have no desire to go looking for one at this moment as I have friends I wish to see." He pushed her to the side.

Lydia followed behind. "But you will drink, and then you will sleep too long." He was always indulging more than he should. If he did not drink so much as he did, his list of debts would not be nearly so long as it was. He was admirably clever when sober, but his wits failed him quickly in the presence of alcohol.

Wickham ignored her and pushed open the door to the inn where he always took a room when in town.

She growled to herself. She did not like to be ignored, nor did she like not having her way. If he thought he could have his way by denying her hers, he was sadly mistaken. She slid up beside him, wound her arm around his, and laid her head on his shoulder as he spoke to the innkeeper.

"Do make it sure it has a comfortable bed, Wickham dear," she inserted into the conversation as sweetly as she could.

"Up the stairs and to the right. Same as always." The innkeeper took the money Wickham gave him and then handed Wickham the key.

"Molly Benson," she introduced herself to the portly man, who was looking at her curiously. "We are on our way to Scotland," she whispered loudly, placing a hand on her belly. "Papa would not agree to our marriage you see, but it really must happen soon, for it would be best if Papa thinks the little one was born a few weeks early." She rubbed her stomach in a circular motion as she had seen many expectant women do. "Mama had two which were early you know, so it would not be so far a stretch to think that I take after her and that this one was also early, now would it?" She blinked wide eyes at the man.

"I am so dreadfully happy to be out of that coach. The motion was nearly more than I could handle, but Wickham has promised to spend the evening reading to me, so I shall be fine by morning." She held her hand out to her maid, who handed her the book she had been holding since they disembarked from the coach. "My favourite." Lydia sighed. "And his voice is so melodic." She smiled up at Wickham. His face was suffused with shock, and it nearly caused her to giggle. "See that our dinner is sent to our room," she said to the innkeeper, who mumbled something in agreement.

Wickham opened his mouth to speak and fearing that he might attempt to refute what she had said, she added, "I fear I may be too exhausted to write that letter to my sister." She removed her arm from his and stretched and yawned.

Wickham's eyes narrowed, but he remained silent as they ascended the stairs to the room they had been assigned. He pushed open the door and waited for her to enter, but she remained in the hall. She would not be locked in a room while he enjoyed his evening and most likely made his escape. She smiled at him and motioned for him to enter, which, after considering her with a hard stare for a few minutes, he did. Then, she followed.

"I will have my way, Mr. Wickham," she said as she closed the door and slid the bolt across.

"And perhaps, I will have mine," he shot back.

She shook her head. "I am afraid not, Mr. Wickham. For if you were to ruin me in truth, you would then have to marry me in truth, and I will not marry you."

"Plenty of ladies are not maidens when they marry," he said, taking a step closer to her.

"This one intends to be." She folded her arms across her chest and refused to be moved. She would not be bullied into appearing weak. However, she did hope that should he be even more of a scoundrel than she thought, Margaret, her maid, would set off a cry of alarm. But, to her relief, he held his ground and did not advance any further.

"You? You, who flutters your lashes at any handsome man and displays your assets to best garner a gentleman's attention?" He laughed.

She placed her hands on her hips and glared at him. A flirt she might be, but that did not make her a light skirt. "Do you not practice marching and shooting?"

"Of course," he replied.

"For what purpose? To start a fight on a Saturday night for entertainment?"

He gave her a puzzled look. "No, so we might be prepared for a fight should one arise, and because if we do not, our colonel might have us flogged."

Lydia shrugged and went to sit in one of the chairs next

to the small table in the room. "I practice so that when a worthy gentleman crosses my path, I shall be ready to conquer him." She laughed. "And I do not go beyond flirting because I do not wish for my father to flog me with his lectures." She motioned to the other chair. "You should make yourself comfortable. No one will be expecting you to leave your room this evening. You are reading to your future wife, after all." She sighed. "This is so much better than spending the evening and night in a carriage, is it not?"

It was not. Neither Wickham nor Lydia enjoyed the evening nor the night, and both rose early the next morning — Wickham from the bed, and Lydia from the mat she had fashioned on the floor before the door — and were well on their way to Derbyshire before her father and Mr. Darcy entered London.

Chapter 10

Mr. Bennet watched Mr. Darcy give directions to his staff as they entered the house. Two footmen were to attend him in his study as soon as could be managed, while a meal was to be laid out in the library. Maids were sent scurrying, preparing a room for their guest. Mr. Bennet's hat and coat were taken from him, and within ten minutes of arriving at the door to Darcy House, he found himself comfortably seated in a study double the size of his own. The walls were filled with just as many books as his were, but here, everything had a more orderly appearance. Piles of papers sat neatly on the desk, some in wooden boxes.

Darcy saw Mr. Bennet eying the boxes of papers and with a sheepish grin explained, "I need things in their place, or I find I get lost. Some have the ability to have things combined in one pile and can remember exactly where an item is, but I cannot. Lists, files, and schedules are of great importance to me. I find I am quite lost without a plan."

Mr. Bennet nodded. "My Lizzy is rather the opposite.

You should be warned. Do not misunderstand me, she can keep a book as well as anyone and organize with the best, but it is not her natural tendency. You may find you will need patience with her."

Darcy smiled. "I have some experience with those not given to naturally ordering things. You must remember Bingley is my friend," he paused and then added with a sigh, "at least, he is currently my friend." He took a stack of correspondence from one box and sorted it. Most of the letters were returned to the box, while a few were placed in front of Darcy on the desk. "These, I must attend to myself," he explained, "although the matters, I am sure, are not pressing, so they will travel with me. The others are merely invitations that will need to be declined by my man."

"Sir," one footman, followed by a second, entered the study. "Mr. Thompson said you wished to see us."

Darcy nodded and motioned for them to take a seat. Thompson had chosen well. These two were probably the largest footmen on his staff. Both were tall and muscular, and neither appeared to be too well-bred to be entering the areas Darcy was about to ask them to enter.

"I need to find someone," he began when the two men were seated somewhat uncomfortably before his desk.

Very few of his servants were ever summoned to his office. Most requests were passed on to them through his butler or housekeeper. However, this was not a topic which could be carried from one person to another. It needed to be contained as much as possible if he wished to keep Lydia's reputation from being further damaged.

"Mr. Bennet's daughter has made an unexpected trip to town," Darcy continued.

"With a scoundrel," muttered Mr. Bennet.

Darcy nodded his agreement with the evaluation of Wickham and then explained the nature of task he wished his men to accomplish, scratched out some addresses on a paper, and after a short rummage through a drawer on the bookcase behind his desk, showed them a miniature of Wickham. "It is rather urgent that we find him as soon as possible, as Miss Bennet's father is desirous to have her back unharmed."

"Of course, sir," both men replied as they stood to leave.

"It is to be private?" asked the second footman.

"As private as a matter such as this can be," acknowledged Darcy. "If you find them, you are to return here and tell us. You do not need to apprehend them, unless, of course, you come upon them as they are leaving. There will, of course, be a bit extra in your pay for doing this for me whether you find them or not."

"Thank you, sir," said the first footman and then turning to Mr. Bennet, he added. "We will do our best."

"As if she were me own sister," muttered the second before he turned and followed the other footman from the room.

Darcy rose from his chair. "And now we wait." He gathered the letters from his desk and walked toward the study door. "I thought the library might be the best place to while away our time. We might not hear back for hours."

"Do you still expect Mr. Bingley?" asked Mr. Bennet as they stepped into the corridor.

Darcy nodded his reply before turning to his butler. "Thompson, well done on the footmen." He handed him the few letters he carried. "Please see that these are placed with my things in my room. I should be packed and ready for a journey in the morning."

"Of course, sir," replied Thompson.

"And, when Mr. Bingley arrives, please show him to the library."

"As you wish, sir. Your meal is waiting, sir."

A small table of cold meat, cheese, rolls and ale had been set out next to a grouping of chairs in the middle of the large room. A further tray of sweets and port sat on a second table, also within the grouping. It was the meal Darcy often took, in smaller quantity, when he arrived home from traveling. He picked up a piece of cheese from the plate and popped it into his mouth as he took a seat and waited for Mr. Bennet to join him. It had been a long day, and despite his concern regarding Lydia, Darcy was hungry. He chuckled to himself as the gentleman turned about, looking at the shelves of books very much like a child might survey a tray of cakes.

"Indeed, my favourite son," Mr. Bennet mumbled as he finally pulled himself from his admiration of the room. "I must say, I am glad you were able to convince my daughter to accept you," he said to Darcy with a grin.

Darcy returned the smile. "As am I, sir. As am I."

They were just tucking into a second helping of food and ale when Bingley was announced.

"Ah, Darcy!" said Bingley as he entered the room. "Mr. Bennet!" His surprise was evident both in his tone and the falter in his steps. "It…it is good to see you, sir," he said in greeting.

"No need to try to hide your surprise, my boy. I am as surprised to be here as you are to see me, but," he leaned back in his chair and gave Darcy an amused smile, "I shall leave the explanation of that to your friend."

Darcy shifted uneasily in his chair. "You are alone?"

"Caroline wished to accompany me, but I managed to escape without her."

"Good," muttered Mr. Bennet. Then, with a sheepish smile, he added, "I do apologize, but I am rather liking being free of females for a time."

Bingley waved it away with a laugh. "We are all happy to be free of Caroline. Am I right, Darcy?"

Darcy shrugged and reluctantly nodded. "Especially tonight." He finished his ale. "I have something to tell you that is not easily done." He rose and paced to the window and back. "It will no doubt be shocking, and I ask that you allow me to finish before you respond."

Bingley's brows furrowed. "I cannot imagine what you might have done that would be shocking, but I agree."

"I truly wish you did not hold me in such high esteem, Bingley." Pain coloured Darcy's words. "It makes it more difficult to admit my errors and how I might have harmed you."

Bingley's brows rose, and he pointed to himself as if questioning whether or not he had heard the statement correctly.

"Yes, you," said Darcy with a sad smile. He paced to the window and back. "I am not sure how to begin," he admitted.

Mr. Bennet leaned forward in his chair. "He is marrying Elizabeth. Lydia has run off, so we must find her, and Jane, whom you were convinced did not love you, did. I cannot say she still does, but she did." He leaned back in his chair once again.

Darcy stared at him, mouth agape.

Mr. Bennet shrugged. "You needed help. I admit it is not the most gentle way to present the news, but we are all men here. And friends." He looked pointedly at Mr. Bingley and emphasized the word. "There is no need to take the long way around as I would with my wife or daughters. I think we are made of sterner stuff than that."

He rose and motioned for Darcy to sit. "I know I said

I would leave this to your friend to explain, but I cannot do it." He chuckled. "I suppose it is not only my wife who likes to meddle, though I do hope my meddling is more productive and useful than hers." He held up a finger as Bingley opened his mouth to speak.

"Love is a sneaky creature. You, Mr. Bingley, are not so easily caught unawares by it. In fact, I would venture a guess that you often think you see it when it is not there." He raised an eyebrow at Bingley and waited for him to agree that such was the case. "However, Mr. Darcy, here, I would dare to say, rarely sees her approach and quite likely never expected her to threaten him at all. Or, mayhap, he did and that is why he wears his scowl so often — as an attempt to scare her away."

Bingley chuckled.

Mr. Bennet with a small chuckle of his own continued without giving Darcy a moment to accept or deny the charges. "He has been well-chastised for his error on your behalf, Mr. Bingley. My Lizzy is not one to allow her sister to be treated ill without showing her displeasure to the one she holds accountable." He chuckled again. "I am not sure how she discovered Mr. Darcy's role in the whole charade, but she did and listed it among other reasons for refusing him."

"But?" Bingley's brows were furrowed deeply in confusion.

Mr. Bennet winked and smiled at him. "The first time he

offered. In the spring, was it?" He waited for Darcy to confirm this. Then, he took a seat, leaned toward Bingley, and, growing serious, added, "For several months, your friend has tried to reorder his thinking and his life in such a way as to overcome the pain of such a refusal. It is the same pain from which he was attempting to keep you safe — mistaken as he was. He had your best interests in mind." He leaned back. "My advice, young man, is to accept his apology when he offers it, and then decide if your heart still prefers Jane or if it was merely a pretty face and pleasant smile that held your attention for a time but not for all time." He sighed. "I will not see her heart broken again," he warned.

Darcy's chest clenched at the words. He shook his head. "I doubt I have ever been so wrong about anything in my entire life."

"Wickham," muttered Mr. Bennet.

Darcy's shoulders sagged. "True. I should revise my words to say that when I am wrong, I am quite dreadfully wrong. Perhaps it is a mistake to trust me with your daughter."

Mr. Bennet shook his head. "She'll not let you go so wrong, so long as you listen to her." He smiled sheepishly at Darcy.

Darcy nodded his understanding while Bingley looked at the two men in confusion.

"That bit has to do with Lydia," Mr. Bennet explained.

"I cannot tell you, Bingley, how greatly my heart has grieved over my actions toward both you and Miss Bennet. I did not know what pain I caused until Miss Elizabeth turned me away." He shook his head. "I am not sure I could forgive someone who had treated me so, but I would be very grateful if you would forgive me this wrong." His breath caught in his chest as he waited for Bingley to respond.

Bingley looked at Darcy and then Mr. Bennet, who gave him a nod and tilted his head toward Darcy as if telling him to accept the apology.

"She loved me?" Bingley asked.

"That is what Miss Elizabeth says," Darcy replied.

"But she may not now?"

Darcy's heart sighed at Bingley's sad tone.

"If it was love," said Mr. Bennet softly, "then she still will. If it was not, then you are far better off to have a season of pain rather than a lifetime of it."

Bingley sadly nodded his acceptance of the fact and turned to Darcy. "You thought you were helping me?"

"I did."

"Never, for the rest of our lives, ever help me in such a fashion again. If I require your help with relationships, I will ask for it — though not for some time, I should think."

"I am forgiven?" Relief, nearly certain that forgiveness had been granted, crept cautiously into Darcy's heart.

"I should hate to ask a father for his daughter's hand,"

Bingley explained, "if I am so fortunate as to gain her permission to do so, when he knows that I was unwilling to take his advice. So, yes, you are forgiven."

Darcy blew out a great breath as relief swelled within him.

Mr. Bennet smiled at them both. "So much easier than daughters." He looked to the tray of sweets. "Some port before we explain about Lydia?"

Darcy agreed and was just handing a glass to Bingley before taking his own when...

"Darcy!" A bellow carried from the entry.

Must Richard always make such a loud entrance? "My cousin," he explained to Mr. Bennet.

"Nearly as loud as my wife," muttered Mr. Bennet with a smile and a wink. "Probably not as fetching in a dress, however."

Darcy and Bingley chuckled.

"Darcy!" There was an impatience to the repeated bellow followed by a tromping of feet growing louder as they approached the library.

A frazzled Thompson scurried into the room behind Colonel Fitzwilliam. "I tried to explain, sir."

"It is quite alright. Richard is more familiar with giving than receiving orders." Darcy glowered at his cousin, who, at least, had the decency to look somewhat embarrassed. "Mr. Bennet, my cousin, Colonel Fitzwilliam. Richard, Mr.

Bennet. Do come in and sit down." He motioned to a chair and added, "And kindly keep your voice to a low rumble."

"I haven't time," Richard replied. "I am looking for a good-for-nothing wastrel for Forrester, and my leave does not start until I find both him and the young lady he took with him." Richard paced a small path in front of the door. His hands clenched and unclenched behind his back. "I need the address of that inn where you said he was last time we needed to find him."

"Sit," Darcy barked the order and Richard complied. "We are just awaiting the men I sent to that very inn. Mr. Bennet is as anxious to have his daughter returned as you are to begin your leave. Will you be spending it in town?"

Once again, Richard looked rather chagrinned. "I apologize. I did not put the name of the young lady and yours together."

Mr. Bennet uncrossed his legs and crossed them again, this time with the left foot on top of the right. "I apologize for my daughter being a cause for your current assignment. She is a headstrong child — smart, but willful. Again, I must apologize for that."

"Ah, I nearly forgot." Richard reached into his pocket. "This is for you," he said handing a letter to Darcy. "There was a man on the steps when I arrived," he explained as Darcy looked at the address with some confusion.

Darcy turned the letter over in his hands and ran a finger

over the seal, unsure if he should read this now or wait until later.

"Read it," said Richard. "You'll be half distracted until you do. Am I not right, Bingley?"

"Oh, indeed," agreed Bingley.

Mr. Bennet raised a brow. "From a gentleman or lady?" he inquired, a slight smirk pulling at his mouth.

"Mr. Dobney," Darcy replied. "Philip," he added to Bingley before explaining to Mr. Bennet who Philip was.

Mr. Bennet chuckled as Darcy turned the letter over in his hands while speaking. "You will not offend me if you tend to your letter. I am the one inconveniencing you with my presence, after all. If it were not for Lydia, I would not be here at all."

Darcy insisted that Mr. Bennet was not an inconvenience, although Mr. Bennet would hear nothing of being untruthful out of politeness. This, of course, led to a discussion of a polite dissimulation and the ills or benefits of such pretense. As Richard waxed eloquent on a third story of the ills of such actions, Darcy excused himself to read his letter. He knew that Richard, once started on a topic, could continue for some time, and that the stories were, without a doubt, ones which Darcy had heard before.

Darcy,

As I have promised, I am writing to inform you of a new arrival in the area. My cousin, Captain Harris, has arrived for a visit. He has called on Willow Hall with my sister. In fact, that is where Lucy and I found him this afternoon — lounging in the garden with the full family. Miss Bennet and the Gardiners have arrived safely. You will be pleased to know that Harris has shown no particular attention to Miss Elizabeth. He does, however, seem taken with Miss Bennet, and I cannot blame him. She is quite lovely.

I am to inform you, for Lucy says I must, that your Miss Elizabeth has eyes only for you, so you need not worry. Lucy also wishes you to know that Miss Elizabeth has had the full story of all that transpired with Lucy's uncle and Wickham. It seems Miss Elizabeth's youngest sister has gone to Brighton and has, according to Harris, been flirting with several officers — Wickham being one of them. You might wish to share what you know of the man with Mr. Bennet when you call on him. If this letter reaches you after you have called on him, I would urge you to write to him. Lucy gives permission to speak of her ordeal.

Looking forward to your return, etc.

P.D.

"Is all well in Derbyshire?" asked Richard as Darcy folded the letter.

Darcy grimaced slightly. "Just informing me that Miss Bennet and the Gardiners have arrived safely, as has Captain Harris. It seems Harris has brought news from Brighton that Miss Elizabeth found unsettling."

"About Lydia?" asked Mr. Bennet.

Darcy nodded slowly. "It seems Harris mentioned some flirtation." Darcy motioned for the footmen, who stood at the door, to enter. "What have you discovered?"

The two men looked at each other uneasily.

"They all know of it," assured Darcy. "You may speak freely."

"They were not at the inn when we arrived, but they had been there, sir," began the first man. "They left this morning."

"They are going to Scotland, sir," said the second man. "It seems they must marry."

Darcy's heart sank to his boots. "They must?" he asked.

The second man cleared his throat. "Yes, sir. It seems the lady is with child."

Chapter 11

Derbyshire

"We have another guest, ma'am," said Mrs. Smith, entering the drawing room where the ladies of Willow Hall had gathered to sew and chat with Lucy, Mary Ellen, and Georgiana.

"Another?" asked Cecily.

"Miss Lydia Bennet, ma'am."

Elizabeth's mouth dropped open as she gasped. "Lydia is here?"

"Yes, miss," replied Mrs. Smith. Elizabeth could tell by the look on the housekeeper's face that she was not entirely pleased with the new arrival. "She's waiting in the entry. Shall I show her in?"

"Oh, indeed." Cecily tucked her sewing back into her workbasket. "We can't have her standing in the entryway, nor can we turn her out."

"Is she unaccompanied?" asked Aunt Gardiner.

Mrs. Smith shook her head. "There is an officer with

her." Her eyes narrowed and her lips puckered slightly in disgust. "Lieutenant Wickham."

Elizabeth was certain her heart had stopped beating for a moment. It could not be. It just could not be. She cast an uneasy glance at Lucy and Georgiana before rising and hurrying from the room. She needed to see the truth of the report for herself.

"Lydia!" she said in surprise. Her sister and Wickham were indeed in the entryway. "What are you doing here? Why are you not in Brighton?"

Lydia pouted. This was not exactly the welcome she had expected. They would be surprised, to be sure, but not displeased. "Are you not glad to see me? I thought you and Jane and Aunt would be delighted. I have gone to an enormous amount of trouble to come for a visit." She crossed her arms. Lizzy was nearly as severe as Mary at times; perhaps the others would be more welcoming.

"How can I be happy you are here when you are supposed to be in Brighton?"

"Brighton is dull." Lydia tried not to reply to her sister's critical tone without snapping, but it was not possible.

"Dull?" Elizabeth repeated incredulously.

"Yes, Brighton is dull, which is why I asked Mr. Wickham if he would escort me to visit you." She flashed a sweet smile at Elizabeth and managed, this time, to keep her tone pleasant. "It was ever so long a journey. I had not realized just how far Derbyshire is from Hertfordshire. It is quite a distance, is it not?"

"Indeed, it is." Elizabeth wished to grab her sister by the shoulders and shake the smile from her face. Had she no idea the impropriety of her actions? "You travelled alone?" She raised a brow and looked at Wickham for an answer.

"No," he replied. "Miss Lydia was accompanied by a maid, and we were on a crowded coach."

"Oh, Lizzy! It was very unpleasant. All those people bouncing around and bumping into one another." Lydia shuddered dramatically. "I shall not like to do that again. It is much better to have one's own carriage."

By this time, Mrs. Abbot had joined Elizabeth in the hall.

"Come," said Cecily. "This would be a far more pleasant conversation to have in the sitting room." She turned to Mrs. Smith. "Please have Mr. Abbot and Mr. Gardiner join us at their earliest convenience."

"I cannot stay," said Wickham.

"You'll stay." There was a steeliness to Cecily's voice. "Until we have this all sorted out, you will stay, sir."

"But I am not welcome –" Wickham attempted again to extricate himself from his present situation, but Cecily would not allow it.

"You most certainly are not, but that does not signify." She turned to Elizabeth. "Take Lydia to the sitting room.

Mr. Wickham and I shall follow as soon as I have a word with him."

Elizabeth did as instructed and had gotten both Lydia and herself into seats before Cecily, accompanied by a somber Wickham, entered. Wickham bowed and greeted each person in turn and then took a seat away from the group of ladies.

Jane was asking Lydia about Mrs. Forrester and the sites of Brighton, and Elizabeth was thankful for it. For the conversation filled what otherwise would have surely been a silent room. Georgiana's eyes did not leave her stitching, and Lucy's did not leave Georgiana. Elizabeth found herself watching Lydia for a moment and then Wickham, who was nervously turning his hat in his hands.

"I would have been here sooner, but Mr. Wickham insisted on calling on some stuffy old friend first."

Elizabeth turned her eyes back to Lydia. "And who was that?" she inquired.

"Mr. Williams," Wickham answered. "I needed to see him. I had promised him that I would call on him first if I ever came back to Derbyshire. It was a promise I dared not break."

"He was such a crosspatch," said Lydia. "I did not think he would let us continue on our way."

"He is the constable," said Lucy. "He is only cross when he needs to be. Normally, he is a rather pleasant fellow."

"The constable?" asked Lydia in surprise.

Wickham glowered at her. "I told you when we were in London that I was not welcome here. I did not lie."

Lydia crossed her arms and scowled at him in return. "Well, it is quite difficult to ferret out when you are lying and when you are not. Perhaps if you were honest more often."

"Ah, Lydia," said Mr. Gardiner, entering the room ahead of Mr. Abbot. "I heard you had arrived. You are well?" He tilted his head to the side and looked at her.

"I am," she replied.

"Tell me of your journey," Mr. Gardiner said as he took a seat near his wife. "Did you meet any interesting people along the way?"

His tone was open and engaging, but Elizabeth noted how he seemed to force his smile and knew that his manners were to elicit the full story from Lydia. She listened for a few moments as Lydia spoke of her departure from Brighton and her stop in London.

"An inn?" The words leapt from Elizabeth's mouth. "You spent a night in an inn with him?" She waved her hand in Wickham's direction. "Have you no idea of propriety?"

"He refused to continue on. I had no option other than sleeping in the street, and I did not give the innkeeper my name." Lydia crossed her arms and scowled at Elizabeth.

Elizabeth huffed and shook her head.

"Perhaps a walk in the garden?" suggested Cecily. "We must hear the full tale, you know," she added softly.

Elizabeth nodded her understanding.

"I would walk with you," Georgiana offered.

"As would I," said Lucy, rising. "In fact, I would like a bit of air. Mary Ellen, will you join us?"

Elizabeth rose to follow the three from the room. Mary Ellen joined arms with Georgiana, and Lucy took Elizabeth's but remained standing near the house until the others were a distance ahead.

"Now," she said with a smile, "tell me what is in your heart."

"She will have to marry him." Elizabeth blinked against the tears that formed in her eyes.

"She may," agreed Lucy. "It would be an unfortunate result but not unlikely. Do you worry for her safety or her happiness?"

Elizabeth nodded. "How could one be happy with such a man? How could one be safe?" A tear slid down her cheek. "If I had not listened to him, if I had not befriended him, this would not have happened."

Lucy drew her close. "He is handsome, and you said she was a flirt. Is it truly impossible that it could not have happened on its own?" Lucy led her to a bench near a tree as Elizabeth allowed that it was not entirely outside the realm of possibility.

They sat silently for a few moments. Lucy watched as

grief played at Elizabeth's features. There was yet something which was disquieting her, and Lucy feared that she knew all too well what it was, for she had, thanks to her uncle, felt the same — twice. So, it was not so very surprising when Elizabeth finally shook her head and voiced her true concern.

"I cannot bear to think of Georgiana having to be related to him, and I cannot imagine her brother would wish it." She drew a shuddering breath as tears flowed down her cheeks. "Lydia has not only destroyed her own happiness but mine as well."

Somewhere between London and Derbyshire

Darcy settled into the carriage again once the fresh horses had been acquired.

"I am not so old that I could not ride a horse," grumbled Mr. Bennet.

Darcy was unsure how many times he had heard the complaint.

"Richard and Bingley are riding ahead of us, and we shall travel as quickly as we can, but the carriage was needed." Darcy had said the same words each time Mr. Bennet had grumbled and shifted uneasily, but this time, he added, "we can ride from Pemberley."

Mr. Bennet nodded and attempted to open his book to occupy his mind. Darcy watched as the man flipped pages and then went back and flipped them again before closing the book and placing it on the bench next to him.

"What a fool I have been," Mr. Bennet leaned his head against the back of the carriage. "How could I have allowed her to go to Brighton? Was my peace truly worth the cost?" His eyes continued to search the top of the carriage as if it would give him the answers he sought.

"A lady of fifteen or sixteen can be persuasive," Darcy replied. "I had wished for my sister to wait for me to accompany her to Ramsgate, but the thought so distressed her that I pushed my better judgement to the side and allowed her to go ahead of me. It was not as if she would be unaccompanied. She had a companion who seemed respectable." He shrugged as Mr. Bennet looked his direction. "I did not know Mrs. Younge's connection to Wickham, and you did not know Wickham's true character. We, both of us, made decisions based on what we knew. Unfortunately, those decisions proved poor."

He shook his head at his foolishness in condemning Mr. Bennet for his neglect of family. True, the man did not appear to put forth enough effort — and Darcy was sure there were improvements that begged making. However, Darcy could commiserate to a degree with the gentleman. "I struggle to do right by one sister. I cannot imagine how much more challenging it would be to have five."

"You are far too generous," Mr. Bennet replied with a sad smile. "It is a challenge, and there are six females in my home, not five." He chuckled. "You are gaining a sensible wife, so your task of raising children, should they all be girls, will be much easier." He turned to look out at the road. The sun was dipping behind the hills and the shadows were growing. "I trusted my wife to guide them. What did I know of daughters? I had only a brother and a cousin." He smiled at Darcy. "My mother was much like Lizzy — a quick wit, a strong character, a love of learning, and a temper strong enough to quell the most stubborn acquaintance who dared challenge her." He chuckled again at the memory.

"You were close to her?"

"Closer to her than to my father." He sighed. "There was no love lost between my father and me. He preferred my brother and my cousin. They questioned less."

The sound of the wheels on the road and the rhythmic fall of horses' hooves filled the carriage for some minutes.

"That is why the estate is entailed," Mr. Bennet said, at last. "My father figured I would do a miserable job of seeing to it. He despised my love of new methods, you see." His chuckle, this time, was a bitter one. "And to my brother and my cousin, it looked like I was fulfilling my father's predictions." An impertinent grin very like Lizzy's played at his mouth. "The estate does well."

Darcy's brows rose. "Why hide your success?"

Mr. Bennet shrugged. "I cared not for their opinion and felt they deserved to keep it. I also did not trust my cousin and feared that if he knew I was a success, he might hasten my demise. He was with my brother when my brother had his fall. That is when the rift in our family occurred. I held him responsible since it was his idea to go out in foul weather. Fortunately, he has not survived me and will not reap the benefits of my labours. Unfortunately, his brother's son will. I would rather the estate not go to such a bumbling fool, but he seems harmless enough if you can avoid his prattling." He smiled. "And Charlotte is a fine young woman. She will do well by the estate and him. Not that I envy her the task."

The sounds of travel once again filled the space between the two men. Darcy considered the man across from him. There was much he had assumed about him, but the more time he spent with Mr. Bennet, the more he realized that not all of his assumptions were true. Again, he shook his head. How much more clearly he saw things since Elizabeth's refusal had caused him to re-evaluate himself and all he knew.

"She did well with the first two, and to a point with Mary." Mr. Bennet's head was resting against the back of the carriage. "But she became overwhelmed when the fourth was another girl." He looked toward Darcy for a moment. "She thought herself a failure, and no matter my assurance, she would not change from her position."

He leaned his head back again. "She was as beautiful as Jane and as lively as Lydia. She still is beautiful, but her liveliness has been misdirected, and I have been unsuccessful in redirecting it."

He drew a deep breath and released it. "That was my error, Mr. Darcy. I allowed myself to accept the failure. My distress is not so much about a poor decision in allowing Lydia to journey to Brighton, although it was unwise." He shook his head. "No, my distress is from allowing myself to find comfort in solitude while my wife seeks comfort in promoting her daughters — in an unchecked fashion. And now, I must feel the full weight of that decision, knowing that it will bring sorrow to my wife and daughters."

"Perhaps, we will overtake them." Darcy knew it was unlikely and even if they did, the damage had already been done.

Mr. Bennet shook his head. "She is with child, and even if she was not, her reputation is tarnished. She will have to marry the man." Mr. Bennet leaned forward. "I would understand if you were to withdraw your offer. I cannot expect you to wish the connection."

"Withdraw my offer?" The idea shocked Darcy. Not once in all of the events of the last two days had he considered such a thing. "I would rather be connected to ten men such as Wickham than to live without your daughter, sir."

Mr. Bennet patted Darcy's knee and then leaned his head against the back of the coach again as he prepared to get some rest. "If I have thought it, Lizzy will as well when she hears of what Lydia has done."

"Then we shall have to take the carriage and your daughter to Scotland with us, and we will marry before a word of this situation is spoken to her."

Mr. Bennet chuckled. "I applaud your determination, but I dare say you'll not get her to Gretna Green without her discovering the truth."

Chapter 12

Derbyshire

"Darcy will not give you up," said Lucy, placing an arm around Elizabeth's shoulders, "and if you are even considering rejecting him, . . . again . . . I shall be quite cross with you."

"But to be tied to Wickham!" cried Elizabeth. How could she ask him to be connected to such a person? It was not that she wished to give Darcy up, but she could not hold him to an agreement that would make him miserable.

"Wickham would be less of a burden for him to bear than losing you would be." Lucy sighed and searched her mind for ways to convince Elizabeth of this truth. Finally, after listening for a few moments to Elizabeth's soft sobs, she decided to share what she knew of Darcy's letters.

"He was beyond despondent after you rejected him." Her words were soft but drew Elizabeth's attention. "Philip feared for him."

"Feared?" Elizabeth sniffled and dried her eyes.

"Philip said Darcy sounded as if he was capable of doing

himself harm, though he would not, for even in his distress he talked about those who were dependent on him." Lucy saw the pain her words were causing Elizabeth and squeezed her close.

"I would not tell you this if I did not think it beneficial." She gave Elizabeth a small smile. "He had not been so distraught over Georgiana's ordeal with Wickham. He was unpleasant to be around, to be sure. He was angry and ashamed, as well as worried for his sister, but never beyond what a good hard ride or an afternoon of chopping wood could not work away." She paused and then shook her head. "That is not entirely true. There was an air about him that was rather off-putting — a facade designed to keep everyone at a distance. His words could be quite cutting at times, but you know that." She was relieved to see Elizabeth's lips curve upwards just a bit at the comment.

"And then, he left for Hertfordshire to assist Bingley as planned, and his letters, which were at first very short, became longer, and his words became gentler. I remember in one that Philip read to me, he told of a lady who had a keen wit and was at the time of his writing, and much to his delight, engaging in a bit of debate about what one might consider an accomplished lady."

Elizabeth's mouth fell open slightly, and her eyes grew wide. She remembered well that afternoon at Netherfield.

"He was quite taken with you," Lucy continued, "so taken that he left Netherfield." She withdrew her arm from around Elizabeth's shoulders since it seemed as if Elizabeth had calmed for the moment.

"Even when he was in London, his letters still spoke of you. He could physically distance himself from you, but he could not separate you from his heart. That is how it is with love. Once it has laid claim to your heart, it cannot be easily removed, not even with well-thought out arguments concerning families or duties.

"Oh, the times I listened to Philip sigh and moan over the letters he wrote in return! He experienced such difficulty in counselling his friend that what one expects in a wife and what one finds are often quite different and that no matter what Darcy's family might expect of station or breeding in his wife, what Darcy desired and needed was far greater."

She took Elizabeth's hand, for the next part was necessarily going to be unsettling for her. "Finally, in one joyous letter, he announced that he had resolved to act as his heart desired. The young lady had once again been placed in his path, and he was determined to offer for her. We anxiously awaited his announcement to call the banns, but the next letter was nearly a month in coming — although we did have one before that from Georgiana telling us of her brother's state."

"Please, I cannot bear to hear it," Elizabeth said through fresh tears.

"But you must," Lucy spoke as gently as she could,

though her tone was firm. She would not allow Elizabeth to cause the same pain to Darcy again. He was a friend, but beyond that she owed him so much for the help he provided her in dealing with her uncle. "His despair when we finally saw him was shocking. No amount of riding or chopping wood could dislodge it. It faded, but it was never gone. Even now, before he left for town, he was despondent at the thought of leaving — fearful that he would lose you. He loves you completely. You mean more to him than an unfavourable connection. You must believe me."

Elizabeth stood and walked toward the tree that the Abbot boys loved to play under. Bits and pieces of Lucy's words replayed themselves in her mind. She leant against the tree and allowed her tears to fall without restraint. She knew she had injured Darcy with the words of her refusal — she had intended them to sting — but she had never imagined him to be so shaken by them. And now, she must either cause him the same unbearable pain or a slightly lesser one of being related to Wickham. How could she decide such a thing? If they did marry, would he grow to resent her because of her sister? As much as she could not bear the thought of not being his, the idea of being his and despised was equally as painful.

The sound of voices drew her from her contemplation, and she turned to look at the house, just as Jane, accompanied by Captain Harris and Mr. Dobney, entered the garden. She took a deep breath and, drying her eyes as best she could, returned to Lucy.

"We thought it best to join you," said Jane, leaving the gentlemen near Lucy and walking a small distance away with her sister.

"How do things stand with Lydia?" asked Elizabeth.

"She is determined that she shall not marry Mr. Wickham." Jane sighed. "She says she has gone to great lengths to protect herself from such a thing happening, but it is Lydia, and though her plan is no doubt a clever one, it is not without fault. Uncle is still attempting to work on her."

"And what of Wickham?" Elizabeth asked.

"He had no part in the scheme beyond that which he was forced to take, and he does not seem willing to be wed to Lydia any more than she wishes to be tied to him. I do not know what can be done unless the matter can be silenced. Uncle will write to Papa tonight, and then, I suppose, we shall wait for his reply."

"And if Wickham leaves before Papa's answer arrives?"

Jane sighed. "That is a sticking point at present; however, Mr. Philip Dobney has gone to call for Mr. Williams, the constable, as he might have some sway."

"It is a fine mess," muttered Elizabeth.

"It is," admitted Jane. She glanced over her shoulder to where Lucy talked with her cousin and brother. "Are you well?"

Elizabeth shook her head. "I do not know until I know how Mr. Darcy will respond. Do Captain Harris and Mr. Dobney know what has happened?"

Jane sighed again. "Not the full tale, but enough. I believe any hope I had of capturing the captain may be at an end." She linked arms with Elizabeth and walked a bit further.

"And Mr. Dobney?" Elizabeth asked hopefully.

"He has yet to pay me any particular attention beyond the expected civilities," Jane said with a laugh. "I do not think our wayward sister shall inspire him to fall at my feet. Besides," she added softly, "what hope have I when you, though you have ensnared a man's heart as completely as you have Mr. Darcy's, fear losing his regard?"

"But there are different circumstances, a different relationship between Mr. Darcy and Mr. Wickham. You know there are."

"Perhaps," said Jane, "but Mr. Dobney and Captain Harris also have a relation who was ill-treated by the man."

"We are beyond hope, then?" asked Elizabeth.

"Never beyond hope," said Jane. "There must always be hope that happiness is not beyond our reach." She looked up toward the clouds that shifted back and forth in the sky above. "Even when the hope is very small."

~*~*~

Elizabeth rose from her bed as the sun stretched its arms across the fields, stirring the birds to sing and the night to flee. It had been a long night of little sleep. Her mind would not be quiet. It continually weighed Lucy's words about Darcy with the fears she had about bringing shame to him through her sister's actions.

She had wished to toss and turn in bed and considered rising and pacing the room, but Jane had fallen asleep with some difficulty, and Elizabeth had been loath to disturb her. So, she had waited, dozing briefly, disturbed in sleep by dreams and in waking moments by thought, until finally concluding in the end that it might be best to break with propriety and write a letter to Darcy, leaving the decision entirely with him.

So, quietly, she slipped from the room, wrapping her robe tightly about herself, and headed to the sitting room where she knew she would find writing supplies and a window that faced the early morning sun.

"Good morning," Mr. Abbot, who was bouncing Aiden on his knee, greeted her. "It is a rather early start to the day after the night we endured."

He smiled at Aiden and poked out his tongue. "I would still be in bed if it were not for this early riser. He was insistent that he see his mama but graciously agreed to spend time with his papa instead. I did not wish to disturb Cecily so early." He placed Aiden on the floor.

Aiden immediately pulled himself up next to his father's leg and stood, swaying slightly from side to side, lifting one foot and then the other before plopping down and beginning the process again.

"He is determined to be on his way," chuckled Mr. Abbot.

"He is," agreed Elizabeth. "I had hoped to write a letter before the day began." Elizabeth looked toward the writing desk.

Mr. Abbot made a small waving motion. "Do not let us keep you from your pleasure."

Elizabeth thanked him and seated herself at the desk.

"Gardiner wrote a letter to your father last night, and I added my observations. It is not sealed yet. We wished to wait until morning — in case some thought for a solution would come after a few hours of rest. You may include yours with ours before we seal it."

Elizabeth held her pen still, hovering above the name she had just written. "I am not writing to Papa," she admitted softly.

"You are not?"

Elizabeth understood the surprise in Mr. Abbot's tone. To whom else would she be writing? Her mother was not to know of Lydia's tale until Mr. Bennet had been notified, and both Jane and Mrs. Gardiner were at Willow Hall.

She looked up from her paper. "I am writing to Mr. Darcy."

Mr. Abbot's smile was understanding. "Do not let us disturb you," was his only reply.

Aiden's response was not so accommodating. After trying to stand and take a step for what must have been the tenth time, he had dropped once again onto the floor. The situation did not please him, and he made his opinion about it known in a loud cry.

"We will go see if Cook has a biscuit, and then it might be time for a visit to Mama." Mr. Abbot scooped up his son. The child's wails softened as he snuggled his head into his father's shoulder, his chubby arms clinging tightly to his papa.

Elizabeth turned back to her letter and began the task of telling Darcy about her sister's arrival with Wickham. She was just blowing her nose for the third time in only twice as many lines when her solitude was once again interrupted.

Mrs. Gardiner hurried into the room, stopped short, and looked very disconcerted to see Elizabeth.

"Is something the matter?" asked Elizabeth. Aunt Gardiner was typically unflappable. Even when Mama would take a spell of nerves, Aunt Gardiner could be counted on to tend to them with a smile and a soft voice. She was much like Jane in that way. But this morning, she looked very much like she could use a dose of Mama's salts.

Mrs. Gardiner sighed and dropped into a chair. "I had hoped when I heard someone in this room that it might be Lydia." She shook her head. "Unless she has taken herself out to the barn — which is an unlikely option — she is gone."

"Gone?" Elizabeth's heart leapt to her throat.

"Gone." Mrs. Gardiner's eyes filled with tears. "Her bed has not been slept in, and her travelling bag is missing with her."

Elizabeth rose and moved to look out the window and down the driveway to the lane beyond. "Where could she have gone? She knows no one, and her sense of direction is paltry at best." Her hand ran nervously from her elbow to her shoulder and back. There was one thing that would be worse than having Lydia married to Wickham, and that would be to have her lost forever.

Mrs. Gardiner shook her head in response. "I do not know."

"Mr. Wickham left with Mr. Williams, did he not?" Elizabeth asked, her letter forgotten.

"He did."

"And he would not return?"

"He holds no fondness for your sister," said her aunt.

"She is not in the barn or the stables," said Mr. Gardiner, coming into the room. "No horses have been taken, and there are no fresh marks on the driveway, nor has anyone heard anything unusual. I have come to get a cup of tea, and then we will begin a search of the estate."

And so they did. After a cup of tea and a few fortifying bites of toast, as many of the party at Willow Hall as could be taken from their duties were gathered and a thorough search of the estate was conducted. No sign of Lydia, save a few footprints near the gate, could be found. And so, it was determined that Lydia had more than likely thought to follow the path of the road she had travelled to reach Willow Hall.

"I do not know what she is thinking," said Jane as she and Elizabeth travelled along the road toward Kympton.

"She was quite adamant that she not be forced to marry Mr. Wickham," said Aunt Gardiner. "My guess is that she is bound for Longbourn and her mother. We have only to check at Mr. Williams' to be certain that she has not gone there to beg Mr. Wickham to accompany her, and then we shall continue on to the coaching inn." She patted Jane's knee reassuringly. "The matter should be all settled before long."

Elizabeth did not miss the uncertainty in her aunt's countenance as Aunt Gardiner attempted to smile at her. With Lydia, nothing was ever settled easily. The logical path never seemed to be one that her sister ventured down. And then, if they were successful and found Lydia or discovered in which direction she had fled, there was still the issue of what to be done about her travelling with Wickham.

The gentlemen had taken horses so their travel to Mr. Williams' home was quicker than the carriage. So, before the ladies could reach where they would turn from the main road, Mr. Gardiner and Mr. Abbot had discovered what they needed to know and had turned back to find the carriage and direct it on to the coaching inn.

There, Mr. Abbot and Mr. Gardiner made inquiries, but to no avail. Lydia had not been seen by anyone, and with heavy hearts and at a slower pace than they had travelled previously, the party began their return to Willow Hall.

Chapter 13

Darcy paced the sitting room at Willow Hall while Mr. Bennet took a place at the window, watching for the return of his daughters. It had been Darcy's plan to stop only at Pemberley to refresh horses before continuing on to Scotland, but when Mr. Bennet had suggested stopping at Willow Hall to speak to Gardiner, Darcy had been happy to oblige as it meant he would have an opportunity to see Elizabeth. Upon arrival at Willow Hall, however, their plans had changed.

"Not gone to Scotland?" Mr. Bennet muttered for the third time since they had been told what news Mrs. Smith had regarding Lydia.

"So it appears," said Darcy.

Mr. Bennet shifted so that he could see Darcy. "Is there a way to inform the colonel of our change in plans?'

Darcy stopped mid-stride and turned to face Mr. Bennet. "Richard said he would stop at Pemberley." He furrowed his brow. "He may still be there."

His gaze fell on the writing-table. He might be able to

send a message and keep Richard and Bingley from riding to Scotland unnecessarily. If he did not stop them at Pemberley, he would have to go after them, and that would take him away from Elizabeth yet again.

He sat down at the desk and lifted the letter which was only partially written to put it to the side. However, his eyes caught the name at the top of the page, and before he could pull them away, he had read the first few lines.

Mr. Darcy,

Forgive my impropriety in writing to you, but there is a disturbing matter which must be brought to your attention. I shall not dither about but shall come directly to the point. My sister, Lydia, has done something quite foolish and has travelled to Derbyshire in the company of Mr. Wickham.

Darcy pulled his eyes from the letter and lay it to the side as intended. Though he desired to read the remainder, he needed to send his message to Richard as quickly as possible. However, he promised himself, as soon as his task was done, he would return to the letter Elizabeth had been writing him.

"A messenger will be needed to carry this." Darcy placed a clean paper on the desk, giving Mr. Bennet the briefest of glances before setting about the business of writing to his cousin.

Before the ink was dry enough for the message to be folded, a lad from the stables had appeared. So, as he folded the message, Darcy gave instruction to the boy about its delivery.

Then, as Mr. Bennet returned to his position of watching at the window, Darcy picked up the letter he had placed to the side and continued reading.

Although her maid travelled with her, they spent more than one night on the road. It is my understanding that they were never parted while they travelled — not even to sleep. I am certain that you can see the gravity of this situation and that the solution for salvaging her reputation is for her to marry Mr. Wickham. However, she has not yet agreed to the arrangement. Indeed, both she and Mr. Wickham seem to be most vehemently opposed to such a suggestion. My uncle has written to my father, and we await his decision.

My heart is grieved not only at the foolishness of my sister and the life to which she is consigning herself but also for you and your sister. The thought of bringing such a man as Mr. Wickham into your family as a relation is nearly too awful to contemplate. To think that I should be the cause of such grief! It is overwhelming. And so, I release you from your promise. I cannot —

There was no more. The letter had been left incomplete, but the portion that was there struck panic in Darcy's heart. She was turning him away? He read it again and then a third time.

"No." He shook his head and stood. "She will not release me." He took up his hat. "I must find her."

Darcy was nearly at the stables before Mr. Bennet caught up to him.

"Elizabeth has broken the engagement?" he asked between laboured breaths.

Darcy handed Mr. Bennet the letter as he ordered a horse readied.

"It is incomplete," said Mr. Bennet to the back of the man in front of him.

"It is complete enough."

Mr. Bennet placed a hand on Darcy's shoulder. "It is never complete enough until the full matter has been told." He smiled gently when Darcy looked over his shoulder. "Allow her to finish her thoughts. They may not be as you assume." He handed the letter back to Darcy. "I will wait here, and I would suggest you do the same, but I am certain such a suggestion would not be heeded."

He chuckled at Darcy's expression. "No, a man violently in love is not one to sit idly by and wait." He removed his hand from Darcy's shoulder. "Be patient with her. Her tongue may be sharp, but her heart is tender." Then, he turned and ambled back toward the house.

Darcy tucked the letter into his pocket and mounted the horse that had been brought to him. With a cluck and a nudge, he urged the horse toward the road. Several minutes later, he drew to a stop before the parsonage.

"Philip," he called in greeting to the man, who was making his way towards him.

"Darcy, we had not expected to see you so soon." Philip looked nervously toward the house.

"Is she here?" Darcy asked. "Is Elizabeth here?" He repeated when Philip did not respond immediately.

"She is." Philip stepped in front of his friend. "Some things have happened –."

"I know," Darcy pushed his way past Philip. "Which is why I must see her without delay."

Darcy hurried into the house. She would not release him from his promise. She would not refuse him again. He would make certain of it, and she could explain the rest of her letter after he had.

There were others in the room, but aside from Lucy, to whom he nodded a greeting, he was unsure of who they were, for he was looking for one person and one person only, and he had found her the instant he had entered.

"Mr. Darcy," Elizabeth said in surprise as he approached her.

He pulled the letter from his pocket. "You will not release me from my promise," he said. "I will not allow it, for I love you, Elizabeth Bennet. I would endure a connection to a thousand men such as Wickham for you."

"You would?" A smile spread across her face and relief washing through her spirit.

"I would if you will but say you will have me."

She nodded as tears formed in her eyes. "I will."

He turned toward Philip. "Call the banns," he said with

a smile. Then, he turned his attention back to Elizabeth. "It seems I shall be marrying." And with that, he gathered Elizabeth into his arms and kissed her soundly.

~*~*~

"It is rarely who you expect," said Philip to Darcy later after all of the party from Willow Hall had left except Elizabeth, who had stayed behind at Lucy's request. Philip knew that it was an effort to give Darcy a few moments of calm before having to face the mix of delight and concern that would hang over Willow Hall. Large groups and high emotions had never been something with which Darcy had been comfortable.

Darcy shook his head. "She is not what I expected. She is far better."

"That is just how I feel about Lucy," agreed Philip. "God works in mysterious ways."

"That he does," agreed Mr. Harker from his chair. "I would not be surprised if the Good Lord provided a ram in the thicket for Miss Lydia."

Darcy shot him an inquisitive look.

"Faith, my lad. That is what trials test and strengthen. Abraham was put to the test and just when the dire deed was to be completed, a ram was provided. And if the Lord could save Isaac from death, I believe He can save Miss Lydia from Wickham. Did He not save Lucy and Georgiana?"

"He did," Darcy acknowledged.

"Well, then," the elderly man pushed himself from his chair, "I shall go home and entreat the Lord for such a miracle."

He stopped in front of Darcy. "Miss Elizabeth seems a fine choice. Your mother and father would be pleased." He held out a hand which, though wrinkled, was steady and strong. "My joy to you both."

He clucked his tongue at Philip as the younger man stood to give his mentor assistance in exiting the house. "Mrs. Barnes will see me home, young man. You have guests."

Philip thought to protest, but from the set of Mr. Harker's jaw, he knew it would be to no avail. The gentleman's eyes might be growing dim, but his spirit of independence was not. So, he merely thanked him for his visit.

"You know, Darcy is a much better choice for her than your brother," Mr. Harker whispered as he waited for Lucy's aunt to say her farewells and join him. "And don't let your sister attempt to match Miss Bennet with Marcus either. She's a lovely girl, but far too tame. Marcus needs a wife with a bit of spirit." He chuckled. "Perhaps he can be the ram in the thicket," he said as he held out an arm to Mrs. Barnes.

Philip shook his head and sighed as he took his seat again.

"Mary Ellen truly was attempting to match Elizabeth with Marcus?" Darcy asked.

"Until you arrived," admitted Philip, "but Lucy set her straight after seeing how you greeted Miss Elizabeth."

"Has she attempted to match him with Miss Bennet?"

Philip shook his head. "He has shown no interest, so she has focused her work on our cousin — although I am not certain much encouragement is needed on either side."

Darcy's heart sank at the news. "Miss Bennet has shown interest in Harris?"

"Some." Philip studied his friend's expression. "Is there a reason Mary Ellen should not meddle?"

Darcy nodded slowly. "Bingley."

Philip scrubbed his hands down his face. "Maybe if Mary Ellen would marry, she would stop her interference with all her single relations."

"Should I speak to Richard then?" Darcy laughed at the surprise on Philip's face.

"You know?"

Darcy shrugged. "I do. It seems the only one who does not is my cousin."

Philip chuckled. "I suppose that is because she is not what he expects."

"She never is, is she?" Darcy asked, smiling at Elizabeth. He heard the crunch of gravel under horses' hooves and carriage wheels approach the house. "My carriage has arrived. I should see Elizabeth back to Willow Hall."

~*~*~

Elizabeth sat on the bench next to Darcy. He watched

her nervously smooth her skirts. Her cheeks were flushed a lovely rose colour.

"I know it is not entirely proper," he began, trying to help her feel at ease.

She shook her head. "No, it is not." She smiled at him impertinently. "But neither is kissing a gentleman in public, and I have already done that today."

"And I hope you might kiss him again in private."

Her cheeks grew even rosier. "I would like that," her admission was barely above a whisper.

He slid closer to her and bent his mouth to hers, kissing her softly at first and then more firmly as he wrapped her in his embrace. Breaking their kiss, he held her close and enjoyed her presence in his arms before he spoke of the letter.

"You thought I was sending you away?"

He nodded. "But your father told me that my assumption might not be true."

"Yet, you accused me of that very thing at the parsonage." She peeked up at him. "Explain yourself, sir."

He kissed her upturned forehead. "I decided it did not matter how you were to conclude that letter. I was going to make certain you could not refuse me."

"So you professed your love for me in the sitting room at a parsonage."

He chuckled. "Yes. Not that it was the first time I have done so."

She squeezed him tight. "I can never apologize enough for how I refused you. It is why I was not going to refuse you in that letter. I lost you once through my foolishness. I would not be the one to send you away again. I released you from our agreement so that you might choose without fear of breaking your promise to me." She looked up at him again. "I hoped you would choose me, but . . ."

"Knowing what you know of my relationship with Wickham, you would not force me to be tied to him."

She nodded. "I could not bear the thought of your growing to despise me for the connection."

He tipped her chin up so that he could kiss her once again. "I will see him well-situated and your sister as safe as can be, and I will do so gladly as long as you are mine."

"You are too good," she said. "You are not what I expected."

"Nor are you what I expected." He smiled down at her. "But Philip assures me that that is how it is with love. And I do love you, Elizabeth Bennet."

"And I love you, Fitzwilliam Darcy," she said stretching up to kiss him.

And so the unlikely pair — he, the nephew of an earl and master of a grand estate, and she, the daughter of a country gentleman and his tenant's guest — passed the last few miles to Willow Hall wrapped in each other's arms, speaking in word and deed of their love for each other, and knowing that, come what may, they had found their happiness both now and forever.

So Very Unexpected

Willow Hall Romance, Book 3
A Pride and Prejudice Variation Novel

~*~*~

When plans go awry, the results, much like the lady
who made them, can be very unexpected.

Chapter 1

Lydia Bennet pulled the door to Willow Hall closed as quietly as she could. She did not want to wake a single person, especially her uncle. Marry Wickham? A lieutenant? A man who cheated and played cards far too often? Did her uncle wish for her to be a pauper? She knew she was not made for such lowly circumstances. Did Uncle Gardiner not also know? If she married Wickham, she might be limited to just one maid of all work! Lydia shuddered at the thought.

Reaching the gate, she turned to take one last look at Willow Hall, and then, biting her lip and summoning her courage, she continued on to the road. Her heart beat loudly in her chest. She had done some things before which required a good dose of fortitude, but none had been so daring as this.

Above her, the moon was only a sliver and clouds blocked many of the stars. Lydia stood looking down the road one way and then the other for a few minutes. Surely, the carriage that brought her to Willow Hall had turned left into the driveway, or was it right? She sighed and crouched down to look more closely at the ground. It was no use; there were grooves from carriages both to her right and to her left. With a shrug, she swallowed her fear and turned in the direction her mind had first told her must be the way to Kympton.

She felt a need to whistle, to fill the silence of the night, but she dared not. She would do nothing to draw attention to herself from anyone or anything. The thought sent a shiver down her spine. This was foolish and far too dangerous. She paused, turned back, and then remembering her uncle's words, "It must be done. You must marry him to save both your reputation and that of your family." She turned away from Willow Hall once again and continued on her way.

For the next twenty minutes, she entertained herself with thoughts of ribbons, lace, and bonnets, describing to herself the perfect hat to accompany the new yellow dress she would have when she reached home. Mama would see to it. Lydia smiled to herself. Mama always saw to what Lydia wanted even when Papa was reticent. Mama would not see her married to a lieutenant. A captain was the lowest rank which Mama, and truly anyone of sense, would find acceptable. A lieutenant's wife! Indeed! Lydia nearly laughed at the thought until she heard something — a scurrying beside the road to her right. Something very like a fit of nerves gripped her heart.

Not wishing to be preyed on by either man or beast, Lydia scooted off the road and into the stand of trees on the left. The woods, indeed, felt safer. She picked her way between the trees, not entirely sure if she was still travelling in the same direction as she had intended, but going back toward that scurrying sound was not an option.

After another twenty minutes of walking and feeling quite turned about and tired, Lydia spotted a cottage. It was a tiny stone cottage with a small structure for storage next to it. Perhaps she could rest there and be tucked away from the notice of any night creatures. She just wished a moment to rest so that this feeling of being utterly lost would vanish.

She rapped lightly on the door to the storage building. She lay her ear against the wood, and after a few minutes of listening intently and hearing no sounds, she opened the door. The structure housed nothing — not a scythe, not a rake, not a bucket. There were no flowers or herbs hanging from the rafters to dry. It was empty. Completely and entirely empty. Lydia studied the perplexing emptiness for a moment before finding a corner and sitting down with her feet tucked beneath her and her head resting, at first, tentatively and then more fully, against the wall as she relaxed.

~*~*~

The first rays of sun poked their fingers through a small gap between two boards on the wall opposite Lydia. The light played with her hair and then crept across her face, tickling first her nose and then her eyelashes. Lydia swatted at the offending light and turned her head to avoid it. Her hair caught on a nail that had not been hammered in completely, and the sharp pain of the tugging woke her. She rubbed her eyes and looked around the shed. In the light of the morning, it was not quite so empty as it had been in lantern light. In one corner, there were five pieces of wood neatly stacked, but that was all — five pieces of wood and a lot of nothing else.

She peeked out the door. There was neither the smell of a fire nor a wisp of smoke rising from the chimney of the cottage. Confident she was alone, she stepped out of her sleeping spot and surveyed her surroundings. Nothing looked familiar. There were fields of grass and flowers beyond the cottage and trees behind her. To her left was a slope that descended for some distance. She had not seen any of this when they had travelled from Kympton to Willow Hall. She would have remembered it, for it was beautiful — the kind of beautiful that caused one to stop and admire it for hours, the kind of beautiful that inspired paintings and poems, the kind of beautiful that brought a smile to her face and peace to her heart.

After several minutes of admiring her surroundings, Lydia decided it was time to explore the cottage. Carefully, she opened the door, calling out a greeting as she did, just in case someone might be within. She waited for a reply, and when none came, she entered. Dust covered the table and the three glasses that sat turned upside down on the small cabinet next to a larger cupboard with doors. In the small sitting room, Lydia took a seat on a large chair in front of the fireplace. The back of the chair wrapped up and around her. She leaned her head against its back. Ah, she sighed with pleasure. Even though the fabric of the chair was worn so thin that the pattern was little more than a shadow, this was much more comfortable than that shed.

She allowed herself to close her eyes and enjoy the comfort for whatshe thought was a moment. However, when one is as tired from travelling in crowded coaches, debating with one's relative to avoid an untenable marriage, and then walking for nearly an hour in a circular path along a road and amongst trees while fearing that some creature was going to attack her, even a moment of rest can stretch into hours.

Lydia's weary body welcomed sleep, and just as it had in the shed, it did not wake of its own accord. However, this time it was not the gentle and playful fingers of the sun which woke Lydia but the banging of a door and a masculine voice.

Lydia tucked herself into the chair as best she could. The back of the chair was nearly turned completely toward the door, so perhaps if she were very still, she would not be noticed. She sucked in her breath and closed her eyes as she listened to the sound of boots thumping through the cottage.

Marcus Dobney peered into all the rooms in the cottage and was about to lock the door and leave when he heard a small, muffled sneeze from the sitting room. He shook his head. He had looked in that room and seen no one. Another sneeze. Ah, the chair by the fireplace! How had he neglected to check there?

He crept into the room, coming up behind the chair. "I heard you sneeze," he said as he stood behind the chair and looked down at the occupant. "Miss Lydia?" he asked in surprise as she squealed and shot to her feet.

She whirled on him. "That was not nice. You frightened me half to death." She placed her hands on her hips and glared at the intruder, who looked oddly familiar. "How do you know my name?"

He chuckled and leaned on the back of the chair. "It is also not nice to be stealing into cottages that do not belong to you." He tipped his head and smirked as her eyes narrowed. She looked as defiant now as she had last evening when they had been introduced. "You do not remember me?"

Lydia shook her head, but then her brows furrowed, and her mouth formed a perfect *o* as her eyes grew wide, and she began to recall why the fine looking gentleman leaning on the back of the tired old chair looked so familiar.

"You were with Captain Harris." She bit her lip as she strained to remember his name.

To be honest, she had not been focused on much yesterday except convincing her uncle that she did not need to marry Wickham. There had been two gentlemen who had come to call, and then Jane escorted them to the garden to find Miss Dobney. That was it!

"Mr. Dobney, is it?" Lydia fluttered her lashes just a bit and smiled sweetly. Most of the men she had met responded well to such an expression.

Marcus nodded and motioned for Lydia to be seated on the settee near the window as he pulled the chair to face it. "Why are you here in my cottage when you should be at Willow Hall?"

Lydia watched his fingers unbutton his jacket as he sank into the chair and swung one leg over the other. This was his cottage? Her brows furrowed once again. Surely, a man who wore such beautiful clothes did not live in this tiny dust-covered cottage. "You live here?"

He chuckled again. It was a sound that Lydia found dreadfully infuriating. There was no need to laugh at her for asking a simple question.

"No, I do not live here, but just the same, the cottage is mine — or will be when I come into my inheritance." He leaned forward. "Now, tell me why I should not call the constable to report a vagrant?"

Lydia pulled herself up and looked down her nose at the

man across from her. "I am not a vagrant. I merely needed a place to rest, and the door was unlocked." She folded her arms. "It seems very careless of you to leave your inheritance unlocked."

He chuckled again, and she huffed. "My steward forgot to lock it yesterday when he was checking on the fields. That is why I am here. I told him I would see to it."

"It is not well-tended," she muttered.

He raised a brow at the comment but let it pass. "You are avoiding my question."

She smiled at him again and rose from her seat. "I am sorry, but I must be on my way. If you could just point me in the direction of Kympton."

This time he laughed out loud. "Sit down."

If she were not so irritated with him, she might have taken a moment to admire his smile. It was very nice. Very nice, indeed. But she was not in a mood to admire his pleasant mouth or his lovely brown eyes that were currently sparkling with amusement.

He pointed to the settee, and she sat. "You were going to Kympton?"

"I may have gotten turned about in the woods," she admitted.

"You most certainly did," he replied.

"It was dark," she mumbled.

His eyes grew wide. "You were travelling at night?"

"Of course," she smoothed her skirts, so she would not

have to look at his face. It was a handsome face and wearing an expression she particularly did not like — especially on a handsome face. Handsome men were to look at her with interest, of course, but not as he was. His expression was one that spoke of him wondering quite loudly about her mental abilities.

"It is far easier to make an unnoticed exit when it is dark and everyone is asleep." She skewered him with a challenging look. "I do not suppose you remember doing anything so exciting in your youth?" There, that ought to grate, but just to make certain it did –"Not that I am calling you old, per se." She smiled and fluttered her lashes. "I am just saying you are not young." The effect was as she had hoped. His smile faded, and his eyes narrowed. Displeasure she could allow on a handsome face.

"I was never so foolish in my youth."

She shrugged.

He could see the anger at his comment by the set of her mouth and the narrowing of her eyes. His sister, Mary Ellen, would often respond in such a fashion when she did not wish to continue a particular discussion.

"Now, tell me why a girl," he emphasized the word, enjoying the darkening in her eyes, "like you is sneaking off in the night? A secret rendezvous? Perhaps with Wickham?" He attempted to keep his tone from growling the name, but his success was only limited.

She shot to her feet, grabbed her bag, and would have left if Marcus had not blocked her path.

She stepped close to him, so close that she had to tip her head up to glare at him. "I am not a girl!"

He swallowed as he looked down at her. Her figure was definitely not girlish. However, the stamp of her foot was.

"And I do not know why everyone insists that I would even consider a man like Mr. Wickham." She visibly shuddered as she said his name.

"Perhaps it is because, as I have heard tell, you flirted with him in Brighton and then travelled with him for several days." He folded his arms across his chest in an attempt to avoid seeing any more of her than her face when he looked down. She rolled her large hazel eyes at him and pursed her lovely lips, causing him to swallow once again.

"As I explained to my uncle, a man such as Mr. Wickham is easily led. A mention of exposing his swindling to the ones he has played for fools and a hint that a rumour of doing harm to me might reach Mr. Darcy ensured me safe passage."

"A lady is never safe with a man like Wickham," growled Marcus.

Her eyes sparkled at the comment — most fetchingly he thought.

"So, I am now a lady?" She smiled at him and raised an eyebrow. Then, swiftly, she took a step to her right and scooted past him. "I really must be on my way, for as you say, no lady is safe with a man such as Wickham, so it is best that I do not remain where I might be forced to be tied to him in marriage." She threw the words over her shoulder as she hurried to the door of the cottage.

Marcus chased after her and grabbed her by an elbow. "You are not leaving. You are returning to Willow Hall. Your family must be worried."

She wrenched her arm free. "I am not returning to Willow Hall!"

He reached for her arm once again, but she pulled it away. "You are," he said as he took two long strides to catch up to her again.

"No. I am not." She began to run.

"You are being a fool."

"I will not marry him, Mr. Dobney. I will not!"

He sighed and ran after her. "Perhaps, but you must return to your family." He pulled her bag from her hand and sat it on the ground behind him.

"Give me my bag!"

"No, not until you are at Willow Hall."

"Oh, you are infuriating."

He smiled as she stamped her foot.

"Very well, I shall go to Willow Hall with you, but I am not staying."

"Yes, you are." He chuckled at her scowl. "You are a

rather adorable girl even when you are put out." He called to his horse. "I will need a way to get home," he explained.

"I am not a girl," she muttered as she stood there, waiting for him to tie her bag onto his horse.

"And I am not old," he retorted and began walking with Lydia scampering behind, trying to keep pace with his long strides.

Chapter 2

Marcus kept his pace quick, glancing over his shoulder now and then to make sure that Lydia was keeping within sight of him. He knew it would be far more gentlemanly and courteous to slow his pace to hers, but he was also certain it would be more difficult for her to berate him if he kept her at a distance and nearly out of breath. If only he had been right!

"You are doing this to vex me," she called. "Ouch."

He stopped and looked back to see that she was well. "Mind the branches."

"If you would slow down, I might be at leisure to do so," she spat back.

"If you would stop complaining, I might willingly slow down." He gave her a crooked smile. "However, it seems a young thing like you should be able to keep up with an old man like me." He ran a hand over his horse. Content that his horse was faring well, he turned and continued walking.

"I did not say you were old," she called.

"Per se," he returned.

Oh, he was as irritating as he was attractive, which made it all that much more frustrating. She should be imagining knives in his back instead of noticing how wide his shoulders were or how muscular, his legs. Why could he not act as every other handsome man she had met? If he did, she would not be marching at a ferocious pace through the woods.

"I am not going any further," she said, stopping and taking a seat on a fallen log. "My feet hurt." She held her breath. Surely, he would not leave her alone in the woods. He took three more steps before turning in her direction once again.

"If you stay there, I will bring your uncle to you," he called.

Her mouth dropped open. He would leave her? She folded her arms across her chest and glared at him. She was positive that he was too far away to see her scowl, but she wore it none-the-less.

"A gentleman would not abandon a lady," she called in an attempt to goad him into staying.

Had her tone not been one resembling that of a willful child, he might have taken the comment as an insult. But since it was most definitely spoken in a tone of one trying to get her way, it did not injure his pride in the least. It did, however, raise his ire. "It is fortunate for me, then, that you are not a lady."

The responding huff was rather satisfying to Marcus.

"Now," he called to her, "will you stay where you are, if I promise to bring a horse with me for you to ride?"

Receiving only a shrug in response, he sighed and said, "Five minutes, and then we move on again." He dropped the reins of his horse and came back to take a seat on the ground closer to where she was. He watched as she stretched out one leg, twirling her foot in a circle before repeating the same activity with the other leg. She rubbed her calves rather vigorously. Her face did look a bit pained.

"If you turn around, I could take off my boots for a minute."

He shook his head. "That would be a bad idea."

She glared at him yet again and began to untie her right boot. She had only gotten it loosened and was beginning to remove it when his hands were on hers, halting her progress.

"If your foot is swollen, you might not get your boot back on."

"You needn't growl at me."

He applied himself to the task of retying her boot and tried not to hear the hurt in her voice. "If they are truly sore, you may ride with your bag."

"Thank you," she said, pulling her foot away from him and tucking it back under her skirts. She considered untying her left boot so that he might also retie it and that foot might feel as lovely as her right did at this moment. She bit her lip. He would just scold her again, but the lovely prickly feeling might be worth it.

"So you will ride?"

He was looking at her with the most concerned look he had given her since their meeting, and it was making it very difficult to be angry at him, although she knew she should be since he was being so demanding.

She sighed and looked toward his horse. "Must I indeed go back?"

He nodded. "Your family will be worried."

She pulled her lip between her teeth once again. "I cannot marry him," she said softly. "I will not."

"Let me help you onto Erebus, and then you can tell me about it." He waited until he saw a small nod. Then, he stood and extended his hand to help her to her feet.

It was odd how, at one moment, he wished to leave her sitting here in the woods, exposed to the elements, and suffering the fate of her foolishness and the next he wished to bundle her up and see her protected. He hoisted her up onto Erebus and situated her bag so that she had enough room to be comfortable.

She grabbed his hand before he could remove it from her bag. "You will stop before we get there so I might dismount?"

His brows drew together. "If you wish it, I can."

She looked away from him, her cheeks growing rosy. "It

is not very ladylike to ride astride. I know what they think of me, but I assure you I am not...that."

He mumbled his understanding. She was a conundrum — worrying about her modesty yet sneaking out at night and travelling with a man such as Wickham — and then there was that perplexing wavering of his own opinion about her.

"Did you name him Erebus because he is the colour of shadows?"

"Indeed, I did. Have you read mythology?" He glanced up at her. She was smiling, and her head bobbed up and down enthusiastically.

"I have. They are such fanciful tales. I quite enjoy them." She laughed. "Although Papa does not know I have read them. In fact, only Kitty knows." She leaned forward and spoke more softly as if what she was going to say was a secret that not even the trees were allowed to hear. "I cannot let Mama know, you see. She is always going on about how Lizzy is far too quick to make a good match, and I should not want her saying such things about me. It would ruin my chances."

"And why would it ruin your chances?"

"Because gentlemen do not wish for intelligent wives. They want only pretty women who smile, flutter their lashes, and agree with their opinions."

She said it in such a matter of fact way, as if all of creation, save him, already knew this fact.

"I would disagree," he said.

"You cannot. It is true. That is why everyone prefers Jane to Lizzy and me and Kitty to Mary."

"Everyone?"

Her head was bobbing up and down again quite emphatically, and his mind was once again perplexed by the disparity of her thinking. She claimed to enjoy reading myths; she had out-schemed Wickham; and yet she could not countenance the fact that some man, such as himself, might wish for a woman with more than just good looks and pleasant manners.

"I would disagree."

Lydia shook her head. "You cannot."

He realized she was quite probably correct. Although he could make a case to refute her claim, he was uncertain as to which Lydia he might be presenting his case. The scheming Lydia might see his logic, but the one that rode his horse did not seem capable of it.

"Very well, I shall not disagree. However, it is not because I agree." His lips twitched in amusement at the look of utter confusion on her face.

"That makes no sense," she said after a few moments of contemplation. "If you do not agree, you disagree, and if you do not disagree, you agree."

He shrugged. "Ah, but it does make sense that I am neither old nor young?"

"It does. You see there are degrees to age. If you were

young, you would not have such a prickly look about your jaw."

He rubbed his hand against the stubble on his jaw.

"It is not a bad look," Lydia added, seeing his brows furrow. "It looks quite good actually, but it does give the appearance of age rather than youth."

"And precisely how does an appearance of age and a lack of youth not equate with being old?"

"I did not say you lacked youth! I said you were not young. The two are very different. One can still have a youthful vigor and be quite decidedly old."

"Very well, continue with your explanation." He dared not ask any further questions, for his mind was already getting rather turned about.

"To be old, I imagine, one must be at least forty. You are not forty, are you?"

"No, I am not forty."

She tipped her head to the side. "Are you thirty?"

He shook his head. "Not yet. I have two more years."

She smiled. "I thought as much." She pointed to the corner of her eye. "There are no little creases."

"And creases happen when one turns thirty?"

"I think so," she replied. "You have no creases; your eyes are bright, and your hair is brown without a fleck of grey or white. It is actually a lovely colour, as are your eyes. And, therefore, you are not old; although, you are not young, either."

He nodded, unsure exactly how to respond to such statements. "Very well, I will allow that you do not find me old."

"As you should," she said with a smile.

He chuckled, and this time, instead of being a sound that annoyed her as it had before, it was a sound that she found rather pleasing. How odd. But then her feet were no longer hurting, so that must account for her better opinion of him. Lydia patted the neck of Erebus. Yes, her feet not hurting must be the answer.

~*~*~

Some time later, as they approached Willow Hall, Marcus stopped as he had promised he would.

Lydia's cheeks puffed out and then flattened again as she released the breath she had drawn. "I cannot go in there," she said, turning to Marcus. "They will make me marry him."

"We discussed this," Marcus replied gently. He had listened at length to why Lydia could not marry a man like Wickham. Much of her reasoning was sound. Wickham was a cad. He drank and gambled too much, and he would surely be the sort that would not remain faithful to his wife. Wickham was also merely a lieutenant, so even if he could keep his money, it was not enough for Lydia. She desired a man with a steady character and a good income.

There were also some ridiculous reasons. Wickham had blonde hair, and Lydia had brown, so they would not look good together. Apparently, it was important that a couple look good together or a marriage would never be happy. It was a concept Marcus had not heard before. But it seemed fitting for one such as Lydia to deduce such a thing. She was, as he was coming to learn, an interesting mix of the astute and the absurd.

He reached up and lifted her from his horse. "You must return. There must be a way to undo whatever scandal you might have created."

She shook her head. "Scandals for ladies cannot be undone. They can only be undone for men."

He waited for her to straighten her skirts. At least, during their discussion, she had finally come to realize that what she had done was, in fact, scandalous, especially if the story should be shared by a man such as Wickham, who knew how to spin a boring tale into something fantastic.

Skirts straightened, she stood there, unmoving, looking every bit like a skittish foal about to run.

"You mean to tell me, Miss Lydia, that you cannot find a solution to this debacle? Other than running away from it, that is." The comment drew her eyes from their focused gaze on Willow Hall as it was meant to do. Why he felt a need to goad her into action and out of despondence, he was unsure. But then, he seemed to have been at odds with himself since discovering her in the cottage.

She shook her head. "I cannot, and I am quite good at getting out of scrapes."

He chuckled and extended his arm to her and began leading her toward the house. "I can well imagine you are."

They had taken only a few steps when suddenly she stopped. "Oh!"

Marcus turned toward her, thinking she might once again be distraught or fearful, but instead, her eyes gleamed, and her lips formed a perfect o that slid into a delightful smile.

"Wickham likes money," she said. "We shall give him some." Her eyes grew wide. "And that grumpy constable, Mr. Williams, can scare him into taking it and remaining silent. Wickham is afraid of him, you know."

"That is an idea," said Marcus. A fairly good one, if he thought about it. Wickham had always been able to be bought off with a bit of coin. "But it could be expensive."

She shrugged. "I cannot marry him," she repeated as they once again began walking toward Willow Hall.

Her mind whirled as they walked. She had very little money of her own, and she was uncertain that either her father or her uncle would be willing to lend her any. There was, however, her dowry. The thought made her sigh heavily, but surely some man might marry her without it. It was not large to begin with, according to Mama. And did not Mama always claim that Jane was so beautiful that no man would care if she had not a farthing?

She glanced at Marcus, wishing to ask him about it but was uncertain if she should.

"Ask what you wish to know," Marcus said as Lydia peeked up at him for the third time.

"Do you think a man of good fortune — enough for a cook, a housekeeper, a butler, a few maids, a couple of footmen." She sighed. What else might be required for a comfortable life? "And a carriage with a driver — would such a man consider a lady without much dowry if she were very pretty?"

He had not been in her company for more than a couple of hours, and yet, he found he had become accustomed to her unusual thoughts and questions. He was almost surprised that it was a question that made perfect sense to him. She must, of course, be considering funding the payment to Wickham out of her dowry. And, although he did not think her father would allow her to part with it, he answered honestly instead of trying to turn her mind from such a suggestion. She was pretty — very pretty — and if a gentleman could get past the randomness of her logic and not mind an occasional fit of temper, he might be sorely tempted to offer for her regardless of the monetary disadvantage. "I imagine if the gentlemen did not need the money to prop up his estate, he might."

"I could replace part of it, I am sure, if I could but go without a new dress or ribbons for my bonnet."

There was a particular tone of wistfulness to her voice

that let Marcus know that to do so would be no small sacrifice.

She sighed. "I will not need my dowry for a few more years."

"You do not plan on marrying young?"

She shrugged. "I had thought it a fabulous joke if I should marry before Jane or Lizzy, but I have not met a man worthy of me just yet. I expect it will take some time to find him. Oh, my bag!" She cried as a groom led Marcus's horse away.

"Have the bag brought to the house," Marcus called after the groom.

"But we are here. Can I not have it now?"

Marcus shook his head and tried not to smile at the pout forming on Lydia's pretty lips. Yes, some gentleman might be sorely tempted to offer for her just to kiss those pretty lips. He shook his head. Clearly, the fatigue of bodily exercise along with the exertion of his mind that had been required to follow Lydia's way of thinking had addled his own logic. "You claimed you would not stay. I do not wish to have to chase after you before I have had a chance to rest my legs." And chase after her he would since his fickle mind seemed determined to see her safe.

Her eyes narrowed. "I was beginning to think you likable."

"I assure you I am likable, Miss Lydia. I am just not a fool."

Lydia pursed her lips.

"Nor am I whatever name it is you are about to call me." He raised the knocker and let it drop.

Lydia lifted her chin and set her jaw. It was rather ungentlemanly of him to be guessing her thoughts unbidden, but she was not willing to admit to him that he had guessed correctly, so she said, right primly, "I am sure I do not know of what you speak."

"I believe you do," he replied with a smile. Then, feeling her grip on his arm tighten as the door began to open, his mind once again flipped from wishing to tease and taunt her to needing to see her well. "Are you ready?" he whispered as the door opened the rest of the way. Her eyes, for a brief moment, said no before she smiled and nodded, and the fear was hidden.

Chapter 3

The sitting room was full at Willow Hall. The searchers, who had left early that morning as soon as it was discovered that Lydia was missing, had returned some time ago. Plans to continue searching were being formed. Mr. Bennet wavered between relief that Lydia had not gone to Scotland and distress because she had gone somewhere — somewhere unknown to them at present. Tea was being shared by one and all. Those who were not involved immediately in discussions of strategy, which was everyone save Colonel Fitzwilliam, Captain Harris, and Mr. Gardiner, were conducting their own conversations on more mundane items. It was into this lot of people that Marcus attempted to direct Lydia. However, upon being announced and stepping nearly into the room, he found his arm empty of his companion.

He shook his head and sighed. "One moment, if you please. Miss Lydia will be with you directly." He nodded to the occupants of the room and then, turning on his heel, ran after her.

Within the room, there was a great deal of exclamation over Marcus, having found Lydia and speculation as to where she had been. A few crowded to the window to watch the chase. Elizabeth moved to follow Marcus, but the restraining hand of Darcy kept her from it. He assured her that Marcus was not a man to be thwarted in his objective, and if Marcus said Lydia would be joining them, then Lydia would be joining them.

It was true. Marcus Dobney was not the sort of man who backed away from a challenge nor was he the sort of man who gave his word and reneged. Over the course of his life, these traits had been both an asset in helping him solve problems and a liability when a hasty promise was made, and the fulfilling of that promise came at great personal cost — it was one of the many dangers of having an impulsive tongue.

Marcus was thankful that his legs were longer than Lydia's and that he was not hampered by petticoats and skirts, for though her feet hurt, she ran quickly. Having had a lead of a few moments, she was nearly at the gate before he grabbed her arm and stopped her.

"Let go of me!" She twisted to get her arm free of his grasp. "You are hurting my arm," she snapped as he tightened his grip.

"If you would stop struggling, I would not have to hold your arm so tightly." He attempted to keep his voice even despite his wishing to yell. Yelling had never worked in a positive way with Mary Ellen or Philip. They had always just dug in their heels and held more firmly to their position whenever he had attempted to sway them with the volume of his voice.

"My father." Lydia shook her head and blinked against the gathering tears. "I cannot go in there."

She had stopped struggling, so Marcus relaxed his grip on her arm but did not release it. Patiently, he waited for her to continue.

"He never listens to me. He only listens to Jane and Lizzy and sometimes Mary. Mama must always plead my case, and then he only surrenders to be rid of the distraction." She brushed a tear from her cheek. "He says I am the silliest girl in all of England." She lifted her chin and glared in the direction of Willow Hall.

"At the moment, I might be inclined to agree." He smiled as she turned her glare on him. "But, that might be my tired legs speaking." Why did seeing her small smile at that delight him? She really was a very vexing girl, and he suspected would be a rather difficult one to convince that returning to Willow Hall was what she needed to do. He was not wrong. They argued over the issue for the next five minutes with him repeating that a solution could be found, and her insisting that it was impossible.

"I am returning you to your family," he said at last as he realized that there would be no swaying of her opinion.

She shook her head. "I will not go."

He clamped his teeth firmly shut and shook his head at her stubbornness. "You will. Either on your own two feet, walking in as the lady you insist you are, or flung over my shoulder like a child. Which will it be? I will not allow you to go gallivanting about the countryside throwing yourself into harm's way at every turn. Most of which, I assume, would be in the wrong direction."

Lydia could tell by his eyes that he was angry, and for a brief moment, she felt something very like remorse before the fear of facing her father chased it away. She shook her head. "I cannot go in there."

Lydia gasped as Marcus hoisted her so that her head was hanging over his back and his arms were wrapped around her legs. She beat on his back and begged him to release her.

Marcus did his best to ignore both her pleas and the fact that she was rather pleasingly formed. Perhaps carrying her in such a fashion was not one of his better ideas, but it was effective. They covered the ground to the front of the house quickly.

Once inside the front door, he placed her on her feet. After a moment of catching his breath, he turned her face so that she was forced to look at him. Her cheeks were flushed, of course. He had expected that. However, he had not counted on her tears. In a moment, his frustration faded and compassion for the fear she must be feeling rose within him.

"I will speak for you." He brushed a tear away with his thumb. "I will speak honestly, but perhaps your father might listen to me. We cannot have you marrying Wickham," he gave her a small teasing smile, "no matter how foolish you have been."

He pulled his handkerchief from his pocket. "Dry your eyes." He waited for her to comply and then, taking her hand so that she could not slip away this time, led her into the sitting room. Crossing the room to where there were two seats nearly together, he nodded to one and whispered. "Sit."

Lydia felt her insides quiver as introductions were made. There were an awful lot of eyes looking at her — an awful lot of curious, critical eyes. She fought the urge to drop her gaze to her lap. She must not look fearful. If she did, they would surely have her wrapped up and delivered to Wickham in an instant, just to be rid of her distraction. She did not even turn toward Marcus as he pulled a chair near her, nor did she turn to him when he began to speak. It was not easy to ignore a handsome man when he spoke of you, even if he was not speaking in a terribly flattering way. It would have been far more enjoyable to watch his mouth and eyes, but she must not. Instead, she must listen to him tell them how she had gotten lost and ended up in his cottage.

"Miss Lydia and I have had a good deal of time to discuss her plight today, and I agree with her that to marry

Wickham would be a poor idea. However, she is aware that she has placed herself in a scandalous position." He nudged her foot with his.

She looked at him. What was he doing? He was supposed to speak for her. He had said he would. Why was he tipping his head toward her father?

"Your idea," he whispered.

She glanced at her father and then shook her head slightly.

Marcus folded his arms across his chest and with jaw set, raised a brow while giving her a hard stare.

He was not going to share it? He knew that her father did not listen to her. She had told him. Her eyes narrowed as the silence stretched. Then, with a very displeased puckering of her mouth, she turned her eyes from him and back to her father.

"Mr. Wickham likes money," she said softly. "If I could pay him, he might keep silent, and the matter would be known by few." She held her breath as she waited for a response.

"And what of the child?" asked her father.

Lydia's heart felt as it was going to race out of her chest. There was no way he knew of that lie.

"What of Colonel Forester and all the people in Brighton who were looking for you?" Mr. Bennet leaned forward. "It is more than just us in this room who know you were travelling with Mr. Wickham."

"Brighton?" Lydia gasped. "I left a message for Mrs. Forester. It told her that my maid and I were going to visit my sisters in Derbyshire. Why would they look for me if I had told them where I was? I even left a gift — a cloth for the little table in the drawing room — as a token of my gratitude for having been their guest."

Mr. Bennet blinked and shook his head. "I cannot say why they were searching if that is the case, although it is still not within your purview to decide when you will travel and where. You were Colonel Forester's responsibility in my stead. You should have spoken to him directly."

Lydia bit her lip, holding back the fact that she knew Colonel Forester would have not allowed her to travel and spoiled all her fun in surprising her sisters.

"And then there is the matter of the innkeeper," Mr. Bennet continued. "Mr. Darcy's men were told that a lady with child had spent the night at the inn with Mr. Wickham on their way to be married in Scotland. Do you wish to explain that?"

Lydia's cheeks burned. "Mr. Wickham would have left. He wanted to go play cards and drink with his friends, and anyone who knows anything about Mr. Wickham knows that he would not have returned to help me find my way to Derbyshire. His word means very little."

Marcus watched the frightened young lady that he had led into the room return to the courageous and defiant one he had met in his cottage.

"I did not use my real name, and the story about being with child and traveling to Scotland was a ruse. Mr. Wickham could not leave his soon to be wife alone and be thought of as a decent fellow, now could he?"

"I am surprised he did not," muttered Marcus. It seemed it would be easy enough for Wickham to leave her for a short while and no one would have thought it odd.

Lydia glared at him. "Well, he already understood what might happen if he did not cooperate."

Marcus nodded. "The forged letter?"

She rolled her eyes. Forged sounded so ugly.

"What letter is this?" asked Mr. Bennet.

"Apparently, Miss Lydia possesses a talent for copying penmanship. She knew of some cheating which had taken place and created a confession of sorts, signed by Wickham, and then sent it along with a letter hinting at the possibility of Wickham doing her harm to her sister." Marcus looked at Lydia. "Kitty, was it?"

Lydia nodded.

"Both of which she successfully used to blackmail Wickham into escorting her to Derbyshire."

She rolled her eyes again. Blackmail was also such an ugly word. Could he have not used the word persuaded?

Mr. Bennet lowered his voice. "So, I am to believe that my daughter, who is capable of forgery and blackmail and who spent several nights on the road with a gentleman, is not pregnant nor has she been ruined?"

Lydia's eyes grew wide. "That is precisely what you are to believe because it is true!"

"And all of this is supposed to go away with a few pounds being paid to a scoundrel?"

Her father's eyes were doing that laughing thing again. He thought her foolish. She knew he would. The thought of it pained her heart now just as it always did. "Yes," she said firmly. "And not a few pounds. My portion. I wish to give him my portion."

Chapter 4

"Lydia, do be serious," Elizabeth chided before anyone else could say a word.

"I can replace it." Ignoring her sister, Lydia continued with her explanation. Of course, Elizabeth would not understand. Elizabeth never did anything foolish enough to be punished by their father. In fact, he had never once called Elizabeth dull or silly. No, to their father, Elizabeth was quick and clever. "I will go without most of my pin money, and I am not without skills. I could take in some sewing."

Lydia saw the look of disbelief on Elizabeth's face and could not ignore the stinging of her sister's words any longer. "Mr. Wickham is not what you think, Lizzy. If you knew what he was like, you would not wish him upon me. I was not taken in by him as you were." She smiled inwardly at the stricken look on Elizabeth's face. "I may look like I am not paying attention at times, but I assure you, I am listening. I have heard plenty of tales about Mr. Wickham."

"Then why did you choose him to accompany you?" demanded Elizabeth.

Lydia sighed. "Because he knows where Derbyshire is, and he is weak enough to be led. I should think you would be able to piece that together." She knew there was a cutting edge to her voice, but she did not care. Lizzy was Papa's favourite. "I am not so stupid as you think." A hand took hers.

"I do not think Lydia's plan is completely without merit," said Marcus, squeezing Lydia's hand tightly. "Wickham has been bought off before. I am sure he could be once again." He returned the small smile Lydia gave him.

"I do not have access at a moment's notice to produce your portion," said Mr. Bennet. "And to replace it will take a great deal of time."

Lydia nodded. "I know. I shall wait to marry."

"A great deal of time," repeated Mr. Bennet.

Lydia swallowed and nodded once again. The thought of remaining at home for longer than any of her sisters presented itself. Well, perhaps she would not remain at home as long as Mary, but — oh, to be just she and Mary and Mama with a father who thought her of little use beyond a good joke was not a pleasant thought! However, the prospect could not be avoided. She would not be marrying Wickham. And there was a small hope. Her looks might save her from such a dire fate as remaining home too long.

She was pretty, so it might be possible to capture a man's attention without having any money. Mama had said it of Jane, and Mr. Dobney had said it was possible.

"Lydia," Jane's soft and soothing voice interrupted her thoughts, "are you certain that this is what you wish?"

"What I wish is to not marry Mr. Wickham," Lydia replied. "So, if this is the only solution, then, yes, it is what I wish."

"It is a lot of money," said Jane.

"I know." Lydia gave Jane a sad smile. "I only hope it is enough. His debts are significant."

"You know of his debts?" Marcus asked in surprise.

"I have a list," said Lydia. "I told you; I listened. It is how I knew that he needed to cheat Denny out of some money. Captain Hopwood was growing impatient to be paid. And since Colonel Forester does not look favourably on his men having such large debts, cheating Denny and risking a fist fight was more appealing than whatever punishment Colonel Forester would have dealt him."

"A flogging, no doubt," mutter Captain Harris.

"No doubt," agreed Lydia. "There are several others who will soon be as impatient as Captain Hopwood. Depending on rank and pay, it seems a month or two is the longest any officer will wait to be repaid by another."

Colonel Fitzwilliam chuckled. "You have been paying attention then, have you not?" He crossed one leg over the other. He rested easily in his chair and wore a rather amused look. It was decidedly different from the serious expressions worn by everyone else. "Colonel Forester might be interested in your list."

Lydia blinked. Of course, why had she not thought of that? A list such as hers might be useful in negotiations. "Do you think we could use it to make Mr. Wickham go away?" She asked the colonel eagerly.

"More blackmail?" asked Marcus, a slight note of trepidation in his voice.

Lydia shook her head and looked at him. "No, blackmail is too ugly a word. I like to think of it as a bit of persuasion or a small guarantee of cooperation. "

"Blackmail," Marcus repeated.

Lydia shook her head again. "Persuasion." She looked at Colonel Fitzwilliam. "I could copy my list and give it to you."

"Copy it?" Marcus closed his eyes and grimaced as her lovely hazel-coloured eyes looked at him as if he should already know why the document should be copied. He was certain there was some scheming reason for it, not that he could readily think of one. He really did need to think more before he spoke. He also needed to release her hand, which he still held. Both seemed things he was incapable of doing at present.

"Of course," Lydia said in surprise, "one does not give away such information without retaining a small guarantee for herself that the information will not be lost and never used." How was it that no one thought of these things but her? Surely, it was not such a difficult thing to think.

"It is what I would do," said Colonel Fitzwilliam.

Lydia was beginning to like the colonel, even if he was rather short and not so very handsome. He seemed willing to consider her as something other than just a silly girl, and that alone made him quite likable and worthy of at least a moment's consideration. She studied him more carefully. His build was muscular and pleasing, and his hair was a respectable honey colour. However, there were little lines near his eyes. He must be at least thirty, which was really too old. But he seemed pleasant. "Then you would like a copy?"

"Indeed," said Colonel Fitzwilliam. There was a glint of excited satisfaction in his eye. She knew that the colonel had not appeared welcoming to Wickham when in Brighton. Perhaps Colonel Fitzwilliam would prove to be a valuable ally, regardless of his relationship to the always proper Mr. Darcy. Lydia cast a glance in Darcy's direction. He was listening intently, but he did not seem as dour as she might have expected. Perhaps that could be credited to his dislike of Wickham.

"And this will save your reputation?" Mr. Bennet spoke in disbelief. "Do you have such articles of persuasion for all of Brighton and whomever else might have heard your story?"

Lydia's shoulders drooped, and her brows furrowed. She had been so focused on Wickham that she had forgotten that problem. "I left a note. If Mrs. Forrester were to find it..."

"A convenient coincidence after the fact?" Mr. Bennet's voice was softening. "You know how the gossips work. True or not, it will only fan the flames of a juicy tale."

Lydia looked from the serious face of her father to equally serious faces of her uncle and Mr. Abbot before looking at her sisters. So this is how it was? Could no one present a plausible solution? Were they all just hoping to be done with her? She shook her head and stood.

"I shall not marry him." She pulled her hand from Marcus's and closed her eyes against the pain that she felt in her heart. "You will have to send me away." The words were barely a whisper. "A new name, in a new place...." She swallowed and blinked her eyes rapidly to keep the tears from falling. "Perhaps I could find a position..." She paused again trying to control her emotions, but it was no use, they would not be controlled. She shook her head as the tears began to fall. "I cannot marry him," she whispered before fleeing the room.

Mr. Bennet began to rise to follow after her.

"No, Papa. I will go," said Jane.

"I do not wish to see her tied to that man, but what can be done?"

Jane patted his hand. "We might think of something."

Mr. Bennet nodded, but the look on his face spoke of his disbelief.

"Another suitor?" suggested Bingley. "Perhaps if there were another gentleman willing to marry her? Would that not lessen the gossip? It was only thought that she had run off with Wickham."

"She has been with few others," said Captain Harris. He smiled ruefully. "It would be easy for anyone at Brighton to believe her gone off with Wickham. She batted her lashes at him often enough."

Mr. Bennet sighed.

Marcus glared at his cousin. How could he speak so meanly of Lydia? She was obviously more than a flirt. She was undeniably pretty, and he had no doubt she was quite capable of flirting. In fact, she had attempted it once or twice while they were on their walk today. It was a tactic, he realized, she was using in an effort to sway his opinion. Even in her flirting, she was clever. Could no one see that? "There must be a way," he muttered. "She cannot marry him. If you knew his character..."

"I do," said Mr. Bennet, casting a glance toward Darcy. "I am very well aware of his character, but I see no way to save her reputation."

"There must be a way," Marcus muttered again as he stood. "Give us some time to think," he suggested. "Surely, one of us might come up with a solution." He waited long enough to get Mr. Bennet's assurance that they would not make any decisions just yet, then he left the room. He needed a good ride. He thought better when he rode. However, before he left Willow Hall, he asked Mrs. Smith if he might have a paper and pen so that he could leave a message for Miss Lydia.

Miss Lydia,

I will not allow you to marry him. Please do not run away. I hope to call on you tomorrow. Perhaps I will arrive at a solution by then. If you do choose to run, have the grooms direct you to Woodhead Cottage, so that I might find you. I am enclosing the key.

He signed the message and wrapped it around the key for the cottage that he had used this morning to lock it up. Then, with an assurance from Mrs. Smith that both the message and the key would be given to Miss Lydia, he bid the housekeeper farewell and left Willow Hall.

He walked toward the stables but stopped when he had only reached the halfway point. Imagining he had heard his name called, he turned and looked toward the house. Again, he thought he heard his name. Ah, in the window.

Lydia stood at the window and called twice to Marcus as he left. In her hand, she clutched his letter tightly. The key was safely tucked in her pocket. Seeing him turn, she called again. Finally, as he lifted his eyes to her window, she waved. She also smiled at him, although she was sure he could not see it. A friend. She had found a friend — not one who wished to use her for introductions to gentlemen or advice on what to wear or how to trim a hat — no, she had found a real friend — one who wished to see her safe and well. It was both a strange and a delightful feeling.

Marcus waved in return and gave her a shallow bow before turning and continuing on his way. She would be safe. He nodded in agreement with himself. He would see that she was safe, for despite her fits of displeasure and her wandering trail of thought, he enjoyed her company. He paused and looked back at her window once more.

"Your horse, Mr. Dobney."

A groom interrupted his contemplation of his pretty, yet vexing, new friend. "Thank you, James." He paused before mounting. "Do you know the way to Woodhead Cottage?"

"Of course, sir."

"And you will be here all night?"

The groom nodded.

"If Miss Lydia decides to leave Willow Hall, lead her to Woodhead Cottage and then find me. Do not tell anyone here that she has gone before you tell me."

The groom nodded.

"There will be something in it for you, of course." Marcus swung up onto his horse. "And before you leave her at the cottage, remind her to lock the door. Oh, and see to it that the fire is lit. There will be wood beside the door."

"Of course, Mr. Dobney."

"And you will come see me first before you tell anyone here that she is gone?"

"Yes, sir."

"Very good." He gave a nod to the groom and set off to prepare his cottage for its potential visitor.

Chapter 5

Marcus straightened his clean cravat and inspected his jacket, ensuring he looked presentable for dinner. Ready, but not yet willing to descend to his father's drawing room, Marcus walked to his bedroom window, which faced the east drive, so that he could see who had or was arriving. There was to be a large group tonight.

A small carriage was just drawing up to the front of the house. Lucy and his brother, Philip, were here, and, Marcus hoped, they had brought Aunt Tess with them as requested. He could go down. He pulled his watch from his pocket as his stomach rumbled. Half an hour until they ate. It was just enough time to enjoy a glass of wine and some conversation.

He was certain there would be plenty of news from the neighbourhood to be shared. He smiled at his reflection in the mirror as he passed it one last time before exiting his room. It was not that Aldwood Abbey's guests would gossip, but they would discuss the various goings on of their neighbours and friends. He was still not entirely certain he saw the difference as clearly as his sister, Mary Ellen, did.

"Ah, you are here," said Mary Ellen as Marcus entered the drawing room. "You have been no more than a shadow to us today. Scurrying here and there on business." She raised a questioning brow.

"There were things to be done," Marcus replied as he placed a kiss on her upturned cheek before taking a seat next to his father. "How are you today, sir?"

"No worse than yesterday. Mary Ellen has done her best to entertain me with books." He sighed. "I wish she would learn to play chess."

"I know how to play," protested his daughter.

"Not very well," her father muttered with a chuckle and a wink.

"Yes, well, if you did not have Marcus to play against, you might not know my skills are lacking." She smiled at him as she said it. It was a frequent discussion.

Mr. Dobney found his greatest enjoyment in a challenging game of chess. His sons, Marcus to a greater degree and Philip to a lesser extent, provided him with a match he deemed worthy of his time and effort. Mary Ellen, on the other hand, would attempt to do her best, but no matter how hard she tried, some thought or another would capture her fancy and cause her to lose the game.

"So what kept you from our game?" Mr. Dobney asked Marcus.

"I was at Mother's cottage." Marcus attempted to make his reply sound as if it were somewhere very natural for him to be, when in reality, it had been some time since he had visited that particular cottage for more than a quick look around the grounds to see that the roof was not in need of repairs and no windows were broken.

"The steward forgot to lock the door when he checked it yesterday, so I went to take care of it." He accepted the glass of wine his sister offered him and swirled its contents slowly before inhaling its fragrance and taking a small sip that he swished between his teeth and allowed to sit on his tongue for a moment before swallowing.

He cast a glance at his cousin and knew that Harris was eagerly waiting to share information about who had been found at that cottage. However, Marcus would rather introduce the topic himself. Harris had already shown himself unable to speak kindly of Lydia, so it was best if Marcus broached the subject. At least then Lydia might be presented in a more flattering light.

"The young lady I found there pointed out that the cottage was in need of attention, and so, I have attended to it."

"You were cleaning?" Shock suffused Mary Ellen's face.

Marcus shrugged. "It was needed."

"Cleaning?" Mary Ellen asked once again.

"I am capable of it." He glared at his sister. "And I had help."

"So that is what Mrs. Yardley was muttering about

today. 'Maids gone off to clean for nobody.'" Mr. Dobney gave his son a pointed look.

"I imagine it was," Marcus replied. "She assured me she could manage without them."

"Oh, she was not grumbling," said his father. "She seemed quite shocked at the idea, and now I understand why." He patted Marcus's arm. "It is yours whenever you choose to claim it," he added softly.

Marcus nodded. The cottage had been a place where each summer for a week or two and for at least one weekend each winter, he and his mother, along with his father and siblings, would, as his mother called it, "escape the trappings and finery of the landed gentleman and remember their blessings." He smiled at his father. "One day soon."

"I would go with you," whispered Mary Ellen. "I miss it, you know."

He nodded and smiled at her.

"You said you found a young lady there?" His father had never been one to miss a detail, especially if that detail might produce some interesting bit of news. He had always been curious, but since his illness had confined him to his home except for an occasional trip to church, he had grown worse. Boredom, of course, was the culprit.

"A lost traveller," said Marcus, taking a sip of his wine. He could have told his father her name and laid out the complete story in a few sentences, but where would be his father's enjoyment in that? "She was attempting to find Kympton but took a wrong turn."

"Does this lady have a name?"

Marcus nodded and smiled as his father grew impatient at his silence.

"Miss Lydia Bennet," said Captain Harris. "Her name is Miss Lydia Bennet."

Marcus shook his head and rolled his eyes. Harris had never been the most patient of fellows when they were young, and apparently, impatience was something that he had not entirely outgrown.

Mr. Dobney's eyes grew wide. Marcus was sure that his father's eyes were not the only ones filled with surprise.

"The one you mentioned had arrived at Willow Hall with that scoundrel?" Mr. Dobney looked at his daughter.

She shrugged. "Apparently."

"You met her?" Marcus asked.

Mary Ellen turned to her brother. "I did, briefly. From what I could gather, she is very different from her sisters. Very different."

Marcus could tell by the emphasis that she placed on those last two words that she did not hold Lydia in high esteem. "Did you talk to her?"

Mary Ellen shook her head. "I did not. I was walking in the garden with Miss Darcy while Lucy comforted Miss Elizabeth, who was certain that a connection to Wickham would separate her from Darcy forever."

"There'll be no connection to Wickham," said Marcus quite firmly.

"I cannot see how there will not be," said Captain Harris before sharing with the group the extent of his knowledge of Miss Lydia's situation from her arrival at Willow Hall accompanied by Wickham to her running away and finally to her return.

"Her poor father," said Aunt Tess. "To be chasing after her under the impression that she is about to marry a scoundrel and in such a state." She referred, of course, to Lydia's claim to be with child, but she was too polite to say such a thing in company.

"If it is a lie," said Harris, looking slyly over his glass at Aunt Tess. "You should have seen the audience she drew in Brighton and the flirting... Not at all proper."

"Indeed," Aunt Tess looked to the others. "Is she such a flirt as to be expected to do more than bat her lashes? Is that what must follow a pretty girl drawing attention from gentlemen?" She looked back at Harris. "She is pretty?"

"Very," supplied Marcus.

"She is," agreed Captain Harris.

"I had no idea that being pretty was so dangerous. I am very lucky it was not so in my day or my reputation would have been well and truly ruined, for I did like to flutter my lashes." She chuckled at the open but speechless mouths of both Marcus and Harris.

"I say it sounds as if our cousin is jealous," said Philip.

"Did she reject you?" Lucy's elbow caught her husband just below his ribs, and he winced.

Harris shook his head. "I would have had to get close enough to be rejected, a feat that was nearly impossible with all the lieutenants buzzing about."

Marcus chuckled, drawing his cousin's attention. "You would have stood a better chance than any one of them since you are a captain."

Harris's brows furrowed. "My rank would give me an advantage?"

Marcus nodded. "A slight one, and an even greater one if you were well liked and worthy of a promotion — an officer with a future, so to speak. You see, a captain's pay really is as low as a lady should go when accepting offers, and then only if she does not think a better rank is possible. However, if a girl is very pretty, she might aspire to at least a colonel. Though," he chuckled remembering how Lydia had told him all this as she rode his horse, "colonels tend to be old and stodgy. A few have been known to be not so terribly old, but nearly all have lines," he pointed to the corner of his eye, "which means they are at least thirty, which is not old, but not young either. And, the more lines and older one becomes, the less enjoyable his company. So clearly, any young lady who does not wish to be a young widow would do well to look at a captain with a good reputation since that is a man who will be promoted."

He looked at the confused faces around him. He must

have explained it just as Lydia did to earn such expressions, and the thought delighted him.

"It is really not so difficult to understand. The older a man, the sooner he dies, and although widows, who are well provided for have a bit of freedom, not all ladies look good in black and to wear it for a full six months would be quite dreadful." He could see her pout as she said that bit. He had felt exactly as his listeners looked – bewildered. "I can guarantee you she is not as you think."

Aunt Tess was the first to recover herself. "It does make sense in a way."

"If you squint your eyes and tilt your head," muttered Marcus with a smile.

"Aye, you may need to do that," said Aunt Tess as she tilted her head and looked at Marcus. "She refuses to marry Mr. Wickham because he is a lieutenant?"

"No," said Marcus, "she refuses to marry him because of his character." He held up a finger. "Which she had deciphered on her own to be deplorable. Forgive my indelicacy, but she can name for you the women he has been with in Brighton and in Hertfordshire. She suspects at least one maid has not truly gone to help a sick relative. And she has a list of his debts — to whom they are owed as well as the amount and an estimated date of when the debt will need to be covered for Mr. Wickham to avoid any unpleasantness. It is information that she used quite skillfully to garner his assistance in finding her way to Derbyshire."

"And yet she travelled with him alone and did not expect to be forced to marry him?" asked Lucy.

Marcus sighed. "She was not alone. She had her maid, but yes, that is the conundrum named Lydia Bennet. Wise to a point and foolish thereafter."

"Misguided," said Mr. Dobney. "Not foolish."

Marcus nodded. "Do you remember Eris when she was young?"

"Earned her name with the strife she caused in the stables," said his father. "Kicked a hole in the gate because the pail of oats had spilled, and she was not satisfied with what she had been given."

"Miss Lydia is like that."

His father patted Marcus's arm. "Eris has become a fine mare, however — after much training." He motioned to the clock that sat on the mantle. "Our meal should be ready."

Marcus handed his glass to his sister and then helped his father to his feet and assisted him in walking the short distance from his father's particular drawing room to the dining room.

"Bring her to meet me," Mr. Dobney whispered to Marcus. "I think I would like her."

"I think you would," agreed Marcus as he waited for a footman to pull out his father's chair.

After Mr. Dobney had taken his seat, he grabbed his son by the arm and pulled him close, so he could whisper one more thing. "This house could use a mistress, and it has survived one spirited lady already."

Marcus looked at his father in surprise.

"Think about it, Son."

"But you have not met her."

Mr. Dobney smiled. "Although I wish to, I do not need to. I see the way she affects you." He patted Marcus's arm and then shooed him to his seat.

Chapter 6

Lydia studied her reflection in the mirror. It was not as pleasing as it could be. Her eyes were dull, and her lips did not care if they smiled or not. They, like the rest of her body, was tired — so very tired.

"I can only do so much, miss," her maid commented, hearing her mistress sigh deeply. "Lack of sleep can only be disguised to a point. Eventually, you will need to sleep."

Lydia sighed again. It was true. She had not slept well in many nights. She thought back: how long had it been? Brighton. That was the last place she had truly had a good sleep. The floors of inns and the cramped interior of the coach had not been conducive to rest, especially when one must keep a hand on the knife in her pocket and an ear listening to Wickham.

Lydia had expected Wickham to find some way to leave her at each turn. It really had been a most trying journey! And then, to arrive to such displeasure and lectures! A third sigh escaped her.

The corner of that shed had been more restful than her

bed the past two nights. She tucked a curl behind her ear. She was certain that the reason sleeping had been easier in that shed was because there, she had been free of the awful possibility of marriage to Wickham. Here, the thought constantly swirled around her. Her aunt and uncle spoke of it. Her father sighed over it, and her sisters whispered and smiled sadly.

"Is being a maid very horrid?"

Margaret looked at her in surprise. "I could not say, miss, with it being the only thing I have known."

Lydia pursed her lips. "Are you content?"

Margaret paused in arranging Lydia's hair. "I suppose I am. Not that I would not like to have dresses as fine as you or beaux, a plenty." She smiled in the mirror at Lydia. "But I would look rather silly in a fine gown and wouldn't know what to do if even one gentleman came to pay me a call." She rested her hands on Lydia's shoulders. "You are made for society, and I am not. It is not my planning," she returned to pinning Lydia's hair, "it is the good Lord's. 'Twas he who selected our parents." She placed one last pin and then, with a true look of delight, declared her work complete.

"Margaret," Lydia called to her as she was about to leave the room. "I am sorry I did not take you with me the other day, but I knew I could not pay for two. You deserve to be better kept..."

"Oh, miss!" her maid exclaimed, cutting off the rest of

Lydia's comment. "Think nothing of it. You have been returned to us safely, and that is all that was needed to put me to right. I was sore afraid for you. Wandering in the night with who knows what monsters lurking in the shadows." She shuddered. "I am pleased you have returned." She dipped a curtesy and scooted from the room.

Lydia looked at the closed door in surprise. A second person had worried for her safety? Neither had been her family. Her family worried only about her reputation, not her safety. If they cared one jot for her safety, they would not keep suggesting she marry Wickham.

She gathered the needlework from her bag and went to the sitting room. Perhaps she would be fortunate, and everyone would be occupied elsewhere. She would spend another day in her room, but Mr. Dobney had said he would call, and she would endure the presence of her relatives to see him.

"Lydia," called Mrs. Abbot as she hurried toward Lydia in the hall. "You have callers." She placed an arm around Lydia's shoulder. "You look tired, my dear."

"I am," Lydia admitted. There was no use denying what was so evidently etched under her eyes.

Mrs. Abbot squeezed Lydia's shoulder. "You will find rest comes more readily once we find a solution to your problem."

"I am certain you are correct." Lydia wished the lady

would release her shoulder. Mrs. Abbott was just another person worried about fixing the problem of Lydia.

"And a solution will be found," Mrs. Abbott said with another squeeze to Lydia's shoulder. "And its name shall not be Wickham." She winked at Lydia as she released her.

"You do not think I should marry him?" Lydia's shock must have shown clearly on her face for Cecily Abbot smiled very sympathetically at her.

"No one wishes you to marry him. They only wish for your reputation to be saved so that you will not face a life of misery."

"Truly?"

"Ah, my dear." Cecily wrapped Lydia in an embrace. "Do you not know you are loved?"

Lydia shook her head and blinked at the tears that formed.

"You are," Cecily said, grasping Lydia's chin lightly. "Very much." She smiled again. "Now, you have guests awaiting you in the sitting room."

"Who are they?" Lydia asked with a slight bit of trepidation gnawing at her stomach. Silently, she wished them to not be Mr. Wickham and that grumbly Mr. Williams. One interview in the sitting room with them had been enough.

"Mr. Dobney, Mrs. Barnes, and Miss Dobney," replied Cecily. "Go on." She waved Lydia toward the sitting room. "And if they ask you to go for a drive, I will tell your father and sisters of it when they return."

Lydia sighed in relief. Her sisters were gone and so was her father. Perhaps for a few moments, she would be able to have a conversation without someone bringing up that horrid man, Mr. Wickham.

"Miss Lydia," Marcus rose as she entered the room and bowed before extending a hand to lead her to a chair. "I trust you have recovered from your journey."

"Not yet," she replied with a smile. "I have had much to think about," she added softly.

"I was pleasantly surprised to find my cottage unused." He smiled. "I even cleaned it some. A friend told me it was a bad show to let one's inheritance sit in neglect."

"And so it is." She glanced at the others in the room, who were watching her curiously.

"My sister, Mary Ellen, and Mrs. Barnes." He turned to Lydia. "Mrs. Barnes is Lucy's Aunt Tess, which is what we all call her."

"Lucy?" Lydia looked at him in confusion. The name sounded vaguely familiar.

"Forgive me. You have not met my brother, Philip, and his wife, Lucy. I forget you have not been at Willow Hall long enough to make friends." He smiled at the surprised blink of her eyes. She might not think she would find friends in Derbyshire, but he knew if they could see her as he did, she would not want for friendship.

Lydia turned and politely greeted each lady.

"Lucy was here when you arrived," said Mary Ellen, "although you may not remember her."

Lydia's brows furrowed as she thought back to her arrival. There had been three ladies with her sisters. "She left the room with Elizabeth?"

Mary Ellen confirmed the fact to be true, and then, the group slipped into an uneasy silence.

Aunt Tess, a small lady with bright eyes and just a few streaks of grey in her nearly black hair, tipped her head and studied Lydia for a moment. "No need to squirm, my dear Miss Lydia," she said as she noted Lydia shifting the position of her crossed ankles, "I am not finding fault. You are as pretty as I was told."

Lydia blushed and ducked her head just a bit. "Thank you."

"I had thought you might be bigger for all the stir you have created, but you are so petite," Aunt Tess smiled at Lydia as she said it. "But, we, who are capable of such things, are usually rather surprisingly short in stature."

Lydia giggled uneasily. She was uncertain if she should like this lady or not, but she did.

"Marcus has told me a bit about your predicament," Aunt Tess explained in a quiet voice as if not wishing to let anyone who might enter during their discussion to know what was being said.

It was, Lydia thought as she turned startled eyes toward Marcus, as if Aunt Tess did not wish to cause her any embarrassment. Marcus's reassuring smile quelled the small flutter of nerves she felt at the topic being broached, and she took a steadying breath. Surely, she could trust him.

"He thought I might be of assistance, you see," continued Aunt Tess in the same soft tone as before. "I am thinking of hiring a companion. I resisted the idea at first, but I find I miss Lucy's company. She was in my care for many years," she said in answer to Lydia's questioning look while straightening a glove.

"I was wondering if you would be so kind as to give me a practice run at having someone about once again. I would like to have you with me for at least three months as that should give me sufficient experience to know if I truly desire a companion or not. However, you would not have to remain with me any longer than you wished, even if that time is less than the three months."

"It would give us time to sort things out," said Marcus. "You could send a note to your friends in Brighton letting them know that you have arrived safely and are happily installed with Mrs. Barnes. It would also," he paused not quite sure of how to proceed with the rest of his thoughts.

"It would give time, my dear," said Aunt Tess, "to prove that your story to the innkeeper was not true."

Intense heat flooded Lydia's cheeks, and her eyes dropped to her hands.

"We may believe you," said Marcus softly, "but if there is gossip..."

Lydia nodded her understanding. "I assure you," she said, glancing at Mary Ellen and then at Aunt Tess. "It is not true."

"We will speak no more of it beyond this," Aunt Tess looked at Marcus, "proving you are not with child does not restore your reputation. There may still be those who will think you ruined. You must know the realities of the situation."

Lydia sucked the right corner of her lower lip between her teeth in an attempt to keep tears from forming and nodded. When she felt she had control of her emotions, she spoke. "If there is gossip and my reputation is ruined, and I have served you well, would you consider allowing me to stay with you — instead of hiring someone else?"

"That is a possibility," said Aunt Tess.

"Might I begin today?" asked Lydia before tilting her head and furrowing her brow. "Although, I do not know precisely what a companion does? How does one learn this?" She turned to Marcus. "And what do I do about Margaret? I am certain a servant cannot employ a maid. Oh, how will I get dressed? I am not as good at fixing my hair as Margaret is... Oh, I will need a cap. Are there particular caps that must be worn? And will my dresses be too fine? Margaret said she would look foolish in such fine dresses. I do not wish to look foolish. And my things from Longbourn..."

Marcus reached over and took her hand. "We do not need to know everything at once."

"Indeed, we do not," said Aunt Tess, there was a hint of laughter in her voice. "Things might work out in such a way that you will not require my assistance." A smile formed on her lips as her eyes flicked briefly from Lydia to Marcus.

"Why do you wish to begin today?" asked Mary Ellen.

"I cannot sleep," said Lydia. "If this means I will not have to marry Mr. Wickham, I wish to begin right away, so that I might sleep. Sleep is imperative, after all, if one wishes to look her best, and I suppose even if I am never to marry, I shall always desire to look my best." She shrugged one shoulder. "Perhaps if I look good enough, someone might one day — after my debt is paid and rumors have faded — be willing to offer for me." She sighed. "A farmer or a merchant, perhaps. I am sure I cannot aspire to higher now." A sadness settled in her heart.

"One never knows about these things," said Aunt Tess, her lips twitched with barely concealed humor, but it was not the sort of humor that laughed at a person. No, from the sparkle in Aunt Tess's eyes, Lydia could tell that the lady was merely enjoying herself.

"I had hoped to spend a bit of time getting to know you this afternoon," Aunt Tess continued, "and I must discuss this proposition with your father. It is his decision as much as it is yours."

Lydia pulled her lips into a smile and nodded politely. She was certain that her father would be happy to be rid of her so easily, and the thought cut deeply.

"My father has heard about you," said Mary Ellen, "and would like to meet you."

"Yes, he has asked that we bring you for tea," added Marcus. "He would have joined us on this visit, but he does not travel, as he is unwell."

"Oh, of course," said Lydia without a moment's thought, her free hand rising to cover her heart in compassion, and the one that still remained in Marcus's hand gave his a small squeeze. "Shall I get my hat? Or will we go later?"

Marcus chuckled and released her hand as warmth crept up his neck. He had completely forgotten that he held her hand until she had squeezed his. He really must learn to not take her hand, for it seemed once he did, he was wont to let it go. He tipped his head toward the door. "Get your hat."

Chapter 7

It was a beautiful day. The sun was shining, and a dry, cool breeze was blowing just enough to make the flowers dance and the leaves on the trees twirl slowly. Marcus had requested that the canopy be lowered so they might all enjoy the fresh summer breeze.

Lydia was quite pleased to be looking about the countryside and exclaiming about this or that. Aunt Tess had insisted that Lydia be given the seat next to Marcus, so she would have the best view of her new surroundings.

"Do you like the country?" asked Mary Ellen during a small gap between Lydia's cries of delight and her brother's explanation of whatever it was that had caught Lydia's attention.

"I suppose, I do." Lydia's head tipped to the side, and her brows furrowed slightly. "I have spent most of my life in the country, so I am not sure if I prefer it because I prefer it, or if I prefer it simply because it is all I have ever known. My aunt and uncle Gardiner live in town, of course, and I have visited them a few times for a day or two, but they prefer to have Lizzy and Jane stay for extended periods. I am not yet, nor, I suspect, will I ever be, invited to do so."

She turned her attention back to the wall that Marcus had pointed out was a new addition to that particular field. There was a small dip in it with steps so that one might climb over with ease.

"Why would they not invite you?"

Marcus rolled his eyes at his sister's inability to keep a question to herself at times. It was a bothersome trait they shared.

Lydia looked back at Mary Ellen and gave her a tight smile. "They do not like me. Not many do. Most prefer Lizzy and Jane."

Mary Ellen gasped at the response.

"Surely, that cannot be true," said Aunt Tess.

"Oh, it is," Lydia assured her. No one paid Lydia an ounce of attention unless she was making a scene, and then, they only noticed her so that they might scold her or scowl at her in displeasure. No, that was not entirely true. There were those who paid her attention for what they might receive from her in return. It was why she was so popular as a dance partner and a conversation companion at assemblies. Gentlemen enjoyed her liveliness and flirting while the ladies enjoyed the notice of the gentlemen who sought her hand for a dance. After all, someone had to dance with the men left standing when Lydia was occupied. But in her family, she was only truly liked by her mother and Aunt Philips. Oh, and Kitty, Lydia added mentally. Kitty liked her, too.

The rest wished she would go away, and her father? Well, he thought her foolish and silly. She knew he did because he often commented on her lack of sense. Again, a pain gripped her heart at the thought that he would be happy to be rid of her. She had longed to be given the attention her father showered on Elizabeth. She would have loved to have been questioned about books and asked to play chess. But, she was just a pretty face destined to make a good match and save her mama from destitution.

"I find it hard to believe," Aunt Tess said.

Lydia shrugged. "It is just how things are. They shall be happy to see me installed with you. I am certain of it." It took some effort to keep the smile in place on her lips.

"That is most dreadful," muttered Mary Ellen.

"I speak the truth," said Lydia with a small amount of indignation colouring her voice. "I am not dreadful."

"Oh," said Mary Ellen, reaching across the carriage to grasp Lydia's hand. "I did not mean you are dreadful. It is dreadful that you should be so little missed. I cannot fathom it."

Lydia dropped her gaze and blinked against the tears that wanted to fall. "It is not so impossible to think when you have been spoken of as I have been." She blinked a few more times and then, feeling the threat of tears was passed, looked up and smiled at Mary Ellen.

"We often only see things as they appear to us," said Aunt Tess. "The challenge is to view them through the eyes of another. While Miss Lydia sees a father who is cross and angry, another might see a man who is grieved at his failing and fearful for his daughter. And while some personalities might mesh well and prompt the like-minded to spend time together to the detriment of those who are not of the same bent, that does not indicate that one is liked while the other is not. One may be favoured, but there is nothing wrong with having preferences."

Lydia pulled the left corner of her lower lip between her teeth and chewed on it slightly as her mind ruminated on what Aunt Tess had said, recalling how Mrs. Abbot had assured her that morning that she was loved.

"Very true," said Marcus. "but then there are those who are too similar, and their similarities lead to disagreements. Take Mary Ellen and me for example. We get on well for being so similar, but both of us get along with Philip better than each other. She and I are similar, but Philip is not like either of us."

Aunt Tess chuckled. "You are very much like your father," she said to Marcus. "You are not afraid of working hard for what you have, nor are you afraid of offending with your opinion."

"Because he always thinks his opinion is right," Mary Ellen said with a smile.

"Oh, it very often is right," said Aunt Tess, patting Mary Ellen's knee. "Much like yours is. Where the struggle comes is in admitting when you are in error." She sighed as she gave Marcus a sympathetic look and Mary Ellen's knee another pat. "That is where your mother worked her wonders with your father. Her views often thwarted convention, but they were not wrong — which was something your father understood."

"What was she like?" Lydia asked.

"Beautiful," Marcus said softly.

"Kind," Mary Ellen said.

"And stubborn as a mule," added Aunt Tess, "and as lively and unfocused as a yearling." She smiled broadly. "And wonderful. She was just wonderful. Such a mixture of beauty and vivacity coupled with intelligence and caring!"

"She sounds lovely," Lydia said.

"She was," Marcus said.

Lydia heard the sadness in his tone. He must have been close to his mother. "I know I shall miss my mother." She sighed heavily. "I was to marry well and see to her comfort, you know. Now, it shall fall to one of my sisters to do so. I suppose it will be Jane as she is so very beautiful and always does what is right."

Mary Ellen chuckled. "Or it might be Elizabeth."

Lydia shook her head. "Oh, Lizzy would not know a fine gentleman if she saw one. She is so critical. I should not say it, but I was certain that Mr. Darcy was all but in love with her, and all she could do was speak poorly of him."

Mary Ellen burst into laughter. "She seems to find him acceptable now. Did you not see them sitting closer than is acceptable at church yesterday?"

Lydia shook her head. "I did not attend. My father thought it best that I not make any appearance in public until he has sorted out my predicament." She turned to Marcus. "Does she really like him now? I knew he liked her — not that she would hear of it, of course."

Marcus looked at her in surprise. "Has she not told you? They are betrothed. Darcy asked her in front of a large crowd at the parsonage, and she liked him well enough to accept him and allow him to kiss her."

Lydia's eyes grew wide, and she looked to Mary Ellen and Aunt Tess for confirmation of these facts. "He kissed her? But that... that is so... improper!"

"You truly did not know?" asked Marcus.

Lydia shook her head again. "I have kept to my room since there are fewer disapproving eyes in my room."

He took her hand. "I am sorry," he whispered. How had her family allowed her to hide away in her room? No wonder she thought none of them liked her. First, she was questioned in the sitting room with few showing any acceptance of her ideas, and then she was kept home from church as if she was an embarrassment. He had not heard a word of gossip, and the ladies who had the pew behind him were not known for their lack of knowledge of anything that might be even slightly untoward. Yet, they had said nothing about Lydia, although they had mentioned seeing Wickham with Mr. Williams. Yes, he told himself, what she had done was foolish, but it was not beyond what could be repaired.

"It was my choice," she said softly. She might have said more, but they had turned off the main road, and a large and elegant home stood before her. "Oh, my! Is that your home?"

"It is," said Marcus proudly. "That is Aldwood Abbey."

"I am certain it is as large as Netherfield! Oh, Mama would be so delighted to see such a house. She is always exclaiming over Netherfield and its many windows..." Lydia stopped and poked the air with a finger. "There are two more windows on each floor!" She sat forward on the bench. "And the front of Netherfield is flat, but yours sticks out further on each end. Is it flat in the back?" She turned toward Marcus, who was enjoying watching her excitement at seeing the house. For some reason, her approval of it made his pride in his inheritance grow.

"No, it is the same in the back as it is in the front."

"So like an upper case h?"

"I had not thought of it as such," he admitted, "but yes, although no tutor would accept such a form since the two side posts are much shorter than the line that connects them. If there is time, I shall give you a tour," he said impulsively.

She smiled at him and clasped her hands delightedly before the smile slipped slowly from her face. "I have not come to view the house. I have come to meet your father."

"He would not be offended. In fact, he would be flattered, I am certain."

"But he is not well and would not be able to join us." Lydia lay a hand on Marcus's arm and looked around the group. "It would be unkind to leave him when he expected to be entertained."

"I will ask him," said Marcus. "Perhaps your presence will induce him to allow me to push him about in the chair that he hates to use."

"Oh, it would be excellent to get him out of his three rooms," said Mary Ellen.

"Three rooms? In a house so large?" Lydia stared, mouth agape at the house. She would not limit herself to three rooms in such a grand house even if she was unwell. Surely there were servants who could help an ill master to each and every room at least once in a fortnight. "How does his spirit manage it?"

Marcus laughed. "You may have to ask him if he becomes reticent about joining the tour." He stepped down from the carriage and assisted each lady in turn to alight.

"Oh, Marcus," said Aunt Tess as she took his arm to enter the house since Mary Ellen, much to Marcus's displeasure, had already taken Lydia's arm, "she is a delight. Lacking in training, but such potential." She patted his arm. "She can stay with me, and you can tell Mr. Williams that Wickham is free to leave. She will not be marrying him. To think anyone would even consider it!" She patted his arm again. "However, I do think she is right. She might be able to capture some gentleman's heart in time."

"She is headstrong and not always sensible," cautioned Marcus.

"Yes," said Aunt Tess, removing her hand from his arm as they entered the house. "So was your mother." She gave him a wink and a playful smile before following Mary Ellen to Mr. Dobney's particular drawing room.

Chapter 8

After the appropriate introductions had been made, Lydia took a seat near Mary Ellen's father as he requested. She carefully arranged her skirts and folded her hands in her lap. His words of welcome had been very pleasant, and he was a handsome man. Her eyes flicked to Marcus, who was just entering the room, and then back to his father. Yes, with a few wrinkles and a smattering of grey hair, they would look very much alike. They had the same eyes, both in shape and colour, and the same slanted nose, but their mouths were not exactly the same. Mr. Dobney's lips were thin, and his mouth appeared smaller than his son's.

"Did you have a pleasant drive, Miss Lydia?" asked Mr. Dobney.

"Oh, it was lovely!" Lydia answered with some enthusiasm.

"I pointed out all the important estate details," said Marcus, taking a seat beside his sister, and Aunt Tess on a sofa across from where Lydia and his father sat. "I believe Miss Lydia was duly impressed." There was a hint of teasing in his tone. His father always wished to know that all visitors were pleased with the estate he loved so much.

Lydia's head bobbed up and down. "Oh, yes. It is beautiful. So much land and then to see the house situated just as it should be..." She sighed. "It is nearly perfection."

"Nearly?" Mr. Dobney asked with an amused chuckle.

Lydia nodded again. "Quite."

"But it is not perfection?" Mr. Dobney wore a smile that Marcus had not seen in a while. His father was obviously enjoying himself thoroughly.

"Perfection does not exist in any estate — not even a palace," said Lydia.

"Perfection does not exist?" The question slipped from Marcus before he could think better of asking. Of course, there would be some round about explanation that would be delightful to him, but perhaps it would not serve to show Lydia in the best light to the others, and for some odd and unsettling reason, it seemed extremely important to him that she be accepted.

On the tail of Marcus's question and before Lydia could respond, Mr. Dobney asked one of his own. "If it does not exist in an estate, where does perfection exist?"

Marcus tipped his head and looked at his father inquisitively. It seemed as if his father had an idea of where Lydia's thoughts would lead.

Lydia pursed her lips and drew her brows together. "Perfection is very rare," she answered in all seriousness. "Few find it." She looked up at Mr. Dobney, who was nodding his head in agreement and looking at her as if he were truly interested in what she had to say. He was smiling, but his eyes were not laughing. A faint blush stained her cheeks at the pleasure that such attention brought to her heart.

He tapped a finger on his chest, and her eyes grew wide in delight.

"Yes," she said, "that is precisely where it is found. Aldwood Abbey cannot be perfection to me, for I have only just met it, and though I find it delightful in appearance and situation, it does not have a place in my heart."

"Not yet," said Mr. Dobney, "but I would venture to say, it will one day when it has become a welcome old friend — if you will visit often enough."

Lydia blinked and a small furrow formed between her brows. Was he just being polite or did he actually wish for her company? His eyes were smiling as much as his mouth, making it appear that he was quite honestly inviting her to visit. "I would like that."

"Would you like to see all of this big old house?" he asked.

Lydia sucked in a quick breath and nodded and, though she caught her lower lip between her teeth, could not help how her smile grew at the suggestion.

"Very well, after we have had a bit of conversation and some tea, I will allow my son to push me around in that confounded chair he has placed outside the door and show it to you myself."

Lydia's eyes grew wide. "It will not be too much?" she whispered, looking at his leg which was propped up on a tufted green footstool. "I do not have to see it all at once. Mrs. Barnes might allow me to return."

Mr. Dobney's fuzzy grey brows drew together slightly.

"I am to be her companion," said Lydia. He nodded at her comment, but his eyes were still puzzled. She opened her mouth to speak and then closed it again. She did not want to tell him of the situation that required her to take a position as a companion. He seemed to like her, but once he heard how foolish she had been, that was likely to change.

"It was my idea," said Marcus. "Miss Lydia has found herself in a spot of trouble, and it seemed a good option for solving the problem."

Lydia could feel the fear climbing up her spine and stiffening it. How could he tell his father about that? Did he not realize that she would no longer be welcome? Her eyes dropped to her hands. Perhaps she might still be allowed to tour part of the house today before she was sent away.

"Ah," said Mr. Dobney. "This will rid us of that scoundrel?"

Lydia's head snapped up. He did not sound displeased.

"That is the plan," said Marcus.

"Then it is a good one."

Lydia blinked. He was smiling at her and not just with his lips. He was not going to call her a fool and send her away.

Mr. Dobney pulled his handkerchief from his pocket and handed it to her. "Marcus is a smart lad, is he not?" he asked softly.

Lydia nodded and blotted the tears from her eyes before they could fall.

"Now, Mrs. Barnes," he continued, turning away from Lydia and toward Aunt Tess, "It appears the decision of how large our tour will be falls at your feet."

It was decided, after a short discussion, that the lower halls and garden would be an excellent amount of the house to be seen this afternoon, and when they called next, Mr. Dobney would meet Lydia and Aunt Tess in the library above and escort them through that level of the house. It was a plan that delighted Lydia, for though her curiosity would have dearly loved to be assuaged in one complete tour of the house, she knew that in dividing the tour, she was being welcomed to return.

Being welcomed just for herself was a new feeling. Lydia had little to offer the Dobneys. She had no societal position that begged their attention nor was she a relation whom they must entertain. Miss Dobney had not inquired once about any matter of fashion, and seeing as Lydia was new in the area, it was quite evident that Miss Dobney did not wish to be her friend merely to gain introductions to gentlemen. And Marcus — Lydia paused to look at him from where she sat on a garden bench next to his father's chair. Marcus had already proven himself a friend. They wished nothing from her beyond her presence. It was really a very novel thing.

"Do you like it?" asked Marcus, catching her eye when she looked at him.

"I do," she said with a smile. "It is so well arranged and the decor is just what it should be."

Marcus came around from behind his father's chair and took a seat next to her, curious to hear her description, for he could tell by the small furrow between her brow and the slight pursing of her lips, she was about to elaborate on her comment as soon as the proper words were found. And he was not to be disappointed.

"The colours are rich and somber where they should be. The deep reds in the chapel and its drawing room give just the proper amount of reverence without being off-putting and austere. And the artwork is such that one cannot but think of things beyond this world. And the grand parlour, which must be used as a dining room or ballroom on occasion?" She looked to Mr. Dobney to see if her guess was correct. He nodded and admitted that it had in the past been used for that very purpose.

"Oh, it must be used once again. A small party is often just the thing to lift the mood and aid in recovery. One cannot feel poorly for long when surrounded by good humor and music. One must have music even if it is just a pianoforte or a harp. There is nothing quite like it to set one to right."

Mr. Dobney chuckled at her enthusiasm for the scheme. "I may have to try your remedy."

"Oh, I shall help you, if you need it," Lydia offered, her excitement growing at the thought of an elegant soiree. "My mother is quite adept at planning parties, and I do think I take after her in that way."

Marcus bit the sides of his cheeks to keep from chuckling. Having met Lydia's father and older sisters and having listened to many of her strange rationalizations, he suspected that Lydia took after her mother in more ways than just planning parties.

"The paintings in that room along with the mirrors must absolutely sparkle when the candles are lit! And with the doors that open onto the garden," she clasped her hands in delight, "the air would not become stuffy and unbearable, even in winter." She leaned toward Mr. Dobney slightly and whispered. "You can open them just a crack when it is cold. The fresh air will come in and the crush of people will ensure the room stays warm."

"I shall keep that in mind," he assured her.

"And lanterns must be lit in the garden along these paths, for I am certain that someone would like to take a stroll along them in the moonlight." She sighed. "It would be quite romantic, but there must be light so that nothing untoward happens."

Mr. Dobney chuckled. "It sounds delightful. Marcus, we must plan a soiree before the summer ends."

Marcus shook his head. As much as he wished his father to leave his rooms and open the doors of their house to visitors, he did not wish to rush the proceedings and tax him unduly. "Perhaps in the autumn."

"Oh, at Michaelmas," said Lydia. "There is always an assembly at Michaelmas in Meryton. It is such good fun." She sighed. She did not mean to sigh, but the thought of missing an assembly and dancing in a new dress with so many willing partners was too much to contemplate without a sigh.

"Then at Michaelmas, we will have a small gathering," said Marcus. Lydia's small cry of delight and the clapping of her hands pleased him greatly, and from the smile his father wore, it seemed he was not alone. "Shall we continue our tour of the garden? I believe Aunt Tess and Mary Ellen will have made a complete circuit twice over before we have completed our first."

"I should like to go just as far as your mother's roses, and then you may leave me there and continue on your way," said Mr. Dobney as Marcus took his place behind the chair. "It is my favourite spot to sit," he explained to Lydia. "The fragrance of the flowers brings back such pleasant memories."

Lydia took his hand and gave it a small comforting squeeze. "Then you shall sit there as long as you wish," she said softly.

How sad it must be to miss someone you loved. Would there be things, after she had been in Derbyshire for a time, which would remind her of her mother and Kitty and which she would seek out just to feel not so far away from them?

Mr. Dobney must have heard the small sigh she tried not to make, for he squeezed her hand gently and he did not release it until they had come to the spot where he wished to sit. Then with a smile, he released her to his son's care and instructed them not to hurry. He would be quite content to sit as he was for hours if need be.

Marcus led Lydia down the path, and as much as he had planned to be quick, the pleasantness of her at his side and her hand on his arm slowed his feet. It was at least half an hour before they returned to escort his father back to his drawing room. Then, after a thorough report from Lydia to Mr. Dobney about the delights of his garden, it was time for Lydia to return to Willow Hall.

Chapter 9

That evening, Lydia tried to make herself as small as possible where she sat next to Jane at the foot of the table. Her visit with Aunt Tess and the Dobneys had been so lovely that she did not wish to have the pleasant feelings it had given her flee before they must. And she knew they must eventually be displaced, for there was still a conversation — a dreaded conversation — to be had with her father regarding her future.

Happily, Mr. Bennet had been occupied with Mr. Gardener in a game of chess, and Jane and Elizabeth had been conversing with callers when Lydia had returned to Willow Hall.

This arrangement of her family members had meant she could say a quick word of thanks to Marcus and Aunt Tess and then slip away to her room unnoticed. In her room, by herself, she could relive the afternoon in her mind, uninterrupted by sad sighs and disapproving looks.

"You are very quiet this evening," said Mrs. Abbot, leaning towards Lydia. "Did you enjoy your visit with Mr. Dobney?"

"I did," Lydia answered and turned back to the pudding that had just been served.

"You have nothing to share of your day?" Mrs. Abbot raised a brow as she asked the question. "I am certain I would not have the strength to keep silent after a visit to such a place. I have been to Aldwood Abbey once for a small dinner just after we arrived at Willow Hall. I was quite struck by its elegance."

"Oh, to be sure," agreed Lydia. "The house is well-situated, and the gardens are well-tended."

"The gardens?" Mrs. Abbot drew in a quick breath. "Oh, I should like to see the gardens. There is nothing quite like a walk through the gardens of a home to get a true feel for the place, you know." She smiled at Lydia. "A well-designed garden affords so many differing and pleasing views of the house." She sighed softly. "And then there are the special flowers that are of significance to some member of the family. Gardens speak volumes."

Lydia could not agree more. Gardens were delightful places, and the one at Aldwood Abbey was perhaps the most delightful she had ever seen — not that she had seen many.

"Mr. Dobney asked to sit by his wife's roses." Lydia could not help but share that fact. It was the one thing, out of all the beautiful views in the garden, that had captured her attention the most.

She had watched him when she could while she listened to Marcus tell her of little things that had happened in this place or that. He, of course, had caught her looking back. He always seemed to see what she was about.

"He loved her very much, did he not?" she had asked in response to Marcus's question as to why she kept peering at his father.

"He still does," Marcus's reply had been so soft that Lydia had looked up to see if he had actually spoken.

Mr. Dobney was not the only Dobney to still love and miss Mrs. Dobney. Lydia could tell by the way Marcus fixed his eyes on some spot in the distance, and by the sad expression which caused his lips to turn down ever so slightly, that Marcus had loved his mother deeply.

That was what had made the prospect so captivating. To be loved so very much as to be sought in the face of a flower after you were gone gripped Lydia's heart and would not let go. She had read and heard of such a love, but to see it — well, it was quite irresistible. Something so rare must be committed to memory.

Lydia sighed and poked at her pudding as Mrs. Abbot waited for further description of the visit, which Lydia gave as briefly and carefully as she could. She did not wish to draw the attention of her father by exclaiming over anything in particular. It was a task which was not easily accomplished, for Aldwood Abbey had captured Lydia's imagination, and she longed to share about the party that was to be held in September. However, she most certainly could not mention plans for the autumn, even to Mrs. Abbot, when Lydia, herself, was not entirely certain her father would allow her to remain in Derbyshire for that long.

"It sounds beautiful," said Jane, who had been listening intently and asking nearly as many questions as Mrs. Abbott. "I should very much like to see it."

"Why?" asked Lydia.

"Because it sounds lovely, of course," said Jane in surprise.

"There is no other reason? You do not wish to make it your home?" Lydia's heart thumped loudly within her chest. Jane was beautiful and proper. She would make an excellent mistress to any estate. Indeed, Jane would care for any home very well, and to have Aldwood Abbey in such good care should make Lydia happy.

However, the thought of Jane as the new Mrs. Dobney was not settling well in Lydia's stomach. In fact, it seemed to be stirring up the contents. Lydia put down her fork. Although she had not finished her meal, the remaining portion was unappealing. And since she was apparently becoming ill, it was best, Lydia decided, to leave a bit of food on her plate. She hoped the apothecary would not have to be called. She detested the taste of his tinctures.

"No, I had not thought to make it my home."

Jane 's voice sounded incredulous at the idea, but her cheeks, Lydia thought, coloured suspiciously. Lydia bit back a grimace as her stomach roiled. She would need to go straight to bed if she wished to avoid truly being ill. She rubbed her temple lightly as Mrs. Abbot stood to leave. A headache due to tiredness should give her the excuse to retire early without causing any great concern and drawing unwanted care. She would just follow Mrs. Abbot to the hall and then plead her excuses.

"Lydia."

Lydia froze and turned slowly toward her father.

"Have a seat. Up here by us." He crossed his arms and leaned back in his chair. The rest of the ladies exited the room, and she thought her uncle and Mr. Abbot would join them, but they made no move to leave.

It was apparently going to be a demanding discussion if they all needed to remain. Lydia rubbed her temple once more as she took a seat closer to her father. She would not need to feign a headache now.

"I had a very interesting discussion with Mr. Dobney," her father began.

Lydia clasped her hands in her lap and waited. Marcus had told her of his plan to speak with her father. In fact, she had sat near the window to watch him depart. He had not looked angry or flustered, so she had dared to hope her father had agreed to Marcus's plan. She had even ventured so far as to write a letter to her mother telling her of the exciting news. However, now as Lydia sat here in the dining room with her father, her uncle, and her host, she wondered if perhaps her hope had been rash.

"You are not going to ask me about what we spoke?" There was a note of disbelief in her father's tone as he leaned closer and peered at her.

Lydia shook her head. "There is no need. I knew of Mr. Dobney's intentions in speaking to you."

"And you are agreeable to them?"

Lydia nodded. She had enjoyed her time with Aunt Tess. It would not be so very bad to do her bidding. She seemed to be a kind and sensible lady. Surely, she would not be overbearing or unreasonable. And, by accepting a position with Aunt Tess, Lydia would be able to visit Mr. Dobney at Aldwood Abbey and help him plan his soiree.

"Shall I have Mr. Philip Dobney call the first banns this Sunday, then?"

Lydia's eyes grew wide, and her mouth dropped open until she saw that his eyes were laughing. She snapped her mouth shut, and her eyes narrowed. Of course, she was the source of an amusing joke. She waited for him to chuckle and continue on with the joke, but he did not.

Instead, her father sighed. The twinkle in his eye faded, and he rubbed a hand across his eyes as if he were very tired. "I should not tease. I know." He smiled at her sadly. "I only wish I were deciding whether or not to give you to such a proper gentleman instead of whether or not to allow you to take a position with Mrs. Barnes."

"She is very kind." Lydia held her breath waiting for her father to either tell her she might stay or that she would be returning home.

"She is, but your mother had such hopes for you..." He rubbed his face again. "I suppose those hopes vanished the moment you stole away from Brighton." He shook his head. "No, they were gone when I gave my permission for you to travel to Brighton. You were too young to be venturing so far from home. I see that now." He drew in a deep breath and released it. "But, that is neither here nor there. It is very unlikely that you will be able to return to Longbourn without some gossip swirling and making you and your mother miserable, so the best option is as Mr. Dobney has suggested." He cocked his head to the side, a small smile tugged at the right corner of his lips. "Unless you would prefer that the banns be called. I really do not believe Mr. Dobney would be opposed to taking you for a wife. He seems keen to see you safe."

Lydia's mouth dropped open again. Marry Mr. Dobney? He was so old. No, she corrected herself, he was not old. He was just not young. But he was handsome, and his estate was beautiful. She pressed her lips together. It was not a suggestion without merit. Perhaps it was something she should consider. After all, he knew her circumstances and yet had not shunned her. Yes, she would give it some thought — later. Right now, however, she needed to secure her place with Aunt Tess. "So I may stay with Mrs. Barnes?"

Her father nodded. "It does seem best. I am not certain how I shall break that news to your mother. She is expecting you to return from Brighton at the end of the summer, and she does not even know you have travelled to Derbyshire."

Lydia sat forward in her chair. A tiny prickle of excitement crept cautiously up her spine. "I can help with that. I have a letter already written."

"You do?" There was no mistaking the surprise in her father's tone.

Lydia's head bobbed up and down. The prickle of excitement had reached the place right between her shoulder blades and waited expectantly to be allowed to wrap around her and touch her heart.

"I wrote it after I returned today with the hope that I was not writing it in vain." She tried desperately to keep a smile from forming on her lips. She was to stay — here in Derbyshire — with people who liked her.

"I should like to read it."

"Of course." She had intended to show it to him. She began to rise and then sat back down. "May I go retrieve it from my room?"

"In a moment." He looked at the other two men at the table. "I have asked Mr. Abbot to stand in my stead while

354

you are here, and he has agreed to take on the responsibility. Your sister Lizzy will also be remaining in Derbyshire and Mr. Darcy, I am certain, will assist Mr. Abbot where needed."

"Lizzy is marrying here? She is not returning to Longbourn? Mama will be sorely disappointed." It was true that Mama and Lizzy did not get on well, but to deny their mother her pleasure in arranging for a wedding breakfast and making all the happy calls associated with such an event seemed selfish to Lydia, and it made her heart ache. "Mama wishes for all her daughters to be married from Longbourn."

"Indeed, she does, but this is what Lizzy wishes. I am certain your mother will be just as pleased to share the news of it as to have organized the affair herself."

Lydia was certain her father was wrong, but it would not do to say so. Papa always saw to Elizabeth's happiness.

"I will send your things when I send hers." There was sadness in his eyes. "I know that Lizzy shall be happy, but will you? Will you be happy?"

Lydia blinked in confusion. Could he truly be sad on her account? "I believe I will be."

He pulled his lips into a smile and rose from his chair. "Then, I shall attempt to bear the separation as best I can." He extended his arms. "Give your old papa a hug before you go get your letter."

Lydia blinked again but slowly rose to do as he asked. She did not remember the last time he had hugged her.

"I am sorry," he whispered as he squeezed her tight. Then he released her slightly and looked into her eyes.

She had never seen his eyes look quite like they did at that moment. Perhaps what Mrs. Abbott had said about being loved was true.

"I am sorry to have to leave you here, but I am glad you are not marrying Mr. Wickham."

Lydia's brows furrowed. "I thought you wished me to marry him?"

He pulled her close again. "Only because I saw no other way to solve the muddle you had created." He gave her one last squeeze and then released her. "Now, I should like to read that letter."

Chapter 10

"This," said Marcus as his carriage came to the end of the drive at Willow Hall and turned toward the right, "is the correct direction to Kympton." He smiled at Lydia as she rolled her eyes.

He was quite happy to be providing her with transportation to her new home, but he had seen her blinking rapidly and biting her lip as she stood outside Willow Hall. He suspected that no matter how much she claimed her family did not like her, they truly did, and it was a sentiment Lydia returned. She had, after all, taken it upon herself to travel a great distance to be with her sisters. Going on a journey, knowing you would be returning to your home with tales to tell was one thing. However, this — leaving your family without a plan to return — was something entirely different and bound to stir emotions in the most reticent of hearts. Lydia's heart and emotions were not reticent. They were well-shrouded perhaps, but what she felt, she felt deeply.

"We shall not need to worry about your finding the

inn and purchasing passage to some unknown destination, will we?" He kept his tone light, but it was not entirely a jest.

"Oh, not until at least October," she replied with an impertinent smile. Her eyes swept the view in front of her from left to right. "Which direction is the inn?"

"October?" he asked.

Her head bobbed up and down. "I hear there is to be a grand soiree at Michaelmas at an estate somewhere about here." Her hand waved around in a circle. "I stumbled upon it once."

Marcus chuckled. "I will personally see that you find it again."

"And the inn?" She smiled sweetly at him and batted her lashes.

"That, I shall not help you find." Her lower lip protruded, and he quickly returned his eyes to the road so that he would not be tempted to think about kissing her. He shook his head. It was too late for that. He had been tempted to kiss her more times than he cared to admit even to himself. It was shocking, really, how much he had thought about her since finding her in his cottage three days ago.

"Then I shall have to discover it on my own," she declared with no small amount of determination in her voice.

He laughed.

She huffed. "I shall soon become familiar with my surroundings, you know."

He chuckled a bit longer. It was true. He was certain that even Lydia would know her way around the small town of Kympton before October.

"I shall just have to trust that you will find your position to your liking and not too boring." He raised a brow, and his lips curled into a smirk as he said the last word.

She shrugged and tossed her head. "I do hope there will be some entertainment to the society in which I will be moving."

"Aunt Tess is well-known and liked. You will not want for society," he assured her.

Lydia grabbed his arm. "Oh, do not tell her what I said. It was merely a jest to provoke you."

He took his eyes from the road and looked into her large, round, fearful eyes. "I would not think of doing anything to put you or your position with Aunt Tess in danger." A smile spread slowly across his face. "Your eyes are very pretty," he said before turning away from them.

"Oh, yes, they are," she agreed most sincerely. "I rather like how they are a mix of brown and green."

"With flecks of gold," he added.

She nodded. "And depending on what I wear or how the light hits them, they can appear more or less of one colour than the other. There is not another girl in all of Meryton whose eyes are as lovely as mine."

"Your sisters do not have the same colouring?"

She sighed. "Lizzy and Kitty do, but mine are the nicest, for they have more green and less brown. Mine could only truly be nicer if they were completely green. Green is one of my favourite colours, you know, but yellow is nice, as well."

"I like green and brown," Marcus made an attempt to follow her conversation and add to it.

She clapped her hands. "Just like my eyes. It is no wonder you like them so much." Her hand flew to her bonnet. "My hair is brown. Do you like it?"

He glanced over at her. She was patiently waiting for his response. Her eyes watched him without a hint of teasing, and she did not appear to be asking just to puff up her vanity. She seemed truly interested in his opinion, and he had no doubt she was already rather confident about the appearance of her hair just as she was about her eyes. He nodded. "It is lovely."

"I knew you would like it. Everybody does." She turned to look at their surroundings. They had reached the edge of town where some small cottages dotted the sides of the road. "Are the people friendly?"

"I find them to be," he assured her. Then, he pointed out a few places that he knew. "And if you turn here," he pointed to a road to their right, "that street will wrap around to the church and then bring you right back to this very road we are on. Where the other end of that street meets this one is where you will be living. Up there, three houses down on the left."

"Oh!" She sat forward on the seat.

"And across from it is where my brother and Lucy live."

She nodded and looked at him. "Your brother, Mr. Philip Dobney, is the vicar?"

"He is. Mr. Darcy gave him the living just last year shortly before Philip married." He slowed the horses as they drew near to Aunt Tess's. "You will have to meet them. I think you will like Lucy. Everybody does."

He was just drawing to a stop in front of Philip's house when Lydia grabbed his arm once again.

"There," she pointed down the street, "that is Mr. William's house, is it not?"

"You remember it?"

She nodded. Her hand still gripped his arm.

"I am to go there after I deliver you to Aunt Tess," he said, covering her hand with his, "to tell Mr. Williams that Wickham can leave."

Lydia nodded again and removed her hand from his arm, allowing him to dismount and then help her down from her seat. It was a relief that she would not have to see Wickham again. She also did not wish to see Mr. Williams. However, he would be a neighbour, which would mean at least an occasional meeting would be inevitable. She sighed. A cranky constable was better than Wickham.

"Marcus!" A familiar looking lady called from her step across the street.

Marcus lifted his hand in greeting. "Come, I will introduce you to Lucy." He took a step, but Lydia did not follow.

"I have already met her," Lydia said as Marcus turned to look at her. "The night I arrived at Willow Hall."

Marcus smiled. There was that Lydia again. The one that stared at her hands when he mentioned her troubles to his father. The one that stood her ground refusing to be returned to her father. The one that cared what others thought of her though she pretended not to. "She'll not judge you."

Lydia's eyes grew wide in surprise.

"I promise," he said, giving the hand that lay on his arm a small squeeze. "Trust me."

Lydia nodded and just as quickly as she had hidden her fear the day he had carried her into Willow Hall, she tucked it away now. And were it not for the firmness of her grip on his arm, he would have thought her completely at ease to look at her expression.

He gave her hand one more squeeze, led her to where Lucy waited, and made a proper introduction.

Lucy glanced over her shoulder. "I would ask you to come in, but Aunt Tess gave particular instructions that I am to join you for tea. Tomorrow, Aunt Tess and you, Miss Lydia, will have tea at my home. It is a bit of back and forth we do." She looked at Marcus. "Your brother wishes to speak with you."

"Am I not allowed tea?" Marcus grumbled. Lydia might look the part of a confident young lady, but he knew she would be much more at ease if he were to be with her when being introduced to her new surroundings.

Lucy shook her head. "Not until you have seen Philip. He says it is important. I will see Miss Lydia safe to her home."

Marcus felt Lydia's grasp tighten for a moment. He was right. She was uneasy. It was not something he could ignore, especially since he had asked her to trust him. "Philip can wait until I see you both safely to Aunt Tess's house," he said as he extended his free arm to Lucy. "I will not take tea until I see him," he added as he waited for Lucy to take his arm. How was he to placate two demanding females?

"Very well," said Lucy reluctantly. "But he is not alone. Mr. Williams has come to call."

"It will be but a moment longer before I attend them," he reassured her.

"Is everything well?" Lydia's voice wavered just a bit.

"It is," said Lucy. "There is nothing to fear. Mr. Wickham left this morning, and he shall not be returning." She tugged Marcus's arm until he leant down so that she could kiss his cheek. "Tell my husband to be quick so that his tea is not cold." She extended a hand to Lydia. "I shall tell you all about it while we eat biscuits." She lay her other hand on her abdomen and winked at Lydia.

Marcus did not miss the small motion. "Keeping secrets are we?" he asked with a grin.

"For a few more weeks," Lucy said with a smile. "Philip knows, as does Aunt Tess, but no one else." She gave Marcus a severe look.

"You glare me into silence and not Miss Lydia?" He lay a hand on his heart as if he were wounded.

Lucy laughed. "Men do not keep secrets as well as ladies."

At that, he laughed outright. "Yes, gentlemen are the chief gossips." He waved and took his leave, assuring them that the secret was safe.

Lucy wrapped Lydia's arm around hers. "We expect the baby to arrive at the end of winter," she said as they entered the house. "I am hoping that you, as well as Aunt Tess, will help me prepare for its arrival."

Lydia felt the importance of such a request made in secret. Lucy, it seemed, was not unkindly disposed to Lydia as Lydia had feared she might be. "I know little of babies, but I am very good with a needle."

Lucy laughed. "I know very little about them either. We shall learn together."

Lydia placed her bonnet on the table that stood just inside the door. "Mrs. Abbot knows about babies, and she seems very nice."

Lucy smiled. This girl, who looked very much like the defiant girl standing in Willow Hall's sitting room that first night she arrived, was not as she presented herself. She might be fierce when provoked and self-indulgent to a fault, but she was not without sense or feelings. Her eyes spoke, no, begged, for acceptance. Lucy was not sure if it was her condition or the moment of being allowed to see such an unguarded expression, but her handkerchief was about to be used for the third time that day.

"I believe you are a good judge of character, Miss Lydia, for Mrs. Abbot is one of the kindest souls I have met, and we will ask her for help when we are ready." She dabbed at the corners of her eyes. "We had best hurry before all the best biscuits are gone. Aunt Tess has a rather large sweet tooth."

Chapter 11

Marcus knocked firmly on the door to his brother's study before pushing it open. He hoped that whatever matter needed to be discussed would be done quickly. He had planned to spend some time with Lydia at Aunt Tess's before returning home. He wished to see her well-settled and happy. He was confident that she and Aunt Tess would rub along nicely, but still, his mind would not be easy unless he saw it for himself.

"Your charge has been delivered?" Philip was leaning back in his chair. His hands were folded in front of him while his elbows were propped on the arms of the chair, and his lips wore a slightly teasing grin.

"Miss Lydia is not my charge." Marcus tossed his hat on the desk. "I believe her care falls under her father's jurisdiction and then transfers to Mr. Abbot on Mr. Bennet's departure. Mr. Williams." He acknowledged the gentleman with a nod before taking a seat.

Philip chuckled softly. "Yet, you seem very intent on seeing to Miss Lydia's welfare."

Marcus glared at his brother. "As I would for any friend. Am I not known for caring for my friends?" He turned to Mr. Williams, who held up his hands in protest of being brought into any argument the two brothers might be starting.

"I will not take sides," he said. "I find caring for one's friends is a family trait, instilled by your father and nurtured by your mother. In fact," he added with a sly smile, "your brother is a fine example of just how far a Dobney will go to care for a friend."

"Would you go so far as I, Marcus?"

This was not the matter they had called him here to discuss, was it? He looked from Mr. Williams to Philip. Philip's expression was smug while Mr. Williams' was unwavering as if the topic was not unexpected.

"It should be considered," said Mr. Williams.

"What should be considered?" Marcus asked tentatively.

"Oh, my boy, you are not so feeble-minded as you pretend." Mr. Williams pulled a paper from his pocket. "Miss Lydia is free of Wickham for now." He handed the paper to Marcus. "I have his account of what transpired on their way to Derbyshire from Brighton." He smiled. "That Miss Lydia is a clever one. I dare say Wickham has never agreed to sign something so quickly in his life as he was that paper. I half expected him to put up a bit of a struggle —

weasel his way into heavier pockets or the like — but he did not."

Marcus read Wickham's account. "Very similar to Miss Lydia's story," he said, passing the paper back to Mr. Williams. "It is my understanding that his pockets were not to be light when he left."

Mr. Williams shook his head. "He would not take a farthing of Miss Lydia's money. Did not wish to be tied to her in any way."

"But his debts," protested Marcus.

"Aye, they were large."

"They have been seen to — or will be shortly." Philip supplied, lifting a hand to stop the question he knew was coming. "I cannot say who has seen to them, nor am I perfectly at ease knowing Wickham has left so peacefully. His debts will not remain cancelled for long. There will be others, and then, he will again be looking for ways to claim his due."

"Aye," agreed Mr. Williams. "Wait three months, and he'll be looking for escape once again and willing to use whatever he must to obtain it."

Marcus shook his head. "I do not follow. You have his account of what happened. He cannot say otherwise."

Mr. Williams shrugged. "A whisper is all it takes. The damage will be done before it can be refuted. It is not fair that a lady's reputation is so fragile, but it is what it is."

"With or without Wickham's accounting of the tale,"

began Philip, leaning forward and propping his arms on his desk, "there is no doubt already talk in Brighton, at least, and when the regiment returns to Hertfordshire, the tale will follow."

"That will not change if I marry her," Marcus protested.

"No, it will not, but it will limit Miss Lydia's chances of marrying as she should." Philip shuffled a few papers. "And she will be, most likely, going home after a brief stay with Aunt Tess."

Going home? Soon? Marcus shook his head again. "Why?"

Philip sighed. "When I spoke to Mr. Bennet this morning, he agreed with Aunt Tess that a separation from what Miss Lydia knows and the responsibility of being a companion will do Miss Lydia good. However, Wickham did not take her money. Her portion is untouched, so there is no need for her to work to replace it. Therefore, after an agreed upon interval, the arrangement will be terminated, and Miss Lydia will be sent back to Hertfordshire, a wiser and more refined young lady."

Marcus scowled.

"We will not lie to her if that is what you are thinking," added Philip. "Aunt Tess is probably telling her about the arrangement right now. Her staying will be couched as a lesson in what could have happened."

Marcus was on his feet. "It will not work."

Philip snatched Marcus's hat before he got it. "Sit down.

Let us finish, and trust Aunt Tess to word it better than I have."

Marcus remained standing but did not move from his spot in front of Philip's desk. "It will hurt her to have her idea — her sacrifice — turned into another reminder of how little anyone thinks of her." His heart ached at the thought.

"Sit down," said Mr. Williams. "I have known Theresa Barnes long enough to know that she will not do or say anything to injure Miss Lydia."

Marcus stared at Mr. Williams for a moment before deciding to acquiesce and sit down. His brother he would defy. Mr. Williams, he would not.

"According to Aunt Tess, Miss Lydia wishes to marry," said Mr. Williams. "Her best chance for marrying, and marrying well, is here in Derbyshire where no one is aware of the commotion surrounding her arrival. She was recovering from her journey last Lord's Day and merely got lost while on a walk. Both perfectly true." He raised his brows and gave Marcus a look that demanded his words be accepted. "So, it will be our business to make certain she has the opportunity to make an attachment if at all possible. And the sooner the deed is done, the better."

"Marriage to some gentleman does not guarantee she will be free from scandal if Wickham does decide to break his silence," argued Marcus.

Mr. Williams shrugged. "No, it does not."

"The scoundrel may attempt to scheme his way into the coffers of whomever Miss Lydia marries." He leaned forward and glared at both men. "You know as well as I that not all husbands will be kind to a wife they think has played them for a fool." His heart beat heavily against his ribs while his fingers clutched the arms of his chair. How could they suggest such a thing? It would be better for Lydia never to marry than to be subjected to such treatment.

"Yes," said Philip, pushing a folded piece of paper across the desk toward Marcus, "we have taken that into consideration. I made a list of men I knew to be upstanding in my estimation. The list was not long, of course. We are not well-stocked with eligible gentlemen here in Kympton at present, so I included those I knew from Lambton."

Marcus attempted to take the paper from the desk, but Philip held it in place by pressing down on it.

"Lucy wishes for me to say that she had only your description and a few comments made yesterday by Aunt Tess upon which to base her opinions when eliminating names." Philip removed his hand from the paper. "However, she also had a few opinions of her own about some of the gentlemen I had included and, therefore, would not allow their names to remain on the list."

Marcus opened the paper. A list of about fifteen names had been whittled down to five. "Harris? I dare say he would not treat her well," Marcus muttered. "It was he who called her a flirt to Miss Elizabeth."

"Would you like to remove his name?" Philip held out a pen. Had Marcus not been so disgusted with his cousin as a choice and therefore so eager to scratch out his name, he might have noticed the amused look that passed between Philip and Mr. Williams.

Marcus scooted to the edge of his chair and, placing the paper on the desk, scratched out his cousin's name. "Besides, he is only a captain." He looked up at Philip. "The bottom of what Miss Lydia finds acceptable for rank. Now, Colonel Fitzwilliam has a better rank and good connections," he drew a line through the name, "but Mary Ellen would not be pleased."

"She should make her interest known," muttered Philip.

"Perhaps, but I will not attempt to steer the object of her affections away from her."

"Just as you refuse to inform him of her affections?" Philip asked with a laugh.

"Precisely." Marcus grinned at his brother. "For the same reasons you have not made mention of it."

Philip inclined his head in acknowledgment of the fact.

Marcus returned his attention to the list and scratched out the next two names. "Not sensible enough. It would be a home filled with folly," he muttered about the first. "Too sensible. She would be thought a fool," he said of the second and looked up at his brother, "which she is not."

He made one last omission from the list and, placing the pen on the desk, sat back in his chair. It had taken some fortitude to omit the last name, for a small flutter in the vicinity of his heart wished for the gentleman to succeed with Lydia.

"You have made our task impossible." Philip's words were stern, but his expression was not. "You did not mention why the last man was unacceptable."

"He is too old, and she is too young."

Philip picked up the paper and motioned to his brother to lean forward. Then, he looked very carefully at Marcus's face. "I am afraid you are wrong." He picked up the pen and added Marcus's name once again to the list.

"I am not."

Philip nodded and pointed to the corner of his eye. "No lines. Therefore, not old." He grinned. "Although not young either."

"I cannot marry her." The words cut at his heart. "She is not ready to take on Aldwood Abbey."

Mr. Williams snorted. "She is not ready, or you are not?" He stood. "Your grandfather said the same about your mother when your father married." His hand rested on Marcus's shoulder. "And she did struggle at first, but ask anyone in your father's employ: she rose to the challenge, just as I expect Miss Lydia would. She is quick enough to see a blackguard for what he is and cunning enough to bend him to her purposes. So, unless you can find a name to replace yours, you will have to accept one of the fellows you crossed off — or take on the responsibility yourself." He gave Marcus's shoulder a pat. "With you, she would, at least, be safe. Gentleman." He bowed and took his leave.

Philip rose. "I suppose my tea will be cold."

Marcus nodded and took up his hat. He really did not care if his brother's tea was cold. In fact, if he had not promised to take tea with Aunt Tess, he would just go home. How could he face Lydia when his mind was in such a jumbled state. Marry her? See her married to another? Neither seemed an acceptable outcome.

Philip reached for the doorknob but instead of opening the door, he turned toward his brother. "Let me tell you something I once told Darcy. The woman you marry may not be what or whom you expect her to be. I know; I never once considered Lucy as a bride until that day in the cemetery when she asked for my help in saving her from her uncle." He sighed and shook his head slowly. "My marriage did not happen as I would have planned, but I am happy for it." He pulled open the door. "God's ways are not always our ways."

Philip followed his brother out of the room. "Miss Lydia must marry someone. If not you, then who? Who would you give her to?" He clapped his brother on the shoulder as they reached the door to the parsonage. "If you can stomach the idea of giving her to anyone, then your name should not be on our list. But if you cannot, then you will never be happy without her."

Chapter 12

"Are you well?" Aunt Tess asked Lydia as they sat later that evening in the sitting room enjoying a cup of tea. "You have been very quiet, and I did not take you to be such a silent person. I hope I do not offend, but you rather seemed more lively than pensive when I met you. And until we were joined by the gentlemen for tea you were animated." She took a sip of her tea. "I rather like animated ladies. There are far too many dull ones."

Lydia returned the smile Aunt Tess gave her. "It has been an odd day."

It had started out pleasant enough. Mr. Dobney had come to collect her as he had promised, and he had been charming on their drive here. And then? Well, she was not exactly certain what had happened, but suddenly, he was no longer charming. He was barely pleasant. She blinked against the unexpected sting of tears in her eyes.

Aunt Tess placed her cup and saucer on the side table. "It is natural to feel out of sorts in a new home and to miss your family."

Lydia nodded. She did feel out of sorts, but she knew it was not from missing her family or being in a new home. She did not miss her family very much, at least not yet. Eventually, she would likely miss them more — especially Mama and Kitty — but not today. Today, she had begun a new adventure, and she enjoyed new adventures. So staying in a new home could not be the cause of her morose mood.

Perhaps her odd feelings could be credited to the number of adventures she had had of late — there had been many. However, she suspected, it was more likely due to Marcus's unusual behaviour when he came to tea. He had taken a seat near her but not the empty one next to her as she had expected, and he had not smiled very often. She sighed. And his eyes — his eyes had rarely fallen on her. They were everywhere else in the room, but not on her.

If she was to make him wish to marry her — for she had thought on her father's suggestion and deemed it a good one — he had to look at her. It was clearly her beauty that would persuade him — was that not what Mama had said?

"Ah, Lydia, every man shall find it hard to resist your beauty," *she would say and then add with a wink, "but you must not allow anyone to claim it unless he is rich and handsome. To be tied to less with such beauty would be a travesty of the greatest sort. Promise me, you will not waste such looks on a man of average means and countenance."*

Lydia had promised Mama each time. It made sense

actually. Beauty should not be wasted. She sighed again. Mr. Dobney was neither average in standing or looks, and yet, he seemed perfectly capable of resisting her charms.

Aunt Tess had returned to her tea. "That is a great deal of sighing."

Lydia's eyes grew wide. She did not wish to offend Aunt Tess, for she did not wish for her stay in Kympton to be shortened any more than it already had been. Drat, that Wickham for choosing to be honorable. It was very unlike him!

"I apologize. I had not meant to sigh, but today was so strange. I cannot make sense of it."

Aunt Tess's head tipped to the side. "Perhaps if you tell me the parts that were odd, I might be able to help you discern them."

Lydia bit her lip and considered sharing her thoughts. She peeked up at Aunt Tess. The lady seemed nice enough, and Marcus had told her that Aunt Tess was to be trusted. Yet there was that niggling feeling in her stomach that made her waiver. She never let anyone hear her inner thoughts save Kitty, but Kitty was not here.

"I promise I can be trusted," said Aunt Tess with a smile.

Lydia blinked. "Did I speak aloud?"

"No." Aunt Tess chuckled. "Your eyes are very expressive."

Lydia blinked again. Of course! Her eyes were very expressive. Many people had commented on that very thing. Although, her brows furrowed, she would have to guard them more closely if they were to be giving away secrets that she did not wish to be guessed.

"You can tell me. I am a very poor gossip," coaxed Aunt Tess once again.

"You agreed I might stay with you until after Michaelmas?"

"I did. I would not deprive Mr. Dobney of hosting a soiree. He has been too reclusive. It is not good, you know."

Lydia's head bobbed up and down. "Solitude can be very taxing."

"For some," agreed Aunt Tess with a smile. She imagined prolonged solitude for Lydia was akin to torture.

Lydia's lips pursed, and her brows drew together. "Is it truly my best option for marriage to look for a husband here?"

Aunt Tess shrugged. "Unless your sister and Mr. Darcy would be willing to sponsor you for a season..." She did not finish the thought as Lydia's expressive eyes had grown wide in horror at the mention of such a thing. "Then, yes."

Lydia would nearly rather be a spinster and wear a tight bun and dingy clothes than spend a whole season with a sister who would always be lecturing. Lydia sighed and shook her head as her shoulders lifted and lowered in a slight shrug.

"But how am I to make a match if he will not look at me?"

It was Aunt Tess's turn to blink, but she was not blinking in surprise. She was confused.

"He has an estate. He is mostly nice to me." Lydia held up a finger as she ticked off all the reasons why Marcus was an acceptable choice. "He is not too old. He is handsome, and I am pretty." She lifted exasperated hands before folding her arms across her chest. "So why would he not look at me? He looked at me on the way here." Lydia's foot stomped lightly on the floor, and she huffed.

"You mean Marcus?" Aunt Tess reined in her smile so that it would not spread across her entire face. That Lydia preferred Marcus was excellent news, in her opinion. "You have set your cap at Marcus?"

Lydia nodded. "Mr. Darcy is marrying my sister, and even if he were not, he smiles far too little. Colonel Fitzwilliam has lines near his eyes, so he is a bit too old. Captain Harris," she lifted a brow, "he gossips." She shook her head in disgust. "He would tell everyone everything. There would be no secrets. It is one thing about my mother that I wish I could change. There should always be some secrets." She sighed. "And Mr. Bingley must marry Jane. They look so good together that it would be a sin for them not to marry. And I know no other eligible gentlemen."

"Well," said Aunt Tess, who was no longer confused,

but not exactly sure how to counsel a young lady with such interesting logic. However, she could see how Marcus had been charmed by it. There was something rather endearing about the girl. Something that, once you got past the hardened outer shell, she, like him, wished to protect. "One poor meeting does not mean the end result must be tossed aside. He had just been told much of what you had. He was probably still processing the information."

Lydia looked thoughtful, so Aunt Tess continued, "Aldwood Abbey is a grand estate. Are you prepared to run it?" She smiled. "Your eyes tell me you do not believe you are, so where should we begin? Accounts? Care for tenants? Meal planning? Schedules?"

Lydia sank back in her chair. Marrying a man with a large estate sounded like it might be more work than she expected.

"Oh, do not give up," said Aunt Tess. "You are clever and, I would guess, a keen learner when you wish to be." She placed her empty teacup on the table. "Care for tenants. That is where we shall begin, for I believe it is an area in which you will excel. You have a kind heart."

Lydia's eyes grew wide. "I do?"

She had never been told that before. She was beautiful. Her hair was to be envied. Her eyes were unique. Her complexion could not be more perfect. She was neither too tall nor too short, nor was she too fat or too thin. Her figure was pleasing. These things she had been told — frequently. But never had she heard she had a kind heart. She felt it to be true, of course, but it is so hard to know if one is accurate in assumptions about one's self unless it is confirmed by the words of another.

"You do. It was you who insisted we not take a tour of Aldwood Abbey because we were there to see the master of the estate and not just his house. And then, you made him comfortable in the garden before you took a stroll through it yourself. And what of the soiree. It is not just for you to enjoy, is it?"

Lydia shook her head. Yes, she would enjoy it, but Mr. Dobney and the rest of his family and staff would as well.

"You see. You care for others, and it is a natural trait. Therefore, that is where we must start." Aunt Tess stood and crossed the room to a shelf of books. "However, caring for tenants is tiring work, so take this book, *The Mirror of the Graces*. It is a guide on what a mistress of a grand estate should be. Read it for a short while and then go to sleep. Lack of sleep does nothing for the complexion, and red, tired eyes will do nothing to inspire a man to an attachment."

"Oh, you are so right," said Lydia, accepting the book. She turned the book over in her hands. "I have seen Mary read this, but I did not know it was for becoming the mistress of an estate." She flipped the pages. "I thought it was just for scolding. That is how Mary uses it."

Aunt Tess chuckled. "I assure you it is good for more than scolding. I have recently read it, and so has Lucy... and neither of us are terrible scolds...at least not often," she added with a wink.

Lydia hugged the book tightly to her chest. If this book could make her into a lady like Mrs. Barnes or Lucy, she would read it thrice over, even if it made her eyes water from boredom. "Thank you."

Aunt Tess opened her arms in invitation to Lydia. "I have not had Lucy to hug before bed in some time. I should very much like it if you would allow me the privilege of hugging you."

Lydia stepped into Aunt Tess's embrace. How good such a small gesture felt!

"I will call you early," cautioned Aunt Tess. "A mistress does not lie abed all day. There is much for her to do."

"Yes, ma'am," said Lydia with a small curtsey. "Sleep well," she added before scooting out of the room and up the stairs.

"Ah, Marcus," Aunt Tess said to the empty room, "you will be happy." She shook her head slowly and smiled. Lydia was wonderful. So full of life and potential. "So much like your mother, Marcus," she again spoke to the empty room. "So very much like your mother."

She picked up the two discarded tea cups and went to find her housekeeper, who would likely be in her room off the kitchen at this time of the evening. There were a few parcels to make ready and a small lunch to be ordered in preparation for her outing with Lydia.

Tomorrow, Lydia would find her abilities to entertain and help others would shine like the sun. And then, with a bit of confidence in those abilities built — for though the girl did not lack confidence in her looks or charms, there seemed to be a hesitancy in accepting abilities beyond that — the teaching of any other skills would fall on more receptive ears.

Chapter 13

Lydia twisted her hair and pinned it as best she could. Turning her head from side to side and studying her reflection in the mirror, she decided it was not dreadfully done. One could still see the long curve of her neck and a few wisps around her ears softened the severity of the style. Though she looked presentably pretty, Lydia would be glad to have a maid once again after her stay with Aunt Tess was over. Margaret was so much better at styling Lydia's hair and at caring for Lydia's clothes than Lydia was herself.

Lydia smoothed the bodice of her dress with a tug and looked over her shoulder into the mirror to see if everything was lying as it should. She had hoped that she might be allowed her maid since she was now merely a guest and not a servant, but Aunt Tess had thought it best to proceed as planned. Lydia was not quite certain she agreed with the reasoning. There seemed no need to demonstrate what life might be like as a servant. Lydia had already definitely decided that it would be horrid. She sighed. At least, she had been given assistance in dressing by one of the maids in Aunt Tess's employ — reaching all your fastenings yourself was not an easy task.

Aunt Tess tapped on the door and pushed it open. "Are you ready?"

Lydia smoothed her skirts, put on her bonnet, and checked her reflection one last time. In her opinion, it was important that she look the part of a mistress even if she was not one yet. "I am."

Aunt Tess held the door open fully. "We shall have a quick cup of tea and then be on our way. I have asked Mrs. Graham to pack us a small lunch, and we shall eat it next to the stream near Aldwood Abbey. It will be too far a drive to come back for a meal."

"Will we stop to see Mr. Dobney?" Lydia asked as she descended the stairs behind Aunt Tess.

Reaching the bottom of the stairs, Aunt Tess turned and smiled at Lydia. "We will — although we will not have time for a tour. Perhaps a stroll in the garden or a chat in his particular room, but there is much to be done." She motioned to the sitting room. "I always take my tea in here in the morning. The sun shines in just so."

As the rays of sun danced across the room to meet her, Lydia could immediately see why someone would enjoy this room in the morning. All was bright and cheery. One could not help but anticipate a day filled with pleasantness in such a room. She would have gladly stayed in that room until the sun had withdrawn the last tips of its fingers and moved over the peak of the house if she had been allowed. But she was not. They spent no more than a quarter hour eating a bit of toast and drinking a cup of tea before Aunt Tess had called for her picnic lunch and inquired if the gig was ready, which it was.

"Have you ever driven?" asked Aunt Tess, climbing into the carriage and arranging the ribbons in her hand.

Lydia shook her head and swallowed. She hoped that she would not be expected to drive. Horses did not particularly like to go where she told them. She supposed it was because she could never remember which way to pull the reins. It would be much simpler if the animal would just go in the direction she pointed, but every time she tried that, the horse went the opposite way. Horses were very uncooperative creatures, and as such, she had decided that riding was not an activity she should like to do very often and that carriage driving was best left to a coachman — someone who had been trained in directing horses.

"You should learn," said Aunt Tess. "It is quite enjoyable to be so independent. If I could but manage the hitching and unhitching of the cattle myself, I would be able to go here and there whenever I wanted much more easily." She flicked her hand and called to the horse — Maggie, as it was named — and with a squeak of a wheel, the gig began its journey.

"Mrs. Bell, whom we will see first, is quite old, and her

son is away on the continent," Aunt Tess explained as they drove away from the house. "She had been staying with her brother, but he passed away just a little over a month ago. She has a servant who is unwilling to leave her, so she is not completely alone, but her income is so little, and her son so far away, that I have chosen her as my particular project."

Lydia watched in amazement as Aunt Tess slowed the gig and turned the horses onto a small lane to their left. Driving did not look so difficult when Aunt Tess did it. Perhaps one day, Lydia would try it, but not for some time.

"Mrs. Bell's eyes are still sharp and her fingers, though not so nimble as they once were, are still adept at sewing," Aunt Tess continued. "As I am sure you can imagine, supplies for such pleasurable activities are often lacking, what with there being no funds to purchase them and few old dresses being available to repurpose. So, today, I have a small packet of material and thread made up for her. She likes to make quilts for the new babies in the church. It is always a gift that is presented after their christening. Mrs. Ross — she is the wife of Mr. Ross, the steward at Aldwood Abbey — will have a new baby in a month's time or so. This material and some more that I will take to her when I call next week will be used for that child's quilt."

She leaned toward Lydia and spoke more softly. "I have the full amount of supplies at home, but Mrs. Bell would be offended to be given such a large gift all at once. There is a pride that does not diminish as quickly as a need arises. As a mistress, you must be aware of such things and be gentle in your approach. Provide what you can, but do not do so to the harm of the receiver. A spirit is a fragile thing." And not so easily repaired, she added to herself as she gave Lydia a sidelong look. She was grateful that Lydia seemed willing to learn, but she was not so foolish as to believe that a spirit so put upon by careless words and lack of care would be easily restored. She smiled as Lydia took a small pad of paper from her reticule and peeked surreptitiously at what Lydia was writing.

Help without harm. Consider the spirit.

Aunt Tess smiled and returned her focus to the road, satisfied that not only was Lydia an eager pupil; she was also a diligent one.

Lydia wrote the note as neatly as she could while moving in a carriage. She knew that her mind was perfectly capable of learning a myriad of new things, but she also knew that to have so many things told to her in quick succession would make it difficult to remember them all. Not even Elizabeth would be able to remember everything, although Lydia was confident she would remember more than her sister would.

She smiled to herself. It was actually something she had tested on a regular basis. Mama would give Elizabeth a list of things to get when in town. Jane would write them down, of course, for Jane always did what was proper, but

Elizabeth would insist that she did not need a list. Invariably, however, when the list would be checked before going home, Elizabeth would have forgotten at least one item. Elizabeth needed the list, but Lydia did not. She would always remember every item, but Lydia never mentioned it, of course. Why should she? Elizabeth would listen to no one but Jane.

In her quest to learn to be a proper mistress of an estate, Lydia would not be like Elizabeth. With this list, Lydia would make certain that she remembered every important detail. There would not be a better mistress of an estate in all of Derbyshire — and that included the mistress of Pemberley.

"Who will we see after Mrs. Bell?" Lydia asked.

"We must stop to see that Old Mr. Atkins is not in need of anything, and then we will move on to the Thompsons and Frasers. There is no particular thing we will be providing them aside from a friendly face and a few moments of conversation. However, the children might like you to read to them, and I did tuck a book or two in next to our lunch." She glanced at Lydia. "You have read to children before, have you not?'

Lydia nodded her head. "I have, on occasion, attended my mother on tenant calls and would often play with the children or read to them."

"Excellent. Then you shall read to the Thompson and Fraser children," said Aunt Tess. She was glad to know that Lydia was not without some training concerning the duties required of the wife of a man in possession of an estate. Aunt Tess had wished to ask exactly what training Lydia had received, but not wanting to either offend with such a question or receive information which Lydia thought to be true but was, in fact, false, Aunt Tess had chosen to assume the girl next to her had no training whatsoever.

"Would a mistress be allowed to read to the children on a visit, or would it be considered poor form if she did?" Lydia turned questioning eyes toward her teacher. Mama had never read to the children, but Mama had always been accompanied by Lydia. She did not know if Mama would have read to the children had she been alone. Lydia certainly hoped that being the mistress and not just the daughter would not keep her from such a delightful task.

"She might," said Aunt Tess. "Her first duty is, of course, to the lady of the house, but then, if everyone is in agreement, a story to the children might be just the thing to provide the lady of the house with a moment or two to see to a task while the children are occupied." She pulled back on the reins and slowed Maggie so that the gig could be turned into a small drive up to a tiny cottage. "You may be the mistress of a grand house who employs many servants, but you are — even in such a position — to be a servant to those under your care. You must provide for them, in part, that which they cannot provide for themselves or, at the very least, add some small amount of pleasantness to their lives. Read to the children. Deliver food or clothes. Help knead a loaf of bread, or..." Aunt Tess drew her horse to a stop and motioned toward the boxes of flowers that sat beside the front door to the cottage, "get up to your elbows in dirt and plant a flower or two. They are very cheery are they not?"

"These are like yours," said Lydia.

"That is because they used to be mine. But, a great darkness had fallen on Mrs. Bell when her brother died, and these brought a bit of light. My garden did not need that light nearly so much as Mrs. Bell's front step." Aunt Tess climbed down from the carriage and secured the horses. "I have a jug of water next to my package of cloth. Would you be so good as to pour it out on the boxes?"

"Of course. I will do it straight away," Lydia replied as she hurriedly scratched another note in her book.

Be light.

Chapter 14

Marcus stopped just outside the door to his father's draw-ing room. He had been at his desk when Aunt Tess and Lydia had arrived and had wished to leave his papers and make his way to this room as soon as he had seen the horses stop, but he had not. His brother's words concern-ing his need to decide if he would give Lydia to another to protect or take on the task himself had held Marcus in his chair. He was determined to attempt to view her just as another lady making a call on his father, which she would be should she marry another. He would sit and work his numbers and be at ease knowing that his father was enter-tained.

It had, however, proven to be an exercise in futility. Marcus had added and check the same row of numbers three times and gotten a different answer on each attempt. Not thinking of Lydia when he knew her to be there was difficult, but not thinking of her while hearing her laugh was more than he could endure, and so, he had finally closed his books and taken himself down the hall to his father's room.

"And this one can move here?"

His father had left the door open just a bit, and Marcus could see Lydia sliding a chess piece across the board.

"Ah, you are a quick study." It was funny how the pride in his father's voice was echoed in his own heart.

"Oh, yes," said Lydia, tilting her head and looking at the board with her brows furrowed. "I have a very good memory."

Marcus smiled and shook his head. To anyone else, her comments would sound boastful, but to him, they were not. She was merely stating a fact. He watched her select a knight, her fingers resting lightly on its head as she tilted her head and pursed her lips in thought. It was an enchanting expression.

"This one hops, does it not?" she asked, after a moment.

"Yes," replied his father, grinning widely. "It jumps just like a real horse might when it comes to a hedge or gate, but in which direction?"

Lydia pulled the corner of her lip between her teeth and moved the piece ahead two and to the right one. She was just about to remove her finger from the top of the horse's head when her eyes widened, and her lips formed an *o* before sliding into a smile. "That was a trick question," she accused playfully. "The knight can move in any direction

it chooses as long as it follows the pattern of two and one
or one and two."

Mr. Dobney clapped his hands in delight. "You know
them all, and with just one lesson. Well done, Miss Lydia.
Well done. We shall have to play a game next time you
call." He leaned forward and lowered his voice just a bit.
"Do you suppose Aunt Tess will allow it?"

Lydia returned his smile and darted a look at Aunt Tess.
"I shall ask, but I have so many things to learn that I cannot
guarantee it."

He patted her hand which lay on the table next to the
chessboard. "I shall talk to her. A day spent with my
housekeeper might be well-worth your while. You did say
you are learning to be a mistress of an estate, did you not?"

Lydia nodded.

"So it seems a fitting lesson." He winked. "And then I
can instruct Mrs. Yardley that you will need to spend an
hour or so with me."

"What are you planning?" asked Aunt Tess with a
laugh.

Marcus watched as Lydia excitedly told Aunt Tess
about the plan to spend the day at Aldwood Abbey learning from Mrs. Yardley. Her smile was mesmerizing.

"What are you watching?"

Marcus jumped at the sound of his sister's voice.

"Nothing," he answered far too quickly as heat crept up
his neck at being discovered watching Lydia.

Mary Ellen folded her arms and raised a brow in disbelief. "Nothing?" she repeated. "Is the room empty?"

Marcus shrugged.

A smile spread across Mary Ellen's face as she heard what sounded very much like a squeal of delight from beyond the door. She tucked her arm through his. "I believe that is something or more accurately, someone. Come along, Brother," she said, pushing the door open and drawing him into the room with her.

"You sound happy, Miss Lydia," Mary Ellen said as she pulled her brother across the room with her to take a seat near Aunt Tess.

"Oh, I am."

Marcus glanced at her quickly before averting his eyes. She was indeed happy from the expression on her face.

"Miss Lydia is going to spend a full day at Aldwood Abbey to learn the duties of a housekeeper," Mr. Dobney supplied the explanation of his guest's delight.

"She is not coming so that you might secure a partner for chess?" asked Marcus with a grin as he took his seat.

Lydia's smile faded somewhat, and she cast a worried look at Aunt Tess.

It was not the reply Marcus had expected, and for a moment, he considered taking himself back to his study. Perhaps, she did need someone else. Coming in here was a mistake. He could not think clearly with her there in front of him. How was he to make a decision about whether he should be the one to marry her or not when she drove all rational thought from his head?

He had been battling that question of whether or not to offer for Lydia for a full day now. He was certain his horse had not appreciated the slow meandering walk they had taken this morning instead of the fast gallop as was his normal habit. He had over poured his cup of tea at breakfast and paced rings around his office. Accounts were not adding up, and he had spent far too many hours staring blankly at the chair in front of his desk, trying not to imagine her there. And his pillow had suffered a great deal of abuse as he had attempted to find a comfortable sleeping position last night — one that would allow him to close his eyes without seeing her. If he were to be honest, his whole world seemed to be at sixes and sevens since his annoying brother and Mr. Williams had cornered him with their suggestion.

"My boy knows how desperate I am for a good game," said Mr. Dobney.

Aunt Tess laughed. "I feared I might not get away so quickly as I had planned when you brought out your pieces, for I know how much you love to play. I should hope that while Miss Lydia is here, she will be allowed to be of service to you in such a fashion. A mistress' life is not all duty. There must be time for enjoyment as well."

Lydia's smile grew again, and Marcus's mind felt more at ease. He settled a bit more comfortably into his chair but kept his eyes from resting for any extended period of time on Lydia's lovely face or figure.

They spent a few more minutes in conversation about the estate and the calls that had been made earlier that day, and then, when Aunt Tess stood, Lydia followed suit.

"We have one more call to make before we return home," Aunt Tess explained.

"I have had a lovely time," said Lydia, extending her hand to Mr. Dobney. "I have always wished to learn about chess."

He took her hand and held it between both of his. "It has been a pleasure, Miss Lydia. You were a very capable student." He squeezed her hand tightly and then let it go. "I will arrange a day with Mrs. Yardley and send word." Then, he turned to Marcus. "Do not scurry back to your desk. See our guests to their carriage."

"Yes, sir," Marcus said with a chuckle. "I promise; I was not going to scurry anywhere." He moved to extend an arm to Aunt Tess, but his sister had already claimed it. "Miss Lydia," he said instead, offering her his arm. She hesitated and then placed her hand very lightly on his arm. There was something that was not right in her responses today. Had they told her of the list? Did she know that his name was on it and did not wish to encourage his suit? The thought made him scowl.

~*~*~

Lydia let out an exasperated huff as the gig moved away

from Aldwood Abbey. Marcus had seen them arrive and not joined them for tea — she knew he had seen them, for she had seen him at the window. Then, when he finally did join them, he had nearly ruined her planned day with his father, and he only spoke of trivial things while, just like yesterday, looking everywhere in the room but at her. Her heart skipped a beat, and she drew a quick deep breath as the reason for his avoidance became clear. He knew she must marry, and now he avoided her presence. There was only one reason.

She placed a hand on Aunt Tess's arm. "He does not want me." Her voice was nearly a whisper. "I am not good enough." The pain of the thought pinched her throat making the words difficult to form.

Aunt Tess drew the gig on the side of the road and stopped. "Whatever makes you say that?"

Lydia shrugged. "He is no different from every other gentleman I have met. They flirt. They tease. They tell you they like your hair and your eyes, and then, when someone," she sighed deeply to cover a sob that wished to be released, "usually my mother, mentions anything that might sound like marriage, I am no longer their favourite. I am no more than a passing entertainment." She clenched her teeth and drew in a breath through her nose to steady her nerves before she continued. "They think me silly and stupid, but I am not."

"Oh, my dear," Aunt Tess wrapped an arm around

Lydia's shoulders, "I am certain Marcus thinks you neither silly nor stupid."

Lydia lifted one shoulder in a sad half-shrug.

"It matters not. I am not what he wants." Tears filled her eyes. She had thought him interested in her. He had looked at her as if he wished to kiss her. He had pulled at his neckcloth. She had been so certain he might like her. He had even acted the part of a friend. A tear slipped down her cheek, and she drew a shuddering breath, willing her tears not to fall and her sorrow to be gone, but neither would listen.

She had thought him different from all the others, but he was not. He only wished for a kiss just like they did. She swiped at another tear that made its escape and rolled down her cheek. Well, he, like the others, would do without. Only her husband would get her kisses. She was pretty and, therefore, her kisses were more valuable than most. They would not be given away!

Aunt Tess watched the softness leave Lydia's features, and her heart ached but not nearly so much as she suspected Lydia's did.

Lydia pulled her lips into a smile as she wiped the remaining tears away from her eyes. She would not allow her heart to break for him. She would not. She straightened her shoulders. "Are there other gentlemen in the area who might wish a silly wife?" There was a hint of bitterness in her tone.

"You will not be a silly wife. You will be a fine mistress of a grand estate."

Lydia shook her head and wiped at her eyes again. Those tears were determined to make her eyes red and her nose swollen.

Aunt Tess patted Lydia's knee and called to Maggie to resume their journey. "Shall we return home?"

"No." Lydia lifted her chin. She could feign happiness. It was not the first time she had done so when she would have rather cried. "We have a duty to do."

Aunt Tess cast a sidelong glance at Lydia. The girl did seem determined. Perhaps a visit to the Ross's would be just the thing. "Are you prepared to read to the little ones again?"

"I am," Lydia replied with a nod. "I enjoy it."

And she did enjoy it. All three stories were read to the Ross's three young children as Aunt Tess talked with their mama about how she was faring and what still needed to be done before the arrival of child number four. Then, with three little people to escort their new friend, Miss Lydia, to her carriage, the ladies said their farewells and returned to Kympton.

Chapter 15

That night, after a sullen evening, Marcus spent two hours wrestling his pillow and his thoughts before he gave up trying to sleep and lit a candle. Pulling on his robe, he paced the length of his room for a few minutes, hoping the movement would distract him and weary his body enough to accept sleep.

He stopped at the window and looked out toward his mother's cottage. The moon was still about half its fullness, so he could see the shadows of the stand of trees that signalled the edge of the cottage garden. He smiled sadly as he remembered finding Lydia in the sitting room, curled up in a chair, attempting to not be seen. She had been a disheveled, defiant mess. He chuckled at how she had attempted to thwart his attempts to return her to her family.

He sank down on the window seat. Somewhere between that cottage and Willow Hall, she had wormed her way into his heart — never, he feared, to be removed. He blew out a breath, clapped his hands on his thighs, and pushed up from his seat.

Taking the candle from beside his bed, he made his way out of his room and down the stairs. Perhaps the numbers in his ledgers would be more cooperative now than they had been earlier, and perhaps the activity would cause his eyes to droop. If it did not, there was more than one tome dedicated to agriculture that might do the job admirably. There was a sofa in his study. He would sleep there.

He stopped outside his study and noted the light that shone from beneath his father's door. His father's candle was nearly always out before Marcus had made his final rounds of the house each night. He should check to make sure the candle had not been left burning.

He crossed to the door and knocked softly before pushing the door open. "Are you well?" he asked, seeing his father sitting up in his bed.

"Merely pondering life," he replied with a smile. He patted the bed. "Join me."

Marcus sighed and joined his father in the bed. "I have had my fill of pondering."

"I want grandchildren."

The comment took Marcus by surprise. "Philip will have a child soon."

His father nodded. "By spring."

"You know?"

Mr. Dobney chuckled. "I do. Philip could not keep the

news to himself, so he confided in me." He shrugged. "I suppose he wished me to know in case ..." The idea of mortality hung in the air, heavy, and unwelcome to both. Finally, after a few moments of contemplation, he continued. "But Philip's child will not sleep in Aldwood's nursery nor run through the garden or fill these halls with laughter every day. Only yours will. I want grandchildren. Here. With me."

Marcus considered the idea of youngsters chasing each other down the stairs and out into the garden as he and Philip had done. "It would be pleasant," he admitted.

"I remember holding you for the first time. I was terrified. You were so small and helpless. Everything I did suddenly grew in importance because it affected not only me but also you and your children." He patted Marcus's hand that lay on the bed between them. "My knees had not shaken that much since the day I asked your grandfather for permission to marry your mother."

"Were you nervous about being accepted" Marcus turned questioning eyes toward his father.

"No. I knew I would be accepted both by her and her father." He smiled. "She was beautiful, but so –" He seemed to be searching for the word.

"Spirited?"

"She was that, and illogical at times. Very much like Miss Lydia, but with a shade — and only a shade — more training. I feared for Aldwood Abbey."

Marcus blinked in surprise. "You did?"

Mr. Dobney nodded. "Very much so. My mother had predicted that the place would crumble around my feet from neglect and over expenditure, and my father insisted our children would be indulged to the point of ruin. However, they only saw the bright, spirited side your mother displayed in public. I had seen her heart. She was not what others thought her, and she proved it time and again over the years." He patted Marcus's hand once again. "Have I told you the story about how your mother's cottage came to be?"

"Not today." Marcus chuckled. He had heard the story many times over the years. "It was a wedding gift. A place where you could begin your life together without grandmother and grandfather's interference."

"It was a bit more than that. It was where your mother could prove to them that I had not made a mistake in choosing her, which is why she insisted that the cottage become yours — solely and completely yours — on your wedding day."

"What?" Marcus had not heard this part before. "It is not just part of the estate."

His father shook his head. "No, it was hers to do with as she willed. She said that you were very much like me, and she knew that one day, you would find a girl who no one else would see as capable, and she would steal your heart and you, being the cautious sort, would need a place to let her find her feet."

Marcus shook his head in disbelief. "So, when I came home with a tale about a spirited young lady –"

"Whom you found in your mother's cottage and who brought a light to your eyes as you spoke, I knew that she would be my daughter." He pulled himself up straighter in the bed. "And then you returned to the cottage and cleaned it — ah — the final piece fell into place. Someone had finally pushed you past your guilt in not spending that last visit at the cottage with your mother."

"Lydia scolded me about not caring for my inheritance, and then, I feared she might need it as a refuge should she flee Willow Hall again." He chuckled. "For some reason, I wanted her to approve of me if she did return to the cottage."

"She watches you with such admiration," his father said softly.

"What?" Marcus had not noticed any such thing.

"When you are not looking at her so that she might bat her lashes at you, she watches you with admiration. Even today, she watched you." He took his son's hand. "I want grandchildren, and I want them to be yours and Miss Lydia's." His grip tightened on Marcus's hand. "Do you think her a fool?"

"No!" Marcus had not known her for long before he knew she was not a fool — perhaps foolish at times, but never a fool. She lacked guidance, and that was something that she was now receiving from Aunt Tess.

"Is she incapable of learning?"

Marcus shook his head. "She is quite bright."

"Do you love her?"

Marcus swallowed audibly and faced the question that had plagued him for the last day and a half.

"You have seen her here," his father continued. "Can you imagine another in her place, sitting in my room, stitching, or playing chess? Do you wish to stroll through the garden with anyone else?"

Marcus shook his head. He could not.

"Then marry her. Aldwood Abbey will not crumble in ruins, and your children will have a loving mother. But most importantly, your heart will be complete."

~*~*~

"Marcus," Darcy took a seat next to Marcus on the bench in the churchyard. "Are you waiting for Philip?"

Marcus shook his head and lifted the small book in his hand. "Reading."

Darcy looked around at the church behind them and the graves before them. "This seems a strange place to be reading."

Marcus laughed. "I suppose it would appear to be." He let the book fall open on his lap so that Darcy could see the contents were written in a fine feminine hand. "It was my mother's. I found it at her cottage this morning when I was seeing to some matters of upkeep."

"Harris mentioned you had finally returned to it." Darcy's tone was understanding. There were places at Pemberley to which he had not returned for several months after the passing of each parent. The memories were too great and caused too much pain at first. Now, however, those places brought a smile because of the memories they stirred.

"The cottage is mine as soon as I marry." Marcus flipped to the back of the book and passed it to Darcy, pointing to a section that told about how his mother expected him to need a place for his wife to find her feet.

"She expected you to marry someone who needed training?"

Marcus chuckled at Darcy's inability to hide his surprise. "She was not wrong."

Darcy passed the book back to Marcus. "You are planning to marry?"

"I am. If I can convince her to accept me." He tucked the book in his pocket.

"I did not know you had been courting anyone." There was a hint of a question in Darcy's voice as if he wished to ask who the young lady was but did not wish to pry.

Marcus chuckled again. "Neither did I until my brother pointed it out to me. I had thought I was just being a friend, but a friend would be willing to see her happy with another and that I cannot do." He could tell by the widening of Darcy's eyes that his friend had deciphered who the young lady was. Marcus nodded in reply to the unspoken question. "If all goes well, we will be brothers."

"Forgive me, but she is so young — the same age as Georgiana!"

Again, Marcus nodded. Her youth had been his first argument with himself. She was young, but she did not have the leisure of time to find a husband. "She is also on the verge of ruination. How long do you suppose it will be once she is home that the tale of her adventure falls on the right ears and is spread far and wide, leaving her without the slightest hope of finding a good match?"

"But a silly wife, Marcus? You would tie yourself to a silly wife?"

Marcus closed his eyes and swallowed the anger that rose in his throat at the comment. A response such as he wished to give would serve no purpose other than to appease his need to defend Lydia and would quite possibly drive away a friend.

"What do you know of her?" He was certain some of the anger he was trying to contain must have come through in his words, for Darcy studied his face carefully before replying.

"Remember that you have asked, and I am only answering." Darcy waited until Marcus gave a sharp nod of his head. "She is a flirt –"

"Apparently," interrupted Marcus, "batting one's lashes and giggling among other things are part of the female arsenal and must be practiced so that when a man of worth — someone who can provide a secure home with adequate staff — catches her fancy, the lady is prepared to snare him. You have been in enough ballrooms to know ladies use such techniques."

Darcy's mouth hung open slightly.

"What else do you think you know of her?"

Darcy shrugged. "She puts herself forward too much and too loudly." He turned to Marcus as if expecting an explanation.

"That is not something to which I can speak with any degree of confidence other than to say I have seen no evidence of it since her arrival. I suspect that it is to some degree her mother's doing, as well as an attempt to outshine her sisters. She has had neither mother nor sisters present when I have seen her in company."

Darcy tipped his head to one side and drawing his brows together in concern, asked with a degree of trepidation, "Do you not fear she will become her mother?"

"Do you fear Miss Elizabeth will?"

It was not the reply Darcy expected from the way his eyebrows rose so high and so quickly. "Miss Elizabeth is not like her mother, but Miss Lydia is."

"Why do you suppose Miss Elizabeth is not like her mother? Is it an innate tendency to be more like her father or is it the fact that her father has nurtured that tendency? Do you not fear that since Miss Elizabeth is like her father, she will eventually become as withdrawn and unengaged with her children as he seems to be with his? I am speaking, of course, with limited knowledge, but I do not think I do him too great an injustice."

"Miss Elizabeth may be like her father, but she sees his failings. I cannot imagine her becoming as you have described."

"Nor would you allow it," said Marcus firmly. He knew enough about Darcy to know that there would be no reason for Elizabeth to retreat from her family.

"Indeed, I would not," said Darcy. "Not that such a circumstance would ever present itself."

"No," agreed Marcus, "it would not. Your marriage will, I imagine, be quite different from that of Mr. and Mrs. Bennet. For one, you are not the sort to give people their way just to be rid of them." Marcus could see that Darcy was about to object to some portion of what he had said, and he suspected it was the disparagement of Mr. Bennet, so he added, "That is what Miss Lydia says occurs. I should not like to think it true of any man, but the grief in her words was too great to be taken as anything less than accurate."

Shock passed quickly over Darcy's face before turning to concern. Marcus knew it was time to lay before his friend all he knew about Lydia. "You have not seen her as

I have. You have not heard her fears or seen her hide them behind a smile. Did you know she reads mythology or that she wishes to learn chess, which my father has agreed to teach her?" He chuckled. "She learned the pieces and their uses in just one lesson. Mary Ellen required three and still occasionally needs to be reminded."

"I did not know," said Darcy. "I would never have expected her to harbour such...such..."

Darcy seemed lost for the correct word, so Marcus supplied a few of his own. "Intelligence? Wit? Sense?"

"I do not wish to be rude," said Darcy, "but yes. She hides it well."

Marcus sighed and nodded his agreement. "She does." He shook his head. He was still surprised by his feeling for her. "I love her, Darcy. I would not have expected to, but I love her."

"Well, Philip once told me that love is — unexpected."

Marcus laughed. "He said the same to me. Who knew my little brother could be so wise."

He pushed up from the bench. "Were you planning to spend time with your parents or would you like to accompany me to Aunt Tess's house? I assume your lady is there with Lucy this afternoon?"

Darcy smiled and rose to join him. "She is, and I spent a few moments with my parents while you were reading." As they exited the churchyard and began their way down the street, Darcy asked, "You say Miss Lydia learned the chess pieces in one lesson?"

"Mmmhmm," replied Marcus, "and their purposes."

"Impressive," Darcy muttered. "What else might I not know of Miss Lydia?"

"She knew the reason for my horse's name, and her eyes are a rare mix of green and brown which makes them the prettiest in all of Hertfordshire." He purposefully mixed a sensible fact with one that was not just as Lydia might.

Darcy chuckled. "I will admit that knowing the meaning of your horse's name is notable, but I will have to disagree on the last part. I believe Elizabeth's eyes are far more beautiful."

Marcus clapped Darcy on the shoulder. "As you should, my friend. As you should."

Chapter 16

"Miss Idia." Three-year-old Susan Ross tugged at Lydia's skirt to gain her attention.

"Miss Lydia. L — Lydia," corrected Susan's brother Frank. "See. Put your tongue between your teeth." He made the sound of an L again.

Susan did as instructed and, with a bit of work and some more guidance from her brother, formed Lydia's name perfectly.

"You are a very good teacher," said Lydia with a smile for Frank before squatting down to speak with Susan. "A book? Do you wish to have your book read again?" It would be the third time the book had been read since Lydia arrived at the Ross home with Mr. Ross this morning. "Might I check on your mama before we begin" The little girl's head bobbed her agreement.

"I can check on Mama," Frank offered. He was trying so very hard to be a proper young gentleman and care for both his sisters and his mother. Lydia saw the wish to be of use in the worried eyes that he turned toward her as he made the suggestion.

"I had hoped you would keep Susan and Edith company for me. I do not wish to leave them unattended."

A smile spread across Frank's young eight-year-old face, and he took Susan's hand. "We can wait for Miss Lydia on the great stump." He turned his face toward Lydia. "It is a good place to read. Papa reads to us there sometimes, but Mama prefers the rocks near the stream. But Edith might get wet if we go to the stream. She likes to chase the little fish."

Six-year-old Edith scowled at her brother and folded her arms. "I would not get wet."

"You would," Frank retorted. "You always do. You do not know how to behave properly yet. Something catches your fancy, and you run away. It is foolish, you know."

"It is not foolish," said Lydia gently. She would not allow Edith to be called what Lydia's sisters and father had always called her. "She is curious."

"Getting wet when you should stay dry is foolish," insisted Frank.

He was right, Lydia supposed, but still she could not allow that word. "I will allow that it is not wise." Not wise sounded so much better than foolish. If one was not wise, she could still be smart. However, if one was foolish, there was no hope for her ever being intelligent. People did not allow for foolish girls to be anything but stupid.

"Are they not the same thing?" asked Frank. "If you are not wise, are you not foolish?"

Lydia shrugged one shoulder. "Would you wish to be called foolish?"

Frank blinked his eyes, and his lips parted just a bit as he shook his head.

"Then do not say it of another," Lydia kept her tone as gentle as she could, and she smiled at him. She wished him to learn, but she did not want to hurt him. Feelings were difficult things to mend.

"I believe we will read at the great stump." She winked at Edith. "I would find it challenging not to chase the fish myself, and I do not wish to have wet stockings. They are very uncomfortable." Lydia's heart nearly burst — in fact, she placed a hand on it to make sure it had not — when Edith's scowl became a smile. Lydia was not certain she had ever received such a smile of gratitude.

"Go on then," she said to Frank. "I will not be long."

As they ran off toward where a very large tree had once stood, she called after them, "Mind your brother."

She was not certain why she felt compelled to shout such an instruction to them, but she did. She watched them for a moment longer to see them settled and then hurried into the house.

"Mrs. Ross," she said, peeking her head into the sitting room. "How are you feeling?"

Mrs. Ross turned her face from watching her children through the window. "You are very good with them."

"Thank you," replied Lydia.

Mrs. Ross held out a hand toward Lydia. "Would you help me up? I find I would like to take a small walk around the room, and then return to my seat with a glass of water. I am feeling so much better than I was."

"The room is no longer spinning?" Lydia assisted Mrs. Ross to her feet. Mr. Ross, with Susan hanging onto his coat tails, had been concerned about his wife when Lydia had met him at the shop on High Street. He had mentioned how she became dizzy and ill when getting close to the time when the baby was expected. As Susan peeked from under her father's coat and smiled at Lydia, Lydia had been unable to resist offering her help.

"No, it is standing completely still," said Mrs. Ross, "Not a stick of furniture has wobbled in nearly half an hour. I am, however, still feeling a tightening of the muscles in my belly."

"You are certain you do not require the midwife?" Lydia asked in concern.

Mrs. Ross shook her head. "This happened before Edith was born as well. She was a few weeks early." She rubbed her belly as she slowly walked around the room on Lydia's arm. "I expect this one will be here before long, but not today."

"Are you anxious?" Lydia asked softly. She did not wish

to be rude, but she was curious. She had not been with any woman who was about to give birth.

Mrs. Ross laughed lightly. "I have done this three times already, so I do know what to expect, but yes, I still get anxious and excited." She squeezed Lydia's arm. "However, I am curious about what this one will be. Will Frank finally have a brother or continue to be outnumbered? Keeping the thought of meeting this little one foremost in my mind keeps my concerns in the back."

"Do you wish for a boy or a girl?"

Mrs. Ross sighed. "The correct answer is for a healthy child no matter the gender, but to be honest, Frank would dearly love a brother, and I would be glad to see him receive one. However, whether his wish is granted or declined, I will love this child as I do my others."

"Frank is a good boy," said Lydia as she assisted Mrs. Ross in returning to her seat.

"That he is," Mrs. Ross agreed with a smile. "He wishes to be like his father."

Lydia arranged Mrs. Ross' pillows and the footstool. "He takes great care of his sisters."

"He does — much to Edith's dismay at times." Mrs. Ross chuckled. "She is a free spirit. Curious and quick. She will accomplish great things."

Lydia could see that in Edith there was a determination that seemed indomitable.

"Frank has not yet realized his sister's curiosity is a

strength to be nurtured, but I believe, he will." She smiled at Lydia. "What you told him just now will help. They were wise words."

Lydia felt her cheeks grow warm. She had never been praised for giving instruction nor has she ever been called wise. She was glad that Edith had such a mother, and she determined that should she ever be given the chance to be a mother herself, she would be like Mrs. Ross, accepting of her children's differences and viewing them as strengths to be nurtured.

"My sister will be here tomorrow," said Mrs. Ross. "I had hoped she would arrive before I began feeling like this, but one can never tell for certain when it will begin. Each child is different."

Lydia filled Mrs. Ross' glass with water from the decanter on the table near the door. "Are you and your sister close?"

Mrs. Ross smiled. "We are now, but we were not always so. Age and experience can change the dynamic between sisters and brothers. Frank and Susan are close, and I expect will always remain so, but Edith drives poor Frank to distraction. She is lively while he is serious, but he, no matter her antics, would protect her with his life. He is that sort, you know." She looked out the window to where her children were waiting for Lydia. "He sees the danger in her curiosity, and it is his love for her that causes him to worry about her safety when she will not worry about it for herself."

"They are lovely children," said Lydia.

Mrs. Ross nodded. "I have been blessed." She took a sip of her water and then nodded toward the window. "I think you might be needed soon. I see that Edith is crossing her arms which means Frank is being demanding." She laughed. "Oh, I shall delight to see what sort of husband, Edith finally snares with that determined spirit!" She continued to chuckle. "I imagine it will be someone very much like her brother."

"But would that not be a difficult match?" Lydia asked in surprise. "Would they not argue and fight?"

Mrs. Ross shrugged. "I am certain there would be some argument, but like I said, Frank loves her and will see to her safety when she will not do so herself. That is the sort of gentleman she shall need. One who gives guidance out of love."

Lydia had not considered such a thing before. She had not considered that scolding and disapproving could be the way some people showed love. The idea was startling.

She peeked out the window at the children after she had made certain Mrs. Ross did not require anything else.

"They are blessed," she said before stepping out of the door to the room. "You are a very good mother." And then, without waiting for Mrs. Ross to reply, she returned to her charges.

~*~*~

Marcus dropped into a chair, his legs not willing to allow him to stand at the news Aunt Tess had just shared. "Missing? What do you mean missing?"

"Exactly what I said," Aunt Tess replied, her tone sharper than normal. She peered out the window again. She had been watching out that window for an hour already. "Miss Lydia is not here. She is missing. Lucy and Philip have gone to High Street to see if she is there and has just gotten distracted by the shops."

She turned from the window with a sigh. "I sent her to place an order for lace. Mrs. Smith will be wanting a bit for the cap she is making, and I wished to provide it." She picked up a package from the side table. "The lace has arrived, but Miss Lydia has not."

"Have you shown her the direction to the inn?" Marcus's heart was beating wildly in his chest. She had promised to not leave until after Michaelmas, but then that was before she had been told about needing to marry. She had been acting peculiar yesterday. But she had promised to visit his father. Surely, she would not leave without seeing his father.

Aunt Tess shook her head. "No, I have not, and she has not taken her bags. All her things are still in her room."

A modicum of relief crept into Marcus's mind.

"She has found something of interest," said Elizabeth, "and forgotten all else. It would not be the first time."

Aunt Tess's brows furrowed. "I cannot agree. She was so eager to learn and do well."

"Lydia?" Jane's question was soft, but there was no mistaking the surprise in her voice.

Aunt Tess nodded. "There was a moment after we left Aldwood Abbey where I thought she might become reticent, but she did not."

"What do you mean?" Marcus had taken up Aunt Tess's spot at the window watching toward High Street, so that he could see if Philip and Lucy returned alone or not.

"Oh, she was upset by something, and I thought she might lose her resolve." Aunt Tess shook her head. "But she did not. She dried her tears, put on a smile, and entertained the Ross children as if nothing had disturbed her."

Marcus's heart sank. In the short time he had known Lydia, he had witnessed her ability to hide her feelings behind a smile on more than one occasion. And so he knew that a smile did not mean all was well.

"But this morning," Aunt Tess continued, "she was up and ready to go about our duties before I was."

"Lydia?" Elizabeth was incredulous. "Lydia does not rise early."

Aunt Tess shrugged. "She has willingly risen early the last two mornings."

"Lydia?" Elizabeth asked once more.

"They are alone," said Marcus. "She is not with them."

"Oh, dear," said Aunt Tess, coming to join him at the window to see the truth of the situation with her own eyes.

"I will ride toward Aldwood Abbey," he said taking his hat. "Perhaps she wished for a game of chess." He knew it sounded silly. It was a foolish idea, but he needed to be out and looking for her. The skies would not stay bright for very much longer.

"Lydia does not play chess," said Elizabeth.

"My father was teaching her," said Marcus.

As he ducked out of the room, he could hear Aunt Tess telling Elizabeth of Lydia's lesson yesterday. Hearing Darcy's voice joining with Aunt Tess's brought a smile to Marcus's face as he swung up onto his horse.

He looked up the street and decided that instead of setting off directly toward home, he would confirm that Lydia was indeed not in any shop on High Street.

Chapter 17

Marcus took a ride toward the church and around again toward the main road into Kympton from Willow Hall. He remembered telling Lydia how that road wrapped around, and though he had been in the churchyard earlier, it was still possible that she might be somewhere along that lane, doing what he did not know, but he felt he must check.

Not finding her there, he decided that the cottage where he had first found her might be a good place to begin his search. She still had his key, after all. So, he turned and rode toward Willow Hall. He had just ridden past the Abbots' home when the thought struck him that Lydia might have stopped there for a rest, so he turned and went back.

"Ho, there, Mr. Dobney!" called Mr. Abbot from the garden, croquet mallet in hand. He approached the hedge that bordered the side garden as Marcus drew his horse close. "I am afraid you have missed all the young people as they have taken the carriage to visit Mrs. Barnes and Mrs.

Dobney. They left about an hour ago and do not plan to return for at least another hour."

Marcus knew it would probably have been more polite to dismount to have a conversation, but he did not wish to waste time. Who knew where someone like Lydia might wander and in what danger she might find herself! "I was just there. Are you certain none have returned?"

"Yes, none have returned." Mr. Abbot's face grew concerned. "Is something amiss?"

By this time, Mr. Gardiner and Mr. Bennet had joined Mr. Abbot at the hedge.

"I went to call on Miss Lydia," he shifted uneasily in his saddle. He probably should have requested permission from her father before going to call on her, but in all honesty, his mind had been so intent on his decision that the detail of requesting permission had completely been overlooked.

"Indeed," said Mr. Bennet, a smile curling his lips in a knowing smile. "Did you have any particular purpose in mind?"

Marcus slid from his horse. "I did." He stood between his horse and the hedge. "But she was not there."

Mr. Bennet tipped his head to the side. "Was she gone out on a call?"

Marcus shrugged and shook his head. "No one knows. She went on an errand for Aunt Tess and did not return. I was riding in this direction in hopes of finding her."

"They have checked all the shops?" Mr. Bennet handed his mallet to Mr. Abbot and began around the hedge. "She has been known to lose track of time when distracted by the goods in the stores. The milliner's shop is her particular favorite."

Marcus rubbed the back of his neck with his hand. "Philip and Lucy checked. She is not there."

"I will return," Mr. Bennet said to Mr. Gardiner and Mr. Abbot.

"Do you wish for us to assist you?" asked Mr. Abbot.

Mr. Bennet shook his head. "I do not know how you could."

Marcus was about to agree when he remembered that Lydia had called on several people yesterday. She had been particularly taken with Mrs. Bell. "If you would ride to Mrs. Bell's house," he said to Mr. Abbot. "She called there with Aunt Tess yesterday. She may have returned to tend the flowers."

"Who is Mrs. Bell?" questioned Mr. Bennet.

"An elderly lady whom Aunt Tess has taken on as a special project of sorts," Marcus explained.

Mr. Bennet pursed his lips and nodded his head. "Lydia always did enjoy making calls with her mother." He began walking toward the stable with Marcus following behind. "I am glad to hear Mrs. Barnes is taking Lydia along."

"I had thought to check at Aldwood Abbey," said Marcus. "My father was teaching Miss Lydia how to play chess, and if she got bored, I thought perhaps she might have ventured in that direction."

Mr. Bennet slowed his steps. "Does she like chess?"

"Very much from what I gathered from my father."

Mr. Bennet stood perfectly still. "I would have never expected her to like it. It requires remaining still and a good deal of concentration. I had not noted those qualities in her." There was a hint of something sad in his tone.

He once again began walking toward the stables. As they drew close, he called for a horse to be readied and then waited in the yard for the animal to be brought to him. He paced a small circle, head down, watching his boots. He stopped in front of Marcus.

"It makes sense with all the other things she has done recently. Strategy, manoeuvring — two skills that chess requires, and I did not realize she had." He chuckled. "Although I imagine her sisters have realized it to some extent. It is quite likely how she has gotten so much of what she wants." He shook his head. "My failures regarding her mount."

He looked back at Willow Hall. "Over the past few days, I have wondered how any of my daughters have turned out as well as they have. It certainly was not due in any large part to my efforts."

Marcus did not know exactly how to respond to such a statement. He had not seen much of Mr. Bennet's daughters, aside from Lydia. Elizabeth had spent some time in his company and seemed assured of herself and her abilities — nearly too assured. He had not thought so at first but seeing and hearing how she thought of Lydia had done it. But then any who tried to disparage Lydia did not stand high in his opinion.

He turned his thoughts to Jane as Mr. Bennet mounted his horse. Jane had not spoken to Marcus more than a dozen times and had always been very proper and pleasant though a trifle dull, in his opinion. However, she was kind to Lydia, so she did stand a step ahead of Elizabeth.

But Lydia — he swung up onto his own horse — well, he had spent time with her and had heard her comments about both her father and her sisters — none of whom seemed to expect much of her. It was a thought that still baffled him. How had they lived with her for so many years and not seen her potential? He shook his head. He had nearly done the same. Was it not he who had dismissed the idea of marrying her just because he thought her unprepared? However, unprepared did not equate to unable.

"I would like to marry Miss Lydia," he blurted. "If I can find her and persuade her to accept me."

Shock mingled with pleasure suffused Mr. Bennet's face. "Do you know what you ask? She is headstrong and spoiled."

Marcus chuckled. It had been no easy task to persuade her to return to Willow Hall. "That she is, along with being far too young and unprepared to take on Aldwood

Abbey. But she is not incapable of learning. She is smart — if a bit illogical — and will get along fine with a bit of instruction."

Mr. Bennet's brows rose, a small bit of incredulity shone in his eyes. "You think very highly of her for all the trouble and stir she had caused. Your life will not be peaceful."

Marcus chuckled again. That was the most incongruous thing. He knew he would never find rest without the commotion Lydia might bring.

"My life — my heart — will not know peace without her liveliness, sir. I will own that there will be pouting and stamping of feet at times. A lady of Miss Lydia's leadership abilities does not often acquiesce without some show of displeasure — some argue and debate while others huff and stamp. And I am not one whit less stubborn, of that my father and siblings will assure you."

Mr. Bennet wore a half-smile, but his eyes still held their disbelief. "You think she will bow to your will and not harass you until she gets her way?"

Marcus blinked at the man, a sudden annoyance replacing his good humor. Did Mr. Bennet know nothing of his daughter?

"I believe she will," he answered. "If I can show her the love and respect she deserves, I believe, she will." He pressed his heels into his mount to speed him.

Mr. Bennet trotted up next to him. "I do love her."

Marcus turned his head in the man's direction. "As do I."

"But you do not think I respect her."

Marcus drew a deep breath and released it. He measured his words carefully before speaking. "Although I cannot speak with authority to that point at all, having only met you, I have not seen it evidenced. She came up with a plan to set things right and few, yourself included, seemed willing to consider it." He blew out another breath. His chances of being allowed to marry Lydia after such a comment were limited, he was certain.

"You prize honesty," said Mr. Bennet.

"I do," Marcus admitted.

"She schemes. Blackmail, forgery, manipulation — that is how she ended up needing a plan to set things right."

Frustration rose within Marcus. It was as if her father was attempting to convince him that he should not marry Lydia. "She has always been truthful with me."

"You have not known her long," Mr. Bennet cautioned.

"Sir," said Marcus, reining in his horse and turning to face Mr. Bennet, "I have known her long enough to know that my heart will not be at peace without her and her challenging ways. I will not be persuaded to drop my suit. If you do not wish for me to marry her, you must tell me directly."

Mr. Bennet's eyes narrowed as he studied Marcus. "And

if I deny you your suit, how long would it be before you would reach Scotland?"

Marcus smiled. Obviously, Mr. Bennet finally understood just how determined he was to marry Lydia. "That depends on how long it would take me to convince her to act so improperly. She has very unusual ideas about what is proper and what is not, so I cannot tell you exactly how long it would take." Marcus raised a brow, his expression becoming serious. "But, no matter how long it takes or if I have to beg Bingley to allow me the use of Netherfield and follow her back to Hertfordshire, I will convince her."

Mr. Bennet clucked his tongue and prodded his horse to walk. "I am satisfied," he said with a smile. "A man of less determination would stand little chance with Lydia. So perhaps, Mr. Dobney, as we are searching for her, you can tell me what you have to offer besides the mulishness to handle my daughter."

They rode and talked, each man getting to know the other better. Though Marcus was uncertain he could ever completely absolve Mr. Bennet of his neglect of a mind such as Lydia's, he did come to understand that the gentleman realized his errors with his daughters. And he could not deny that had Mr. Bennet taken the care he needed to take with Lydia, she would have never stumbled into Marcus's cottage and heart. So reluctantly, Marcus allowed that although Lydia had suffered for her father's neglect, the results were not all bad. And he knew that, if he should be so fortunate as to earn Lydia's acceptance, he would see that neglect replaced with regard.

Marcus took Mr. Bennet to Woodhead Cottage and showed him where Lydia had been discovered, then the two continued on to Aldwood Abbey and after an explanation to his father about Lydia being missing and a time of discussion between Mr. Bennet and Mr. Dobney concerning Lydia, Marcus and Mr. Bennet returned to Aunt Tess's house.

~*~*~

"You were unsuccessful?" Aunt Tess, who had taken a position once again at the window, asked as Marcus entered the room.

"I was," said Marcus taking a seat. "I have no idea where to look next." He ran his hands down his face as the desperation of the situation settled into his heart. "I had Mr. Abbot look for her at Mrs. Bell's, but she was not there. Is there anywhere else she might have gone?"

Aunt Tess turned from the window. "Mr. Harker's perhaps. She was going to read to — " she did not complete her thought as the noise of a horse and carriage caught her attention. She clapped her hands. "Oh, she has returned," she said as she scurried from the room.

Chapter 18

Lydia took Mr. Ross's hand and stepped down from his carriage.

"Thank you for your help, Miss Lydia. I know Frank thought he could handle the care of both his sisters and mother, and I am certain his sisters would have been well-behaved, but I would have worried."

"And Susan would have been a hindrance as you did your work. She did not seem willing to let you do what you needed when you were in town."

He chuckled. "Indeed. I had hoped she would be more complacent to just wait quietly, but it is not yet a strength."

"I was happy to help," said Lydia. And she meant it. She had not had such a pleasant time that she could remember. Reading stories on the great stump, foraging for bears in the garden, and attempting to catch fish in a net at the stream — with shoes and socks off and remaining dry — had been delightful, as had been assisting Mrs. Ross with her comfort. They had all accepted her as someone who was capable. It was a very singular feeling, and she knew she wanted to experience it again. Perhaps when she had a home and children of her own, she would feel that way again. She stood on the step and waved to Mr. Ross as he drove away.

"Lydia," Aunt Tess cried as she pulled open the door. "Come in, come in. We have been beside ourselves with worry." She looked down the street. "Was that Mr. Ross?"

The question startled Lydia. Of course, it was Mr. Ross. Had not her note explained that she would be at the Ross home until Mrs. Ness completed whatever it was that she was doing? Lydia had not paid particular attention to that bit of what Mr. Ross had told her, partly because there was a young girl winding circles around her father's legs and peeking at her from under her father's coat. "It was," she answered.

"I am so glad you are back." Aunt Tess put an arm around Lydia's shoulder and drew her into the house. "I only wish I had known where you had gone. I am afraid we have had people out looking."

Lydia's hands stopped their work of removing her bonnet. "But I left a note with the lace."

"Lydia," Elizabeth rushed into the hall. "Where have you been?"

Lydia rolled her eyes. Of course, it would be Elizabeth who would accost her first. Mary was not here to do it, so it must be Elizabeth.

Jane pulled Elizabeth back and gave her a stern look and

shake of her head. "Let Lydia freshen up, and then, she can tell us about her day."

Lydia smiled her appreciation to Jane. Jane could scold, but it was never so severe as Elizabeth or Mary.

"I would like to repair my hair and rinse my face," she looked toward Aunt Tess and waited for permission, which was readily granted.

No more than a quarter hour later, Lydia, feeling less dusty and wearing a clean dress, entered the sitting room. All conversation stopped as she did. A twisting began in her stomach much as it had on her return to Willow Hall. She swallowed her fear and, lifting her chin, made her way to sit next to Aunt Tess. At least whatever they were thinking about her had caused Marcus's eyes to not roam the room. This time his eyes were focused only on her as he held a teacup halfway to his lips. However, she could not tell exactly what his eyes were saying. They did not look angry like Elizabeth's had nor did they look sadly concerned like Jane's did.

"Was the lace what you wished?" Lydia began. It seemed silly to sit so silently and be stared at.

"It was," said Aunt Tess. "Your eye is as good as you claimed."

Lydia smiled. "It is a gift. Not everyone has an eye for the correct embellishments. One time Miss Maria was about to buy the entirely wrong lace for trimming her gloves, but I stopped her. She received so many compliments on those gloves, that she asked me my opinion the next time she needed to pick trim."

"Lace?" The question escaped Marcus before he could clamp his mouth shut on it.

A pain stabbed at Lydia's heart. Ah, that was his game, he was going to prove that she was not good enough. However, that was something she would not allow. She turned a patronizing smile on him. He had ignored her two days in a row and the first thing he was going to do was criticize her? She thought not!

"Yes, lace, Mr. Dobney. I would not expect you to understand."

"As if that is a deficiency," he muttered. Drat, his mouth's inability to stay closed!

"It would be if you were a lady, but you are not, so it is just an expected shortcoming of your gender."

His eyes narrowed. Why was she being so — so — angry? And with him? He was not the one that had disappeared without a trace for the second time since arriving in Derbyshire. He took a sip of his tea and then set is aside.

Good, she thought with a small toss of her head. He was put out as he should be.

Aunt Tess placed a hand on Lydia's arm. "Knowing the correct lace for a project is a good thing to know." She shot a displeased look at Marcus, warning him, Marcus suspected, to hold his tongue. "And after you found the perfect lace, what did you do?"

"I brought it here and placed it on the table along with a note letting you know that I would be assisting Mrs. Ross for the afternoon. She did not expect to feel so poorly this soon. Her sister is coming tomorrow, and Mrs. Ness was unable to be with her and the children all day — she is back now, however, which is why I was able to return earlier than I thought I would."

"There was no note," said Aunt Tess in a soft voice. "The lace was on the table as you said, but there was no note."

"But there was," Lydia insisted. "I left it right on the table next to the vase of flowers. I had it standing up like the peak of a roof. It looked very nice next to the flowers and the package of lace."

Elizabeth made a noise very like a huff, and Lydia scowled at her. "It was there."

Elizabeth raised a brow.

"There was a note both here and in Brighton," she said in answer to the unspoken accusation. She turned her eyes toward Aunt Tess again. Fear that she might be sent away early crept into her heart. She liked Aunt Tess and wished to learn all she could before she returned home to find a husband. "I swear to you, it was there."

"I did not see it."

Lydia rose and twisting her hands together, walked over to the table. "It was right here," she pointed to the spot on the table where she had left it. "Did a servant take it?"

Aunt Tess shook her head. "No one seemed to know where you were."

Lydia closed her eyes as a thought pushed its way into her mind. She drew a shaky breath. "I should have let Ruth tell Mrs. Graham where she and I were going. She suggested it, but I thought it would be faster if I just left a note." She turned tear-filled eyes toward Aunt Tess. "I am sorry."

Aunt Tess's smile was soft, but her words caused the tears to spill over the edge of Lydia's eyes. "We were worried."

"I am sorry," Lydia whispered again. She turned to look out the window. She could not look back at the eyes staring at her in the room. She had seen those accusing looks before. She did not need a reminder that she was stupid. Perhaps she should just pack her things and go home. What hope was there of ever learning to be a proper lady?

"You said Mrs. Ross is not well?"

It was Marcus's voice. She nodded and stiffened her spine for whatever he might throw at her to prove without doubt that she was unfit to be considered by a man like him.

"And you gave up your afternoon of visiting to assist her?"

She wiped at her eyes and glanced over her shoulder at him in confusion. He was not going to say how she should have sought someone with more sense to care for a lady who was not well? "I did. The children needed someone."

He shrugged and gave her a small smile. "That was well done."

She blinked in surprise.

Marcus looked at Lydia's back as she stood in front of the window with her arms wrapped tightly around herself. Then he looked around the room at the faces that stared at her. It felt very much like that first day in Willow Hall's sitting room. She had not run out the door yet, but he suspected she wished to do just that. His eyes fell on Mr. Bennet, and Marcus knew that he must prove both to her father and to Lydia that he not only believed her but respected her as well.

"It was a lovely day. Did the children play outdoors?"

Her head bobbed up and down.

"Did Edith end up in the stream? Ross is always telling me how much she loves to fish."

Lydia laughed lightly. "We caught three small fish, but our shoes and stockings remained dry." She glanced over her shoulder at him again and smiled. "We took them off and tied up the hems of our skirts."

Marcus's eyes dropped to look at her feet. A very tantalizing image of her with her ankles and feet exposed as she waded in the water caused him to lose his train of thought momentarily. "Did you use a –" His thought was once again disrupted by a corner of a paper poking out from under the settee.

Lydia turned from the window to see why he had stopped talking. To her surprise, he had slipped from his chair and was on the floor in front of the settee fishing something out from under it. He sat back and triumphantly held the note above his head. "Was the window open when you left this on the table?"

Lydia turned back to the window and then toward the table. "I think it was."

"There was a beautiful breeze today, was there not?"

Lydia smiled and nodded. "It pulled at my bonnet."

Marcus handed the note to Aunt Tess and stood. "Perhaps placing the parcel on top of the note next time would save some trouble." He said it gently and with a smile. He straightened his jacket and joined her at the window. "Would you tell us about your day? The Ross children are delightful. I imagine they had you playing some interesting games."

"Why are you being nice?" she asked in response.

"Why would I not be nice?" he asked cautiously.

"You ignored me the last two days. I do not like being ignored."

"I was not ignoring you. I was thinking."

She crossed her arms and looked at him as if she did not believe him. "You could not look at me and think?"

Marcus glanced around the room uneasily. Darcy and

Philip, as well as Mr. Bennet, looked as if they were going to laugh while Jane and Elizabeth looked mortified, and Aunt Tess and Lucy wore decidedly smug smiles. He shook his head. "No. I could not."

"That seems unlikely," Lydia muttered. "What could you be thinking of that would not allow you to look at me?"

"Might we have this conversation somewhere else?" Marcus ran a finger around his cravat. This time, one of the other gentlemen in the room did chuckle, and it sounded a good deal like his brother.

"If you wish," said Lydia with a small huff, "but I do not see why. A person should be able to think and look at another person. I do it. It cannot be all that hard. You looked at everyone else in the room. What could a person possibly be thinking about that would require him not to look at one person?"

"Marriage," said Marcus through clenched teeth. "It was brought to my attention that you and I might suit well, and I was considering the possibility." There was a small gasp both from the lady in front of him and her sisters behind him.

Lydia's eyes were wide, and her mouth hung open. Her heart felt like it had risen to her throat, and her breath caught in her chest.

Marcus ran his finger around his collar once more. "I think they were right."

Lydia blinked, and her mouth snapped shut. They were right? Did he mean that he wished to marry her or just that they would suit well, so it was a viable option?

"I think we should marry." He took her by the arm. "Please," he pleaded, "might we finish this conversation somewhere else?"

"Why?"

"Because declaring your love in front of an audience is rather awkward," he answered without thought.

"Oh." She tipped her head to the side, her lips puckered, and her brows furrowed. "You love me?"

He nodded. "I do."

She pointed at herself. "Me?" she squeaked. "You love me?"

He nodded again.

A smile began to form on her lips, but then it faded. "I cannot marry you."

Marcus felt as if he had been punched hard in the stomach. "Why not?" he managed to ask.

"I have not finished my lessons."

He shook his head. "Lessons?"

Her head bobbed up and down. "Aunt Tess is teaching me how to be the mistress of an estate. I cannot marry you until I know all her lessons. I have been writing down what she says — not exactly how she says it, but so I will remember — but I have had only two days of instruction, and there is so much to know."

"How long do you think it will take for these lessons?" She had not refused him, and joy was tentatively creeping its way into Marcus's heart. "Would you say you might know enough by Michaelmas?"

Lydia peeked around him at Aunt Tess. He smiled at how serious her expression was.

"Would that be long enough?"

"I think," said Aunt Tess, "that we might be able to finish a week before. But there is a soiree to plan."

Marcus could hear the laughter in Aunt Tess's tone.

"Oh, you are correct." Lydia tapped her lip. They could certainly plan a wedding and a soiree at the same time, could they not? She sighed and her brows furrowed. "Would a wedding in the morning and a soiree at night be too much for your father?" she asked. Her eyes grew wide, and she placed both hands on one of Marcus's arms. "We could get married in the chapel at Aldwood Abbey. I know my mother wished for us all to marry from Longbourn, but this way your father could attend. Oh," She squeezed his arm. "You must get a special license that will make it so much more acceptable to Mama." Her head tipped to the side. "Can you afford one?"

He laughed and nodded. "So you will marry me?"

She nodded a joyous yes.

He moved to take her in his arms, but she pushed him away. "It is not proper," she darted a significant look at Elizabeth, who blushed. Then, with a smile, she tilted her head and said, "However, if you would like to take a walk in the garden, I would accompany you."

Much to everyone's amusement, Marcus did not waste a minute in removing Lydia from the room and to the garden. Then, with one last declaration of love, he kissed her.

Lydia wrapped her arms around his neck and held him close. Kissing was quite as pleasurable as she had expected it would be, but the fluttering of her heart and the emotions that flooded through her, though pleasant, were not expected. She pulled back from him and looked up into his eyes. "I love you." Her eyes were wide with surprise.

He laughed. "It is rather unexpected when it hits, is it not?"

She nodded. "Yes, very. It is so very unexpected."

He brushed a hair back from her temple. "But not unpleasantly so?"

She shook her head. "No. It is rather delightful."

"Yes. Yes, it is," he said against her lips before claiming them once again.

At All Costs

Willow Hall Romance, Book 4

A Pride and Prejudice Variation Novel

~*~*~

She's trying to forget him, but he'll stop at nothing to reclaim her heart.

Prologue

George Wickham balanced on the back two legs of his chair. A smile curled his lips as he saw the man who entered the upper room at the inn. This was the man they sent to deal with him? He chuckled inwardly. This man was all charm and smiles. This was not the usual sort of man with whom Wickham dealt. Well, at least, not as the victim. No, when dealing with anyone as malleable as this man, it was Wickham who would be the aggressor, and the poor blithe chap would not realize his folly until Wickham was well away and in possession of something that the man formerly possessed — money, jewels, a maidenly sister. Wickham's smile grew at the thought. This man had a sister — a bit of a shrew but a wealthy one.

Mr. Williams raised a brow in his direction as if he knew what Wickham was thinking.

With a thud, Wickham dropped his chair to the ground and took up a proper position and demeanor for negotiations. His lips twitched with a barely contained smile. Perhaps Miss Lydia had not done him a disservice after all in conscripting him to take her to Derbyshire.

"Mr. Williams," Charles Bingley stuck out his hand in greeting, "I trust you are well today." Bingley motioned for his companion, Philip Dobney, to take a seat at the table before taking his own place.

"I am well and will be better once I have rid myself of this cad," grumbled Williams.

"Understandable," agreed Bingley with a smile. "Mr. Dobney has agreed to sign as a witness." Bingley spread out some papers in front of him.

"Very good," said Mr. Williams. "The sooner we can have this business concluded, the better. Although I do not like the idea of giving any assistance to an associate of Tolson." He narrowed his eyes at Wickham. "Deserves the same fate if you ask me."

Wickham swallowed. He would have to keep an eye behind him as he travelled. It was one of Mr. Williams' men who had found Tolson after his fall. The events of that accident had never sat well with Wickham. It was why he had attempted to do just as required while in Derbyshire.

"Miss Lydia will be free of you, and you shall be free of your debts. Are we agreed?" Bingley produced a small pen and ink set from his bag.

"We are," Wickham agreed, pondering just how much

extra money he could extract from Bingley when telling him the number of what he owed.

"This is the record of debts I will pay." Bingley slid the list Colonel Fitzwilliam had obtained from Lydia across the table.

Wickham looked at the paper in surprise. "Where did you get this?" His eyes scanned the paper, falling on a small flower constructed of hearts at the bottom of the page. "Miss Lydia?" he asked in surprise.

"She is resourceful," said Bingley.

Wickham's jaw clenched. Resourceful was not exactly the word he would use for the vixen.

"I just need a signature from you to show your agreement and from Mr. Dobney as the witness to said agreement," said Bingley. He waited as Wickham signed the document and then slid it to Philip. "The money along with a further copy of this list has been sent to Brighton. All will be settled before your return and without Colonel Forester knowing."

Bingley blew lightly on the signatures to dry them. "Mr. Williams will post this to my solicitor." He folded the paper and, after addressing it, sealed it before handing it to the constable.

"I do have a bit of something for your trouble in escorting Miss Lydia to Willow Hall." He nodded to Philip. "I will be only a moment more. I know you were expected at

Aunt Tess's for tea and had business to conclude before then, so I will delay you no longer."

Wickham shifted uneasily in his seat. He could sense a change in the atmosphere as Philip Dobney left the room.

Bingley's smile faded, and he looked to Mr. Williams for permission to proceed.

"You'll find no resistance or condemnation from me — no matter the results." He stood and moved to take a place at the door.

"Mr. Wickham," Bingley began, "the Bennets are very dear friends of mine. I would find it particularly unsettling if something were to happen to any of them."

Wickham eyed the man across from him suspiciously.

"You will leave Derbyshire, and you will not mention a word against Miss Lydia or her family, not in London, not in Brighton, not in Hertfordshire, not in any place in this world where word of your having done so might reach me."

That did not seem so difficult. Bingley moved where Wickham did not — in Darcy's circles. None of them would ever hear a word he spoke about anything. He smiled and nodded.

"No, Mr. Wickham, I do not believe you understand what I am saying. I am giving you the contents of this bag — five hundred pounds to do with as you choose. You will not come looking for more from me or anyone else associated with the Bennets, or you will find yourself in one of two places." Bingley cast a glance over his shoulder toward Mr. Williams, who only smiled and found something outside the door to be of particular interest. "You will be either dead or wishing you were."

Wickham's eyes widened at the comment. He had not expected Bingley to threaten him in such a way. In fact, he had not expected Bingley to threaten him at all. Ah, but then he relaxed, Bingley was not capable of making good such a threat.

Bingley's smile became predatory as he saw Wickham relax. "I am from trade, Mr. Wickham. I assure you there are unsavoury men of my acquaintance who, for a shilling, would see the matter resolved. And you mustn't forget that my uncle's ships have many interesting ports of call where you might be able to find a home if a wave does not sweep you off the deck." Bingley slid the pouch of money across the table but did not lift his hand from it. He waited for Wickham to look him in the eye before he continued. "Five hundred pounds to keep silent, or you will repay it with your life. Have I made myself clear?"

"And if I do not take your blunt?"

"And not remain silent?" There was a slight growl to Bingley's tone.

Wickham shrugged.

"Coaching inns and London streets are not safe." Bingley's glare was unwavering. "A loose step, a footpad — so many things can happen." He pushed the packet of money closer to Wickham and removed his hand. "Your choice, Wickham. Five hundred quid for your silence or..." Bingley shrugged.

Wickham picked up the money, shifting the pouch from his right hand to his left before slipping it into his pocket. "I shall not say a word about any of this."

Bingley stood. "See that you do not. My associates will be watching and listening." He placed his ink and pen back into his bag and then gave Wickham one final hard look. "Do not mistake me for having the same scruples as my friend. He is a gentleman's son. I am not." Bingley took up his hat, and as he placed it on his head, the charming smile from earlier returned. "It has been a pleasure doing business with you gentlemen." He gave a small bow and left the room.

"You are free to leave," said Mr. Williams. "Do take care on the steps."

Wickham patted the money in his pocket and blew out a breath. He was free to leave Derbyshire, and so he would, after a quick call on a friend who owed him a favour. He smiled. He would not be outwitted by the likes of Lydia Bennet and Charles Bingley. There were ways to remain silent and still exact his revenge — Darcy, Bingley, the Bennets, and the Dobneys — he chuckled. Not a one would be left unaffected.

Chapter 1

Charles Bingley folded the last of two letters he had spent the past hour composing. The first had been quickly dashed off, but this second one...

Bingley blew out a breath, unfolded the letter, and gave it a third reading. The news this missive contained would not be well-received. He only hoped he had written his wishes in a fashion that would leave his sister Caroline with little option but to comply.

"You look rather fatigued," said Darcy, entering the library and taking a seat near the window.

"What keeps you here?" asked Bingley.

"It is my library," replied Darcy with a grin. "I am allowed to use it whenever I like."

Bingley's eyes narrowed. "That was not my meaning, which you very well know."

"I cannot spend every moment at Willow Hall," Darcy said with a grimace, "no matter how much I might wish to do so. There were some matters of business here that required my attention, and after Mr. Bennet leaves this morning, Elizabeth is to come here for another, more extensive, tour than the one she had during the soiree three nights ago. And I have arranged a meeting with Mrs. Reynolds. There are not many days left to prepare Pemberley to receive its mistress." His grimace slid into a pleased smile at the thought. "Now, tell me what has you looking as though you have gone three rounds dodging swords?"

Bingley lifted the letter in his hand. "There is not much time to prepare Caroline for Pemberley to receive its new mistress — seeing that it is not she, that is. I have told Hurst to accept the invitation to Hadaway's house party. It is time that my youngest sister get on with her duty of securing a husband." Bingley sealed the letter. "I shall not be staying past the wedding breakfast."

"You are welcome to remain as long as you wish," Darcy said with some concern. "Miss Bennet will be in Derbyshire until at least Michaelmas."

Bingley nodded slowly. "It may be best if we both realize that you were correct, and her feelings for me were not what I imagined." He blew out another breath. "Which is why this will likely be my last visit to Pemberley."

Darcy sat forward in his chair. "I was not correct. She loved you and still may."

"I will give it until your wedding, but if I see no more encouragement than I have seen since arriving nearly ten days ago, I shall wish her well and move on."

He stood at the window to the library. The garden was

cheery and the day, bright, but he did not feel it. Indeed, he had not felt the loveliness of any day since he arrived. How could he when Captain Harris kept acting the part of a cloud blocking the sun?

"It can be done, can it not?" He glanced over his shoulder at Darcy. "I can find another happiness eventually?"

"As much as I do not wish to encourage your line of thinking, I would dare to say that if anyone could accomplish such an arduous feat, it is you." Darcy rose and crossed to the window to stand next to his friend. "I am sorry."

Bingley shrugged. "You did not know." He sighed heavily as he shifted to lean against the wall next to the window. "My sister, however, would have known more. Ladies always do. I am glad not to be seeing her."

"You cannot be certain she knew. Miss Bennet was very circumspect in keeping her attachment unknown."

Bingley laughed. "I dare say it would appear to be so to you, but you are not a lady. They have their own understandings of each other about which we gentlemen know nothing. I have witnessed it many times with Caroline and Louisa." He shook his head. "No, Caroline knew and whether she wished to separate me from Miss Bennet or you from Miss Elizabeth is my only question regarding the whole matter."

"Why would she have wanted to separate me from Elizabeth? I had declared nothing in Elizabeth's favour. In fact, I was rather rude at times."

Bingley chuckled again. "I do hope for your sake you have more sons than daughters. A gentleman cannot declare a lady's eyes to be fine and not be suspected of marking that lady for marriage." He raised a brow, challenging Darcy to deny it, but Darcy did not and admitted he supposed that such a thing was possible.

"What are your plans for the afternoon?" Darcy asked. "It is warm, so I would advise against a ride for both your sake and that of your horse. Miss Bennet is to accompany Elizabeth."

"What of Harris and Fitzwilliam? Is either of them to accompany Miss Bennet?"

He had seen Miss Bennet on the arm of one or the other of the gentleman whenever an opportunity arose for a stroll. He had been relegated to escorting Mary Ellen Dobney — not that there was anything particularly wrong with Miss Dobney. She was a lovely lady and were Bingley's heart not attached elsewhere, he might have considered her as a match. Her humour was pleasant. Her figure was all that it should be. Truly, her only imperfection was that she seemed to have a modicum of a fiery temper, which, having endured the peevishness of his youngest sister, Bingley was inclined to avoid even in small doses in a prospective wife. He had had his fill of fits and tantrums —

and meddling interferences, he thought with a scowl. Caroline could not marry soon enough to suit him.

"It is my understanding that it is just the ladies of Willow Hall who are to call. Georgiana has arranged to have tea in the garden with Mrs. Gardiner and Mrs. Abbot as well as Miss Bennet and Elizabeth."

"Very well, if Harris and Fitzwilliam will not be present, then it might serve me best to join you." And so he did. He smiled and acted the part of a charming gentleman enough to make all save one of the ladies from Willow Hall smile and laugh in reply. Unfortunately, it was that one lady, Miss Jane Bennet, whose refusal to act as anything more than a person forced to be civil, who coloured the whole event with a deep stroke of grey and sent him in search of a strong drink later that evening.

~*~*~

Jane Bennet sat on the window seat in the room she was sharing with Elizabeth at Willow Hall. She rested her head against the wall, pulled her legs up so she could wrap her arms around her knees and watched the sunset paint the sky with brilliant hues of purple and red. She turned her head to look at Elizabeth, who was lying on the bed, reading a book that Darcy had lent her from Pemberley's library. "I should have gone home with Papa," she said.

"But if you had gone with him, you would not be here for my wedding," reasoned Elizabeth.

Jane nodded. It was the only reason she had stayed. "But

after you marry, I will be quite alone," she said softly. Alone here in this room and at Longbourn when she returned there.

"You will have Aunt and Uncle as well as the Abbots, and if Captain Harris keeps calling as he has, you will spend very little time alone," assured Elizabeth.

Jane shrugged and attempted a smile, but smiling was not something she felt capable of doing much anymore — not since last fall before Mr. Bingley had left Netherfield. She had made an effort to remain cheerful and not give any hints about the pain that resided in her heart, and for the most part, she had been successful. However, it was so much more difficult when the man you wished to love, but dared not, was constantly in your presence.

She was attempting to love another, and Captain Harris was not without merit. He was handsome and pleasant, and his inheritance would be sufficient for a good life. But he was not Mr. Bingley, and her heart was still unwilling to forget that fact. Perhaps with time, it would. Marriages were often formed without the deepest affection. Captain Harris seemed to respect her; that was a good thing, was it not?

She sighed. She had never imagined she would have to settle for such an arrangement. She had always thought her heart would be engaged in such a way that the man she married would be her one true delight, the one person with whom she longed to spend her days.

"What of Mr. Bingley?" Elizabeth had come to join Jane on the window seat.

Jane shook her head. "He made his choice, and it was not me."

"But what if he made the choice based on faulty information?"

Jane drew a deep breath. "I wish for a husband who will choose me no matter the advice he is given. I wish to be the one person he craves...the one he would put before his sister — before life itself." She smiled sadly. "But that is not to be."

"But what if he did love you with his whole being?" Elizabeth leaned forward toward her sister and placed her hands onto Jane's knees.

"No," said Jane, pushing Elizabeth's hands away and standing. "I will not even contemplate it. I have not the strength to do so. I am sick to death of longing for what cannot be. You must not ask me to consider such things. I will be happy enough with Captain Harris, should he decide that I am indeed worthy of his regard."

"But you do not love him," argued Elizabeth.

"One can learn to love," replied Jane.

"You will not give Mr. Bingley a chance?" Elizabeth asked in surprise.

Jane shook her head. "I cannot, for I cannot survive another disappointment."

"Disappointment?" cried Elizabeth. "You do not know that it would be a disappointment."

Jane crossed her arms and set her jaw firmly. She knew of what she spoke. Her sister had been fortunate in love; there was little Elizabeth could know of the disappointment Jane had suffered in London when she had been spurned. "It is not as if I did not give him a second chance. I did call while I was in London."

"You cannot be certain he knew of your call," argued Elizabeth.

"He knew. Caroline made it clear that he did."

"And you believe her — the very same woman who led you to believe you had an intimacy with her and later showed herself to be false — you believe *her*?"

"He did not call," said Jane, going to brush her hair out at the dressing table in preparation for plaiting before bed.

Elizabeth threw her hands up in frustration. "And why would he call if he had no knowledge of your being in town? Mr. Darcy knew nothing of your being in town until I told him, and you had been there for three months by then."

Jane's brush stopped just above her head where she had intended to begin the next stroke. Slowly she lowered the brush and laid it on the table. Then, just as slowly, she turned on her stool to face Elizabeth. "You spoke to Mr. Darcy of me while you were in Kent?"

Elizabeth's eyes lowered to look at her hands. "I did. I asked if he had seen you, but he had not."

Jane nodded slowly as this information settled into her brain. It was entirely possible that Mr. Bingley did not know of her presence in town if Mr. Darcy did not. Miss Bingley would likely not keep it from one and not the other, would she?

Elizabeth had come to take up the job of brushing Jane's hair.

"Did he speak of Mr. Bingley?" The brush stuttered in its progress through her hair, and Jane turned so that she could see Elizabeth in the mirror. "What are you not telling me?"

Elizabeth concentrated on three more slow strokes of the brush through Jane's hair before replying.

"I did not wish to cause you pain," she began, placing the brush on the table and turning away. "He loved you." She turned back toward Jane, tears in her eyes. "Mr. Bingley loved you, but Mr. Darcy feared you did not return his friend's affections."

Jane blinked and stared at her sister with her mouth hanging open. Mr. Bingley had loved her? And Mr. Darcy was to blame for the separation? She shook her head. It could not be true.

"I did not wish to tell you because you were so sad already, and I did not think we would ever see Mr. Bingley again." The tears in Elizabeth's eyes had begun rolling down her cheeks. "Mr. Darcy was sorry — *is* sorry — for having had any part in your pain. He truly thought you indifferent to Mr. Bingley and wished to save his friend from a disappointment. Had he known you were in town and had called on Miss Bingley, I am certain he would have seen that he was wrong and would not have kept Mr. Bingley from you."

Jane's shoulders rounded forward as her spine curved in a sigh. "That is why Miss Bingley would not have told Mr. Darcy of my call."

Elizabeth nodded.

Jane stood and walked the room, pacing down to the window and back to the wardrobe and wash stand. "What am I to do? What am I to think? He loved me only enough to be persuaded away from me? How great a love is that? Can one forgive such capriciousness? Is it not a flaw in character? Had we married, would he have eventually been persuaded by another that he loved her and not me? How am I to think?"

Elizabeth wrapped her arms around her sister. "I do not know, though I wish I did. Come, let me finish your hair, and then, we shall lie in bed and attempt to decipher the answer."

And they did but to no avail. As first one and then the other sister drifted off into a less than restful sleep, the question of what was to be done about Mr. Bingley remained unanswered — that is to say, no answer was spoken aloud, but in the breast of each lady a heart pled in his favour.

Chapter 2

"What has you looking like you ate a piece of bad fish?" asked Richard as he took a seat in Pemberley's game room next to Bingley.

Bingley shrugged and gulped the last of his drink. "You did not stay at Matlock?"

Richard sighed and scrubbed his face with his hands. "My sister is the center of a house party, and although her friends seem to enjoy my company, I do not enjoy theirs. The last of the guests should leave by week's end. I shall visit for a longer period of time after that. As it was, yesterday and this morning were long enough for my mother to begin speaking of my marrying."

"It is a sad lot for us men," muttered Bingley.

"You mean marriage?" Richard unbuttoned his waistcoat.

Bingley's head bobbed up and down slowly. "I suppose it is not only a sad business for men." He rose on shaky legs to refill his glass. "It is only a happy business if you can persuade the lady you love to accept you, but if you cannot."

He made a slashing motion in front of his throat. "All the pleasures of life are at an end, for there is little joy in a marriage of convenience." Port sloshed back and forth, nearly spilling over the rim of the glass that Bingley handed to Richard.

"You have seen it. I have seen it. All those sad men drinking and gambling in the clubs or trotting off in closed carriages and entertaining who knows what disease in an attempt to feel some joy." Bingley huffed and shook his head. "It never works. Have you ever met one that was happy?" He sloshed another glass of port to the table next to his chair before taking a seat. "And the ladies — not any happier. It's a sorry business, marriage is." He heaved a great sigh and rested his head against the back of the chair. "And yet, we must do our duty."

As he drank, Richard studied Bingley. "Miss Bennet is still not warming to your presence?"

Bingley scowled and huffed. "As warm as a pond in January." He turned angry eyes toward Richard. "Not that you would know: she is all that is pleasant around you and that blasted Harris."

"I have only meant to be civil," retorted Richard.

Bingley grunted.

"Harris, however, seems enamoured," Richard admitted, "although, I do not see Miss Bennet returning his affections in equal measure."

Bingley laughed bitterly. "Yes, but that does not mean they are not returned."

He shook his head. Why had he listened to his sister and Darcy? He had been nearly certain Jane favoured him. He sighed. That was why he had listened. He had been nearly but not completely certain, and he had been wrong before.

"What of your prospects for marriage? Besides the debutantes at your parent's estate, that is. Are there any of your sister's friends who might settle for an almost gentleman such as myself?"

"I admit to having no particular prospects in mind," said Richard, rising to refill his glass. "My lot is not all that much rosier than yours. I am a second son, after all."

"Of an earl," Bingley scoffed. "That alone makes you valuable. Your brother could die."

"A pleasant thought," Richard said dryly. "I have no desire to claim the title."

"Your inheritance cannot be nothing," said Bingley. "What will you have on the completion of your career? A small estate? A piece of land?"

"Aye," said Richard. "A small estate. Are you not going to purchase an estate?"

Bingley shrugged. "Perhaps, once Caroline is married, so I can guarantee it is not too close to her." He held his glass a few inches from his lips. "She has twenty thousand pounds you know."

"I have met her, Bingley, and as much as I like you, I do not wish to be tied to you by marrying her."

Bingley nodded. "Wise choice. She is disagreeable and spoiled. I blame our aunt for it — filling her head with impossible dreams of grandeur." He leaned forward in his chair. "You know she does not wish to marry for love?" His voice was filled with incredulity. "She only wishes to marry for money and position."

Richard shrugged. "That is not an uncommon desire."

"Well," said Bingley, falling back in his chair, "I find it disturbing. Louisa wished for a fondness of affections, but Caroline does not even care for that! She follows Darcy around like a lost puppy only for his estate. It is so grand and well-situated, and the staff is impressive — or so she has said. But Darcy?" He shrugged. "She thought him handsome — she is not blind or entirely stupid — but," he shook his head and frowned, "she thought him too grave. She cared for him little beyond the connections he possessed." His chuckle was humourless. "The way she fawned over his every word and deed — empty, hollow praise. That's all it was. I do not know how she can be so very shallow. It is not as if our parents did not instill good principles in us." Once again he shrugged. "Again, I blame our aunt, and that school Caroline attended. She was too young to be left without a mother."

Bingley lapsed into silence. It had been ten years since his mother had passed away and three since his father had joined her, but still, the thought of their departure left an unsettled feeling in his chest. It was a void that he had at one time thought Jane would fill.

Bingley sighed. His happiness would never be complete without Miss Bennet. "How do I do it?"

"Pardon?" asked Richard in surprise.

"See myself happily married to Miss Bennet," Bingley clarified.

"I cannot say I have ever pursued any lady in particular, so I might not be the best person to ask for advice."

Bingley rolled his head, which was resting on the back of his chair, so that he could see Richard. "But you are skilled in developing strategies to win a battle, are you not?"

Richard shrugged. "I know a thing or two, yes."

"Then how do I win this battle?"

Richard steepled his fingers and rested his chin on them as he thought. "Ladies are unpredictable."

Bingley nodded. "That they are."

Richard took another drink of his port. "They often want what they cannot have, do they not? I mean my sister will whine more about some dress she cannot have and claim it is the latest in fashion and better than anything she already possesses."

"True!" said Bingley. "Caroline is the same. So is Louisa."

"Then, you must be the dress she cannot have," said Richard with finality.

Bingley's brows furrowed. "How am I to be a dress?"

"If my sister sees that dress — the one she was denied — on another lady — " Richard rolled his eyes and let out a low whistle.

"Ah," said Bingley, a smile curving his lips. "I must pay attention to another lady."

Richard tapped his nose. "Precisely. But you must do it with care. You do not wish to be obligated to marry this other lady."

Bingley nodded. A small amount of hope began to grow in his mind. "Who?" he asked, turning again to Richard. "I only know Miss Darcy and Miss Dobney."

"Miss Darcy will not do," said Richard sharply. "She is too young, and Wickham has left her heart fragile."

"Then," Bingley lifted his nearly empty glass in salute, "Miss Dobney it shall be." He paused with the glass nearly at his lips. "Do we tell Miss Dobney of our scheme?"

"Only if necessary. Ladies tend to talk," he drained the remaining liquid from his glass. The plan had seemed a good one as he spoke it, but now — his brows furrowed — he was not entirely certain.

~*~*~

When the sun crept its way over the horizon, Bingley slept in a chair in the game room at Pemberley, a stiff neck and headache would be the gift of his indulgence when he awoke.

At Willow Hall, Jane was also awakening with a sore head. She had spent too long last night thinking about what to do in regard to Mr. Bingley to have slept well enough to rise refreshed. Elizabeth, from the wince she made when opening her eyes, was in no better shape.

Jane rose first and tended to her needs and was sitting at the dressing table when Elizabeth got out of bed.

"He is quite perfect," she said, glancing over her shoulder to where Elizabeth was splashing cold water on her face.

"Mr. Bingley?" Elizabeth asked from behind a towel.

"Mmm hmm." Jane unraveled the last of her braid and was about to begin brushing her hair. A maid could be called to assist, but as at home, she liked to do as much of her preparations for the day on her own. There was a peacefulness to starting the day without anyone to fawn over you or tell you to sit straight or look this way or that. "He is handsome and agreeable. I do not think a life with him would be dull."

Elizabeth could only agree with such a statement. Mr. Bingley was, after all, all that a young man should be. Jane had declared such to be true shortly after meeting him.

"He affects me as no other man has — not even Captain Harris, and I am fond of the captain in a friendly sort of way," reasoned Jane. It was the same reasoning she had used sometime in the early morning hours while the moon still shone in the sky. "I shall give him a second chance to win my affections." She plunked the brush down on the table and gave a sharp nod of her head in agreement with her own determination. "I will stop avoiding him. I shall even be more than civil, and I shall no longer hide my smiles from him."

Elizabeth sat on the edge of the bed, pulling on her stockings. "Are you going to stop spending so much time with Captain Harris?"

Jane shook her head. "I shall not actively dissuade him, but I shall offer no encouragement either — unless I am unsuccessful with Mr. Bingley."

"And you will encourage Mr. Bingley?"

Again, Jane shook her head. "I will not unless he is agreeable. I do not want to appear to be throwing myself at him, especially if he does not, in fact, still love me."

Elizabeth reached around Jane for the brush. "You must not be so circumspect as to leave him in doubt."

"I shall not be," said Jane.

And she was not. Later that day, when callers came to Willow Hall, Jane made certain to smile and openly welcome each of them as warmly as she could. However, no matter the number of times she smiled at Mr. Bingley or asked his opinion on some topic, he merely answered courteously in return before turning his attention to Mary Ellen Dobney. By the end of the visit, Jane was growing quite cross and felt her lips forming a pout equal to those produced by her youngest sister.

"That did not go as planned." Jane sat, arms crossed and looking very disgruntled on a bench in the garden at Willow Hall.

"No." Mary Ellen, who had stayed after the others had left, so that she could spend time with Elizabeth and Jane, agreed with a sigh.

"You looked happy to be doted on."

Elizabeth's brows rose at the grumble from her sister. Jane was always pleasant — always, and she never grumbled — never.

"I was not," Mary Ellen assured Jane. "I had hoped by appearing to be happy, someone would make more of an effort to claim my attention away from Mr. Bingley." She slumped forward and, propping her elbows on her knees, rested her chin in her hands.

"Someone?" asked Elizabeth.

"Colonel Fitzwilliam." Mary Ellen said the name as if every frustration of the afternoon was summed up in it.

"You do not like Mr. Bingley?" asked Jane hopefully.

"He is pleasant, but no, he is not who I wish to marry," answered Mary Ellen. "Colonel Fitzwilliam." This time the name was spoken with a sigh, "He is just so...so...perfect. Strong, amiable, intelligent, entertaining. The only thing he lacks is the good sense to swoon at my feet." She turned to Jane. "But what of my cousin?"

Jane's face pinched slightly at the question. "He is pleasant, and I thought I had lost my chance with Mr. Bingley. So –"

"You were looking for a replacement," said Mary Ellen with a knowing nod. "I have tried that. Mr. Jacobson was an excellent dancer and a fine conversationalist as well as possessing a great deal of manliness, but there was something he was missing."

Jane nodded her understanding. "He was not Colonel Fitzwilliam."

"Precisely!" cried Mary Ellen. "Oh, it is good to know there is another who understands. Lucy claims she does, but she fell into her marriage without much effort."

"I understand," said Elizabeth. "I thought I had lost Mr. Darcy."

"True," agreed Jane.

"But you did not have to struggle to gain his attention," Mary Ellen said with a smirk. "Not that you were not fortunate to be reunited, of course."

"How did you gain his acceptance after abusing him so abominably?" asked Jane.

"You abused him?" Mary Ellen's eyes sparkled with curiosity.

"I was not very kind in my first refusal." Elizabeth's cheeks flushed. "And nearly everything I accused him of was not true. I prefer not to repeat any of that horrible scene."

Mary Ellen shook her head. "I have not even been given a chance to make a refusal. Have you?" she asked Jane.

"No. Neither of us has been so fortunate."

"I did not think it fortunate at the time," countered Elizabeth. "The things I said were so wrong that at my first opportunity after meeting Mr. Darcy again, I apologized."

Jane's brows furrowed and her pout returned. That would not work for her. She had nothing for which to apologize. In fact, now that she was thinking about it, it was Mr. Bingley who owed her an apology. It was he who had played with her affections and then disappeared.

"Perhaps, you should continue to be happy to receive Mr. Bingley's attentions," she suggested to Mary Ellen. "The colonel did seem a bit uneasy today. That may be the reason."

"But what of you?" Mary Ellen asked.

"I shall divide my attentions between your cousin and Colonel Fitzwilliam," Jane replied. "If we both appear to be of interest to another gentleman, it may make them take notice."

Elizabeth shook her head. "This sounds very much like a Lydia scheme. I cannot say I approve."

Jane's brows rose. "You do not have to approve. You are happily attached. We," she waved a hand toward Mary Ellen and then back to herself, "are not."

"But, Jane," said Elizabeth, "you have already been in Mr. Bingley's presence and welcomed Captain Harris's and Colonel Fitzwilliam's attention. Surely, if this scheme was to work, it would have already."

"And it was working, although it was not my intention at the time. Mr. Bingley looked quite dejected the last time we were all together, but today when I was willing to welcome him, he was no longer interested in gaining my approval."

Mary Ellen nodded. "I had noticed his gloom on other calls but not today's."

"So, we are agreed?" asked Jane.

Mary Ellen smiled and extended her hand to Jane to shake. "Yes. We shall make them jealous."

Chapter 3

Jane placed her hand in Captain Harris's hand and allowed him to help her from his carriage. Mary Ellen had invited Jane and Elizabeth to join her on a drive to Lambton. There was a particular shop that Mary Ellen wished her new friends to visit with her. According to Miss Dobney, this particular shop had the best trimmings, and a greater selection than could be found in Kympton.

As it happened, it was a shop that was well-known to both Elizabeth and Jane as their aunt's brother was the proprietor. Although neither Bennet lady had been to the shop itself, they knew of the goods and had met their aunt's brother and his wife several times when in London. Lydia had no knowledge of the shop and was intrigued when the outing was proposed a day ago during a dinner at Aldwood Abbey.

So, the entourage of patrons was not a small one. Not a lady from Willow Hall, Aldwood Abbey, Pemberley, the vicarage, or Aunt Tess's home was left behind. All, with gentlemen in tow, squished and squeezed into the several carriages and made the journey to visit this one shop, in particular, and others as time would allow.

Mary Ellen had arranged that Mr. Bingley might join her and Jane in Captain Harris's carriage. Captain Harris had, on returning to Derbyshire and finding a lady worthy of driving about the countryside, inquired of his father for the use of the family's barouche. Since Harris had not shown interest in any particular lady for nearly three years, the request was greeted with great enthusiasm.

"An estate must one day have an heir, after all," his father had said while slapping his son on the back.

"Pris was a lovely thing, but it is time to move on," agreed his mother.

And so it was that Jane found herself seated on the soft seats of the Harris's well-sprung carriage. Had it not been for Jane's need to pretend favour to Captain Harris while Mary Ellen smiled and laughed with Bingley, it might have been a pleasant trip. However, as it was, the trip had been frustrating, and not just for Jane. Bingley found his dislike for Harris growing with each syllable that passed through the man's mouth. Consequently, both were thankful for the change of scenery and companions that disembarking in Lambton brought.

As they stood gathered in a rather large group on Lambton's High Street, Mrs. Abbot suggested that the gentlemen find a means of amusing themselves while the ladies perused the goods in the shop. Mr. Abbot took up his wife's cause, whether this was in support of her idea or just a means to escape the discussion of lace and frills, it cannot be said, but with a little persuasion, he found himself leading the men to a tavern just down the street and around the corner.

Jane wrapped her arm around Mary Ellen's as they made their way into the shop. "I am uncertain I can continue this charade and not grow to dislike you."

This was the third day of their scheme. First, there had been an afternoon of rambling about the countryside. Then, there had been a dinner at Aldwood Abbey, and now, there was this trip.

Mary Ellen sighed. "It is true. I have wished at least once to remove your dazzling smile from your face when you have turned it on Colonel Fitzwilliam. A sampling of your lace, if you will." This last was said to the clerk before Mary Ellen turned back to Jane. "You have not discovered that you care for him, have you?"

Jane shook her head. "I most decidedly have not! What of you? Mr. Bingley's charms are hard to ignore."

"His are not the charms I wish to claim," assured Mary Ellen. "Must men be so slow to act?" she asked with a sigh. "I should have thought they would have grown at least a little uneasy and ill-tempered, but both still act the part of the perfect gentleman. There has not been a huff or a cross word. It is quite remarkable."

Jane agreed that things were not progressing as they

wished. "How long shall we continue before we declare defeat?"

"Defeat?" Mary Ellen laughed. "I shall not quit the field without my colonel! However, we may need to adjust tactics." She ran a finger over the fine lace that the sales woman had brought out. "Two more days? Can we endure until Sunday?" She lifted the lace. "This is lovely, is it not?"

"It is," agreed Jane. "I think it would be exceptional on my blue fichu."

"Sunday?" Mary Ellen asked.

Jane sighed and nodded. "I believe, I can endure for that long."

"What will happen on Sunday?" asked Lydia, who had joined them to look at the lace.

"Nothing." Jane attempted to smile and act as if she was not concealing anything, but the blush which stained her cheeks was all the encouragement Lydia needed.

"It is something," Lydia tipped her head to the side and studied her eldest sister.

"Truly," said Mary Ellen. "It is of little significance."

Lydia's eyes narrowed. "If it were of little significance, none would seek to hide it — particularly Jane." She crossed her arms and waited as if expecting an answer or retort of some sort.

Jane fidgeted and lowered her eyes.

"Very well. I know people do not trust me."

The sadness in Lydia's soft voice caused Jane to look up, and when she did, she saw that the expression on Lydia's face as she turned away matched the tone in her voice. Jane's heart could not bear to be the cause. "It is not that," she said.

"It is always that," Lydia returned. "Lydia is too stupid and foolish to be trusted." She shrugged. "I had hoped, perhaps, that..." She shook her head. "It does not signify. Everyone is entitled to their own little secrets."

"We do not think you stupid or foolish," said Mary Ellen.

Lydia's head cocked to the side again, and she gave Jane a questioning look.

"I am sorry, Lydia, but you have not always been wise," said Jane, accepting her parcel of lace and turning to leave with Mary Ellen.

"You have not always been wise either," said Lydia, following Jane out of the store.

"Pardon me?" Jane asked in surprise. Lydia said harsh things to Elizabeth but rarely to Jane.

"Forgive me, Mary Ellen," said Lydia before turning to Jane. "You should be married to Mr. Bingley, and had you fluttered your eyes or allowed your hand to brush past his when passing, instead of being so entirely proper, he would not have been able to stay away from Netherfield. You are beautiful, but you are..." her shoulders rose high and fell sharply as she drew and released a breath. "You are bland. It is like having a ball gown in the perfect shade of blue — like the midnight sky." She turned to Mary Ellen. "Blue is lovely on Jane, much like red is on you." She turned back to Jane. "Instead of wearing that gown and being the most sought after, you have hung it in the wardrobe and rarely wear it — and when you do, you hide it under a wrap of gray."

"He left," said Jane. "It was his choice."

"Perhaps," said Lydia, "but did you give him reason to return?" Lydia shook her head. "Again, I must apologize, Mary Ellen," she said before continuing. "Do you really wish to marry Captain Harris?" Lydia did not allow for Jane to answer. "It would be a sin, really, if you did. His colouring does not match yours at all, and he is a gossip." Lydia shook her head again. "No, you must marry Mr. Bingley, and Mary Ellen must marry Colonel Fitzwilliam."

Jane's brows furrowed, and her mouth dropped open slightly.

Mary Ellen sighed and rolled her eyes. "That is precisely what we are attempting to arrange."

"It does not look like it." Lydia's eyes were wide with astonishment.

"We are attempting to make them jealous," Mary Ellen admitted in a whisper.

"Then, you are doing it wrong," said Lydia. "You are giving your full attention to the other gentleman when you should flirt a bit with the object of your interest and then turn away from him. Entice and retreat." She shrugged her shoulders.

"Entice and retreat?" repeated Mary Ellen.

Lydia nodded. "Precisely, but if it does not work, tell me, and I shall arrange it all. It is really not so very difficult to get a gentleman to come up to scratch," she paused for a moment, "well, most of them. I did think for a time that Marcus was not going to comply." She smiled as she saw him approaching. "But, thankfully, he did." She was about to flounce off to greet him when a thought stopped her short, and she turned with a very serious look on her face. "But not until he was told he should. That might be the answer."

Jane snatched Lydia's arm. "Please, do not say anything."

Lydia patted Jane's hand. "I can keep secrets, you know. I am actually very good at it."

Jane gave her sister a thankful smile and released her arm.

"Were you successful?" Bingley asked as he approached.

Lydia gave Jane a meaningful look as she tipped her head in Mr. Bingley's direction.

Jane smiled and heartily admitted that the trip had been well worth the effort. "I found a lovely piece of lace to go on the collar of my blue fichu." As she spoke, Jane placed a hand on the side of her neck and ran her fingers lightly along where the collar might lay, stopping and resting her hand just at the base of her throat. Then, turning from Mr. Bingley to Captain Harris, she opened her parcel to show him, and only him, the contents. She bit her lip and glanced toward Lydia who winked and smiled.

Bingley knew that he now wished to squeeze every last ounce of breath from Harris. The man's eyes had only momentarily dropped to inspect the lace before returning to look where Jane's hand lay — or was Harris looking a bit lower?

Bingley clenched his teeth together firmly and forced himself to smile and turn to Mary Ellen to inquire about her success. As he did so, he offered her his arm and with a small word of excuse, drew her away from the group, an action that to his delight was not missed by Jane. He must be more direct with his attentions to Mary Ellen if he was going to cause Jane to forget Harris. He congratulated Mary Ellen on her fine choices and declared that he was certain no other lady of his acquaintance had quite such good taste in trimmings.

"I say, Bingley," said Richard, "I had not taken you for such a dandy."

Bingley raised a brow at the brusqueness of Richard's tone. "I am not. It is just that I have been schooled in all the finer things of fashion by my overly zealous sisters."

"You should have joined the militia," replied Richard with a laugh. "You can be assured there is very little talk of the finer points of fashion among the men."

"Your men never notice what the ladies are wearing?" Mary Ellen fluttered her lashes and feigned a look of innocence.

Richard laughed again. "I did not say that, Miss Dobney. They are not without excellent powers of observation, but their discussion never delves into the latest colour or the particular style of sleeve."

Mary Ellen leaned into Bingley's arm. "Then, I am fortunate to have found a gentleman of such refined talents." She again fluttered her lashes before turning to smile up at Bingley.

"Yes, very fortunate," Richard ground out. "If only we could all be as superior as Bingley."

"Indeed," said Mary Ellen.

"It is not a refinement I have sought. It is rather a serendipitous result of the hours of torture I have endured listening to my sisters on the subject."

Bingley looked questioningly at Richard. Why was that gentleman so gruff? This was the plan they had contrived. He, Bingley, was to play the part of a smitten swain, but it was only a part — and yet, Richard was acting very much like a jealous beau. Bingley opened his mouth to add a comment about the number of times one or the other of his sisters had placed projects before him and asked his opinion, only to tell him where he had gone wrong. However, before he could utter a sound, he clamped it closed again and shifted his body away from Mary Ellen.

Well, this was a fine kettle of fish, he thought to himself as he watched Richard warily and Harris with contempt while the group walked down the street, stopping here and there for an exploration of one shop or another.

Much to Bingley's relief, it was finally suggested that they gather the few things they needed for a small al fresco meal. This was quickly done — Mrs. Abbot and Mrs. Gardiner being very proficient in organizing and orchestrating such tasks. Before long, the party was gathering at a small grove they had passed on the trip earlier that day.

"Why did you not tell me?" Bingley whispered as he and Richard spread blankets on the ground.

"Tell you what?" demanded Richard.

Bingley accepted the gratitude of Mrs. Abbot for having done such a fine job of preparing a place to sit, and then, with a nod of his head, removed himself and Richard a distance away from the others. "Why did you not tell me you cared for Miss Dobney?'

Richard blinked. "Why should I tell you that?"

"Because it is true!"

Richard's brows furrowed and his lower lip protruded slightly as he frowned and shook his head.

Bingley chuckled. "You do not like her?" There was disbelief in his voice. "Then why did you act as if you wished to see my head on a pike when we were in Lambton?"

Richard shrugged. "I do not know."

Bingley shook his head and chuckled once again. "I think I should ride with Darcy on our return."

"You mustn't," said Richard. "Our objective will not be met if you do."

Bingley sighed. "No, it will not. However, I am rather more concerned about your jealousy than I am hers. She may break my heart, but she will not run it through as you might."

"I would do no such thing," scoffed Richard. "I am only disagreeable due to the warmth of the day."

Bingley's brows rose in disbelief. The day was warm but not without a cooling breeze. "Very well, I shall continue as we have, but if you find that it is not just the weather making you cross, you have only to say so." He paused before turning back to take his place with the picnickers. "Have you seen any indication that our plan is working?" he asked.

Richard shrugged. "Miss Bennet is watching us. I dare say that is something, is it not?"

Bingley was not certain it was, but he allowed it to be. As the day ended, Bingley still could not tell whether their machinations were working or not. The one thing of which he was certain was that he disliked Captain Harris immensely, and it was on this thought that he was dwelling later as he and Richard rode to Kympton to find a place other than the game room at Pemberley to wash away the aggravating mental dust of the day.

Chapter 4

As the Saturday sun climbed over the horizon, Bingley once again found himself slumped in a chair at Pemberley instead of in his bed. At least this time, he had made it to his room before succumbing to inebriated sleep. He squinted at the sun and cursed his throbbing head. Frustrated or not, feeling like this in the morning was not worth the short period of memory loss that alcohol provided.

"Never again," he declared to the room before flopping face-first onto his bed and enjoying another hour and a half of sleep before his man came to begin the process of making him presentable.

After enduring the raised brow and unspoken reproach of his valet, as well as the loud rebuke of stiff muscles and a sore head as he dressed, Bingley entered the breakfast room, gathered a piece of dry toast and a cup of tea without milk, then took a seat near Darcy and across from Richard.

"How can you eat so much?" Bingley's face pinched into

a look of revulsion at the eggs, ham, and rolls that were mounded upon Richard's plate.

"I did not drink as much as you did." Richard nodded at Bingley's sparse breakfast. "Only took eating two of those breakfasts to teach me when I should stop." He stabbed a piece of meat with his fork and lifted it to his mouth.

Bingley turned his eyes away. He could not even witness the eating of so much food without his stomach roiling.

"This is twice in a week," commented Darcy with raised brows.

"Yes, I can count," snapped Bingley before apologizing for his short temper. "My head is beyond sore," he explained.

"I find a good bit of fresh air and a nap are conducive to speeding recovery," said Richard. "And water — you should drink plenty of water."

Bingley raised his cup. "Will this do?"

"Aye," said Richard, "but water is better. Take a flask with you when you go for a walk."

Bingley did as Richard suggested. He took a flask of water with him when he went for a long ramble — through the gardens and out into the fields and woods. The breeze of the morning felt good, and he drew great deep breaths to try to clear his mind.

Coming to a stream, he removed his boots and outer clothing and slipped into the cool water. Then, finding a pleasant spot in the sun, he lay down to dry out — first his front and then his back. The sun warmed him and attempted to lull him into sleep, but having sustained more than one sunburn in his youth, he knew better than to allow himself to surrender to the desire to sleep until he had redressed and taken a seat under the shade of a tree. Then, he cocked his hat over his eyes and was soon buzzing like a large angry bee.

Such a time of relaxation and refreshment as this morning had provided was just the thing to clear his head of most of the effects of last night's indulgence. It had also given him time to ponder his situation, and on his return to Pemberley, he came to the conclusion that games were not what was needed. He would, at his first opportunity, call on Miss Bennet, declare his love, and beg her acceptance. At least, then, he would know one way or the other where he stood. This shifting between hope and despair might be tolerable for some men, but not for Bingley. He liked things decided. It was why he listened to advise from those he trusted and often followed their leading.

"It looks like your walk has improved your countenance." Richard sat near the entrance to the garden. He motioned for Bingley to sit. "I think we should end our campaign."

Bingley smiled. "I would agree. I find that I do not like being a dress."

Richard laughed heartily at the comment. "I find I do not like your being a dress either."

"So you have come to realize that I was right about your feelings for Miss Dobney?" Bingley could not help his smirk.

"I have come to the conclusion that it is not entirely impossible that I was feeling jealous. I will admit to nothing further."

Bingley shrugged. He understood the reticence of speaking of feelings. It was not an entirely comfortable thing to do, even for someone like himself who was not so squeamish about such things as other gentlemen, such as Richard, were.

"I am going to speak to Miss Bennet as soon as I find an opportunity to do so."

Richard cocked his head to the side. "Forming your line and marching into battle rather than scouting about the edges?"

Bingley nodded. "Something of that nature."

"It is probably best." Richard rose from his seat. "Miss Bennet and Miss Elizabeth are expected in about an hour, according to Darcy."

"Harris is to leave with you when you leave Derbyshire, is he not?" Bingley cut a sidelong glance at Richard, who nodded, as they walked. Harris was an ever-present annoyance that Bingley would gladly see gone. "Is it not possible to send him back to Brighton early?"

Richard laughed. "I have no reason to do so."

Bingley sighed. "That is unfortunate."

And it was unfortunate indeed, for that very gentleman happened to be the one that brought Miss Bennet and Miss Elizabeth to Pemberley. It was also Harris who took Jane's arm as they strolled around the garden, and it was Harris who claimed the seat next to Jane when they all finally paused for a rest. And it was also Harris who was now monopolizing the conversation.

"It is a lovely day, is it not?" Harris asked as they sat in the shadow cast by Pemberley across the side garden at this time of day.

It was the consensus that it was indeed a fine day — for the weather was pleasant. However, for two of the party, the day was not so fine as it could have been. Bingley was in general annoyed by the presence of Harris and, in specific, irked by Harris's attentions to Jane.

That lady was also not best pleased by the presence of Captain Harris. For, upon their return to Willow Hall yesterday, Jane had confessed to Elizabeth that she could no longer bear the guilt of playing one gentleman against the other. The techniques that Lydia had mentioned seemed to work as Mr. Bingley did look put out, but she feared Captain Harris was beginning to think there was a greater attachment on her part than there was. And so, she sat now wishing to dissuade that particular gentleman while longing to know if she had any hope with Mr. Bingley. The frustration of the situation was enough to cause her smile to fade and to keep her rather silent.

This change in Jane's usually cheerful countenance did not go unnoticed by Mr. Bingley. What could the cause of her silence and sad expression was, he did not know, but seeing her so saddened his heart and made him long for a great wind to sweep away all the others so that he might speak to her in private.

"The summers here are rather pleasant," Harris was saying, "but there is nothing like a sea breeze on a warm day. When I was a child, my father would often take us to the sea for the summer. Ramsgate was his favoured spot. You have been there, have you not, Mr. Darcy?"

"Yes, we had a small cottage there, but it is gone now." Darcy's tone was one that spoke of not wishing to discuss the matter further. Harris, however, seemed not to notice.

But then, thought Bingley with a small sigh, nothing appeared to gain Harris's attention except himself and, to a lesser degree, the lady seated beside him.

"Gone?" Harris said in surprise. "I should not like to give up such a piece of paradise." He added with a grin, "Mother continually asks Father to purchase a place there. However, Father sees it as an unnecessary expense since it is easy enough to rent a place, but, to me, having a place in Ramsgate to be used at your convenience and leased when you are not in residence seems the best of all things — pleasure and income. Father does not agree, nor does he like to travel so much as I do. He is content to be contained within Derbyshire except for the occasional foray

into town or to indulge mother with a time beside the sea."
He turned to Jane. "What of you, Miss Bennet? Do you
enjoy the sea?"

"I do not know," said Jane. "I have never been there."

"But your sister has been to Brighton."

"Yes, Lydia has been to Brighton, but she is the only
one of us who has. And, had it not been for her particular
friend inviting her to visit, she would not have seen the
sea either. We are not great travellers. Our father prefers
to stay at home." Jane saw Elizabeth's brows rise, but Jane
did not care if her tone was not so pleasant as it normally
was. She wished for Captain Harris to both stop speaking
and leave her side for just a moment.

"This is what assumption does," said Harris, clearly
unaffected by Jane's less than sweet response. "We tend to
see the world and everyone in it as our experiences teach
us, but we must not assume that all have had the same
experiences."

"No," said Jane, "we should not."

"Your father was in trade," said Harris, turning to Bingley. "He had ships, did he not?"

"He did."

"So you have been to the sea?"

"I have." Apparently, Harris was desperate to have
someone agree with him on the superiority of a summer
beside the sea to one in Derbyshire. He would not find

such a person in Bingley, even if Bingley did prefer the sea — which he did not.

"And what was your opinion of it?" Harris leaned forward in his chair as if eager to hear what tales Bingley would have to share.

"It is vast and full of water."

Harris blinked. "Is that all? Were you not captivated by its beauty? Did you not like to listen to the calls of the gulls?"

"The gulls will steal your lunch, and the beauty of the sea can turn in an instant to a fearsome monster that snatches life. While I do have some fond memories of the sea, Captain Harris, the most enduring is far from fond, for, you see, my father perished in a storm in the Irish Sea."

"Oh," Jane's hand rested on her heart. "That is very sad indeed."

Bingley gave her a grateful smile. "To be fair, the sea has carried great wealth to our family, for which I am thankful, but it has also carried away that which was most dear. So, I cannot look upon the sea with the same tranquility that another might. If you will excuse me." He rose and walked away from the group. His father had been gone for three years, and yet the pain of his sudden departure had not dulled enough for Bingley to speak of it with great equanimity.

Jane watched Mr. Bingley go and yearned to follow after him, to lend him an arm for comfort and her presence to fill the void he must feel. Colonel Fitzwilliam was shar-ing some tale of having been aboard a ship when the wind had come up and waves had tipped the vessel this way and that, but Jane was not listening. Her eyes were still with Mr. Bingley, who was being called to by a footman and hurrying away.

"Are you well?" Elizabeth whispered to Jane. "You are so somber."

"My head is beginning to hurt," Jane replied. It was not a lie, her head was hurting just a bit, but it was her heart which hurt more.

Elizabeth whispered something to Darcy and soon, when Richard had completed his tale and before Captain Harris could begin another topic of conversation, Darcy asked if Georgiana would like to show Miss Bennet and Miss Elizabeth her new piece of music. "Perhaps after a while, you might even play it for us all?" He smiled at her and winked.

Her eyes darted from him to Jane and then back again. "I am uncertain how long it might take for me to be ready to perform."

"Take whatever time you need," he said with a meaning-ful look. "Gentlemen, if you will excuse me, I would like to escort my sister into the house and speak with my house-keeper about some refreshments for when Georgiana plays for us." With that, he stood, and, offering his hand to his sister, escorted her into the house, followed by Elizabeth and Jane.

Chapter 5

By the look on Caroline Bingley's face, she had not expected her brother to be the one opening the carriage door. "Ch...Charles," she stammered.

"Caroline, you are not expected here." He turned his attention to Mr. Hurst, who was gripping the top of his walking stick so firmly that his knuckles were white. "Did you not receive my letters?" Bingley asked him.

"We did," said Louisa, "but –"

"I did not ask you," Bingley snapped, causing his eldest sister to gasp and cover her mouth in surprise.

"We did," said Hurst uneasily, "but you know how your sisters can be." There was a note of pleading for understanding in his voice. "I accepted the invitation to Hadaway's house party, and we are expected there, but..." He shrugged and looked at Bingley apologetically. "There are two of them and only one of me."

As angry as Bingley was to have his sisters arrive unannounced, he did understand how they could wear a man down. Is that not how they had often gotten their way all their lives?

"When are you expected?" Bingley asked.

"Tomorrow," Hurst replied. "I had thought to stop one more night and then continue on so that we," he nodded his head toward Caroline, "would appear to best advantage when arriving."

Bingley nodded his approval of the idea. He knew that Hurst was equally as anxious to be rid of Caroline, for though she was the youngest of the Bingley siblings, she was the most overbearing. Louisa had not the temperament to stand up to Caroline, and so, what Caroline suggested, Louisa did, even now as a married woman.

"There is an inn in Lambton. There would be a greater distance to be travelled tomorrow, to be certain, but it could be accomplished."

"An inn?" said Caroline in shock.

"Yes, an inn." Bingley gave her a hard, unwavering look.

"Might we stretch our legs?" Louisa asked. "Please. I am quite stiff."

Bingley looked first at one sister and then the other and back again. "You may get out of the carriage, but you are not entering Pemberley." He stepped back and allowed Hurst to help his sisters from the carriage.

"But, Charles," said Caroline as she exited the carriage, "a little refreshment is needed."

Bingley shook his head. "No, you may refresh at the inn. It is not so very far to Lambton."

"Seriously, Charles, an inn?" Caroline gave him a look of amused disbelief. "There are plenty of rooms at Pemberley. It would not be an inconvenience for us to stay the night."

"I am not jesting, Caroline. You may stretch your legs and then be on your way. Did I not explicitly say you were not to come to Pemberley?"

Caroline waved his words away. "There was no reason for us not to come. Pemberley is on the way to Hadaway's, and Darcy is our friend as much as he is yours."

"Darcy is polite and tolerates you." Bingley gave a bitter laugh. "And I have been no better, forcing him to put up with the likes of you."

Again, Louisa gasped and covered her mouth. Bingley could well imagine her surprise at his actions this afternoon. It was not often that he allowed his anger to get the best of him in the presence of ladies — even if those ladies were his sisters.

"Me?" Caroline blinked wide eyes at him. "It is not I who has done him the disservice of seeing him connected to those beneath him."

Bingley's eyes narrowed. So, they were to come to it. "Do you dare stand before his home and disparage the lady he will call wife in one week's time?"

"Charles," Caroline's tone was cajoling, "even you must

admit she is not of his sphere. It will become apparent to one and all soon enough, and then do you think he will remain your friend? You, who led him to such a place as Hertfordshire?"

Bingley stepped close to Caroline and lowered his voice. "You go too far, Sister."

"Oh, I do not think I have gone far enough. Had I done more, this travesty might have been prevented. Indeed, it still might." Caroline smiled slyly.

Bingley's jaw clenched and relaxed. "Darcy is marrying Miss Elizabeth. Take one last look at Pemberley and be gone. You shall not see it again."

Caroline cocked her head and patted her brother's arm before stepping around him. "Mr. Darcy, it is good to see you."

Bingley closed his eyes and shook his head. Of all the unfortunate times for Darcy to appear! Two minutes longer and Caroline would have been gone.

"We are on our way to Hadaway's," Caroline explained in her sweetest voice, "and since Pemberley was on our way, we could not resist the opportunity to call and wish you joy."

"Indeed?" Darcy's eyes looked to Bingley in question. "I had it from your brother that you would not be visiting."

Caroline laughed lightly and shot her brother a triumphant smile. "It was not planned. We only wished to stop for a few minutes before continuing on to the inn in

Lambton for the night. We are expected at the house party tomorrow, you see." She looked about as if expecting to see someone. "Would we be so fortunate as to see Miss Eliza and Miss Darcy?"

Bingley shook his head when Darcy looked his direction.

Darcy gave a small incline, barely a tip, of his head in acceptance of Bingley's unspoken suggestion. "They are occupied at the moment. Miss Bennet felt a headache developing, and Miss Elizabeth and Georgiana are seeing to her needs."

"Miss Bennet? Miss Jane Bennet?" Caroline cast a concerned look toward Bingley.

"Yes, she is visiting the area along with her aunt and uncle Gardiner. It seems my tenants at Willow Hall are related to the Gardiners."

"Oh," said Caroline, "how fortunate."

Bingley smiled at the disappointed tone in her voice.

"Indeed, it was most fortunate. I had not thought to see Miss Elizabeth again so soon after leaving her in Kent this spring." Darcy cut a glance toward Bingley and, catching his eye, winked at him and flicked a brow up quickly.

"In Kent?" Caroline could not contain her surprise at this bit of information.

"Yes, her cousin is my aunt's parson," Darcy replied. "I believe you met Mr. Collins, did you not?"

Caroline nodded.

"He married Miss Lucas. You remember her, do you not?"

Again, Caroline nodded.

"Miss Elizabeth and Mrs. Collins are good friends, so it was only natural that a visit must take place. Happily, it was the same time my cousin Colonel Fitzwilliam and I were visiting my aunt Lady Catherine."

"How fortunate," muttered Caroline.

"My cousin is here now. We are gathered in the garden. Perhaps a stroll before you are on your way would be beneficial?" He motioned to the side of the house.

Bingley breathed a sigh of relief. Darcy was not going to play the gallant and insist on Caroline and the Hursts staying at Pemberley. Bingley would have to thank him for that later.

"That would be lovely," said Louisa, "I have always enjoyed the grounds here. They are so well designed."

Darcy gave a bow of his head in thanks and led the way toward the garden.

~*~*~

Caroline accepted the arm of Captain Harris when he offered to escort her on a stroll.

"I have heard your name mentioned," said Harris as they began their walk, "and I am most happy to now have made your acquaintance. The militia has kept me away, you see."

"You said your father lives near here?" Caroline asked as she studied his features. Captain Harris was nearly a head taller than she was, and his shoulders were wide while his waist was narrow. The arm on which her hand rested was firm, and she guessed him to be very strong. His hair fell around his ears in wisps of golden brown, and his face was angular but not harshly so. Overall, he was quite attractive, but looks were not the salient point when judging a gentleman. No matter the perfection of the physical specimen, it was his accounts and holdings that truly defined his worth to Caroline.

"He does. Not six miles from Aldwood Abbey. Mr. Dobney is my uncle — my mother's sister was his wife." He glanced down at Caroline. "Have you been to Aldwood Abbey?"

"Yes, once."

"Well, then, I shall compare my father's estate with it since you might remember how large Aldwood Abbey is?"

"Oh, I remember every estate I visit. I am very good at that sort of thing. I admire architecture and finishings, you see. The way they lead the eye and present themselves is of great interest to me. So much can be said of a man and his character just by the state of his garden."

She hoped from the smile he favoured her with that he understood her meaning. She would not even consider a man without a proper estate that was well-tended. There were areas where appearances were important, and the impressing of callers, the care of a garden, the right drapery and paintings, and a proper placement of furniture must all be considered as necessities.

"I quite agree, and should you ever visit my father's home, you would find gardens as fine as these," he waved his hand toward the garden, "they lack only size in comparison. My mother has a fine eye, and father dotes on her — though not to extravagance." He shook his head. "Oh, no, Father is far from extravagant."

"So your father's estate is well-tended?"

Harris nodded. "Yes, quite. But, we digress. I was to describe to you the size of the estate."

Caroline looked at him eagerly. He seemed to possess a proper understanding of the importance of appearances and holdings. In fact, he seemed to be a man who would use his money wisely to increase his standing, and she found this fact to be almost as attractive as his face — and the longer she looked at him, the more she had to admit that his face was handsome.

"The lands attached to my father's estate are equal to those of Aldwood Abbey, but we have a greater number of fields, and an attached farm to the west that is let out...but land holdings are not what most ladies find of interest about the estate." He again smiled down at her. "As I said the gardens are magnificent, but the house — ah, there is the true beauty of the estate. The house shines like a jewel surrounded by its gardens and backed by the stand of woods. The drive is not so long as the one here, but there is ample time when a carriage is spotted at the turn for tea to be ordered before the guests arrive at the door. And then, well — my mother's eye is as good at interiors as it is at exteriors. The rooms, and there are only two fewer than at Aldwood Abbey- we have no chapel or chapel anteroom — are so well furnished in a traditional classical style. If you were to be visiting longer, I would insist that you come visit. I am certain you would not be disappointed."

"I dare say you are correct! You have described such a place as I would find every pleasure in seeing. Tell me, what were the impressions of the Bennets on seeing it?"

"Oh, I could not say. I have yet to persuade them to visit."

There was a distinct note of disappointment in his tone that did not evade Caroline's notice. Perhaps, Captain Harris might prove handy in creating a trying environment for Miss Eliza to be entering.

"Do not tell me," Caroline cried, "that Miss Bennet and Miss Elizabeth limit themselves to Pemberley when there are estates such as your father's to visit!"

"No, no. They divide their time between here, the Abbey, and Kympton."

Caroline's brows rose. Was Jane attempting to ensnare Marcus Dobney? "They visit Aldwood Abbey?"

Harris nodded. "Their sister is to marry my cousin Marcus, so it is only natural that they would."

"Miss Bennet is to marry Mr. Marcus Dobney?" she asked in surprise.

Harris laughed. "No, Miss Lydia is to marry Marcus."

"Miss Lydia?" Caroline's eyes grew wide, and her brows rose.

Harris chuckled again. "It is quite the story how it came to be."

"Indeed?"

Harris's lips curled upward slyly as he nodded.

"Do tell," Caroline encouraged.

And he did.

Caroline could not believe what she was hearing. Such tales that could be shared! Oh, the pleasure of tickling Louisa's ears in the carriage! The thought was nearly enough for her to wish to leave that moment, but one must not ignore an opportunity to add to succulent secrets.

"I should say I am surprised, I suppose," Caroline peeked up at him with a coquettish smile and flutter of lashes, "but I am not. The way the Bennets present themselves in public!" She gasped and shook her head. "Oh, the eldest girls present themselves quite well, but the mother and the younger girls — it is quite embarrassing."

"I have no doubt," said Harris. "Miss Lydia was the most determined flirt in Brighton. I heard rumors that she was not ungenerous with her charms."

Oh, this was the opening that Caroline had longed for! A place where she might be able to see Jane and Elizabeth lowered as they should be. And so, she leaned closer and whispered, "I should not say this since he is my brother, but you seem the sort of person who can be trusted." She looked at Harris and waited for the agreement that was not long in coming. "Miss Bennet and Miss Eliza stayed at Netherfield, the estate my brother leased in Hertfordshire, for several days. I cannot say for certain, but there were whispers amongst the staff that not everything was proper."

"Do you mean, Miss Bennet or Miss Elizabeth was not proper?" He asked in surprise.

"I know it is shocking," Caroline agreed. "I cannot say it was one or the other — some things are best left unsaid. However, I can tell you that Miss Bennet was whisked away to her aunt's home only a little more than a month thereafter, and, well, Mr. Darcy is excessively enamoured with Miss Elizabeth, so..." she let the story end there as Harris's eyes grew wide.

"But your brother is not engaged to Miss Bennet. Is his honor not injured by not offering for her?"

Caroline shrugged. "I do not know that my brother did not offer and was rejected. Nor do I know if he found her — hmmm," she tapped her lips with her finger, "untouched. Miss Bennet smiles very easily at all the men she meets."

They walked along in silence for a few strides. "I fear

I have fallen prey to her smiles," Harris finally admitted, "but she seemed so decorous."

"That she does," Caroline said sadly. "I, of course, broke off my friendship with her as soon as I knew."

"As you should!" declared Harris, "And as I will."

"You will not say anything about what I have shared, will you? She is a woman in need of a good home at some point. Her father is not well to do."

Harris looked toward the house that was now just before them. "I shall not whisper a word," he assured her.

Caroline thanked him but knew that this secret would not stay hidden. How could it? It was tantalizing. Miss Bennet would not succeed with any gentleman in Derbyshire, and Charles? She shrugged mentally. It was possible that his reputation might come into question, but he was a man and as such, indiscretions were forgivable. However, she thought as a smile curled her lips, if it did hurt him, it was no more than he deserved for first, ruining her chances with Darcy and then, turning her away from Pemberley to sleep at an inn.

Chapter 6

Bingley was relieved when he could, at last, stand on the steps of Pemberley and watch Hurst's carriage driving away. Finally, when the coach could no longer be seen from the house, he went in search of Darcy, who had gone to check on Georgiana's progress with her music. Bingley smiled. He doubted that Georgiana was little more than a passing thought to his friend. Darcy would no doubt be more interested in Elizabeth, but that was as it should be. He sighed. How he longed to be so besotted! He nearly was — indeed, he would be just as smitten if Jane would accept him.

"Would you be willing to see the ladies returned to Willow Hall?" Harris was asking Darcy as Bingley approached the music room. "I had not thought we would be so long in our call, or I would have allowed another to escort them."

"You are leaving?" Bingley asked in surprise.

"I have another commitment," Harris darted a nervous glance toward the music room, "and I would hate to be the cause of snatching Miss Elizabeth away, for Miss Bennet will not wish to leave without her."

"I can see them home," said Darcy. "It will be no trouble."

"Thank you." Harris scooted back a step. "If you will make my excuses, I shall be on my way. I truly should not delay another minute." He turned and walked away — nearly trotting down the stairs — before anyone could either agree or disagree to do as he requested.

"I am not sorry to see him gone," Bingley said to Darcy once Harris was out of sight.

Darcy laughed. "I can imagine you are not." He slapped Bingley on the shoulder. "It has been a trying afternoon for you, first with Harris arriving and then your sisters."

"Indeed," agreed Bingley.

Richard, who had just joined them, chuckled. "Should Darcy have toast and tea delivered to your room in the morning so that you will not have to watch us eat?"

Bingley scowled. "I have learned my lesson on that front and expect to eat a hearty breakfast — unless my sister returns; then I shall not emerge from my room until she is gone."

"You are not pleased with her, I take it," said Richard, holding open the door to the music room, so that Bingley could pass through ahead of him.

"No, I am not. The sooner I can be rid of her the better." He smiled and nodded a greeting to the ladies, who were gathered near the piano. Elizabeth and Jane sat on a couch, and Georgiana, on the piano bench. The music they held was quickly gathered and returned to a tidy stack on the instrument.

"Was that Miss Bingley who was here?" Elizabeth asked as Darcy took his place next to her.

"It was."

"Was she not supposed to join Mr. Bingley for a time at Pemberley?" Elizabeth's eyes darted from Darcy to Bingley, and Bingley thought he saw Elizabeth squeeze Jane's hand before releasing it.

"Our plans have changed," Bingley said. "Caroline has been invited to a house party, and I will be returning to town next Saturday." He took a seat in a chair that was next to the couch and at Darcy's left elbow, but turned in such a way as to allow the person resting in it to converse easily with those on the couch. "There was no wedding planned when the original arrangements were made."

"I am sorry," said Elizabeth.

"Oh, do not apologize for such a joyful event." Bingley smiled reassuringly as he crossed one foot over the other, trying to appear as at ease as he could. However, in truth, he was anything but easy. He still longed to have a private word with Jane to plead his case and her forgiveness. He had wished for such an arrangement since he had returned from his walk. Unfortunately, Harris's continual presence this afternoon had afforded no such opportunity — that is, until now, if he could manage to break away from the group and draw Jane along with him.

"Then, you will come to visit at another time?" Elizabeth asked.

With some effort, Bingley kept his smile in place and gave a small shrug of his shoulders. "I am uncertain." He could not keep from glancing meaningfully at Jane. "However, if events allow me to return, I will."

Jane did not miss the look Bingley gave her. Was he saying that her acceptance of him was the hinge on which his plans swung? "It would be a travesty to never return to such a lovely place as this," she answered.

Bingley's smile faded slightly as he looked at her. "Undoubtedly, it would be."

Jane's cheeks reddened, and she dropped her gaze for a moment.

Richard cleared his throat and looked at Bingley uneasily. "Can we discuss plans for visits and whatever else you are not saying after Georgiana plays? I have heard enough chatter for one afternoon, and we are not allowed to eat or drink until the performance has ended, and I am hungry." As if it had been prompted by the words, his stomach rumbled.

"You do not have to wait for me to finish," said Georgiana with a giggle. "We would not want you to perish from hunger — or, worse, become bearish because of it."

"I say," Richard began with a feigned look of displeasure, "I should like to protest such a comment, but if it will gain me a biscuit or two earlier than I might have gotten them, I shall be content to be thought of in such a disagreeable way." He winked and waved his hand to indicate she should begin her performance, which she did after sending one last teasing smile in his direction.

Bingley tapped his fingers silently on the arm of his chair while Georgiana played. He was not keeping time to the music. In fact, he was not paying attention to the music in any particular detail. He was merely enjoying it as it washed around him and filled the room so that he could think without having to attempt to keep track of any conversation.

Jane had seemed to welcome him just now. That was what she was doing, was it not? He darted a look in her direction and smiled as her eyes flicked away from watching him. Yes, it did seem he was welcome. He rose and quietly made his way to the tea tray to retrieve a cake. Then, he walked behind the others and took up a place leaning next to the window. Here, he could enjoy the breeze and watch Jane without being obvious — or he would have been able to had she not thought to bring him a cup of tea.

"Are you well?" he asked softly as he accepted the cup.

"I am recovered." She pulled her lip between her teeth and looked briefly at where the others were seated. Then, deciding she was indeed brave enough to do so, she smiled and leaned against the wall across the window from Bingley. "However, I suspect a bit more fresh air might be beneficial."

"Indeed, it might," he agreed, happy to have her stay there with him.

"I have spent a good deal of my time recovering here." She motioned to the bench that was between them and in front of the window.

Bingley's brows rose as he looked out the window to where he and Caroline had spoken earlier that day.

Jane dipped her head. "I did not mean to overhear."

He shook his head as if it was not a big thing to have been overheard being so cross with his sister while inwardly he felt the sting.

"I did not find anything improper in what you said." Jane looked down at her hands.

"You did not?" Bingley was not positive he had heard that correctly. He had not been kind. Was that not improper? Did it not show a man of poor character?

"No, I did not." Jane smiled at him before lowering her gaze once again. Her fingers twisted uneasily around each other. "Did you know I was in town?"

Bingley swallowed. "No," he whispered.

"Then you did not know I called?"

Bingley's mouth dropped open. Jane had called? Why had he not been informed?

"Your sisters eventually returned my call."

Bingley's mouth moved as he unsuccessfully attempted to form words.

"I had hoped you would accompany them." Jane ventured a quick peek at him.

Bingley dropped onto the bench and shook his head. "I had no knowledge of any of it. If I had, I would not have been so polite to Caroline today." Indeed, he might have throttled his sister instead of just speaking harshly.

The music from one song faded, and Georgiana began another.

This was the moment Bingley had desired — the moment when he might beg her forgiveness. He looked first at her and then at the others whose backs were to them before taking her hand and drawing her down to sit next to him.

"I should never have left Netherfield and you. I acted abominably. I was nearly certain your heart was affected as much as mine."

"I should have been less guarded," Jane whispered in return.

Bingley shook his head and smiled sadly at her. "No, I should have stayed until I knew the truth even if the truth would have crushed my soul, for leaving has done just that. Until this moment, I feared I was doomed to a miserable and lonely future." He grasped her hand more firmly. "Please tell me that I have a chance to win you."

Jane blinked against the tears that threatened. "I will, if only you will tell me that I have a chance to be won."

Had the room been empty, Bingley might have allowed the joy, which swelled in his heart, to have overwhelmed his sense and drawn Jane into his arms, but knowing that they were not alone, he refrained from such overt signs of his delight. Instead, he lifted her hand, kissed it, and continued holding it. They sat so for the remainder of the present song and half of the next before Bingley found the words to express what he felt.

"You have made me the happiest of men, and I shall strive to show myself as worthy of you. Then, when I have proven my worth, I shall speak to your father if you desire it."

"Must you wait?" asked Jane. "As time passes, I shall only love you more, not less."

As Bingley searched her eyes, his smile faded slightly. "You fear I will leave you again."

Jane blinked and shook her head, but her cheeks reddened.

"It is a natural concern," said Bingley as calmly as his hurting heart would allow him. "That is why I must wait. I would not have my wife ever doubt my steadfastness."

"But," protested Jane, "you are to leave again — in one week's time."

Bingley blew out a breath, and his shoulders sagged. She was correct. He had planned to leave after the wedding. He could not stay at Pemberley and impose upon his friend at such a time. "I will speak with Marcus, perhaps something can be arranged." He squeezed her hand and released it as the song began to draw to a conclusion. "I will not be persuaded to leave you again, and if I must travel for a time, I will always return."

Jane smiled and nodded her acceptance of his words, for she would not trust herself to speak. Her emotions were too great to be easily regulated.

Bingley stood. "I shall see you home."

Jane's eyes widened, and she looked around the room. "Oh, but what of Captain Harris?"

"He asked Darcy and me to give you and Miss Elizabeth his excuses," Bingley explained. He had been so distracted by the thought of Jane when he entered the room that all other thoughts had been forgotten. He imagined it was the same with Darcy. "It seems Captain Harris had a previous engagement," he added.

Jane laughed in surprise. "I had not even noticed he was not here. How very dreadful of me!"

Bingley grinned. "I find it to be a perfectly acceptable oversight."

Jane laughed again. "I should not say it, for you will begin to think very ill of me, but I am glad he has gone."

Bingley looked at her with a puzzled expression. "I thought you enjoyed his attentions."

"Oh, he was tolerable, perhaps even obliging," she

sighed, "but his regard was not truly what I sought." She lowered her eyes in embarrassment.

"It was not?" Then why had she smiled so often at the man and taken the captain's arm so eagerly when he offered it?

She shook her head. "Oh, what will you think of me?" She sighed again and looked away. "It was a ploy to make you jealous."

Bingley chuckled. "So, you were also being a dress," he said as he helped a confused Jane to her feet and tucked her arm into the crook of his elbow. "You see, Richard had a theory. He had noticed that his sisters always desired a dress they could not have above any they might possess. So," his cheeks grew warm, "we decided that I should be the dress you could not have."

Her eyes grew wide, and a smile spread across her face. "So you have no particular fondness for Miss Dobney?"

"I do not," he admitted.

"I am glad."

"As is Richard," muttered Bingley.

Jane halted their progress toward the door. "Colonel Fitzwilliam is fond of Miss Dobney?"

Bingley could not help but notice the excitement in her voice. "He has not admitted such, but he will not deny it either." He tipped his head, studying her pleased expression. "I take it Miss Dobney will not be injured by my defection?"

"I cannot say." Jane pressed her smiling lips together.

Bingley did not question her further, for though Jane had not spoken a word, the delighted twinkle in her eye gave him to know that he was indeed correct. And he was glad. He had not considered how their plan might have caused injury to Miss Dobney. He would have to be more cautious when making plans in the future, and, he thought with a wry grin, it might be best to make them without the assistance of port.

Chapter 7

Harris' heart raced as his carriage drove away from Pemberley. How fortunate to have come to a solution to his problem in such a convenient way!

He had thought he would have to draw Bingley out — causing him to act rashly and thereby exposing himself as less than a gentleman to one and all in the hopes that Darcy would have little choice but to break ties with his friend. But try as he might to provoke Bingley to irrational jealousy — and he could clearly see that Bingley was jealous — the man had proven to be more controlled than expected.

Harris smiled. Playing the part of the smitten lover of Jane Bennet had not been a hardship. That lady was beautiful! Indeed, until his present trouble had come upon him, Harris had hoped he might convince Jane to marry him. He mentally ticked off the reasons for why he had chosen to favour her with his attentions — she would do justice as mistress of his estate, everyone seemed to adore her, and she was so trusting that she would never suspect his true reason for travelling occasionally to Warwickshire. Yes, Miss Bennet would have made a fabulous Mrs. Harris — not that she was his first choice, no, that choice had been snatched away three years ago. But, that mattered not now, save in keeping the reason for the disappearance of that lady a secret, which Miss Bingley's intelligence should guarantee.

Harris continued to thank his good fortunes all the way to a small pub tucked away around the corner of a street in Lambton. It was not on the familiar path, but it was always busy with a particular shade of customer. He jumped down from his carriage and with a few words to his driver, went in search of his quarry.

"Fisher," Harris greeted a man of middling age as he took a chair at the table where the man sat.

"Harris?" Fisher seemed surprised to see him. "You've got all your teeth and eyes and not a tinge of blood on you." He raised a brow as he lifted his glass. "Not coming to break off our arrangement now are you? Wickham will not be pleased to hear it — and you know what he will do if he is not pleased."

Harris leaned back in his chair and drummed the fingers of his right hand on the edge of the table as a smile spread slowly across his face. "I have come to collect my papers."

"It is done?" Fisher's eyes grew wide in surprise.

"Nearly," said Harris. "I will give you the stories you need to spread about as soon as I have seen the papers."

"You don't expect me to have them with me now do you?" Fisher's empty glass clunked heavily on the table.

"I'm quite certain you do, since Wickham charged you with them in a rather threatening fashion."

Wickham had shoved Fisher against the wall in the room where they had met, holding him in place with a forearm pressed firmly against Fisher's throat and only released Fisher to gasp for air after he got an assurance that the papers would be seen by no one besides himself, Fisher, and Harris until the three week period of time had been completed. At the end of that time, if Harris had not done his best to meet his end of the bargain, the papers were to make their way secretly to Mr. Williams.

Fisher's eyes narrowed, and after waving with his hand to the barkeep for a refill of his drink, he pulled the papers out of a pocket inside his coat and placed them on the table in front of him. "Tell me why I should give these to you?"

Harris' eyes fell on the papers that stood between him and a potential noose or transportation and then lifted his gaze to Fisher with a raised brow.

Fisher flipped the papers over so that Wickham's seal could be seen.

Satisfied that these were the papers he needed, Harris leaned forward and, after a glance around him, began sharing all that Miss Bingley had said about Miss Bennet and

Miss Elizabeth, and then added all he knew of how Miss Lydia had come to Derbyshire.

Fisher laughed. "Wickham did not mention being bamboozled by some pretty skirt."

"Do you blame him?" Harris replied with a smirk. "To meet her one would not think she could string two ideas together in a cohesive fashion...but she is a flirt." His brows flicked upwards quickly. "And from what I hear, her skirts are not precisely heavy." Although they had not been light enough to favour him with any of her attentions. He gritted his teeth — no she kept those for Wickham and his lot.

"Aye, seems a family trait." Fisher slid the papers across the table.

Harris placed a hand on his freedom. "I expect Bingley will be in Miss Bennet's company now that I am stepping away. He will not wait to take up his place next to her, and I imagine hearing her ill-spoken of will bring out an uncharacteristic burst of anger." He stared hard into Fisher's eyes. "He is not to know that the information you received came from me, or I will tell one and all about your connection to Wickham."

Fisher nodded. "He'll only know of his sister being a source. I keep myself to myself."

"See that you do." Harris took the papers and left. His part was done. Not that he would not add to a story about Miss Lydia should he hear one. He would gladly see her shunned as she had done to him in Brighton even if it meant hurting his cousin.

Hopefully, Miss Bingley would have the opportunity to share such a tale about Miss Lydia with her friends at the house party she was to attend. He smiled. That would surely bring raised brows and whispers behind fans whenever Miss Lydia was introduced to finer society — and she would have to be introduced. Darcy was marrying her sister, and there were gatherings even in Derbyshire and Matlock to which his cousin, Marcus, and Lydia as Mrs. Dobney would be invited.

Ah — there was one small pang of regret — Colonel Fitzwilliam was more a brother to Darcy than a cousin, and anything that grieved his cousin would necessarily bring sorrow to the colonel as well. Harris blew out a breath and patted the papers in his pocket. It could not be helped. He must keep his sweet Priscilla safe.

"Was not Captain Harris with you?" Mrs. Abbot stood near the hedge that bordered the garden at Willow Hall to greet Jane and Elizabeth. Her sons played happily on the grass behind her, carefully watched over by Mrs. Gardiner and their nurse.

"He had to leave early for another commitment," Jane explained.

Cecily's head tipped to the side, and her lips pulled into

a small smile. "You do not appear distressed by this development."

"I am not," Jane said simply, schooling her features to only smile slightly and not broadly as she wished. However, her eyes shone with delight.

Cecily's brows rose, and she turned inquisitive eyes toward Elizabeth. "It was Mr. Bingley and Mr. Darcy who attended you home, was it not?"

"Indeed, it was." Elizabeth clamped her lips closed.

"Oh," Cecily's eyes narrowed as she shook her head, "no, you are not going to hide this from me. I will know if Mr. Bingley has spoken about whether he still holds Jane in regard or not. There will be no tea and biscuits until I have heard the full tale." She laced one arm through Elizabeth's and the other through Jane's. "Now, come sit with us and tell me all about your adventure at Pemberley, and you will not finish your tale until you have arrived back at Willow Hall. I must know all."

Madeline Gardiner chuckled. "There is no use trying to deny Cecily what she wishes. She may smile like you, Jane, but I assure you, she is as stubborn as Lizzy." She winked at her sister, who huffed at the description. "And I find I am quite curious as well to know what has transpired to make our Jane's countenance glow as it does."

Jane gasped and placed a hand on her cheek.

Cecily laughed. "It is quite the thing to glow when one

is happy." She took a seat on the blanket which was spread out on the lawn.

Jane took a seat next to her and pondered for a moment how to begin to share all that had happened. One thought kept coming to mind over and over as it had for the entire ride back to Willow Hall, and so, she decided to begin there. "He loves me and always has. He never stopped." This confession, of course, drew exclamations of delight and a flurry of questions.

Patiently and with more joy than she had felt in some time, Jane answered each one.

No, she had never truly felt her heart engaged with regards to Captain Harris. He was a pleasant fellow, but he was not Mr. Bingley.

Yes, the day had been pleasant, but she had found Captain Harris to be rather full of words and then when he had not shown proper sadness at the news of Mr. Bingley's father's death, well...it had been too much to bear. Her heart had ached so! She was ever so thankful to have been given the opportunity to retire to the music room.

She had been shocked at the arrival of Miss Bingley and pleasantly surprised by Mr. Bingley's harsh words to his sisters. Oh, goodness, yes! She was so thankful to not have had to speak with either Mrs. Hurst or Miss Bingley. She really was not certain how she could have countenanced a meeting with them after being treated so abominably.

There was a pause here to consider what it would be

like to have them both for sisters and then a determination that Miss Bingley must marry as soon as possible.

It was the only solution, Elizabeth declared, to keep Jane from having a truly miserable life.

"I am not certain it would be so bad as that!" cried Jane. "I am more forgiving than you, Lizzy. I can abide more foolishness than you can."

Elizabeth allowed this to be so. "Still, I think it would be hideous to have to house and feed her forever. She really must marry if anyone can be found to accept her."

"Oh, Elizabeth," said Cecily with a laugh, "surely, she cannot be beyond finding a husband."

"You have never met her," said Elizabeth. "She can be very unpleasant."

"True," said Jane, "I had not thought so at first, but she did prove to be both unpleasant and untrustworthy."

"Perhaps there will be a man in need of a fortune at this house party," commented Mrs. Gardiner.

They all hoped that would be the case.

"Are we to hear three sets of Bennet wedding bells, then?" asked Cecily.

Jane could not help but smile at the question. "I hope," she replied. "He has not asked. You see — though he would wish to and I would welcome the question — he has asked for a time to prove himself."

Cecily sighed, and Jane nodded her agreement. Having a

gentleman declaring he must show himself worthy of you was just the sort of thing to make a lady swoon just a bit.

This, of course, led to an explanation of Mr. Bingley not knowing that Jane was in town or that she had called. It was his sisters who were to blame. In fact, when Elizabeth mentioned Mr. Darcy's part, Jane could not bring it upon herself to implicate him in any of her misery. He was acting, she said, with the best interest of his friend in mind. Truly, if she had listened to Charlotte and been less circumspect, neither Mr. Darcy nor Mr. Bingley would have doubted her attachment. The blame lay entirely at Miss Bingley's and Mrs. Hurst's feet. They were the ones that made Jane feel as if she were expected to be part of their family, and they were the ones that kept her visit to town a secret. No, there was no use in trying to dissuade her. They were, without a doubt, the injurious parties.

"And what of Captain Harris?" asked Mrs. Gardiner. "Has he made any overtures that he might make an offer? Have you led him to believe one might be welcomed?"

For a moment, a cloud passed across Jane's beautiful and bright horizon. It was never easy to let down a suitor. She had done so once before and had felt the sting of his displeasure for some time afterward. Yet, Captain Harris was not someone she would often see after he returned to Brighton. Perhaps she would see him on occasion if he should visit the Dobneys at the same time she did, but that would be at a time so far in the future that surely, he would have forgotten any disappointment she caused him. She had no reason to believe he valued her as anything more than a pretty conversationalist. He never spoke to her as if she were the only one present. Nor did he ever silently smiled at her with his eyes across a room when they were separated.

"I shall be friendly, of course," she said in reply to her aunt's question. "But I shall not show him any particular attention, for Mr. Bingley shall have it all. He will not doubt my feelings again."

"And you will speak to Captain Harris if the need arises?" Mrs. Gardiner knew of Jane's propensity to avoid unpleasant conversations.

"I will." Jane smiled. "The prize is worth the discomfort."

"Good girl." Mrs. Gardiner patted Jane's knee. "You do love Mr. Bingley, then?"

Jane nodded. "Yes. Very much."

Chapter 8

"I publish the Banns of Marriage between..."

Bingley felt an unusual tingle of excitement skitter up his spine and across the skin on his arms as Philip began to read the first banns for Marcus to be followed by the final banns for Darcy. Soon, it would be his turn to have such a service rendered him. As soon as he could prove to Jane that he was worthy of her trust.

"This is the first time of asking." Philip paused and then began again. "I publish the Banns of Marriage between..."

Bingley glanced across the church and catching Jane's eye, smiled. The way she bowed her head and the colour that stained her cheeks were charming. How had he ever listened to Darcy and his sister? He lifted his shoulders in an imperceptible shrug. Listening to Darcy was perhaps understandable. Darcy was, after all, slightly older and therefore, supposedly, wiser. But listening to Caroline — if there was a character flaw amplified in this whole ordeal, that was it! He had been far too willing to listen to Caroline and Louisa. It was a trust that was sorrowfully misplaced but would not be again.

"This is the third time of asking." Philip once again paused.

"Mr. Darcy is betrothed to another," a voice called out from the back of the church.

Bingley saw Darcy's spine stiffen and the brilliant hues of anger creep up his neck.

Philip's eyes grew wide as he looked first at the well-dressed woman at the back of the church and then Darcy.

Darcy rose and turned toward the woman who accused him. "Lady Catherine, have you come all this way to speak lies?"

Every eye in the church was fixed on either Darcy or the woman Darcy had addressed as Lady Catherine.

"I believe she is his aunt," some woman whispered to the left of Bingley.

"It is not a lie," Lady Catherine countered. "Mr. Darcy is betrothed to my daughter."

"We are not betrothed," countered Darcy with a look toward Philip. "It was merely a wish of my aunt's. There are no papers signed. There has not even been an offer made or an overture of preference shown to my cousin on my part." He turned back to Lady Catherine but looked past her to the ashen-faced girl trying to hide in the depths of the pew. "Cousin Anne, what have you to say?"

"She is not well," said Lady Catherine. "The trip was

long and taxing, but when I heard the news that you were to be married." She clucked her tongue. "That you would defy your own mother in such a way as to marry," her eyes swept the church until they landed on Elizabeth, "her." She glared at Elizabeth before returning her focus to Darcy. "I could not sit by and allow it."

"Is there a record of a betrothal?" Philip asked. "Is there documentation that I might see?"

Lady Catherine raised a brow at Darcy and pulled a folded paper from her reticule. With a flourish of skirts, she marched up the aisle, handed the paper to Philip, and waited as he scanned its contents.

"This is an agreement between yourself and your sister," he said in a hushed voice.

"But you can see, young man, that it is an agreement that my daughter and Darcy are to marry."

"This is merely a wish that it might happen," Philip countered still in a hushed tone. "It is not legally binding."

"You are too young and appointed by him." She attempted to snatch the paper away from him, but Philip held the document out of her reach.

"Would you accept the opinion of one who is older than I and was appointed by Mr. Darcy's father?"

Lady Catherine shifted uneasily and after a moment's consideration nodded.

"Mrs. Dobney, if you would so kindly help Mr. Harker

to the anteroom. Mr. Darcy, Lady Catherine, if you would join me. We shall have this sorted out in no time."

"Anne," Lady Catherine called.

The frail young lady in the last pew on the right-hand side of the church jumped, rose swiftly to her feet, and followed her mother to the small room on the side of the church.

"Come with me," Darcy said to Bingley. "And try to keep me from doing anything foolish that will land me in jail."

~*~*~

Bingley slid into the room and stood behind Darcy where he could poke him if necessary without being seen by the others. This was not the first time that he had stood behind his friend like this. But, at those moments, Darcy had not looked so displeased as he did now. There were degrees to Darcy's foreboding look, varying from the leave me be, I could not be bothered with the likes of you to his current pistols at dawn expression. Bingley leaned forward and whispered near Darcy's ear. "I'll not be your second. Besides, I am certain you cannot call out a lady."

Despite the tense mood, Darcy let out a quiet laugh and shook his head. Bingley sighed in relief. Darcy was no longer looking murderous.

"I do not see why we could not have done this out there," grumbled Lady Catherine.

"I am afraid that is my fault," said Mr. Harker. "My eyes

are not good, so Mr. Dobney will need to read the paper to me."

Lady Catherine huffed.

"I assure you, my lady, that my mental faculties have not left me. It is just my eyes that are dim. I shall be able to judge wisely and fairly."

"You are agreed that Mr. Harker has the final word on the legitimacy of this protest?" Philip asked.

Lady Catherine looked from Darcy to Mr. Harker and, finally, Mr. Dobney. "I feel I have no choice."

"We could call for the magistrate if you prefer," said Darcy.

Lady Catherine narrowed her eyes. "No doubt a friend of yours."

"There are not many who are not." Darcy flinched and clamped his lips closed as Bingley poked him between the shoulder blades. Such comments would do nothing to help the situation. If anything, they would only serve to exacerbate Darcy's aunt.

"I will begin," said Philip. "It is hereby declared on this third day of May in the year of our Lord 1792 that it is designed and intended that Fitzwilliam George Darcy will upon or before the twenty-first birthday of Annella Catherine De Bourgh join with her in marriage." Philip folded the sheet. "It is signed by Lady Catherine and Lady Anne."

"I was seven, and Anne was not one!" Darcy's shoulders twitched at the jab from behind.

"Your age does not matter," said Mr. Harker. "Let us not discuss that it was a contract formed by females but instead consider that Mr. Darcy has not signed it. Anyone could create such a document. I could write on a piece of paper that Miss De Bourgh is to marry Mr. Bingley here, and I could even have Miss De Bourgh sign the paper. However, it would not hold an ounce of power if Mr. Bingley had not signed it. Mr. Darcy is not bound by the law to marry your daughter unless he wishes to marry her. Do you?" Mr. Harker turned toward Darcy.

"No, I wish to marry Miss Elizabeth."

"And you, Miss De Bourgh, I cannot see your face very clearly, but I see you shifting," he smiled kindly at her. "Do you wish to marry Mr. Darcy?"

Anne turned frightened eyes toward her mother.

Mr. Harker nodded. "As I thought. All will be well, Miss De Bourgh. I understand that you only wish to please your mother."

"But it was planned!" protested Lady Catherine. "Will you deny your mother her wish?" She turned her eyes toward Darcy.

"Even if I believed my mother still held such a wish these twenty years later, I would deny it, for I will not marry a lady unless she has captured my heart. And Miss Elizabeth possesses it now and will for all time."

"Her mother is a tradesman's daughter," countered Lady Catherine. "It is unseemly."

"Her father is a gentleman just as I am and just as my father was," retorted Darcy.

"I will not stand for it," said Lady Catherine.

"You have no choice," said Mr. Harker.

Lady Catherine huffed in displeasure and lifted her chin just a touch higher. "I will not accept her."

"You do not need to accept her." Darcy crossed his arms and glowered imperiously back at his aunt.

Again, Lady Catherine huffed. "Mr. Collins was right about her. That woman is an adventuress. She would not have him and his living because she saw you and your fortune. She was the same with Mr. Wickham — pleasant and even a bit of a flirt, but what is he in comparison to your wealth? And her youngest sister is no different, I hear."

"Mr. Wickham?" Darcy snarled, and Bingley allowed him to do so without as much as a nudge as a reminder to Darcy to contain his anger. If Wickham were involved, he wished to hear how.

"I did not see him, of course." She raised her chin enough that she had to look down her nose at anyone to whom she was talking. "He is too far below me, but Mr. and Mrs. Collins were hospitable and saw to his needs. Mr. Collins is not too far above anyone in his behaviour."

"Wickham called at Hunsford?" Bingley asked.

Lady Catherine barely deigned to spare him a glance. "Mr. Wickham called on his way through Kent. He is stationed at Brighton, I believe — or was it Portsmouth?"

"Brighton," Anne offered quietly.

"Ah, yes. Brighton is where he is stationed. He knew Mrs. Collins when she was still Miss Lucas, and he thought it his duty to wish her joy on her marriage." She shook her head. "Mr. Collins relayed to me that his wife was greatly distressed when she heard the extent of Mr. Wickham's trip. He was to go as far as London, but your betrothed's," she gave Darcy a pointed look, "youngest sister — quite the wild thing from Mr. Collins's description — charmed Mr. Wickham into conveying her to Derbyshire under the pretense of an elopement." Her brows rose nearly to her hairline as her scowl deepened. "He claims there was never an arrangement or anything improper between them, and Mr. Collins assured me that he believed Mr. Wickham to be true — and Mr. Collins is very good at judging character. However, they did travel alone. And this, this family of wanton women, is the one with whom you wish to align yourself?"

"Mr. Wickham told all that to Mr. Collins?" Bingley tried to keep his tone cool so as not to betray the anger he felt. He had warned Wickham about speaking of Lydia.

Lady Catherine swept her eyes from Bingley's toes to his face and with a slightly sour look assured him that Mr.

Collins had indeed heard that very thing from Mr. Wickham.

Darcy, whose shoulders had been lifting and lowering at a steady pace as he drew deep breaths, finally, spoke. "You will leave and not return. I never wish to see you again." His voice wavered, and the murderous look had once again returned.

"You would choose her over family?" Lady Catherine asked in surprise.

"Go," said Darcy in a low growl, pointing to the door.

"I will see you out the side door and safely to your carriage," said Lucy, stepping between Darcy and his aunt. Thankfully, with a final look and huff at Darcy, Lady Catherine complied and was soon gone.

Bingley wished to be off after her — not to Kent, but to Brighton. However, rash decisions were not what was needed. So, instead, he looked at the men in the room with him and smiled at Darcy.

"She drove from Kent to make a false claim? Do you think she might be related to my sister?" The question did as it was intended, sending a diffusing chuckle around the group.

Chapter 9

Jane stood beside her sister as they waited for Darcy's carriage. After the morning's service with its interesting interruption, it had been decided that an afternoon near the stream at the bottom of the hill, not far from Willow Hall and in the direction of Aldwood Abbey, would be just the thing. Each group of people had hurried off to their respective homes to divest of their fine clothing in favour of something more conducive to walking and sitting under trees while eating a light picnic. It was to be nothing formal, Mrs. Abbot had instructed, just a time of refreshment and pleasure. She would even bring the children. Darcy had insisted that he would supply transportation for Miss Elizabeth and Miss Bennet, and so the two ladies stood waiting for him.

"It still amazes me," said Jane. She was speaking, of course, of Lady Catherine's appearance at the church. It had been the topic of conversation ever since the service had ended. Jane leaned against the window frame in the sitting room. "I thought our family was the only one to have such silly women." A small smile pulled at her lips. "Can you not see Mama doing the same?"

Elizabeth chuckled lightly. "I can, but it would have been a much bigger to-do with fluttering fans and fainting."

Jane giggled at the image, then tipped her head and said as she saw the smile fade from Elizabeth's face. "We shall both have relations who do not approve of us." She reached out and took Elizabeth's hand. "Promise me that you will not let this affect you too greatly. Mr. Darcy loves you, and that is what is most important."

"But to be the cause of a breach such as this," said Elizabeth.

"No," Jane said firmly. "This breach is not your doing. It is Lady Catherine's choice. You no more forced her to be unreasonable than I have been the cause of Miss Bingley's scheming."

Elizabeth gave Jane a grateful smile.

"It is true." Jane stood up straight and, releasing Elizabeth's hand, straightened her skirts and checked her bonnet as a carriage came into view. "You cannot believe I would have contrived to make Miss Bingley dislike me and cause me sorrow for these many months, can you?"

"Of course not," said Elizabeth as she followed Jane from the room.

"And you did not decide when Mr. Darcy came to Hertfordshire that you would ensnare him with the intent of displeasing his family, did you?"

"I did not even like him!"

Jane smiled. "Precisely. And I am certain that you did not bat your lashes and simper when you were in Kent to draw his attentions and lead him down a merry path." She paused just outside the door and before they were to descend the steps. "I believe a sound refusal of an offer of marriage would be proof enough of that."

"I should think," agreed Elizabeth.

"And after refusing him, did you arrange to meet him here in Derbyshire and expect him to renew his addresses?"

"I did not. I had hoped that should we meet, it would be as friends, but I would not have blamed him for hating me after how I had abused him."

"Then, can you see how this is not your doing?" Jane lifted a brow in question and then, with a smile, turned to greet Mr. Bingley.

She knew what Elizabeth was like when she got an idea in her head that she might be the cause of someone she loved being unhappy. A small crease would form between her brows, and her lips would purse while she looked unseeingly at some object and tried to reason out how she could fix whatever wrong had been done. However, as quick-witted as her dear sister was, there were times when Elizabeth was decidedly dull. It was usually just a momen-

tary lack of judgment and clear thinking unless she stub-
bornly refused to listen to reason — which, thankfully,
she did not seem determined to do at present. Elizabeth's
error with the man currently helping her into the carriage
was likely the reason. Ever since her return from Kent,
there had been a wiser air to Elizabeth. Mr. Darcy would
be good for her. His steadying influence would draw her
along where their father could not.

"Are you well?" asked Bingley.

"I beg your pardon," said Jane, her cheeks coloring at
having been caught woolgathering, "I am well. I was just
lost in thought."

"Pleasant thoughts, I hope," he replied with a smile.

Jane assured him that they were. "I was merely thinking
how good Mr. Darcy will be for my sister." The admission
was barely louder than a whisper.

Bingley nodded his agreement. "And she will be good
for him," he added in a whisper as he helped Jane into the
carriage where she took a seat on the bench with Elizabeth
and Georgiana.

"I feel I must once again apologize for my aunt," said
Darcy as the carriage began moving.

"If we are to take the role of bearer of all the ills of our
relations, then you might have the driver stop near the
deeper end of the river, and I shall cast myself into it," said
Bingley with a playful smile. "Did I tell you that my loving

sisters treated Miss Bennet very ill when Miss Bennet was in town?"

"No," said Georgiana, eagerly, earning a glare from her brother.

"Well, they did. Miss Bennet was kind enough to call on them, and they repaid her kindness by not telling me about her call and then waiting an inexcusable length of time before returning the call."

Georgiana gave a little gasp.

"Precisely," said Bingley, crossing his arms in front of his chest. "Miss Bennet was, of course, left to think we were no longer friends." He smiled. "Which, I assure you, is not the case."

Jane blushed prettily and looked away.

Georgiana's eyes grew wide, and she leaned forward toward Bingley. "Are you more than friends?" she asked in a whisper.

"Georgiana," snapped Darcy.

Georgiana immediately apologized for the impertinence.

"See," said Bingley, with a wink at Georgiana. "If anyone is to be found guilty of having ill-behaved relations, it is I. Caroline would never have responded to a reminder so well." He then leaned toward Georgiana and whispered, "I believe, we are."

"You are quite impossible yourself," Darcy chided Bingley.

"Do not worry on my account," said Jane softly. "I am not offended, nor am I unacquainted with sisters who do as they wish instead of as they should. I have four such sisters."

Elizabeth gasped.

"The three youngest are the worst for it," Jane added quickly, "but none of them do as I would think they should, and do you know why?"

Georgiana shook her head.

"For the same reason your brother does not do as you would always wish he would. He is not you." She smiled at Mr. Darcy, who had inclined his head in acceptance of her argument. "And yes, I also believe we are more than friends," she whispered to Georgiana, "which, I suspect, was exactly the thing Miss Bingley wished to prevent by her behaviour."

Georgiana opened her mouth and then with a glance at her brother closed it again.

"What is it?" Jane encouraged her. "You may ask if I give you permission. May she not, Mr. Darcy?"

"It is impertinent," explained Georgiana.

"I am not a stranger to impertinence either," assured Jane. "Remember, I have four younger sisters," she whispered. "And we are to be sisters in a roundabout way." Jane looked to Mr. Darcy. "May she ask?"

"You are certain you wish it?"

"I am not unaware of what sort of box I might be opening," Jane assured him.

"Very well, then you may ask, Georgiana." Darcy held up a finger. "But, Miss Bennet may choose not to answer if she wishes."

Georgiana's head bobbed her agreement. "I was merely curious about Captain Harris. He has called on you so many times that I thought perhaps..." her voice trailed off.

Jane smiled. "You thought I preferred him?"

"Yes."

"I did not." She drew a deep breath. "Since last September, I have not preferred any gentleman above Mr. Bingley." Her cheeks, she knew, were a brilliant shade of red as she looked at Mr. Darcy. "I may not have been obvious in my preference — in fact, a friend, in concern for my happiness told me I should not be so cautious — I, however, did not listen. It is not an error I will make a second time."

"Which is how it should be with errors." Darcy's smile was understanding and perhaps a bit sheepish. "We should strive only to make them once if we must make them at all."

"Indeed," said Jane.

The carriage rolled along for a few turns of the wheels in relative silence as conversation naturally took a respite.

"We will have to walk from here," said Darcy when the vehicle began to slow. "It is not far, however."

The passengers disembarked, and as the men saw to the

baskets, Georgiana, Jane, and Elizabeth joined arms and walked on ahead.

"I am glad you do not prefer Captain Harris," said Georgiana. "Mr. Bingley is a much finer choice."

"You," Jane began and then stopped.

"Yes?" prompted Georgiana.

"You have never..." Jane was not certain how to ask what she wished to know.

"Miss Bingley wrote a letter," said Elizabeth, looking at Jane, who nodded that that was the topic she was trying to broach. "In this letter, Miss Bingley insinuated that your brother hoped to see an arrangement between yourself and Mr. Bingley."

Georgiana's eyes grew wide, and her mouth dropped open. She looked first to Elizabeth and then to Jane. "Mr. Bingley and me?" She shook her head. "Oh, you will not cause me an ounce of pain!" she cried. "I assure you, I see him as nothing more than another brother."

Jane sighed in relief. "I had thought it might be another ploy of Miss Bingley's, but I had to be certain."

"I should not say it," said Georgiana with a glance over her shoulder towards her brother, "but I do not like Miss Bingley, and she does not truly like me. She likes my brother because of his money. I do not think she is capable of liking anyone but herself. So, I am certainly glad Miss Elizabeth will be my sister and not her." Her face pinched as if in pain. "I am sorry that she will be yours." Her eyes grew wide as if realizing she had misspoken. "That is, if you marry Mr. Bingley."

Elizabeth laughed. "If she does not marry him, I shall be very surprised."

"He has only to ask me," whispered Jane.

Georgiana glanced over her shoulder again. Seeing that her brother was far enough away to not overhear, she continued. "I also do not like Captain Harris."

Jane's brows furrowed. "You do not?"

Georgiana shook her head. "He talks too much. I prefer quiet to excessive conversation."

Jane had to agree with that assessment. It was something she had also noticed.

"And I know my brother would scold me for this, and rightly so, but about three years ago, Captain Harris was nearly engaged to a lady." She glanced again at her brother. "The lady disappeared, and her father was found dead."

This information was shocking to both Elizabeth and Jane.

"It was so long ago now that no one speaks of it, but at the time, I heard the maids whispering that Captain Harris had some part in it."

"Captain Harris?" Elizabeth asked in surprise.

Georgiana nodded. "No one was sorry the lady's father died. He was not kind to any of his servants, nor was he kind to his daughter. They say he wished to break her heart, so he sent her away and when Captain Harris called and found out that she was gone, he strangled her father in a fit of rage. It is only a story, of course, and likely not a whit of it is true, but I have never felt completely at ease around him."

"He seems so pleasant," said Jane. "I cannot imagine him being violent."

Georgiana shrugged. "He is pleasant, and as I said, the story is likely just the work of someone's imagination. But I do not like him and am glad you are not going to marry him."

Jane smiled. "Well, I have to agree with that last bit. I am glad that I am not marrying him either, for my heart would have never been truly happy."

This statement turned the conversation toward love and what each thought was important in a match.

Chapter 10

Bingley took his turn perched on a rock next to the stream, net in hand, attempting to catch a fish.

"There," Lydia pointed to the right, "get him."

Bingley drew the net through the water, but the fish darted away just as he reached it. "You have a good eye for this, Miss Lydia."

Lydia smiled. "I do, but then, I have always noticed details. There." She pointed to the right again. "He has come back."

Bingley once again tried to scoop up the fish in the net.

"Perhaps if you were to move your net next to that pile of rocks and just wait, he will come back again," suggested Lydia, and then she sighed. "It is rather hard to just sit and wait, though."

Bingley had to agree. Waiting was not something which came easily to him. He tended to be impatient and wish for quick action, but he also knew that sometimes, patience was precisely what was needed. He had learned that from watching his father. His father was an accomplished negotiator with a calm demeanor and a longsuffering temperament — at least in the presence of those with whom he wished to strike a deal. Often, he would come out of the transaction the victor, having secured exactly what he wanted, but other times, he would come away only nearly satisfied.

"You must know the most important items and not waiver on those, Son, but you must also have a list of things which are of marginal importance." He would chuckle. *"Indeed, you should include at least one thing that you do not wish for at all. Then, it will be the first item to be shifted; followed in order by the other items on your list of margins. But never compromise on the items of greatest importance. Walk away if necessary. No deal is worth giving up what is most important to you, your business, and your family."*

How often had he heard this same lecture from his father?

Bingley's eyes shifted from the net in the water to where Jane sat. He had compromised what was of greatest value once, but he would not do so again.

"Now," whispered Lydia.

Bingley swiftly drew the net up and under the fish, lifting it victoriously.

Lydia clapped her hands, drawing everyone's attention to the fish she and Mr. Bingley had caught.

Bingley chuckled. He had not thought much of Miss Lydia when they had first met. She was just a young, flirtatious girl, given to outbursts of impropriety, but now that he had seen her several times in company, he had to admit that although she was still not always sensible, he preferred her sweet nature to that of his own sisters. There was little pretense with Miss Lydia — oh, there was scheming to be certain, but for the larger part of their new acquaintance, he had found her to be quite forthright.

He allowed her the privilege of carrying the net to Mr. Abbot, so that the fish could be put into the basket, while he sat for a moment longer on the rock near the water's edge and turned his attention back to Jane.

Patience had won him the fish, and patience would prove his worth to Jane. He must deal with Wickham's breach of contract, but he could write to a friend. He did not need to see to it himself. Indeed, it might be best if he did not see to it himself. He rose and rolled his shirtsleeves down over his forearms.

"Nice work," said Richard, coming to take Bingley's place with the net.

Lydia was not far behind. It seemed she had appointed herself fishing instructor. No matter how Marcus scowled or attempted to draw her away, she was determined that everyone who wished a turn to catch a fish would be successful. Besides, she had said on more than one occasion with a bright smile, fish were delicious, and she would not be eating cold meat and cheese for supper.

Bingley bowed his head in acceptance of the compliment. "I shall wish you the same success."

"Oh, he shall not fail," Lydia assured Bingley. "Colonel Fitzwilliam is a very disciplined sort of man. He will have the skill and patience to accomplish the task."

Richard smiled broadly. "A fine assessment."

Lydia's eyes sparkled. "I also heard him say he was as fond of fish as I am, and a man's stomach will often rule his will."

Bingley could not help the laugh that escaped him at her comment. "So, you think him both clever and hungry?"

"I do," Lydia replied. "Perhaps at a different spot — we might have completed our run of good fortune at this spot." She placed her hands on her hips and looked up and down the stream. Then, with a clap of her hands and what Bingley considered a rather self-satisfied smile, she suggested that they try the spot near Mary Ellen.

"An excellent idea," agreed Bingley with a smirk at Richard, who had yet to come to terms with his particular regard for that young lady.

Richard's brows drew together. "How can you be certain that it will be a good location?" he asked Lydia.

"Oh, I cannot make a guarantee," her eyes were fairly dancing with contained delight, "but I am certain with a bit of patience and attention, there might be something to be caught there." She laughed lightly and walked away. "Come along," she called over her shoulder.

The furrow between Richard's brow deepened. "What does she mean?" he asked Bingley. "What else could be caught besides fish? A frog? I do not care for frogs."

Bingley shook his head. "I believe she means you might catch Miss Dobney, or, more likely, Miss Dobney might catch you."

"Miss Dobney catch me?" Richard looked toward Mary Ellen and then back at Bingley. "Does she wish to catch me?"

Bingley nodded. "Although I am not to say."

"Come along, Colonel," Lydia called again.

Richard tipped his head to the side, his lips pursed and his eyes narrowed, as he studied Mary Ellen. "I suppose," he said at last, "being caught might not be such a bad thing."

"Aye," said Philip, who had come to join them right before Lydia had called to Richard the second time, "it would certainly make her happy."

Richard blinked.

"Come along, Colonel," said Philip. "You must do your duty and allow yourself to get caught so that Marcus and I might be free of a lovelorn sister."

"Lovelorn?" Richard asked as he followed Philip.

Bingley chuckled and went to find Jane.

~*~*~

Later that evening, Bingley tapped his fingers on the table next to the letter he had written. He was uncertain if this was the best course of action. Perhaps he should just take a trip to town to speak with Mr. Newman. Letters were tricky items. There was no guarantee that the intended recipient would be the only recipient of the news in a missive. He scanned the words again.

"A breach of contract has occurred. Please detain the party who is in neglect and extract payment as needed. The packet may be shipped from Portsmouth."

"That is a serious look you are wearing," said Richard as he slipped into the library at Pemberley. "Letter of business or pleasure?"

"Business," said Bingley with a sigh. "An agreement has been breached, and I am uncertain of the best method for rectifying the situation."

Richard settled into a large leather chair and tossed one leg over the other. "What are your options?"

Bingley shrugged and folded the paper without sealing it. "Write to an associate and have him deal with the issue or go see it done myself."

Richard pondered this information for a while. "Is it a serious breach?"

Bingley nodded. "Damaging," he blew out a breath, "but the remedy is not without significant risk either."

The comment caused Richard to raise a brow and look eagerly at Bingley. "Is this remedy something that would fall outside of the law."

Unwilling to admit such a thing, Bingley tilted his head and gave a half shrug.

Richard smiled. "I had not thought you capable of such." There was a note of pride in the colonel's voice.

"You do not condemn me?"

"I would need to know the particulars before I could pronounce any sort of judgment," Richard replied with a grin. "However, I am not a strict judge if you are worried about that."

Bingley blew out a breath and rose from his chair. "It is not that," he said, moving to join Richard in the chairs before the unlit fireplace. "I wish to keep the number of people who know about any of this as small as possible."

Richard's eyes grew wide, and he let out a low whistle. "So, it is a fair distance on the opposite side of the law?"

Again, not willing to admit it aloud, Bingley gave a half shrug.

"A pound of flesh?" Richard asked in a whisper.

Bingley was almost positive he heard a hint of excitement in Richard's voice.

"Something of that nature." Bingley sighed again.

He longed to discuss this with someone who could advise him on the best course of action. If Wickham were to meet with an accident here in Derbyshire, Bingley knew that no one would ask questions, and if they did, Mr. Williams would confirm that it was merely an accident.

Elsewhere, Bingley was uncertain if events would play out so cleanly.

He shook his head. "Life and death are not mine to award." He rubbed his chin with his right hand. "I should tend to it myself."

"I wish you would tell me what it is." Richard's tone was disappointed. "If you are not indeed planning on killing someone, then I do not see the need to be quite so secretive."

"What of transportation?" asked Bingley.

"For you?"

Bingley shook his head in response to the startled question. "Lady Catherine knew of Darcy marrying because of Mr. Collins."

Richard wore a look of confusion. "Darcy mentioned that."

"Collins learned of the wedding from Wickham."

Richard's eyes grew wide. "Darcy did not mention Wickham."

Bingley smirked. "And why do you suppose that would be?"

Richard's features grew hard. "Because I need very little reason to be persuaded to do harm to that man. Darcy is far too patient."

Bingley nodded. "I quite agree. It is the same with my sister. I cannot understand how Darcy has managed to suffer Caroline's attentions all these years without telling her to leave off." He paused for a moment. "Although he did not ask her to stay yesterday."

Richard gave a low chuckle. "She has reached her end. There is always a limit to Darcy's patience but reaching that limit does not mean he is willing to leave all reason behind. He will always take what he thinks is the noblest road."

"Which means sacrificing himself and not the other person," said Bingley.

Richard nodded emphatically. "Precisely. Cutting off of friendship, the paying off of debts, the buying of property — all helpful and not without merit, but they do not eliminate the problem."

"Like Wickham."

"Yes, like Wickham," agreed Richard. "It was only a fortunate accident that Darcy's purchasing Willow Hall worked out so well for Lucy. I am certain that Tolson would not have stayed clear of her."

Bingley's lips twitched.

"You think not?" asked Richard.

"Mr. Williams would not have allowed it." Bingley had spoken to Mr. Williams long enough before presenting his deal to Wickham to know that the man was willing to bend the rules to see justice served in swift order.

Richard allowed this to be true.

Bingley rose to return to the desk and collected his letter. He slipped it into his pocket. He would consult with Mr. Williams before taking any action.

"What agreement do you have with Wickham?" Richard asked.

"I paid him for silence," said Bingley. "About Lydia," he added in reply to the question Richard was about to ask. "Lady Catherine knew about Lydia travelling to Derbyshire with Wickham."

Richard nodded his understanding. "He does not believe you will carry through on your threat. He has not said a word regarding Georgiana because he knows I would not hesitate to relieve him of his life. "

Bingley tapped the letter in his pocket. "How would you do it?"

Richard's smile grew wide as if it was a topic he had considered at some length. "He has a good seat. I have seen him ride."

"A transfer from the militia to the regulars?"

Richard nodded. "The cavalry, to be precise. I have connections enough to see him on his way to meet Old Boney within a fortnight."

Bingley took his seat next to Richard once again, interested to hear exactly what he would have planned to dispose of Wickham. "But you have no guarantee that he would die."

Richard shrugged. "Being of a lowly rank, he would be cannon fodder, but should he manage to return with his life, it would not be as a whole man. He'd no longer be pretty enough to pose any danger to a gently bred young woman. And I suspect, if he did not die of disease, he would eventually drift up along the Thames." He nodded his head slowly as if satisfied with this result.

"And if the war should end before you have a chance to dispose of him on the continent? Then what?"

Richard's face scrunched up as he considered his options. "That would take some thought," he muttered at last. "I suppose, there could be a loose rock on a steep path where he might lose his footing."

"What about transportation to one of the colonies?"

Richard's brows rose. "It would relieve us of his presence, but what about the ladies there?" He again scrunched up his face as he considered it. "The journey might be hazardous."

Bingley swallowed. He knew precisely how dangerous a sea voyage could be. "More so at some times of the year than at others."

They sat in silence for a time.

"I would want to string him up for harming Georgiana and run him through if he harmed Miss Dobney," said Richard, "but I would do neither."

Bingley looked at him in disbelief. "You had a plan to see him done away with. Why this turnabout?"

Richard shook his head. "It is not a turnabout. I would still see him off to the war if I could. But if there is no war, I would not risk losing my life to avenge my angel." He smiled. "I could not be the cause of her sorrow." He shrugged. "I would persuade him to take a voyage, and then, I would spend my time comforting those he had wronged."

Bingley understood the sentiment. "So, we are agreed that Darcy's ways might indeed be the wisest?"

Richard groaned. "I will need a drink before I admit such a thing."

Bingley laughed and rose to fetch the needed refreshment. "Shall I make it a large dose? Are you also going to admit your admiration for Miss Dobney?"

"Miss Dobney? Why should I be admitting to admiring her?" His tone was questioning, but his look was sheepish as if he were asking a question to which he very well knew the answer.

"You cannot call a lady an angel unless you admire her."

Richard sighed. "Then make it a large dose."

Chapter 11

Darcy looked up from the letter he was reading as Bingley and Richard entered the breakfast room the following day. He gave the briefest of nods in greeting and tossed the letter on the table.

"Not a good morning?" Bingley asked as he filled his cup with tea.

"No, it is most certainly not a good morning." Darcy leaned back in his chair, arms folded, eyes narrowing as he scowled. "Do you know where our aunt went when she left yesterday, Richard?"

Richard slowly lowered the forkful of food he was about to place in his mouth. There could only be one place Lady Catherine could have gone. "Matlock?"

"Precisely." Darcy uncrossed his arms long enough to take a large gulp of his tea. "Your father is attempting to calm her, but she has told him the same tales she shared with us at the church. He wishes to see that I am not being taken in by a fortune hunter and so has requested that I put off the wedding until he has had a chance to mollify our aunt and meet Elizabeth."

Richard's brows rose. "He is questioning your decision?"

Darcy's jaw clenched as he nodded. "It appears he is, although he claims he is only doing what he thinks will work best to appease Aunt Catherine and cause the least amount of disunity."

"Are you going to do it?" asked Bingley around a mouthful of toast and jam.

Darcy shrugged. "I will speak to Elizabeth, and if she is amenable, then yes — but for no more than a week. And it will only be a postponement. I will be marrying Elizabeth."

"Father is usually quite reasonable," Richard assured Darcy. "He is merely attempting to keep the peace as much as possible. His visit will be a mere formality. He knows, as well as anyone, that you are your own man."

Darcy relaxed slightly. "I do hope you are correct."

"I am." Richard returned to his plate of food. "He allows her to feel she has been heard and then tells her what will be."

Darcy nodded. He had seen his uncle use that very tactic with Lady Catherine, and it usually worked with only a small amount of stomping and snorting from his aunt.

He picked up the letter, read it once more, and rose to go write his reply. He would give his uncle until the day after tomorrow to meet Elizabeth, and he would not agree to a postponement until he had discussed the issue with her. He drained the last of his tea as he stood next to the table.

"Sir," the butler said, entering the room before Darcy could do more than place his empty cup back on the table, "you have a visitor."

Darcy checked his watch. "It seems early for callers."

"I am told it is not a social call, but one of great importance which requires your attention, as well as Mr. Bingley's."

Darcy's brows rose.

"It is Mr. Williams, sir," continued the butler.

"Shall we meet him here?" Darcy asked Bingley, who was still devouring his breakfast.

Bingley wiped his mouth. "No, your study might be best. You have that letter to write." He motioned to the paper in Darcy's hand.

"But your plate is not empty."

Bingley grimaced. "I have had enough." He emptied his cup of tea and stood. "Richard, you will join us, will you not?" He gave him a significant look.

Richard's eyes grew wide. "You think I will be needed?"

"If it is about whom we discussed last night, yes."

Richard popped the last morsel of his toast into his mouth and finished his tea before following Bingley and Darcy from the breakfast room. He was just a step or two behind Mr. Williams in entering Darcy's study.

"I had planned to come see you later today," Bingley said

quietly to Mr. Williams. "It seems Lady Catherine learned of Miss Lydia's trip to Derbyshire from Wickham."

Mr. Williams' face grew even more grave than it had been when he first entered the room. "Did Lady Catherine mention anything about Miss Bennet's and Miss Elizabeth's stay at Netherfield?"

Bingley's eyes grew wide. "No. She only spoke of Miss Lydia's journey to Derbyshire with Wickham."

"Then," said Mr. Williams, turning to include Darcy and Richard in the conversation, "we have an additional problem. I had thought it might be Wickham who had begun such a rumor as I heard." He scratched at the stubble on his cheek. "I suppose it might still be him, but he has been gone for some time, and this is the sort of thing that does not take very long to circulate."

Bingley swallowed as his stomach roiled uneasily.

Mr. Williams looked first at Darcy and then Bingley. "There is no easy or gentle way to say this, gentlemen, but your honor and that of your ladies have been called into question."

"What?" Darcy's roar was low.

"How?" Bingley added in a dangerously cool voice. He drew deep, deliberate breaths. He would know the details before he allowed himself to feel the full force of his anger.

"The insinuation is that things were not entirely proper during the ladies' stay at Netherfield."

"How improper?" Bingley's voice was still low and controlled, belying the tumult within. He could feel the truth of Richard's comments last night. He did feel the urge to run through whoever was endeavouring to harm Jane.

"There is speculation as to why Miss Bennet left Hertfordshire for London within a month of her stay and why her stay in town was for an extended time."

Bingley's drew a great breath and held it as he waited for Mr. Williams to continue.

"She returned in a state of sadness that indicated some loss. Whether it was because Mr. Bingley refused to do his duty by her or due to the loss of a child is up for discussion."

With a whoosh, Bingley expelled the breath he had been holding.

"I have heard that some think it is due to both." Mr. Williams turned toward Darcy. "There is no talk of Miss Elizabeth ever having been with child, but there is speculation that you are marrying her due to..." he shifted a bit uneasily, "certain charms."

"They think Miss Elizabeth has seduced Darcy?" Richard's voice held as much astonishment as his face.

Mr. Williams nodded. "That is what one of my men heard and relayed to me."

"It is not true," said Darcy when he could finally find his voice.

"I never thought any of it was true," Mr. Williams assured him. "I just knew you should be made aware of the tales before you heard them elsewhere." He glanced at Bingley. "I had also hoped that the source of the rumors might be Wickham since his reputation is not for honesty; however, after what Bingley has said about your aunt not mentioning this, it seems unlikely."

"Who would know such detail and conjure such a story?" asked Richard.

Bingley slumped slightly in his chair as the weight of understanding settled on his shoulders. He closed his eyes and shook his head against the thought. It was a painful recollection of Caroline leaning on Harris's arm and seeming pleased to be doing so. She had been scheming her revenge even then.

"Caroline," he whispered. He looked at Darcy. "Who else could it be?" He rose and paced the room. "She left far too easily on Saturday. She even smiled when saying her goodbyes."

Darcy sank back in his chair and nodded his agreement.

Richard's brows drew together. "But your sister was only here and then gone — unless she spoke to someone at the inn."

Bingley stopped mid-stride as he realized that it was not only his sister who was to blame. No wonder Harris had run away from Pemberley so quickly.

"I will kill him," Bingley muttered. "How –" Bingley shuddered. "It is disgusting! To make love to a woman and then to turn on her and defame her! It is beyond the pale!"

"You know who is to blame?" asked Mr. Williams.

Bingley nodded. "Without a doubt."

"Who?" Mr. Williams asked.

Bingley's face twisted in disgust as he spat the name. "Harris."

Richard moved to the edge of his chair. "How do you figure?"

"Do you remember how cozy Caroline and Harris looked when walking in the garden?" Bingley shook his head. He should have known his sister was up to no good. She was far too pleasant for having been denied the chance to stay at Pemberley — and that on the heels of learning of Darcy's engagement and, ergo, his unavailability to herself.

"And, then," Bingley continued, "Harris could not remove himself from the premises fast enough. He did not even deign to bid farewell to Miss Bennet. He just foisted her off onto Darcy and me — not that I minded his departure or the foisting. I thought him rude to do it, but this?"

Again, Bingley shook his head. He had wondered at Harris's willingness to walk away from Jane that day. Harris had been doing an admirable job of placing himself between Bingley and Jane at every meeting. The fact that he had left the field open for Bingley should have sounded warning bells, but Bingley had been just too glad to be rid of the buffoon.

"How widely spread is this rumor?" Richard asked Mr. Williams.

"Assessing the lay of the land are you?" Mr. Williams smiled conspiratorially as Richard nodded. "My man heard it in Lambton at the Black Crow."

Richard's brows rose. "Not the sort of place I would have expected Harris to frequent, but then I did not think him the sort to start ruinous rumors, either." His eyes grew the smallest bit wide as he looked from Darcy to Bingley when both men growled. "Perhaps we should leave Harris to me," he suggested.

"No. It is my fault that there are any rumors at all. If I had stayed at Netherfield or even returned –"

"If I had not persuaded you to leave!" Darcy interrupted.

"Caroline is my sister." Bingley was not about to allow Darcy to wear the blame for this. "Nor did I have to listen to you. It is my mess, and I will see to it."

Darcy stood and crossed the room to where Bingley paced. "No," he said, grabbing Bingley's arm. "We will see to it. Harris has maligned my name and Elizabeth's as well as yours and Miss Bennet's. I will leave your sister to you, but I will be part of the rest."

"Perhaps," suggested Richard again, "Harris should be left to me."

"Why?" Bingley and Darcy swung toward him and spoke in unison.

"He is under my command. I am able to do more than you might without risking my neck." He gave them a small smile. "We cannot have Miss Elizabeth and Miss Bennet crying at the bottom of a gallows, now can we?"

Bingley glanced at Darcy and raised a single brow in question.

Darcy shrugged.

"We need to know why he did what he did," said Mr. Williams. "I know that you may not agree, but, as you said, the Black Crow is not a place Harris would frequent, but it is not unfamiliar territory for Wickham — nor was it for Tolson."

"You think Wickham is involved?" asked Richard.

"I do." He turned to Bingley. "Which, I believe, brings us to what you wished to see me about today."

Bingley looked warily towards Darcy. He had not wished for Darcy to know about the arrangement with Wickham. Darcy had wanted to pay off Wickham, but when he had presented his idea to Williams, Darcy had been told that the matter had been settled. However, Williams would not say by whom.

Bingley cleared his throat and took a step away from Darcy. "He has breached our agreement." Bingley pulled the letter he had written last night from his pocket and handed it to Williams. "What would you advise? Do I send that or see to it myself?"

"You?" Darcy grabbed Bingley by the shoulder and

attempted to turn him, but Bingley shrugged out of his grasp.

"Yes, me," he replied without turning. "I paid his debts and gave him a small sum to remain silent."

"And a warning." Mr. Williams shifted his eyes to look up at Bingley. "A warning must not be given in vain."

"It has not been," Bingley assured him. Wickham was not going to walk away from what he had done.

Richard reached over Mr. Williams' shoulder and took the letter. "You have access to ships?" he asked as he reread the letter.

Bingley nodded. "I do."

Richard pulled in a deep breath and released it. "Wickham will be expected back with his regiment..." he furrowed his brow as he calculated the leave he knew that Forrester had allowed his men, "two days hence."

"So he was not returning to his regiment when he visited Kent?" Darcy asked in surprise.

Richard shook his head. "No, I suspect he went to Kent with the purpose of sharing what he knew with Mrs. Collins and at the same time notifying Lady Catherine of your betrothal. He would know about Anne."

Bingley cursed. "Can we use your plan?" he asked Richard. "Transportation seems too kind."

Richard gave him a minatory smile. "Not if he can never return, and as you said yourself, voyages can be dangerous."

Bingley cocked a brow. "Explain."

"Abandonment of duty is a serious offense." Richard handed the letter back to Bingley. "Detain the party who is in breach of contract longer than two days hence and then offer him a means of escape to some godforsaken destination. He'll take it."

"Kidnapping?"

From Darcy's tone Bingley could tell he did not agree with Richard's plan, but to Bingley, it seemed a worthy scheme.

"A bit of ale, a smidge of rum, perhaps some brandy," Bingley said with a smile. "It is not kidnapping if one is simply too drunk to remember the day. I have a few quid I could allow to be lost in a game or two."

"Throw in a light skirt," said Mr. Williams, "and it will be like boiling a frog — cooked before he knows it."

"I do not like this," said Darcy gravely.

Bingley turned toward his friend, taking a wide stance and crossing his arms. "He has sullied the names of you and me as well as Miss Lydia, Miss Elizabeth, and Miss Bennet. Do you wish me to trick him into leaving the country or do you prefer me to kill him? His days of causing harm to those we love are done. He will be leaving England either on a ship or in a casket. Your choice, Darcy."

Darcy studied Bingley's face for a moment. "You would kill him?"

"I told him I would."

Darcy's eyes widened.

"I am from trade. I know people who could cause an accident," Bingley explained. "We from trade are a rough lot, don't you know?" he added with a smirk.

"You would seriously kill him?"

"I would prefer not to." Bingley held Darcy's gaze.

Darcy sighed. "Can we not just purchase passage for him on a ship and send him sailing?"

"You would trust him not to return?" Richard asked.

Darcy sighed again. "No. He is not trustworthy."

"Then shall we ply him with liquor, cards, and women for a couple of days before buying him passage?" Bingley asked.

"Aye." Three heads bobbed their agreement as their voices joined as one.

Chapter 12

"It was quite odd," said Jane, "almost as if they did not wish to serve us."

Aunt Tess rested the teapot on the edge of the table between pouring cups. "The shopkeepers were curt?"

Elizabeth nodded as she accepted a cup of tea from Lydia. "And there were people whispering as we went by." She took a sip of tea. "It was not everyone, but several people."

"And watching us," Jane added.

Aunt Tess resumed pouring. "I know that this village is not without its gossips, but what could they have to say about you. You have not been here long and have done nothing worthy of gossip."

"I have," said Lydia as she passed a cup of tea to Lucy and came back to get one for Mary Ellen.

"But no one knows of your indiscretion," said Lucy.

Lydia shrugged. "I am the only one of the three of us that has done anything worthy of gossip — aside from Lizzy kissing Mr. Darcy, that is. But that is not whisper and scowl worthy. That is more of a giggling and smiling sort of secret. It must be related to me." After scanning the group to make certain she had delivered a cup of tea to everyone, she sat down with her own cup.

"It might be," agreed Aunt Tess, "but we have not shared anything about your arrival with anyone. I do not know how it would have become common knowledge."

Lydia wrinkled her nose and pursed her lips. "Oh," she said after a moment of pondering. "Captain Harris enjoys sharing stories. I heard a few good tales being told by him when I was in Brighton. One that seemed to get the most attention was about some poor girl he knew that only lasted half a season and had to return home in shame — something about an imagined compromise — although, to be honest, he did not make it sound like it was imagined at all." She tipped her head and furrowed her brows. "He did not give a name — he was careful not to do so — but he did refer to her as Misty, I believe. Although I was not part of the group when he was telling it, so I might have mis-heard from my position."

"Was there a reason that particular story got so much attention?" asked Mary Ellen.

Lydia nodded. "It seems he knew the young lady and the other officers were curious to know if he would introduce them to her."

"Why did they wish introductions?" Jane asked.

Lydia's brows rose as she shrugged. "I really do not

know why. It was quite odd. They all seemed interested in her shoes."

"Her shoes?" asked Aunt Tess.

Lydia nodded. "Something about the heels."

Aunt Tess bit back a smile. For all the worldly knowledge Lydia seemed to possess, there were moments such as this that showed the girl was still at least partially on the right side of naivety. "I do not think they were referring to her shoes," she said softly, "especially if they were referring to lifting her heels?"

Jane gasped. "How horrid!"

Lydia blinked and gave Jane a questioning look.

"It is like lifting her skirts," hissed Elizabeth.

Lydia's eyes grew wide, and her cheeks flushed. "Oh, if I had known, I would not have mentioned it. It is very improper."

Aunt Tess gave Lydia's hand a reassuring pat. "I am glad you did not know," she assured her.

"Well, I like him even less now." Lydia placed her cup on the table and crossed her arms. "I know he is your cousin, Mary Ellen, but I just cannot abide a gossip who shares hurtful things."

Mary Ellen nodded her acceptance of Lydia's words but refused to lift her eyes from her cup.

"I apologize," said Lydia. "I did not mean to offend."

Mary Ellen shook her head. "It is not that." She took a small sip of her tea. "I suppose we are all going to be family, and you do seem to be the sort to treat something of a delicate nature appropriately," she glanced at Lucy, who gave her a small nod to continue. "Did he perhaps say Miss D rather than Misty?"

"He may have," said Lydia. "As I said, I was not in the group to whom he spoke. I just happened to overhear."

Mary Ellen drew a deep breath. "I am Miss D."

Lydia's eyes grew wide, and her mouth dropped open before she snapped it closed.

"I assure you it is not what he made it out to be. I have never done...that." Her teacup shook a bit as she raised it to take a sip. "I had gone to town for my first season — do you remember that Lucy?"

Lucy smiled and nodded. "You were so excited to go to the dances and show off your new wardrobe."

Mary Ellen laughed. "I drove my brothers mad with my demands that they help me practice my dances." She looked at Elizabeth. "They even tricked Darcy into taking a turn just so they would not have to do it."

"What happened?" Lydia asked.

"I had a lovely time in town. The soirees were all I had dreamed they would be. I enjoyed many strolls in Hyde Park and a carriage ride or two. I did not ever want for a partner at a ball. It was idyllic until," she paused and took another shaky sip of tea, "I fell. While on a walk at the fireworks display, I slipped and fell. The gentleman on whose arm I was walking toppled with me. He landed on top with me beneath him. Someone saw and the next thing I knew, I was only asked to dance by those gentlemen with a certain reputation."

"Rakes?" asked Lydia.

"Yes, rakes," said Mary Ellen, "and known fortune hunters since my dowry is not small."

"That is horrid." Lydia's voice trembled with anger.

"It was, so I left. I asked to return home."

"Did the gentleman who fell on you offer for you?" asked Lydia.

"No, he was already promised to another. He was only strolling with me because we were friends."

"And your cousin shared this?" Jane could not hide her surprise. "How could he share that?"

Mary Ellen brushed a tear from the corner of her eye. "I do not know. I did not realize he was sharing it."

Lydia's lips were puckered in a scowl. "Dueling is illegal, is it not?"

"Oh, my, yes," said Aunt Tess quickly. "And I am not certain Marcus or Philip would wish to call out their cousin."

Lydia blinked. "Why would they do that?"

"They are Mary Ellen's brothers," said Aunt Tess.

"You cannot call him out either. You are a lady," said Elizabeth.

Lydia scowled. "But I am a fair shot."

Aunt Tess laughed. "I have no doubt you are, but your sister is correct. Ladies do not call out gentlemen."

"Not even if they have disparaged a dear friend and sister?"

"Not even then, though the gesture is noble," Aunt Tess assured her.

Lydia sighed and returned to her tea.

~*~*~

Captain Harris jumped down from his horse in front of Aunt Tess's house. He could see the group of ladies through the window and hear the lilt of female voices. No doubt they were talking about something as important as what ribbon to wear with which dress. He chuckled to himself. Women were such easy creatures to cozen about so many things — a little flattery, an extra bit of attention, a feigned look of sympathy, and if one could share some fascinating story, well, they were as easy to lead along as a dog on a leash.

He smoothed his coat and adjusted his hat. It had occurred to him just last evening that he did not need to give up his pursuit of Miss Bennet. In fact, his chances of success would be even better once it was found out that Bingley's sister had spread such hateful rumors about the Misses Bennets.

He gave his lapels one more tug and made his way to the door. He was certain Miss Bennet would want nothing to do with Mr. Bingley after such knowledge was made known. Wickham would be pleased to know that not only had he been able to do damage to the Bennets, Bingley, and Darcy with the stories he had shared, but he would also be breaking Bingley's heart by marrying Miss Bennet. The poor sod.

He chuckled as he lifted the door knocker.

And Miss Bennet? Well, he would see that she was happy enough to provide him with the heir that he needed, but beyond that, she would be left alone.

In fact, he would insist she stay in Derbyshire while he completed his time with the militia. There was no need to dampen his fun by dragging a wife along with him. Now if it were Priscilla, he would be glad to have her about, but Miss Bennet was too particular. He would feel as if he were being watched by his mother or a governess — and that would not do.

Harris waited outside the sitting room as he was announced. It was strange how quiet the room became at the mention of his name, but then, he had not said he would call, so he expected they were merely surprised and delighted. He put on his most charming smile as he entered the room.

"Good morning, ladies." He sketched a gallant bow. "I am happy to have found you all. I stopped at Willow Hall, but Mrs. Abbot informed me you had come here." He took a seat.

"Yes, please, a cup of tea would be lovely," he said to

Aunt Tess's offer. "I understand you were to do a bit of shopping — some trim for a gown or some such thing?"

"Yes," said Jane, "Lizzy needed a piece of lace for her wedding gown."

"And were you successful in finding what was needed?" he asked as Lydia handed him his cup of tea. "Oh!" He jumped a bit as the tea sloshed over the edge of the cup.

"My apologies," said Lydia. "The toe of my slipper caught on the rug." She smiled sweetly. "I am grateful the saucer saved your trousers." Her lashes fluttered.

"No harm was done," he assured her, but his smile was not so brilliant as it had been. Lydia had never been pleasant to him — not in Brighton and not since her arrival in Derbyshire either. He was certain the spill had not been an accident, but he would not call her on it at present.

"We were very successful," said Elizabeth. "Details for the wedding are falling into place as they should."

"Is it a very overwhelming task?" Harris asked over the rim of his cup. He truly did not care, but such a question would make it appear as if he did. Now, if it were his own wedding, he might care a trifle more, but as it was, it was only Darcy getting married, so the details did not particularly interest him.

"No, not very," replied Elizabeth. "Mrs. Abbot and Aunt Gardiner are very good at organizing fetes."

"It must be a relief to have such capable help since you are marrying so far from home." He lowered his cup. "Why did you not wish to marry from Hertfordshire? It seems it would have been more convenient, and I have heard Netherfield is quite grand and would make a lovely place to host a wedding breakfast. Mr. Bingley being a friend and all, I am certain he would have been delighted to be of service in such a fashion. Surely you will miss having some of your friends attend."

"My particular friend no longer lives in Hertfordshire, I am afraid. She married this past winter and is happily settled in Kent."

"You have no other friends?" he asked in surprise.

"None who are close," answered Elizabeth. "And Mr. Bingley has not been in residence at Netherfield for some months now."

"Oh, that is correct. Mr. Bingley left Netherfield, when was that? December?"

"End of November," said Elizabeth.

"Right, that is what I had heard. Miss Bennet left for town with your aunt in December, was it not?" He smiled apologetically. "So many stories that have been shared in our acquaintance that I have managed to mix up the details." He had done no such thing. He knew precisely when Mr. Bingley had left and when Miss Bennet had followed. But showing a sound knowledge of events would not serve him well when he wished to plead ignorant of any rumors that might surface.

"That is to be expected. They are not your life events or

even those of a family member, so one would not expect you to keep every detail straight," said Elizabeth.

Ah, an opening to broach his intent. He took a sip of his tea and then, with a smile at Jane, said, "True, they are not details related to me yet."

He saw Jane's eyes grow wide. Good, she understood him. However, the way she shifted uneasily in her chair did have him somewhat concerned until he decided that being a shy sort of lady, she was merely uncomfortable with having a gentleman declare himself so openly.

"Do you intend to marry my sister?"

"Lydia," Elizabeth hissed.

Lydia scowled at Elizabeth and then returned her focus to Captain Harris.

"I believe that is a topic to be discussed in private with Miss Bennet," said Harris.

"Was that not the meaning of your comment?" Lydia asked.

Harris cleared his throat. There was a certain gleam in Lydia's eye that was unnerving. "I believe Miss Bennet understood my meaning, and that is all that is required."

Lydia turned to Jane. "Did you understand his meaning to be that he was planning to offer for you?"

"Lydia," scolded Jane.

Lydia shook her head and shrugged. "Well, if no one will answer my questions, I will assume that Captain Harris does indeed intend to marry Jane." She sighed and said, with a scowl directed at Harris, "I do hope you are more straightforward in your speech when you become my brother. I do so dislike it when people are purposefully duplicitous. Jane, too, prefers people to be forthright and honest. I believe all my sisters do, as does my father."

Harris cleared his throat again. "As I said, Miss Bennet understood my meaning. I am sorry if you were not able to do the same."

Lydia's eyes narrowed at the insult. "I understood your meaning, sir. I just wished to see if my assessment of your character was correct."

Harris's cup stopped for a brief moment in the air before he continued to lift it, take a sip, and return it to its saucer. "And what assessment have you made of my character, Miss Lydia?"

Lydia's lashes fluttered, and a smile spread across her face. "Oh, I believe I made it obvious to those to whom it is important. If you missed it, well, that is too bad."

Oh, she was an infuriating little tart! He would be glad to see her brought low. That thought brought a smile to his lips. She would not be so superior when one and all knew how she had travelled with Wickham, and he would not refrain from sharing about her flirting in Brighton.

The next few minutes were spent on meaningless trivialities — the weather, the flowers and how they were blooming, when he would be returning to Brighton, and the like. Everyone seemed to be participating in the discussion to some degree except, Harris noticed, his cousin Mary Ellen. She was unusually quiet and kept blinking as if she were trying to overcome the threat of tears.

"Oh," said Lydia with excitement, "before you return to Brighton, you must introduce me to that lady of whom you spoke." She scrunched up her face and tapped her lip. "Misty. I believe that was her name. I should like to hear about her season. I have never had one, you know, and now that I am to be an old married lady, I fear I never shall. Even if I do, it will not be with the excitement of the hunt."

The ladies of the room held their collective breath when Lydia finished her little ramble and looked expectantly at Captain Harris, whose eyes had grown wide.

His gaze flicked briefly to Mary Ellen. If Miss Lydia had been speaking of that story, he knew exactly why his cousin was upset. "I do not think she is home," he hedged. "Perhaps another time."

"That is too bad." Lydia pouted. "I had so hoped to meet her, but it cannot be helped, I am sure. She can call on me at Aldwood Abbey after Michaelmas. Be certain to tell her if you do see her."

"Oh, I will," Harris replied, "although I do not know when I will see her."

"I am not going anywhere," Lydia assured him with a smile. "I am here to stay unless I visit my mother or Marcus decides to take me to town. Oh, would that not be fun,

Lizzy? We could go together — you, me, Georgiana, Mary Ellen ... " She clapped her hands in delight.

Harris checked his watch and rose. "I believe I have stayed over my time, but before I go, I must apologize for my haste in leaving you ladies the other day. I had an appointment."

"Mr. Darcy explained," said Jane, "and we were delivered home safely as you can see. Will we see you tomorrow?"

Harris affected a downcast look. "I am afraid I have promised myself to a friend tomorrow, but perhaps the day after, I might be available." If he had expected Jane to look disappointed, he was to be disappointed himself, for Jane simply smiled politely and wished for him to have a safe trip.

It was odd how she looked so very serene and nearly happy that he was not going to be calling. The thought disquieted him for some time after he left. Something about the whole meeting had been off, and if he had to guess the cause, he would have to say it was due to Miss Lydia Bennet and her big mouth.

He might not be available to call for a few days, he decided. It might be best to bide his time until the rumours he knew to be circulating reached the ears of the Bennets. Then, with Mr. Bingley discredited and Jane desperate for a match, he would dutifully play the part of her hero. He chuckled. Her hero — that should be a useful thing once they were married, for how could she deny him a thing when he was the one to save her from spinsterhood despite her ruin?

Chapter 13

Bingley paced the length of Pemberley's great hall. From one of the rooms at the far end, a clock chimed out the hour. Georgiana would now be preparing for dinner. Richard would be finding a glass of port and setting up the billiard table in anticipation of a game before bed, and Darcy would be busily tucking papers and ledgers back into their proper places before dashing up to dress.

At least that is what they would be doing if this were a normal day; however, today, things were different. Georgiana was preparing for dinner. Richard was probably longing for a glass of port, and Darcy was accompanying his coach to Willow Hall to gather his guests.

At the end of yesterday's picnic, it had been decided that the whole lot of them — the Dobneys, save for Mr. Dobney, the Bennets, the Abbots, the Gardiners, and the Darcys, including Bingley and Richard — would gather for dinner at Pemberley. The ladies would perform. They would walk in the garden. It would be a most delightful time. But that was yesterday, before Mr. Williams' visit and before Bingley's decision to deal with Wickham himself.

Bingley paused in his circuit to look out the window across the front lawn toward the road that led to Pemberley. His bags were packed. He was ready to leave as soon as the sun rose in the morning. He would have left earlier, but he could not — would not — leave without seeing Jane first. His letters had been sent: one to his associate in town and another to Hurst. All that was left now was to meet with the scoundrel responsible for this mess and see him off to a foreign port.

He turned and resumed his walking. And Richard would see to the other blackguard with the flapping jaws. Harris. Bingley scowled even at the thought of his name.

"May I join you on your walk?" Richard asked.

Bingley gave a sharp nod of his head.

"I have written the necessary letters and had them posted. I will proceed as if the response is favourable," said Richard.

Bingley nodded again. "You do not expect any trouble, do you?"

"He will be gone," Richard assured Bingley. "It is simply a question of where he will go." He stopped at the window again with Bingley. "I could go with you."

Bingley shook his head. "No, you must not delay your discussion with Harris."

"I will not receive word for a few days, and if I am in town, I might receive it faster."

Bingley leaned against the window frame. "They are here," he said as a carriage could be seen just beyond the stand of trees at the beginning of the park.

"My bags are ready," said Richard.

"I must be the one to follow through on my word." Bingley's face was grave. "He does not think me a serious threat."

Not that anyone ever had. His classmates had not until he had sent one or more of them sprawling. Caroline, obviously, did not think him capable of anything unpleasant. And to be honest, as he thought of it now, he had been much too pleasant where she was concerned — but she was a girl and his sister. It was not as if he could punch her in the nose, even if he wished to do so.

Richard clapped Bingley on the shoulder. "He would be wrong, and I would not interfere — unless you requested my help. He's a slippery louse."

Bingley nodded. It could be helpful to have Richard as a companion.

"And you can attend me when I see Harris."

Bingley's brows rose. "You would trust me not to level him?"

Richard smiled. "No, I would expect you to give him his due, and I would not interfere. He should also know that he has underestimated you."

The corners of Bingley's mouth curled slightly as he pushed away from the window. "Then be ready to leave at dawn."

Grinning, Richard gave him a salute.

Bingley shook his head and chuckled as he went to meet the carriage.

~*~*~

Darcy had explained about his uncle to Elizabeth on the drive to Pemberley, and though she was not happy to have the wedding postponed, she was understanding of the need. So it was that when they entered the drawing room to await the arrival of the others, it was the topic of discussion. Things could easily be shifted. Philip would have to be informed, of course.

"And Bingley should be returned by then," Darcy said.

"Mr. Bingley is leaving?" asked Elizabeth in surprise.

Darcy grimaced. "My apologies, Bingley. That was your news to share."

"No harm done," said Bingley as cheerfully as he could. "I have a bit of business to attend to in town. It is rather a sudden thing and truly cannot be delayed. I would be sorry to not stand with Darcy, so it is fortunate that Lord Matlock is insistent on this pause in plans."

"You will return?" Jane asked softly.

"Always," Bingley said, grasping her hand. "I will always return to you as long as you will allow it."

No one batted an eye or made a motion of any sort other

than to smile when he tucked Jane's hand in his elbow and excused himself from the room. He led her down the hall to the library.

"I wrote to your father. I have not sent it, for I need your consent." He turned and took both of her hands. "Jane, I cannot be patient. I will not lose you again. This time you will know my heart before I leave."

Jane smiled brightly at him. "I believe I already know it."

"I should hope that you do, but there will be no misunderstanding me this time. I love you, Jane Bennet. From the moment we met, I knew there was no other lady so well suited to me. I would have sworn my undying love to you last November had I not been persuaded to do otherwise. I have been a fool. I am not even a true gentleman, and I do not deserve someone as good as you, but I would beg you to allow me to spend the rest of my life proving to you that I am not completely unworthy. Marry me."

Jane's heart fluttered, and tears stung her eyes. How had she been so fortunate to receive a second chance at such happiness? Had she been more forthcoming with her admiration, he would not have been persuaded away. This time, she would leave him without one shadow of doubt as to her feelings. She pulled one hand free of his grasp and laid it gently on his cheek.

"You are no fool," she began. "Nor are you unworthy of my love. What must one do to earn love? Is it not freely given?" She brushed her thumb against the fine stubble on his cheek. "Must I earn your love?"

He shook his head and would have spoken if she had not lain a finger on his lips.

"I love you, Charles, and I have since last autumn when we met. You are everything that I think a gentleman should be — honorable, amiable, admirable, patient, and loving. And once you have purchased your estate, you will be a gentleman to everyone else. But know this. You were my gentleman in my heart long before society deigned to grant you the title. It is I who is fortunate to have received your attentions."

And then with only a moment's hesitation and a heart that raced at the thought of being completely improper, she rose up on her toes and, leaning forward, kissed him lightly on the lips. "I will marry you. Send your letter, my darling, and make me your wife."

A smile split Bingley's face. "You are certain?"

Jane laughed. "I am. I do not go around kissing gentlemen. In fact, you are the first."

Bingley sighed and wrapped her in his embrace. "And the last."

"And the last," she assured him. She peeked up at him. "You could kiss me."

He smiled at the bright flush of her cheeks. How could anyone believe this woman a wanton seductress when she blushed at the thought of a kiss? The thought almost made him pause and begin the next necessary discussion before he kissed her. It almost made him pause, but it did not.

With a joy that he thought would overwhelm his heart and cause him to do something quite embarrassing like cry, he captured her mouth and granted her request with several pleasurable kisses.

"How long will you be gone?" Jane asked sometime later as she stood still wrapped in his embrace.

"No more than a week," he said, rubbing small soothing circles on her lower back. "Less time if I can manage it."

"Is it a very pressing matter?"

"Mmm hmm," he mumbled. "I would have been gone already except that I would not go without seeing you first."

"Oh, I should not keep you from your responsibilities," she argued.

"You are my responsibility, Jane, my greatest, most important responsibility." He placed another kiss on her lips when she tipped her head up to look at him and give another argument. "You are also my greatest joy."

She smiled. "Then, I am glad you did not leave before now. We should get back. I think I hear Lydia in the hall-way." She bit her lip, and her eyes sparkled with a dash of impertinence. "She is drowning out the beautiful beat of your heart, which," she lay her head against his chest again, "may be my favourite sound."

"It is yours," said Bingley, releasing her and taking her

hand. "Forever and always yours." He held open the door to the library. "There is a bit of unpleasant news that will be shared now that Lydia has arrived."

Jane stopped and turned toward him.

He drew a deep breath, and as he released it his shoulders sagged. "Perhaps, I should not have asked you to marry me before you knew."

"What is it?" Jane's heart raced with fear.

"Rumors started by my sister. They are terrible. I would not blame you if you chose to change your answer, and you may. I will not hold you to our understanding." He kissed her lightly. "Come. It is best if it is all dealt with before we eat."

"You are frightening me," said Jane.

Bingley could not move another step without sharing with her the essence of what Caroline had said regarding Jane's abrupt departure to London.

Jane's face paled, and Bingley quickly moved her to a pair of chairs on the side of the corridor. "That is what the whispers were about this morning?"

"What whispers?" Bingley asked as he sat next to her, holding her hand.

"At the shops. It was as if they did not wish to serve us." She stood slowly. "Lydia thought they must have been about her because she said she was the only one to have done something worthy of gossip. I had forgotten that you do not have to do anything to be worthy of gossip when someone wishes to do you harm."

"I am sorry," said Bingley.

"It is not your fault," said Jane firmly.

"But she is my sister," said Bingley.

"And Lydia is mine," said Jane. "The Lord knows I have scolded her for her behaviour, but she has not listened. Sisters are sisters. They will often do as they wish regardless of the wishes of their sisters or mothers or brothers or fathers."

"You do not blame me?"

She smiled and shook her head. "No, but I will expect you to take some action in response."

He lifted her hand to his lips. "I am truly not worthy of such an angel."

She blushed again.

"I have already written to Hurst. Caroline is to be married this season — I shall not pay for another. I will continue to send her pin money to her, but she will be responsible for all her bills. I will not cover even a farthing of overages."

Jane could not help smiling at his determined, serious tone. It wrapped around her heart making her feel protected. "And if she does not marry?"

"Her funds will be transferred to the care of either Hurst or our aunt in Manchester. She will not be returning to my house unless she apologizes to both you and Elizabeth.

And then it shall only be for brief visits until I have assessed that her behaviour is changed, and then, only if you wish for her to stay longer." He paused outside the drawing room door. "Your happiness is of greatest importance to me."

"I shall only be happy if you are," Jane replied.

"At present, I would happily never see her again," Bingley said with a smile.

Jane's eyes were once again tinged with impertinence. "We seem to agree on a great many things, Mr. Bingley."

He chuckled and then nodded to the footman to open the door, but he did not enter before giving Jane one more soft kiss. "Come, my love, let us traverse into the fray."

Chapter 14

The discussion in the drawing room followed the party into the dining room. It was completely beyond anyone's comprehension how any person could be so devious.

"It does not surprise me," said Lydia as she scooped a bit of soup up from her bowl. "Mrs. Long can be just as cunning and cutting." She quietly slurped the soup from her spoon. "And Sir William is known to spread a tale — not that he would tell one that would harm someone. No, that job must be left to his wife."

She placed her spoon on her charger. "I am wrong. Captain Harris does surprise me. I know plenty of women who would tell a tale to shred someone into ribbons, but I do not believe I had met a man who would do it until I met Captain Harris." She placed her hand on her spoon. "No, I am wrong again. I had already met Wickham — and we know he would say anything as long as it ended with him smelling like a rose and not the fertilizer he is."

Marcus coughed to cover a laugh.

"It is why I did not like him — Captain Harris," she clarified. "He was an insipid gossip." She spooned a bit more soup into her mouth. "He called on us this morning."

"He did?" Richard asked.

"He most clearly declared he wished to marry Jane — Oh, not in those words, but that was his meaning even if he would not admit to it when questioned." She took another spoonful of soup. "I do not like him." Another spoon of soup. "I prefer Wickham."

Richard nearly choked on his own soup at that statement.

Lydia looked up at him. "Wickham is stupid and easily led. Captain Harris is not. He is dull and an oaf, but he is not stupid."

"Is not an oaf stupid?" asked Mary Ellen.

Lydia shrugged. "I suppose one could say that, but by stupid, I believe I mean predictable, easy to follow, not crafty. Wickham is predictable to a fault. It is how I managed to *persuade*," she looked at Marcus and emphasized the word, "him to help me. Captain Harris has no patterns. He shifts as he needs for a situation."

"Give a for instance," encouraged Richard. He had come to appreciate Lydia's powers of observation.

Lydia continued eating for a moment while she thought. "Oh, I know! He is all that is charming and proper when he is in company with those he feels he must impress. I dare say he has never said a rude word to you, Colonel, yet he tells the most interesting tales when you are not around.

Things that are not fit for the ears of a lady — or so I have discovered." Her cheeks tinged pink. "I truly did not know that it meant that," she whispered to Mary Ellen.

"Indeed," said Richard. "I must say, I had not thought him the type."

"Precisely," said Lydia. "Captain Harris is what he wishes you to believe, and he will tell any secret if the prize is right." She placed her hands on her lap as the soup was taken away. "And the prize need only be popularity," she continued.

"Any secret?" Richard asked in surprise. Harris had struck him as a trustworthy sort of soldier, and to hear that Harris was willing to share secrets so freely was disturbing to Richard, not just as a man, but as a military leader. "That is not good for a military man," he said gravely.

"It is not good for any man," said Lydia, taking a sip of her wine. "Captain Harris even told disparaging stories about his relations, although I did not realize it was a relation of whom he spoke." She bit her lip and looked contritely at Mary Ellen.

Mary Ellen's cheeks flushed, but she smiled at Lydia. "It is true."

"It is?" asked Marcus in surprise.

Mary Ellen nodded. "You remember my season?"

Marcus's eyes grew wide, and his jaw clenched. "He did not!"

"Oh, he did. Apparently, to his regiment I am the sort of

girl who will lift her heels for a gentleman even if he is spoken for. That is how he said it, is it not, Lydia?"

After Harris had left, and Mary Ellen had gotten over some of her shock in hearing that her cousin had been gossiping about her, she had asked Lydia to relate the story as Harris had told it.

Lydia nodded. "I did not know who Miss D was, nor did I know to what lifting one's heels alluded." Her cheeks flushed a deep red, and she lowered her voice to a whisper, "I thought he was talking about her shoes."

"Lydia let him know that I know of his indiscretion," said Mary Ellen with a smile for Lydia. "It was very well done. I just wish I could have been more composed when he called, so I could have had a go at him."

"It was the least I could do," said Lydia. "Apparently, since I am a lady, I cannot call him out." She shrugged. "And dueling is illegal."

Marcus's mouth opened and shut and opened again. "You were going to call him out?"

"I am a fairly good shot," Lydia countered.

"You are?"

Lydia nodded as she poked a carrot with her fork. "James Lucas taught me, and it only cost me a lock of hair. He wanted a kiss, but a lesson in shooting was not so valuable as that. No, kisses should be saved for your husband." She smiled at Marcus. "Of course, if I had known how nice kisses could be, perhaps I would not have saved them."

"Well, I am glad you did," muttered Marcus.

"He told people about your fall?" Richard asked Mary Ellen.

Mary Ellen nodded. "And about how I ended up going home in disgrace."

Richard drew and released a breath. "It is a pity duels are illegal." He lifted a brow and looked at Marcus.

"Indeed it is." Marcus's eyes flashed as he shook his head in disbelief at his cousin's self-serving duplicity.

Richard chewed his food slowly. While it was shocking to learn that one of the trusted men in your company was less than trustworthy, the thought that this man had blackened not only the name of his own cousin but also that of the lady he seemed determined to marry was truly repugnant.

"You say he came to call and declared his intent to marry Miss Bennet even though he had begun spreading rumours about her?" he asked after a few moments of contemplation.

Lydia's fork stopped halfway to her mouth. "That is odd, is it not?"

"It most certainly is," he turned toward Bingley, who sat just a chair away on the other side of the table. "Is there any chance we can see Harris before we leave tomorrow?"

Bingley, who was sitting solemnly, holding Jane's hand throughout Lydia's accounting of Harris's call, nodded. He would be very pleased to see Harris, and the sooner, the better. He would not leave Jane in Derbyshire with such a man prowling about. Harris would know his boundaries before Bingley left the area.

"Oh, you cannot," said Lydia. "He is going to visit a friend. I assume it is the one he speaks of who lives in Warwickshire — that is not so very far from here, is it? He said he visited her whenever he was home. I think he also sends her letters."

"A woman friend?" Richard's brows rose in surprise. Not only was Harris courting a lady about whom he was spreading sordid tales, but he was also, apparently, keeping another lady on the side. It was reprehensible!

Lydia nodded, and then her brow furrowed. "Oh, that cad! Claiming to love my Jane when he has a lady with whom he corresponds!" She shook her head. "I do not like him. Not one whit."

"The feeling is mutual," muttered Richard. "Tonight, Bingley. We pay him a call tonight."

Bingley nodded.

"He will not treat you that way," Richard mumbled.

"Me?" asked Mary Ellen.

"Yes, you," Richard retorted.

"It is not different from how he has treated Jane, Elizabeth, or Lydia. In fact, he has treated me better than Jane," argued Mary Ellen with a small smile for Lydia, who winked in return and turned her attention to her food.

"It is different," snapped Richard.

Marcus coughed to cover a laugh, and Richard glared at him.

"How so?" asked Mary Ellen.

"Because it is you," said Richard.

"Yes, you have already told me that, but you still have not told me why it is different just because it is me."

Richard blew out a breath. What she was saying was true. It really should not be different if Harris were insulting one lady or another. Bad was bad. So what exactly made this worse? "I do not know," he said at last. "I just know that it is different."

"Very well," said Mary Ellen, patting his hand which rested on the table. "When you have considered it and have an explanation, I will be willing to hear it." She gave his hand one more pat and then returned her hand to her lap. "I will satisfy myself for now with the knowledge that you care about me enough to defend my honor."

Richard nodded and pushed a piece of meat around his plate before stabbing it and chewing it with great determination. That was it. He cared for her. Of course, he cared for the Bennets as well. They were friends and soon to be part of his extended family, but she...he swallowed...she was different. He slipped his hand under the table and took hers.

A warmth spread through his chest, calming him as nothing ever had. He had always been restless, even as a child — searching for his calling, seeking to be better and do more, all in an effort to find peace in knowing he was where he belonged. Nothing had satisfied him as her hand in his did. Some things such as his position of command in the militia had come close, but nothing had ever caused his muscles to relax as that small hand inside of his did. This was where he belonged. He turned to look at her. "You are my peace," he whispered. "I will allow nothing to destroy that."

The smile she favoured him with caused his breath to catch. She was beautiful. He had always been aware of that. And she was spirited — no one had ever said any different. She was not like any other lady he had ever met, and he had done his duty in attending many soirees over the seasons.

Oh, he was a fool! How many times had he sat in a drawing room conversing with a lady and wished she would challenge him as Mary Ellen did? How many times had he rolled his eyes at some fit of nerves that a young debutante had taken while thinking to himself how Mary Ellen would have just laughed and carried on with whatever needed doing? Not many of the ladies he had met could have withstood the whispers that circulated after her fall for as long as she did. He shook his head. It had always been her. She was his friend, this was true, but she was more than that. She was the missing piece to his heart, and without that piece, he would never know peace.

He returned to his meal and only released her hand

when he needed both of his to cut a piece of food. As the meal finished, Darcy suggested that they not separate but that all retire to the drawing room.

"An hour," said Richard to Bingley as they rose to leave the dining room, "I will not pull you away from Miss Bennet for an hour, but we cannot wait much longer than that."

Getting an agreement from Bingley, he allowed those around him to precede him from the room. That is he allowed everyone but Mary Ellen to leave before him. "Marcus," he said when nearly all the others had left the room, "does your father retire early?"

Marcus's lips curled into a knowing smile. "He should be up and about for another two hours, and Aldwood Abbey is on the way to Harris's."

"Why do you wish to call on my father?" There was a teasing tone to Mary Ellen's voice.

He placed the hand that he still held on his arm. "I have decided to marry."

"You have?"

"Yes, if you will have me." He paused just inside the door to the dining room. Servants scurried about collecting dishes and pretending not to listen to or notice the couple standing at the door.

"Because I am your peace?" she said softly.

"Precisely so," he replied. "You make my heart whole."

"Do you love me?"

His lips curled upwards at the impish look on her face. "I think since I wish to kill one of my own men because he has disparaged you, it is safe to say that I love you."

"You think I am safe?"

He laughed. "No, no, my dear girl, I did not say that. You are anything but safe."

"And yet, though I am not safe, I am your peace?"

He pulled her into his embrace. "Yes. You are my peace, and I love you. Now, do I speak to your father or not?"

Her head tipped to the side and delight danced in her eyes. "I suppose, if you kiss me, then you must speak to him, or I shall be ruined. My reputation is already in a precarious position, and even Darcy's servants might talk."

He chuckled and did as she requested, kissing her thoroughly enough that should any servant carry the tale, her reputation would indeed be tarnished.

Chapter 15

"Colonel Fitzwilliam, Mr. Bingley," Captain Harris greeted as he entered the sitting room where Richard and Bingley had been placed by a rather displeased butler. "What brings you to call at this hour?" He motioned for the gentlemen to be seated.

"A matter of some delicacy," said Richard, attempting to settle into his chair and look at ease. There was no point in making Harris any more suspicious than he already appeared. "I had thought to call tomorrow during more acceptable hours but was informed by Miss Lydia that you were off to visit a friend on the morrow."

Harris's brow rose at the mention of Miss Lydia, and he shifted forward in his seat. "I intended to leave quite early actually and was about to retire for the night."

"I do apologize for keeping you from your repose," said Richard. "However, I do believe we can conclude our business quickly." He leaned forward.

Harris nodded but did not settle any further into his

seat. "By all means then," he said with a sweeping motion of his hand.

"I have heard rumblings of a captaincy or two coming open in the regulars and have put forward your name." Of course, the rumblings had been of Richard's own creation, and his recommendation was not based on Harris's skill as an officer. However, Harris did not need to know that yet.

Harris's eyes grew wide, but a moment later he wore a pleased expression. "I thank you for thinking of me, but I have no ambition to join the regulars. I have nearly completed my duty to the militia and, on its conclusion, intend to take up my place here."

"You are not interested in the least?" Richard asked. It had only been a hope, and a small one, that Harris could be easily disposed of.

Harris shook his head. "I am afraid I am not."

Richard sighed. "I think you should not brush the opportunity away so quickly."

Harris smiled. "I am not a second son. I have no need of a career in the military."

"But it will be years before you come into your inheritance," countered Richard.

"True, but the estate is well-managed. There are funds enough to support both my father and mother and myself and any family I might have." His gaze moved from Richard to Bingley as he mentioned his family.

Bingley's eyes narrowed. "It will not be with Miss Bennet."

"You think not?" Harris's eyes laughed at Bingley.

"I know," said Bingley.

"As I understand it, you had your chance and squandered it." Harris settled into his chair slightly.

Richard smiled, folded his arms, and took a position to watch what might unfold.

"It was a misunderstanding," said Bingley. "One that has been cleared up."

"But what can you offer? Ties to trade? A leased estate?" Harris chuckled. "You are no gentleman. Even if you purchase an estate, your father will always be a tradesman."

Bingley drew a breath and released it slowly. As much as he wished to yank the fool from his seat and throttle him, Bingley knew that Richard would find it easier to discover what he wished to know if Harris were still conscious. "My fortune is not insignificant."

"You would call her a fortune hunter?"

"And you would call her a wanton seductress," Bingley growled.

Richard nearly laughed at how quickly Harris shifted from a position of ease to one of wary watching.

"I have said no such thing."

"Have you not?" Bingley stood and took a step towards Harris, who jumped to his feet.

"I have not," Harris assured.

Bingley moved so that his toes were nearly touching Harris's.

Harris swallowed and shifted backward a partial step.

"This is the matter of some delicacy," Richard said, joining them in standing.

Harris glanced briefly at Richard before returning his attention to Bingley. "Has someone disparaged Miss Bennet?"

"As if you do not know!" Bingley's right fist connected with Harris's abdomen, causing Harris to gasp and bend forward. Bingley pushed Harris backwards into the chair behind him.

"Before you call to have us thrown out," said Richard, placing one hand on each arm of Harris's chair and leaning down to speak very closely to the man's face, "you will wish to hear what we know. And if you are smart — a level to which I believe you might be able to rise — you will fill us in on the details we have not yet discovered."

Harris's eyes darted from one angry face to the other.

"Will you listen?"

Harris nodded.

Richard stood and relaxed his position but remained standing over Harris. "Today, I have heard stories circulating about Miss Bennet, Miss Elizabeth, and Miss Dobney, and they all have one person in common. Do you wish to tell me of whom I speak?"

"It was Miss Bingley," offered Harris. "His sister." He pointed at Bingley.

Colonel Fitzwilliam looked at Bingley. "Will you deny that?"

Bingley shook his head. "No. I am certain she did share most of what we heard with Harris, but how it spread from my sister to Mr. Williams's ears is the question, is it not?"

"Indeed," said Richard, turning back to Harris. "Would you like to inform us as to whom you spoke?"

Harris's eyes grew wide, and he swallowed. "I cannot."

Richard leaned over him again, taking note of the increased level of fear the mere mention of this unnamed person had caused in Harris. "Tell me why you cannot."

Harris shook his head.

"Tell me," demanded Richard.

"I cannot."

Richard glanced at Bingley. "Perhaps we should move this outside. I would hate to bloody the furniture."

"I cannot say," pleaded Harris. "I am not withholding the information for my sake alone."

Richard's brow rose in interest at the comment. His lips curled in a slanted, sly smile as he once again stood and looked at Bingley. "I would wager a month's pay that if there is a reason to fear for the safety of any person, Wickham must be involved." He took a step away, hoping that his hunch about Harris's fear of Wickham was correct.

"Thank you for your time, Captain Harris. We will consult with Wickham regarding this matter. "

"No!" Harris was on his feet and had hold of Richard's arm. "I will tell you as much as I can if you promise to neither share it with Wickham or Mr. Williams."

Richard studied Harris's face. There was no trace of anything but fear in the man's eyes. "Very well, we will not speak of this to Wickham or Mr. Williams. Sit and tell us your story."

Harris released Richard's arm and returned to his chair. "Three years ago..."

~*~

Priscilla wiped her eyes with the corner of the shawl she held tightly about her shoulders. "Is...is he dead?" she asked, peering over Harris's shoulder at the white face of her father.

"I am afraid he is," Harris replied. He looked up toward the top of the stairs. "Did he fall?"

She nodded.

"Is no one here?"

"He was in his cups," she whispered.

Harris knew what that meant. Priscilla's father became violently angry about everything when he was in his cups. No doubt the servants had scurried to find places to be busy and hidden so as not to accidentally become the target of the man's ill temper.

"And none came to investigate the noise of his falling?"

Priscilla's lips trembled.

Harris rose and pulled her into his embrace. "Shhh...all will be well."

She flinched when he began to rub her back.

"Did he hurt you?" Harris attempted to pull the shawl from her shoulders.

"No, please."

"Pris, you must let me see." He gently tugged the shawl from her grasp and unwrapped her. He turned her and froze. The buttons of her dress had been torn from their places, and the material gapped revealing the unmistakable marks of a whip. "Is this the only damage he did?" If her father was not already dead, Harris would have killed him himself.

She shook her head. "Please do not make me tell you."

"Pris, you must." He wrapped her in the shawl once again and, taking a seat on the stairs, pulled her onto his lap.

She rested her head against his shoulder. "You will not leave me?"

"I love you, Pris. You know this."

"Even if I was ruined? Would you love me then?"

Harris's blood ran cold. He had heard how more than one maid had fled her place of employment with Priscilla's father. He forced the question from his lips. "Did he give you to one of his friends?"

"He tried, but I refused and locked myself in my room." She shuddered. "When he came in, I told him that I was going to marry you — that you were the only man who was ever going to know me in that way." She drew a shaky breath. "He said I would

earn my keep. He had gambled beyond his means, and I was the payment."

"Oh, Pris," Harris kissed her forehead.

Her lips quivered, and she shook her head. "I thought he would only beat me, but after he had lashed me thrice, he said I would lift my skirts for his friend. I again told him I would not. I expected another lashing, but instead, he thought to rid me of my hesitance to be with a man." She buried her face. "I am ruined. He ruined me."

"He...your father...ruined you?"

She nodded. "I was so angry. I screamed, but no one came. I tried to not let him do it, but ..." Her body shuddered at the thought. "When he left, I followed him and watched until he got to the stairs, and then..."

"You pushed him?"

She nodded. "I did not mean to kill him. I just wished for him not to be able to send for his friend."

"Pack a bag, Pris. You cannot stay here."

"Where will I go?"

"Somewhere where only I shall find you," said Harris.

~*~

"I told Mr. Williams that Priscilla had been sent away because her father did not wish for us to marry. When the servants finally came out of hiding, it was one of them who discovered the body."

Richard sank back in his chair. The story was nearly

enough to wipe the anger of the rumors that Harris had started from his mind.

"Apparently, there was a maid who was not ignorant of what happened, and with the right kind of persuasion, she told the story to Wickham." Harris gave Bingley an apologetic look. "I had to find a way to harm you, or he would have told Williams that Priscilla killed her father."

"Does Wickham know where she is?" Richard asked.

Harris nodded. "He does."

"Then," said Richard, "it is even more important that you consider my offer. The Canadas are in need of soldiers. Take your young lady and find a new life in Canada."

"But what of my place here."

Richard ran a hand through his hair. "She was sent away. Could she not have had a relation in Canada? If she had remained in England you would have hunted for her until you found her, would you not have?"

Harris nodded slowly.

"I can make arrangements for you to spend a short term in Canada and when the skirmish with the Americans is resolved, you can return with the wonderful prize you found — Miss Priscilla. We can find passage for the two of you."

"It is not two. There is a child."

Richard's brows rose. "Yours, I assume."

Harris shook his head. "Her father's."

Richard blinked. "Well, then, it will be passage for three, if you will go."

Harris looked at Bingley and then back at Richard. "And if I do not wish to go?"

"She will never be free from the danger of Wickham." It was unlikely that Wickham, after this week, would be in a position or country to cause any serious danger, but Richard was not willing to share that bit of news with Harris. There was still the matter of the rumors that were started. "And there is still the fact that you have disparaged the future Mrs. Darcy and Mrs. Bingley." He smiled as Harris looked at Bingley in shock.

"I did say the misunderstanding had been sorted out," said Bingley with a grin.

"And," said Richard before Harris could recover to make a comment in return, "beyond that, you have also shared tales of your cousin, and since she has had the good sense to accept an offer of marriage from your commanding officer, things could become decidedly unpleasant for you."

"You...you...," he stammered. "She finally caught your attention? I did not think she would."

"Women will surprise you," Richard replied. "Now, as to my offer to you, will I be off to make the arrangements tomorrow?"

Harris's shoulders sank with his sigh. "I see there is very little choice but to accept."

"See," said Richard, rising from his chair, "I knew you could rise to the level of intelligence of which I suspected you were capable." He picked up his hat from the table just inside the sitting room door. "Tell your friend tomorrow that she should expect to travel with you in a fortnight." He paused. "A trip to Gretna before might be advisable." He motioned for Bingley to exit before him.

Bingley blew out a breath as they rode away from the Harris estate. "And I thought Wickham evil, but that poor girl's father..." Bingley shook his head in disbelief.

"The depravity of man is hard to fathom at times," agreed Richard.

"Indeed," said Bingley, "I almost feel sorry for Harris."

Richard chuckled. "I would be lying if I said I am not slightly persuaded to show him compassion. However, since he had intended to marry Jane even though he loved Miss Priscilla, I believe we have done him a favour in sending him away with the woman he loves."

Bingley shrugged. "Perhaps we have."

"It was a good meeting," said Richard. "Very little force was needed, and the results were favourable. Hopefully, the next meeting will go so well as this one."

"No," said Bingley with a dark smile, "the next meeting shall be successful, but I expect and hope a bit more force will be needed."

Chapter 16

The sun was setting as Bingley and Richard wound their way through the streets of London. They had paused long enough upon arrival to leave their bags at Bingley's townhouse and for Bingley to stop at his solicitor's to check on the progress of marriage papers and a special license. Now, however, they had left the favourable portion of town and slowly made their way down toward the river.

Bingley waved to some chap who was seated on a crate marking things off in his notebook.

"She sails at dawn," the man called.

"Where to?" Bingley called back.

The man wore a large grin. "Portsmouth."

A gull swooped and called as Bingley drew his horse close to the man. "And my package?"

"Plenty of room," said the man standing, "and not a question to be answered. Always looking for an extra set of hands to man the ropes and hoist the cargo."

"He'll not be a willing worker." Bingley knew how hard the men on these ships worked. His father had made him take a turn at it a time or two. It was, according to his father, the best way to learn about and appreciate the business his family oversaw. It had been weeks before the blisters had healed completely. But his hands were not fated for calluses; his were destined to write in ledgers and see others do the things that needed to be done. He was to be master — not of a company, but an estate. Still, his father thought it best to teach him about those who were less blessed with prosperity.

"Not the first reticent squab I've dealt with." The man swore as a dog with a piece of bread in its mouth raced between his legs attempting to escape the lad who chased it. He eyed the colonel cautiously. "As long as the cur can stand and function, he'll be of use." There was a hint of a warning in the man's voice.

"No promises," muttered Richard. He would like nothing better than to send Wickham off to sea without two good legs or arms.

The man raised a brow and chortled. "Not just you wishin' to see him off?" he said to Bingley.

"We are but two," Bingley replied. "It would be best if he were kept below until you have set sail."

"Aye, a sneaky scoundrel, is he?"

"Among other things," Richard replied. His horse stepped sideways as impatient as his master to be going.

"If you see my uncle while in port, give him my greetings." Bingley gave a bow of his head and moved a short distance down the road before dismounting and tying up his horse. He waited for Richard, then ducked into a tavern and wound his way through the establishment and out a side door. Across the alley, a large man leaned against the wall of a building, smoking. Seeing Bingley, he nodded and tipped his head toward the door to his right. Bingley gave a look up and down the narrow passage before entering the building.

"You continue to surprise me," whispered Richard as he ducked through the door behind Bingley. "Ever considered espionage?"

Bingley chuckled. "No, although covert imports did cross my mind when I was younger."

Richard raised a questioning brow.

Bingley shook his head. "All legal, nothing covert." A slow smile spread across his face, "Well, until now, I suppose."

Richard chuckled softly and followed Bingley down a hall and into a room where Wickham sat slumped over a table, a bottle of rum three-quarters empty and a scattered deck of cards framing where his head lay.

Bingley motioned for Richard to take a seat and then took one himself as he picked up the bottle of liquor, wiped the top, took a draught, and passed it to Richard. Richard took the bottle and a gulp of his own, all the while eying Bingley with a mixture of intrigue and appreciation.

Bingley gathered the cards and gave them a shuffle. He also gave Wickham's leg a nudge with his foot.

"Leave me be," Wickham muttered.

"I am afraid that is impossible," said Bingley, discarding the deck of cards and, catching the legs of Wickham's chair with the toes of his boots, upset it, sending Wickham sprawling backward.

"What is the meaning of this?" Wickham sputtered as he clambered to his feet. He swayed slightly as he stood, blinking his eyes as he attempted to focus on the men before him.

Bingley waited patiently until Wickham's eyes grew wide, and he took an unsteady step backward.

"I've heard stories," said Bingley, rising and moving toward Wickham, who matched Bingley's every step with a retreating step of his own. Bingley only smiled and continued to advance, steadily moving his prey toward the wall. "Lady Catherine visited Derbyshire."

"Did she?" Wickham replied, attempting to sound surprised by such news. However, it was a feeble attempt as the fear in his eyes grew.

Bingley nodded. "She was displeased with Darcy's choice of bride."

Wickham's eyes shifted to look at the door behind Bingley.

"Her curate is a gossip, it seems, but then you knew he would be." Bingley placed a hand on each of Wickham's shoulders and pushed him against the wall. "You told him about Lydia," he hissed close to Wickham's ear.

Wickham attempted to push Bingley away, but Bingley placed his right arm across Wickham's neck, pushing against it firmly enough to make the man gasp and cough. "You thought I would not follow through on my promise." He pressed a bit harder. "You misjudged me."

Bingley released Wickham and stepped back. As he expected, Wickham lunged toward him, attempting to make his fist connect with Bingley's face but only being successful in making contact with the air as Bingley ducked and with a swift jab to the abdomen, doubled Wickham over. Bingley's fist caught Wickham's jaw and sent him staggering. He caught Wickham by the lapels of his jacket and shoved him against the wall once again.

"You have two choices," he growled, leaning close to Wickham's ear. "I leave my associate, who is waiting outside, to do as he will with you, or you accept my offer to leave England and never return."

"You were to be in Brighton yesterday." Richard sat at the table with his legs outstretched and ankles crossed as he flipped through the deck of cards. He was quite content to see Bingley roughing Wickham up a bit. "Dereliction of duty is frowned upon, and I shall make it known that you deserted. Returning to England is not an option."

Wickham's attention shifted from Bingley to Richard, as if seeing the colonel for the first time.

"There is a boat at the dock which sails for Portsmouth at dawn." Bingley released Wickham. "You will be on it." He waved to the toppled over chair on the floor. "Sit."

Wickham did as instructed.

"I said you would pay with your life if you did not remain silent," said Bingley, taking his own seat. "You accepted my money but did not hold up your part of the agreement; therefore, your life belongs to me." He pulled three folded documents from his pocket and placed them on the table.

He tapped the first — "fish." He tapped the second — "sugar." He tapped the third — "spice and tea." He passed a hand over the documents. "Newfoundland, the West Indies, or India — your choice, but the third would seem to have the greatest potential for seeking your fortune and have the benefit of removing you furthest from me."

Bingley leaned forward. "Before you make your decision, hear me and hear me well. You will not return. As Colonel Fitzwilliam, has said, you will be labelled a deserter, and rumor has it that you spent the last two nights in the bed of a French woman known to harbour sympathizers."

Bingley smiled as Wickham's eyes grew wide. "Yes, she was selected for you for that very reason. You did not think you just happily met such a beguiling woman and were successful in bedding her based on your luck and charm alone, did you?" He motioned to the papers on the table. "Choose."

Wickham studied his choices, finally, settling on the third option.

"Very good," said Bingley, gathering up the other two papers and placing them back in his pocket. "Give this to the captain of the ship in the morning. He will see that you make your connection in Portsmouth."

Bingley rose to leave. "Your things have been removed from Brighton. They will join you in Portsmouth." He turned to leave, but then turned back to Wickham once more and tossed a small bag of coins on the table. "That with the money you were allowed to win is one month's pay. It is the last you will get from me. Any further meetings will not end so agreeably."

He gave a nod of his head. "Good day. I would wish you a safe journey, but frankly, I do not care if you survive it."

Richard followed Bingley from the room and back out to the alley where he waited while Bingley relieved himself against the wall as he gave instructions to the burly guard near the door. His business concluded, he turned to Richard. "Would you care for a pint here, or would you rather wait until we are closer to Mayfair?"

Richard studied Bingley's face. "We need to drink here, do we not?"

"It would be best to have a reason for our horses to be out front," agreed Bingley. "Besides, the proprietor was a friend of my father. It would only be polite to pay our respects."

Richard clapped Bingley on the shoulder. "Then a pint on me."

They entered the tavern again through the side door. "Does Darcy have any idea how deviant you can be?"

Bingley's lips twitched. "He might."

Richard's brows rose.

"How do you expect a tradesman's son becomes so well acquainted with a man of Darcy's standing?"

Richard sat down at a table in the corner with Bingley. "It was not just his penchant to be honorable?"

"No," Bingley said with a laugh, "although that was part of it." As they drank their ale, Bingley regaled Richard with the story of a young Darcy, who had stumbled into a compromising position and was in need of a means of escape. "A few well-contrived distractions and a knowledge of the servant's passageways, and we were laughing in the stables with a bottle of pinched port and sharing it with the grooms when the young lady's mother found us."

Richard guffawed. "I cannot see Darcy sitting in the stables drinking port with the grooms."

"Darcy would have done worse to avoid Miss Thacker."

"Miss Thacker?" Richard let out a low whistle. "That was no small escape. She is terrifying."

Bingley nodded. "And in need of a wealthy gent."

"So, the grooms vouched for your being in the stables?"

Bingley grinned. "As did the son of a peer whom we found in a state of dishabille with the lady with whom he has since sired an heir."

"Anyone I might know?"

Bingley laughed. "Being the son of a peer yourself, I am fairly certain you would know him; however, I swore to never reveal what I saw, and it is a promise I intend to keep." Bingley's brows flicked up and back down quickly. "I keep my peace not just because it is the right and proper thing to do, but by doing so, I have an ally should the need ever arise."

Richard snorted and drained the last of his ale. "Ah, the depths that lie behind such a pleasant exterior. It is probably best that Darcy befriended you. I shudder to think if you had come under the influence of a less responsible man."

Bingley's lips curled into a crooked smile. "Such as yourself?"

Richard rose from the table. "Indeed."

Laughing, they exited the tavern, and with a lightness at having rid themselves of a heavy and disagreeable burden, rode off on a weaving path back to Mayfair.

Chapter 17

After half a week in London, one day in Hertfordshire, and two more on the road, Richard and Bingley finally returned to Derbyshire. Wickham had been delivered to Portsmouth and set sail. Mr. Bennet had been called upon, and, with a minimum of teasing from the man, permission for Bingley to marry Jane had been granted. All that remained to be done was for Richard to give Harris his new documents and instructions, and that would be accomplished within the next two days.

Harris was not who either gentleman desired to see first upon their return. However, that is exactly whom they encountered upon their arrival at Willow Hall, for he was just departing and met them on the road.

"I was just sharing my news." Harris glanced nervously back at Willow Hall. "I have located Priscilla. My parents are well-pleased to hear that she is well and has been caring for her cousin, who was orphaned not long after she arrived to live at her aunt's home. I did surprise them, however, by not waiting to marry as one should but impulsively snatching her away to Gretna Green."

Richard tipped his head and studied Harris's face. The captain's expression appeared to be open and honest if a tad bit uneasy. "And have you informed any of them about your desire to sail to Canada?"

Harris swallowed. "Is it still necessary?"

Richard nodded. "I have the paperwork in my satchel. The arrangements have been made. Your signature is all that remains to be added."

"But Canada?" asked Harris. "Could I not be sent to Newcastle?"

Richard blew out a breath. "You sullied Bingley's name, as well as all the Bennets' name and your own cousin's."

Harris nodded slowly. "Yes, I know. It was wrong, but I had a reason for part of it — not that it makes it right or more acceptable even, but surely, you can understand the need to protect a person you love." Harris looked down at the reins he held in his hand. "Would it not be worse for me to be here where I can feel the full weight of my sin?" He looked up at Richard. "I shall always be reminded of my error if I must face the ones I have wronged."

Richard's brows drew together, and his lips puckered slightly. Harris had a point. Richard very much doubted that Marcus, Darcy, or Bingley would ever let Harris forget what he had done. A small smile pulled at one side of Richard's mouth. If any of those men did soften towards

Harris, there was always Lydia to take up the cause. Yes, perhaps Harris was correct. It might be best if the man were exactly where he could constantly be reminded of his failing. Richard's brows flicked upward.

"It is an idea that is not without merit. However, it was not just I who was offended. I must discuss this option with all whose names you dishonored." He gave a tip of his head in dismissal. "I will contact you after I have had all the necessary discussions."

"I thank you, Colonel," said Harris.

Richard watched him go. "Was I too easy on him?" he asked Bingley.

Bingley chuckled as they started up the drive. "I think not. He had a good argument."

Richard sighed. "Aye, but was he being honest?"

Bingley shrugged. "There is no way of truly knowing, I suppose."

"True," Richard agreed.

"But there will be many around to keep him on the straight and narrow." Bingley turned toward Richard with a smirk. "And I do have access to a ship or two if we should need."

Richard laughed as he slid from his horse and tossed the reins to a waiting groom. "It was a heady time sending one scoundrel packing." He clapped Bingley on the shoulder. "I would gladly do so again with you if needed."

Bingley nodded his thanks but whispered as the door

to Willow Hall opened, revealing Darcy coming to greet them, "Just do not tell Darcy that."

Richard chuckled. "Have no fear, my friend. That is one lecture I do not wish to hear."

"Nor do I," said Bingley. "Darcy! Have you missed us so much that you must be the first to greet us?"

Darcy laughed. "No, I just know, since your ladies are within, that as soon as you are in their presence, I will not be able to get the information from you that I need."

"And what information is that?" asked Richard. He knew precisely what it was that Darcy wished to know, but giving the information without at least a small amount of taunting seemed rather a dull method.

"Was your trip a success?" Darcy asked.

"Indeed it was," Bingley replied. "Wickham set sail for India, Mr. Bennet gave me his blessing, and Harris — well, he seems repentant. Oh!" Bingley patted his pocket. "I have also secured a special license. All I need now is a home for my bride."

"You saw Harris?" Darcy asked.

"We did. Just at the road," said Bingley. "He said he is married."

Darcy nodded. "Will you not be keeping Netherfield?" He turned and began walking toward the house with them.

"I shall allow Jane to decide. If she wishes to be near her parents, then I will keep Netherfield, but if she prefers to remain close to Elizabeth, then we will search for an estate within a day's drive of Pemberley."

"That seems reasonable." Darcy turned toward Richard. "Your father found Elizabeth to be delightful and has returned to Matlock to tell your mother that you are betrothed. I had to produce Mary Ellen and allow her to confirm the fact before he was willing to accept it." Darcy chuckled. "I believe he had come to the conclusion that you would never marry. He wishes to know your intentions regarding your inheritance and your commission. I told him that I would mention it and that you would answer as soon as you were able."

Richard drew a breath and released it. "I am certain Mother will have given him my answer for me before I have even thought of it."

Darcy chuckled. "So you will also be within a day's drive."

"Soon," said Richard. "But not immediately. I cannot just leave my men to anyone." He stepped into the house behind Darcy. A smile wiped away any arguments that might have followed, for there, standing in the entryway next to Jane was Mary Ellen. "Miss Dobney," he said, taking her hand and lifting it to his lips.

"Mrs. Abbot thought you and Mr. Bingley might wish to stretch your legs in the garden before sitting for a cup of tea," explained Mary Ellen.

"Did she?" Richard lifted a quizzical brow; a spark of mischief gleamed in his eye. "Can I not just kiss you here?"

Mary Ellen blushed. "You may kiss me both here and in the garden." She lifted onto her toes and placed her lips on his. "I have missed you."

He smiled and wrapped his arms around her, pulling her firmly against his chest. "And I have missed you," he said before kissing her in return. It was just a brief kiss — nowhere near the sort of kiss he wished to give her, but with his cousin, as well as Bingley and Jane, as an audience, a proper greeting that told her exactly how much he had missed her would have to wait. "Shall we?" he asked as he released her and offered her his arm.

"There is a lovely path through the woods," Darcy offered with a chuckle before ducking into the sitting room.

"Your journey was good?" Jane asked as she and Bingley followed Richard and Mary Ellen from the house and around to the garden.

"It was. Everything has been settled," Bingley answered with a smile. "I stopped at Longbourn. Your mother was pleased to see me."

"Just my mother?" Jane asked in surprise.

Bingley chuckled. "Your father was welcoming as well. In fact, he has given me permission to marry his eldest daughter."

Jane wrapped both arms around Bingley's and laid her head on his shoulder. "That is very good news."

He looked down to see her looking up at him. There was a happiness in her eyes that outshone her lovely smile. "You will still have me then?"

"Most happily."

The sense of being fortunate beyond what he deserved nearly overwhelmed him, and he said as much to Jane. She, of course, did not agree. It was not he who was fortunate but herself.

"My darling Jane," he began as they circled the large tree at the far end of the garden and stopped just where it stood between them and the house. "I shall not always be disagreeable," he turned to face her, taking her hands in his, "but on this one point, I must be. You, Dearest, deserve better than a man who was so easily persuaded to desert you." He placed a finger on her lip to prevent her protest. "But I will be hanged if I am going to allow you the opportunity to find such a man. You are mine."

"Indeed, I am," Jane agreed.

Bingley lifted her hand and brushed his lips across her knuckles. "I have a special license." The way her eyes grew wide in surprise was delightful. He was certain he would never get tired of watching her face.

"How do you do that?" he asked. "There is a peace and serenity about your expression even when you are startled, happy, or even hurt. It is as if nothing stirs your composure."

Her cheeks flushed, and she ducked her head. "It is my nature, I suppose, as well as years of practice." She peeked up at him, a mischievous smile on her lips. "You have met my mother, have you not?"

Bingley laughed. "I have."

"If I were to become distressed and out of sorts every time she did or said something shocking," Jane shrugged, "it would be frowned on more greatly than it is, and my father would be spoken of as lacking. It is easier to calm the waters with a smile than a frown." She laughed lightly. "But, I assure you, I possess a temper and am quite capable of being in a bad humor. You may ask Lizzy. She has borne the brunt of it; however, compared to Lydia, Kitty or even Lizzy, my temper is mild."

"I believe your temper to be perfect," Bingley said with a smile, "for if you were not so gentle and forgiving, I would not be so happily attached to such a wonderful lady, which once again proves how very fortunate I am." He chuckled at the way her delightful lips pursed in displeasure briefly, and then, unable to resist the urge any longer, he gathered her into his arms and kissed her.

"I do not wish to wait to marry you," said Jane when Bingley finally allowed her to speak.

Bingley smiled. "We are of the same mind then. It is why I obtained the license, after all." He held her close and rested his chin on the top of her head. "But there are matters to consider. I would not have our wedding be a patched up affair — especially with the rumors that are circulating."

Jane squeezed him tightly. "I do not care about the rumors. Those who matter know the truth, and everyone else will soon figure out that they have been duped. You are an honorable man."

"And you a virtuous woman." He kissed the top of her head. However, he was not as certain as she that the rumors would die so easily.

"We could marry with Lizzy and Mr. Darcy," Jane suggested. "I know Lizzy would not mind."

Bingley leaned against the trunk of the tree, pulling her with him. It did feel good to have her here in his arms. A bit of hurry and a few rumors seemed small prices to pay for this pleasure.

"I am certain Darcy would be happy to share his day as well, but where are we to live? There is Netherfield..." He felt her head shake against his chest. "Or we could find something in Derbyshire." Her contented sigh told him that Derbyshire was her favoured location. "It will take time to find an estate."

"Philip may know of a place that could be rented," Jane suggested hopefully, "if it would not be too great an expense," she added. His chuckle rumbled through his chest below her ear. "You already have the expense of Netherfield," she argued.

"Are you attempting to persuade me to stay in Derbyshire or return to Netherfield, my sweet."

She pulled away slightly, so that she could look at him. "I am merely attempting to be wise. Just because one has money does not mean one should spend it without careful consideration."

"My accounts will not run dry. I believe we can afford to rent a place and still purchase an estate even with the upkeep of Netherfield until such time as the lease ends."

Her brows furrowed. "You are certain?"

"Have you so little faith in me?"

Her eyes grew wide. "No, it is not that. I trust you completely, but my mother has always spent without thought, and I do not wish to be my mother."

He kissed her forehead. "You could never be your mother."

"Thank you," she said as she placed her head back on his chest. "I love you," she said softly.

"And I love you," he replied. They stood just as they were discussing what each might wish for in an estate, and then, finally, as Richard and Mary Ellen appeared from the woods, Bingley pushed off the tree, gave Jane one more kiss, tucked her hand in the crook of his arm, and returned to the house to let Darcy and Elizabeth know of their plans.

Chapter 18

Having the connections Bingley did to Darcy, the Dobneys, and Mr. Williams, two days proved to be sufficient time for Bingley and Jane to acquire a house in Kympton. It was not a grand house, but it was not tiny either. There were three rooms for sleeping, a fine, though not spacious, dining room, a study, and two small sitting rooms — the larger one for entertaining and the other for quiet evenings at home.

Aunt Tess saw to the staffing, and Cecily and Aunt Gardiner made certain that the house itself was ready to receive its new master and mistress, while Mary Ellen and Lucy helped Jane alter one of her dresses to make it more fitting of a wedding ceremony.

So, it was on the third day after Bingley and Richard had returned from town that Jane found herself standing at the front of the church next to Bingley and Darcy and Elizabeth. Philip conducted the ceremony, and then, they all travelled to Pemberley for the wedding breakfast.

The feast was set out in the garden, and after they had

eaten, many guests and the happy couples enjoyed a stroll along the garden paths. Eventually, Bingley and Darcy relinquished their holds on their ladies as others claimed them for a few moments.

Darcy wandered to a quiet corner, while Bingley ventured further down the path toward the middle of the garden. There were two guests in particular with whom he wished to have a conversation.

Richard must have seen him, for Bingley was not many steps into his pursuit when the colonel fell in step with him.

"You have not yet told Harris of your decision, have you?" Bingley asked.

"No, I had thought to call on him tomorrow." He tipped his head and looked at Bingley. "Am I correct in assuming that my call will be unnecessary after this."

Bingley smiled. "You may still call. I am certain there are papers that require signatures."

"There are, but not quite yet. The ones I had, I have sent back with my regrets in being unable to secure a man for the position." It had not been something he had wanted to do, but after consulting with all the injured parties, it had become clear that it might be the best course of action. If it were not for a slight uneasiness that Harris might still be playing a role, Richard would have been happy to send the papers back, but that uneasiness was still there.

"Mrs. Harris," Bingley greeted the lady in front of him

with a bow. "I am pleased to finally have a chance to speak to you beyond a how do you do."

Mrs. Priscilla Harris dipped a curtsey.

"Might we take this path?" Bingley extended an arm to Mrs. Harris and motioned to his left. Harris looked nervously at Bingley but allowed his wife to take Bingley's arm. They walked along for a few feet commenting on the weather and the flowers as well as extending words of congratulations to each other regarding their marriages.

Then, when they were far enough away from any other guests, Bingley began his true purpose for seeking out the Harrises. "I am not normally an unpleasant man, Mrs. Harris, but I find I must be slightly so. I do apologize for any discomfort my words may give, but they are necessary."

Mrs. Harris looked at Bingley and then over her shoulder at her husband. "Of...of course," she stammered.

Bingley led her to a grouping of benches tucked under a tree with a sprawling canopy. "There is no easy way to ask this, I am afraid, but you should know that your answer will go no further than this spot. I am not the sort to spread tales." He gave a significant look to Harris. "Do not answer for her." There was a gentle warning in his voice.

Harris nodded.

"Mrs. Harris, I have been led to believe that your cousin, who is in your care, is not truly your cousin. Oh, there is a family resemblance, to be certain. In fact, she looks very much like you." He was watching Priscilla's face closely and did not miss the fear in her eyes before she dropped her gaze. "The story I was told was most horrific, and I will not repeat it. However, I must verify that it is true and not a tale invented to garner sympathy and avoid just punishment." He paused for just a moment. "Is the child yours?" he asked softly and then waited until she responded with a small nod. "Who is the father?"

She shook her head.

"Forgive me, but I must know. It is important in regards to your husband's future."

Large questioning eyes looked from Bingley to Harris and back, then flicked away to look down the path as she whispered, "my father."

"Forgive me," Bingley said once again. "Was the child conceived through force on the day your father died?"

Mrs. Harris covered her face and nodded.

"Thank you," Bingley said softly, laying a gentle hand on her shoulder for a moment. "I truly would not have put you through this pain if it were not necessary." He looked at Harris. "It seems you did indeed do what you did to protect the one you love."

"That is what I said," Harris replied. "I would do whatever is necessary to protect her."

"But you must understand," said Bingley, "you have acted dishonorably, so your words and actions naturally fall under more severe scrutiny. Not only did you gossip, but you loved one while courting another."

There was a small gasp from Mrs. Harris.

"I shall allow you to explain that last bit to your wife, Harris, but the rumors, I will address. Miss Bennet is as pure as the driven snow, as are her sisters. Not one has ever seduced a man."

"But Miss Lydia..." Harris began.

"No." Bingley's voice was firm. "She is many things, but a light skirt is not one of them." He drew a breath and released it. "She is now my sister, and I will abide no disparagement of her. What was said of me matters little to me except where it pertains to my wife."

He leaned forward toward Harris. "You see this is where you and I are alike. I will do whatever is necessary to protect those I love — Jane, her sisters, and all attached to them. My own sister, I have effectively disowned for her role in this whole affair. And Wickham — well, he will not be able to harm either my family or yours."

Harris's eyes grew wide.

"He is not dead," said Richard.

"Although by now, he probably wishes he was," replied Bingley with a small grin. "The rolling of the sea for days on end can be unpleasant at first."

Harris eyed Bingley cautiously. "He is no longer in England?" he asked.

Bingley shrugged. "Technically, it is still part of the empire, but no he is not in England. However, that, just like the story about your wife's father, goes no further than here. I will repeat. I will do whatever is necessary to protect those I love." There was no mistaking the threat in Bingley's voice.

"Understood," said Harris. "Wickham is truly gone?"

Bingley nodded. "He is." He turned to Mrs. Harris. "Which means you are also safe." He smiled as she looked toward him. "I do not blame you for your actions. I believe they were justified."

He turned back to Harris. "Now, this is the bit where you find out your fate. I have convinced Colonel Fitzwilliam that there is no need for you to be transferred to any other unit. Your point of it being more effective to have you where you could be reminded of your transgression was valid. You will remain under the authority of the man betrothed to the lady you disparaged and eventually, you will return here to live among us. There will not be a day that passes where you will not be reminded of your good fortune in being allowed to live where you please with those you love." He rose. "There is only one thing remaining. I have chosen to believe you repentant of your crimes."

"I am," said Harris.

Bingley smiled at Richard. "Then you will find it therapeutic for your soul to do your best to repeal the mischief you and my sister have created."

"I will," Harris assured him.

"Very good," replied Bingley. "I should not like to have

to deal with you as I have Wickham." He held Harris's gaze.

"You shall not have to," said Harris. He opened his mouth to speak and then closed it again as if unsure if he should continue. Then, obviously deciding it would be acceptable to speak, he added, "You are not what I thought. You are very gentlemanly."

Bingley inclined his head in acceptance of the compliment and then with a smirk added, "I may have been taught good principles, but do not forget that the blood of a tradesman flows through me. And we tradesmen are a roguish lot when we need to be." He lifted a brow, and although Bingley spoke playfully, Harris's expression showed that he understood the full weight of the words. "Now, I must get back to my wife. I will leave you to explain your intentions where Miss Bennet was concerned to your wife."

Richard chuckled as they walked away. "You could be terrifying if you ever claimed political power."

Bingley shuddered. "There is no need to fear that. I have no desire to be bored endlessly with lectures and debate."

"Nor do I," said Richard. "Thankfully for you, you do not have an earl attempting to convince you that a seat in parliament is a thing to be desired."

Bingley grinned. "Having a friend with political clout could be useful."

Richard groaned. "It will not happen."

Bingley clapped him on the shoulder. "Well, if by some stroke of ill luck you find yourself with a political position, I promise to help make it more interesting."

"I shall hold you to that promise," Richard said once he had finished having a good chuckle at the comment.

"We found you." Jane greeted them with a brilliant smile, dropping Darcy's arm and taking Bingley's.

"I hope you did not think I had abandoned you," Bingley said, covering Jane's hand which lay on his arm with his own. He had been gone for an extended amount of time and without telling her where he would be. "I had a small matter of business with which to deal."

"Business?" Jane blinked in surprise.

"The rumors — or more precisely, the source of the rumors," Bingley explained.

"You approached Harris about those rumors at our wedding breakfast?" Darcy's brows were lifted high.

"I did," said Bingley. "It seemed a most effective place to do so. Harris was not expecting it, and so, I had the advantage."

Darcy shook his head. "And I suppose Richard went along to scare the man into submission." There was a playful smile on Darcy's lips and a knowing look in his eye. Although he would not admit it aloud at this moment, Darcy was not unaware that Bingley was capable of uttering and carrying through on a threat. Neither Bingley nor Richard had been allowed to rest until Darcy had had the full story — or at least as much as Bingley was willing to share of the story — about how Wickham had been convinced to board a ship to India.

"Bingley needs no help from me," said Richard with a wink. "A fierceness lies behind that pleasant facade."

Bingley could feel his face flush at the compliment. "My father taught me many things, but the one he stressed more than any other was that a man must protect that which is dear to him at all costs." He looked down at Jane. "It is a principle that I will neither forget nor ignore." He lifted her hand to his lips. "Shall we go home, my dear?"

Her lips quivered slightly, and her eyes shimmered as she nodded.

So with a word of farewell to Darcy, Elizabeth, and Richard, they began to make their way to Bingley's carriage that stood ready on the driveway in front of the house.

"You threatened Captain Harris for me?" Jane asked as they walked.

Bingley shrugged. "I reminded him that I would not allow him to harm the ones I love. It may have been threatening."

"That is sweet."

Bingley chuckled. "I have never heard a threat called sweet, but if you insist, I will allow it to be."

Jane stopped walking. "You defended my honor. That

to a lady is sweet and noble and..." she sighed, "quite worthy of a kiss."

"I will not argue," he said, dipping his head to kiss her.

Her face fairly glowed with happiness as they resumed walking. "Was your business in town truly business, or was it like today's business — another attempt to defend my honor?"

Bingley shook his head.

"You will not tell me, Husband?"

He smiled at the appellation. "I cannot deny you a thing," he answered, "but it must remain between us." He handed her into the carriage.

"I can keep a secret," she said as she settled into her seat. "You may tell me."

He took his place next to her. "I will, but not until we are home." For if threatening Harris was worthy of a kiss, then banishing Wickham was certainly worth far more.

Jane furrowed her brows, and her lips puckered slightly in displeasure before serenity once again washed over her features. His breath caught in his chest at her loveliness, and his heart felt as if it would burst from the joy he felt in having won such a woman.

He placed an arm around her shoulder and pulled her close. "How fortunate I am," he said.

She looked up from where her head rested on his shoulder. "How fortunate we both are."

He smiled and then dipped his head to kiss her. She was

a jewel — rare and valuable, far more dear than anything could ever be, and she was his. Theirs would be a happy life. He would see to it. She would want for nothing, and she would never have reason to doubt him again, for he would see her heart protected at all costs.

Epilogue

A cool breeze blew softly through the garden, causing the lanterns to sway and flicker on the posts where they hung along the garden paths. Music spilled out the doors of Aldwood Abbey and traipsed down the terrace steps following behind those who chose to stroll instead of dance.

"It is a fine fete," said Mr. Harker to Mr. Dobney. Both men had finally persuaded the ladies, who insisted on seeing to their every need, that a quiet spell next to the roses would be refreshing. And so here they sat. Mr. Harker on a stone bench and Mr. Dobney in what he liked to refer to as his confounded contraption.

"My Lydia has a talent for these things," said Mr. Dobney with a large smile.

Lydia had spent hours discussing details and arrangements with him. Sometimes they held their discussions over a game of chess, while other times, they toured the garden, and still other times, they sipped tea and watched the raindrops race each other down a window — always in a different room of the house. He had grown to love her as much as his own children, and if he were to be completely honest, perhaps a bit more, simply because she reminded him so much of his late wife. He had often said a prayer of thanks to the Lord that He had guided this bright and shining spark of life to Woodhead Cottage.

"She has a great many talents, it would seem," agreed Mr. Harker.

"That she does." Mr. Dobney sighed happily. "I feel as if I have accomplished all for which I was needed and, having done so, can now sit back and look on it with pleasure."

Mr. Harker laughed. "Much as the Lord did on the seventh day."

"Precisely," said Mr. Dobney, joining his friend in a laugh.

"I would be lying if I did not say I felt much the same. Philip has found his footing, and the parish continues to thrive under his guidance — and that of Lucy, of course."

Mr. Dobney gave his greetings to a couple who strolled by before replying. "My boys have done very well for themselves."

"And so has Mary Ellen," said Mr. Harker, "as well as Darcy, and that friend of his, Bingley, is a delightful addition to our community — his wife is perhaps the most pleasant lady I have ever met."

Bingley had had no trouble settling into the community of Kympton. Though he was still searching for a perfect estate, he was quite happy to be living in town, surrounded by neighbors who came to call.

Jane had found herself spending a good deal of time with Aunt Tess and had begun assisting her with some of her projects — the ones Lydia had not claimed as her own. Elizabeth also lent her aid as she could but had spent a good bit of the last month learning all there was to know about running an estate the size of Pemberley.

Mr. Harker extended his legs and crossed his ankles. "You are not in a hurry to return to the festivities are you?"

Mr. Dobney shook his head. "No, I am quite content to take my ease and leave the busyness of the night to the younger set. I am certain under Lydia's watchful eye all will run well, or if not, it will be entertaining."

Both men laughed and then lapsed into companionable silence for a few moments before turning their discussion to other news from the area; while inside, Lydia flitted about the room, ensuring all was well and everyone had been attended to.

"She is quite remarkable." Darcy nodded his head in Lydia's direction as he stood next to Marcus and Philip.

Marcus smiled and added his agreement as his wife stopped to talk to two elderly ladies. She ran a finger over the hem of a sleeve and delighted them with a compliment on the fine workmanship. She was indeed remarkable, and he was fortunate enough to claim her as his own.

"I admit I did not see her potential," Darcy continued.

"Having now met her mother, I can see why you did not," said Marcus.

Mrs. Bennet had arrived in Derbyshire three days ago and was to stay at Willow Hall for another fortnight before returning to Longbourn. Lydia had been insistent that her mother would be able to attend the wedding. After all, she had reasoned, Mama had missed both Jane and Lizzy's wedding and, with Lydia being her favourite, missing such an occasion would be far too grievous an injury to bear. She had said it with eyes wide and serious, and although it sounded as if it could be a dramatic ploy, she had been serious. She could not leave Mr. Dobney and forget about his soiree, but neither could she justify her mother being left out of such a happy event as seeing her youngest daughter married.

Bingley chuckled. "Mrs. Bennet is an exuberant lady."

"I am glad Lydia inherited some of her father's intelligence along with that exuberance." Marcus could not keep his eyes off his new wife as she was now seeing to her mother's comfort. He smiled and nodded as she gave him a small wave. "Aldwood Abbey will do well under her care," he added.

"I believe all of Derbyshire, save Harris, will do well under her care," agreed Philip. "She has scowled at him more than once this evening, and he has not done anything wrong to my knowledge."

Bingley again chuckled. It had been as he has suspected,

having Harris stay here, where he could be reminded of his folly, had proven to be a most fitting punishment. "It seems she has appointed herself the defender of all of us."

"Us, the Ross children, Aunt Tess, Mrs. Bell, and half of my parish, I believe," said Philip.

"I have locked up my pistols," Marcus said with a laugh. "All the rapscallions in the area are safe for the moment."

Marcus had taken Lydia out shooting shortly after he had learned she knew how to shoot. He wished to know if she was correct in her assessment of her skills, and as always, she was. She neither overstated nor hid her accomplishments. She was indeed a fair shot.

The musicians were just returning to their places after a short break, and Lydia turned delighted eyes toward him. It was a waltz that would be next, and the dance she had promised him. He excused himself from the gentlemen standing beside him and made his way towards her.

"Mrs. Dobney, I believe this is our dance," he said, holding out a hand to her. He led her out onto the dance floor and took her in his arms. "You have done very well. There is not a sour looking face amongst the crowd this evening."

Her eyes sparkled with impertinence as she looked up at him. "I must have done well indeed, for even Mr. Darcy is smiling and dancing."

Marcus chuckled. "Must we stay for the full evening?" He had asked several times. He was most anxious to get his wife alone, but she had nodded her head at each inquiry, just as she was doing now.

"A hostess does not desert her guests." She stepped a little further into his embrace. "Even if the incentive to do so is as wonderful as her husband."

The word sent a shiver through her from her head down to her toes. Her husband — a man of wealth with a grand estate, just as Mama had wished, but beyond that, he was a man who loved her, not for her beauty, but simply for herself and treated her with the respect she had always craved.

She tipped her head as she smiled up at him. Tears hung on her lashes. "Thank you," she whispered.

"For what?" he asked.

"For loving me." She blinked rapidly to keep the tears in their place.

"How could I not," he pulled her closer and kissed her forehead. "Are you certain you cannot desert our guests even for a few moments? I should very much like to kiss my wife."

She giggled. "I think we might be able to slip into the garden for a few moments." She arched a brow. "I know which paths are not well lit."

"Have I told you how brilliant you are, Mrs. Dobney?" he asked as he tucked her hand into the crook of his arm and led her onto the terrace.

"No, I do not believe you have," she replied. "Down this

path." She pulled him off to the right and around a corner behind a bush.

He pulled her into his embrace. "You, Mrs. Dobney, are brilliant."

She smiled. "Not many have ever called me that."

"I suppose not everyone can be as wise as I," he tilted her chin up and looked into her eyes. "If they saw what I see, they would agree."

"Are you going to kiss me?"

"Are you eager to return?" he teased, caressing her cheek with his thumb.

She shook her head. "No, just to be kissed."

She lifted to her toes and pressed her lips to his. Kissing, she had decided, was one of her favourite things to do. She loved how he pressed her against his firm body and deepened the kiss until the world around them faded into the night, and she was left with only the pleasure that his love brought her. Lydia had found her happy beginning.

And a beginning it was, for there were many events to take place in the next year. Mary Ellen and Richard, who had stood in the chapel in front of Philip along with Marcus and Lydia earlier that day, would return from Brighton to an estate not far from Aldwood Abbey. Jane and Bingley would eventually decide on an estate closer to Pemberley. Lucy and Philip would add a healthy baby girl to their numbers, and this child would soon after be joined by five others — sons for Marcus and Darcy while Bingley would welcome twins — both a son and a daughter, and Richard would become the overprotective papa of a beautiful daughter. But before those children could make their debut, Miss Darcy would make hers in the circles of London with Elizabeth to stand at her side and Lydia's advice about finding a good husband in her head.

While the Dobneys, Fitzwilliams, Bingleys, and Darcys enjoyed the happiness of these events, there were others who were reaping their fair rewards.

Captain Harris would feel the consequences of his gossip for years to come, but with a penitent heart, he would eventually prove himself not fully unworthy of even Lydia's good opinion.

Caroline Bingley was far more fortunate than she deserved. For within a se'enight of her arrival at Mr. Hadaway's house party, she met a man who promptly petitioned Hurst for permission to offer for her, and through this gentleman's instruction, she came to view her actions in a new, humiliating light.

Lady Catherine would eventually come to accept that Darcy was married to someone who was not her daughter and would speak most civilly to Elizabeth whenever they were in company at Matlock. However, Darcy never again travelled to Rosings, and Lady Catherine never darkened Pemberley's door. To admit she was wrong was not easily done, and accepting Elizabeth at Matlock was as far as she was capable of moving toward reconciliation.

And just one year later, when children were filling the nurseries of our couples, Harris was earning his forgiveness, Caroline was beginning to be restored to her family, and Lady Catherine was ruling her domain at Rosings, a letter arrived on a sunny day when the Abbots, Dobneys, Fitzwilliams, Bingleys, and Darcys were gathered in the garden at Willow Hall.

Bingley opened the missive and, after a quick perusal of the contents, shared it aloud with all who were gathered.

Sir,

It is my duty to inform you that one of your uncle's ships on its journey to India was caught in a storm. Most of the cargo and crew made it through, but not all. Among the dead is counted a Mr. George Wickham.

Bingley gave Richard a crooked smile. "A fitting ending, I should say."

"Aye, aye," agreed Richard, looking around at the group that was gathered who would never again have to worry about the likes of Wickham. He smiled and raised his glass of lemonade in salute. "It is a very happy ending indeed."

Before You Go

If you enjoyed this book, be sure to let others know by leaving a review.

~*~*~

Do you want to know when the next Leenie B book will be available?

You can always know what's new with my books by subscribing to my mailing list.

(If you'd like to know what happened to Caroline, you could read her story, *Better than She Deserved, A Willow Hall Romance Sequel,* for free as it is part of the welcome package when you join my mailing list.)

Book News from Leenie Brown

(bit.ly/LeenieBBookNews)

~*~*~

Turn the page to read an excerpt of another one of Leenie's books.

With the Colonel's Help
Excerpt

Another book which began it's journey to publication as a Thursday's Three Hundred story on my blog is With the Colonel's Help. In this story, Colonel Fitzwilliam has put his foot in it while attempting to improve Elizabeth's opinion of his cousin. Now, he must try to fix the trouble he has caused. However, it is not just the mess he has made that Darcy and Elizabeth will need his help to overcome.

CHAPTER 1

The sun shone bright and warm on Colonel Richard Fitzwilliam as he stood before Rosings. He turned and looked back in the direction from whence he had come. The slow but persistent twisting of his stomach continued its work in making him feel very uneasy. There was something not right in how Miss Elizabeth Bennet had responded to his information regarding his cousin Mr. Fitzwilliam Darcy.

He took off his hat and ran a hand through his hair. The

story he had told had been told with an intent to promote his cousin — for it was a viable example of the caring sort of friend Darcy was. However, Richard had the distinct impression that his comments had, in fact, done just the opposite.

He paced toward the side of the house, thumping his walking stick in a very intentional fashion on the ground. He had just lifted the stick to give the earth another resounding thud when the path of what must be done became apparent. He beat that one last note on the path and then, with a twirl, tucked the stick under his arm and hurried to the house.

"Darcy, we need to talk." Richard deposited his outerwear with a footman and taking his cousin, who fortunately was in the passage, by the arm, nearly dragged the poor fellow down the hall and into the billiards room.

Closing the door behind him, Richard placed himself between it and his cousin. It was time to have a discussion that was well past due. However, he knew it was a discussion in which his reserved cousin would not be an eager participant, and that, coupled with the man-handling Darcy had just received, would likely cause his cousin to seek escape. But escape was not an option.

"What are your intentions regarding Miss Bennet?" Richard began.

Darcy sucked in a quick breath and looked at Richard warily before folding his arms and, to Richard's amusement, attempting to look nonchalantly annoyed. "I know not of what you speak. I assure you I have no intentions in regards to Miss Bennet."

Richard cocked a brow. He had not thought his cousin able to prevaricate without some show of distress. "No intentions?" His tone was doubtful. "Come, now, Darcy. It is not like you to tell such falsehoods," he said, pressing his point.

Darcy swallowed. "I speak the truth. I have no intentions toward Miss Bennet."

Richard's lips curled into a small smile. Darcy was shifting from foot to foot, which was a sure indication that while what he said was true, it was done in an attempt to conceal something else. "No intentions toward Miss Elizabeth Bennet?" He asked. "Miss Elizabeth Bennet, the lady in whose presence you become a blundering fool and whose person your eye rarely leaves — you have no intentions towards her?"

Richard crossed his arms and leaned against the door. "Might I remind you that you can answer my questions forthwith, and we will be on our way about the remainder of our day; or I can call for some port and we can enjoy enough of it to make your tongue more easily persuaded to tell me what I wish to know. Either way, as I am certain you are aware, I will get my answers. Therefore, I suppose the correct question is, do you wish to have a headache tomorrow or not?"

Darcy eyed his cousin cautiously.

Richard's gaze was unwavering as Darcy again shifted from one foot to another and his jaw clenched and unclenched. "Which will it be, Darcy?"

With an exasperated sigh, Darcy shook his head. "Very well, I shall answer your questions. I have no desire to spend an entire trip to London in a closed carriage with you while feeling as if the carriage has run over me." He gave Richard a severe look. "My answers go no further than us. Is that understood? If Aunt Catherine even thinks we are hinting at the things about which we are about to speak, things could become quite uncomfortable for many people — you and me foremost."

Richard nodded his consent. The seriousness of the situation magnified in his mind as he realized his cousin was likely considering marrying Miss Bennet. "I would not ask if I did not think the answer imperative."

Darcy crossed to the window and stared out across the lawn toward the groves. He ran a hand through his hair. "I like her, Richard. I like her very much — in fact, I am quite certain I love her."

He turned to look at his cousin and shook his head. "But, it cannot be. I must not love her. She is not an acceptable choice," his shoulders slumped, and he turned back to the window. "However, I am also convinced that I will be utterly miserable without her."

Richard shook his head. The situation was indeed serious, for he suspected that the lady who had stolen his cousin's heart was little disposed to the same emotions written in Darcy's posture and voice. "I neither see why you must not love her, nor do I see how she is an unacceptable choice."

He knew what Darcy's reply would be, of course, but he also knew it was time to challenge the way in which his cousin thought. For if Darcy did not change his thinking, he would be as he had just claimed he would be — miserable. That was not something Richard wished to see happen. His cousin had endured enough heartache.

Darcy turned to face Richard again. "You know what is expected of me when I marry."

"You mean you are expected to marry Cousin Anne?"

Darcy shook his head. "You know very well that I do not intend to marry Anne, nor does she intend to marry me." Disdain coloured his tone as he continued. "Only Lady Catherine wishes for such an arrangement."

He paced a circle around the billiard table. "I had always hoped to find a lady among the ton who would fit the criteria of having both wealth and position and who would be someone whom I would be able to love. However, I have been through several seasons and have found none. Many have the pedigree, but none have captured my heart." He stopped and stared past Richard to the door as he continued. "And then..."

"You met Miss Bennet," supplied Richard.

Darcy nodded slowly. "She is enchanting." He smiled as he said it and then turned grim once again. "But she has no connections and very little wealth. I have turned these things over in my mind — day and night, truth be told — arguing the side of my heart and then the side of duty. I have come to no acceptable answer."

Richard's voice softened as he saw the turmoil of such thoughts etched on his cousin's face. "You cannot reason away love. Even you must be able to fathom that?"

He had left his position at the door and now stood close enough to Darcy to lay a hand on his cousin's shoulder. "You cannot give up a life of happiness out of a sense of duty."

He moved away and began setting up the billiard table. "Consider. Who will be affected? Lady Catherine — she will not be happy unless you marry Anne, no matter what the lady's pedigree. Perhaps my father — but even if he does not approve at first, he would be hard-pressed not to be charmed by Miss Bennet."

"You have not met her family," Darcy interrupted. "Her oldest sister is just as well-bred as Miss Elizabeth, but her younger sisters are extremely silly and ill-mannered. And her mother." He closed his eyes and shook his head as if pained by some memory. "Her mother, Richard, is always going on about things in the most inappropriate fashion. Her father is intelligent and possesses a quick wit, but he is neglectful in his duties, and both his family and his estate suffer for it. In addition to all that, she has an uncle who is a county solicitor and another who is involved in trade. How would connections such as these be thought of as anything but an affront to our family and a disadvantage to Georgiana's prospects in the future?" He sighed deeply. "It is not just my happiness with which I have to be concerned."

Richard's tone was once again firm. "And how happy will Georgiana be if she knows you have sacrificed your happiness for hers? She will be devastated." He held up a hand to stop Darcy's rebuttal. "No — do not tell me she will not be aware of your unhappiness. She has already suspected something is not right with you. She has told me so in her letters, and she thinks it is her fault."

Richard looked at Darcy levelly. "If you do not follow your heart, you will seriously damage hers, and I think you know that. For once, Darcy, put duty second and do something for yourself. It will not make you a lesser man. In fact, if Miss Bennet is involved, I would wager it would make you a better man. She is suited to you like no other and will be the making of you, I am certain of it."

Darcy narrowed his eyes, took up his cue, and studied the table.

Richard waited patiently. He knew his cousin was not just studying a shot. Darcy's mind was weighing what Richard had told him, but the agitation of that mind needed to be released in movement so that clarity could be achieved.

Darcy took his shot and circled the table once more. "You are likely right."

Richard bit back a smile at Darcy's unwilling admission.

"I could not put Georgie in that position," Darcy continued. "She would never forgive herself. There is but one choice, and, as foreign as this sounds and feels, I must put duty second."

Richard did not attempt to hide his smile at his befuddled cousin's countenance. "While I am happy you have finally come to the right conclusion, I must now move on to why I asked for such a confession in the first place." Richard shifted uneasily. "In my desire to help you appear in the best light to Miss Bennet's eyes, I may have put my foot in it."

Darcy sagged and closed his eyes as he shook his head. While Darcy was uneasy and rather silent in the presence of ladies such as Elizabeth, Richard was often quite the opposite — at ease and loquacious nearly to a fault.

"What did you say to her?" Darcy asked.

Richard took the cue from Darcy's hand. "It would be best if we sat for this and that you were not armed."

Darcy raised a wary brow but took a seat as Richard had suggested.

"I met Miss Bennet today while touring the park." Richard lay Darcy's cue on the table. "We walked and talked for some time, and from what I gathered from her comments, you have not made a favourable impression on her. ”

He came to take the chair next to Darcy. “I might like to know what you did or said when in Hertfordshire to so sour her impression of you, but I suppose that can be delved into later.”

“The point, Richard,” Darcy said in exasperation.

Richard grimaced. “The point is I wanted to leave her with some positive note regarding your character, and so, I chose to tell her about your loyalty to your friends.”

Darcy's brows furrowed, and Richard could see that he was attempting to figure out why such a story would cause an issue.

“I may have told her about how you helped Bingley avoid an imprudent match.”

Darcy's eyes widened, and Richard hurried on with his explanation.

“Miss Bennet did not approve of the interference. She thought it was rather high-handed of you to decide such a thing for your friend. And then she became a bit withdrawn and quiet, claiming a headache from fatigue as the reason. She was not fatigued. It was apparent that what I said had distressed her greatly. Her sister, who has been in town — the one she asked if you had seen — is Bingley's angel, is she not?”

Darcy held his head in his hands. "Yes," the anguished reply was soft.

Richard's own heart broke at the sound of that word. He had definitely made a jumble of things. "Why did you separate them?"

Darcy shook his head but did not lift it from where it rested in his hands. "Bingley would do better to establish himself with a lady of higher connections, but I would not have denied him his heart had I not suspected that Miss Bennet — Miss Jane Bennet, " he clarified as he finally lifted his head, "was indifferent to him. I did not wish to see him hurt." He scrubbed his face. "So I have lost my chance at happiness?"

"You have not lost." Richard grasped Darcy's shoulder. "I do hope you can forgive me for telling Miss Bennet about Bingley, but I truly was doing it as a service to you, not as a disservice — as it turns out to have been. But you have not lost," Richard repeated. "As my father always says, 'what is done is done; now, how are you going to fix it?'"

It was a phrase Richard had heard many times over the course of his years, and it had become a part of his very fiber — a maxim by which to live.

Darcy chuckled at Richard's imitation of Lord Matlock's voice.

"It must be set right, of course," Richard continued as he rose and began pacing a path from his chair around the billiards table and back again. "First, we must ascertain how much damage has been caused to Miss Jane Bennet."

Darcy nodded. "And inform Bingley of my interference."

"If necessary," Richard agreed and then added with a rueful smile, "which I believe it is." He took another turn around the billiards table. "Were you your normal reserved and proper self when in Hertfordshire, or were you more reserved and a bit uncivil?"

"I was constantly in Miss Bingley's presence."

Richard groaned. He had seen Darcy with Miss Bingley. The woman always put Darcy on edge with her fawning and posturing. It was as if she expected something she possessed in manners, countenance, or position could suddenly sway Darcy to develop an unquenchable desire for her! Richard shook his head. How many times had he himself heard her supposed qualifications woven into a conversation? "Miss Bingley is an understandable reason for being less civil than is your normal wont."

Darcy nodded. "She was insufferable."

"When is she not?" Richard asked with a small laugh.

"I am sure I have never observed such a time," Darcy grumbled, causing Richard to chuckle once again.

"Very good. We have established that you most likely need to speak with Bingley in an attempt to undo the wrong caused by your interference and that you were driven to incivility by the presence of Miss Bingley, which I will assume was accompanied with a lofty air." He stopped on the far side of the billiards table and, looking at Darcy, waited for confirmation that his assessment so far was accurate. Receiving Darcy's acceptance of the facts, Richard continued, "Well, then, besides your off-putting countenance and Miss Bingley, are there any other reasons why Miss Bennet might have a dislike for you?"

Darcy expelled a deep sigh as he nodded slowly. "Remember Wickham?"

Acknowledgements

There are many who have had a part in the creation of this story. Some have read and commented on it. Some have proofread for grammatical errors and plot holes. Others have not even read the story (and a few, I know, will never read it), but their encouragement and belief in my ability, as well as their patience when I became cranky or when supper was late or the groceries ran low, was invaluable.

And so, I would like to say *thank you* to Zoe, Rose, Betty, Kristine, Ben, and Kyle, as well as the readers who read all those Thursday posts on my blog. I feel blessed through your help, support, and understanding.

I have not listed my dear husband in the above group because, to me, he deserves his own special thank you, for without his somewhat pushy insistence that I start sharing my writing, none of my writing goals and dreams would have been met.

Leenie B Books

You can find all of Leenie's books at this link
bit.ly/LeenieBBooks
where you can explore the collections below

~*~

Other Pens, Mansfield Park

~*~

Touches of Austen Collection

~*~

Other Pens, Pride and Prejudice

~*~

Dash of Darcy and Companions Collection

~*~

Marrying Elizabeth Series

~*~

Willow Hall Romances

~*~

The Choices Series

~*~

Darcy Family Holidays

~*~

Darcy and... An Austen-Inspired Collection

About the Author

Leenie Brown has always been a girl with an active imagination, which, while growing up, was both an asset, providing many hours of fun as she played out stories, and a liability, when her older sister and aunt would tell her frightening tales. At one time, they had her convinced Dracula lived in the trunk at the end of the bed she slept in when visiting her grandparents!

Although it has been years since she cowered in her bed in her grandparents' basement, she still has an imagination which occasionally runs away with her, and she feeds it now as she did then — by reading!

Her heroes, when growing up, were authors, and the worlds they painted with words were (and still are) her favourite playgrounds! Now, as an adult, she spends much of her time in the Regency world, playing with the characters from her favourite Jane Austen novels and those of her own creation.

When she is not traipsing down a trail in an attempt to keep up with her imagination, Leenie resides in the beautiful province of Nova Scotia with her two sons and her very own Mr. Brown (a wonderful mix of all the best of Darcy, Bingley, and Edmund with a healthy dose of the teasing Mr. Tilney and just a dash of the scolding Mr. Knightley).

Connect with Leenie Brown

E-mail:
LeenieBrownAuthor@gmail.com
Facebook:
www.facebook.com/LeenieBrownAuthor
Blog:
leeniebrown.com
Patreon:
https://www.patreon.com/LeenieBrown
Subscribe to Leenie's Mailing List:
Book News from Leenie Brown
(bit.ly/LeenieBBookNews)